I0699660

These Treacherous Lies

SIRI SANDFORD

*In dedication to the people who have felt lost in this
ever changing world.
You are and always will be enough.*

Entrance to Metarock
Brockade Forest
Hidden Caverns
Wyntryn
Dragon Isles
Dire Town
Wyntryn Manor
Fynger Isles
Entrance to Rebynrock
Pheyais
Grymyr
City by the Sea
Iyer City
Capital of Grymyr
Goldryn
N
NW
NE
W
E
SW
SE
S

THE TWO CONTINENTS OF
Kanaleigh
Gladlyn
Crystal Lakes
Eastern Eventyr
Aysand
Gana ta Itzaale
Central City
Ygr
Western Eventyr
Southern Dunes

PART ONE

The City on the Sea

The Lightning

Raiden

Rings of blue in an ocean engulfed by fury. Eyes that deceive him. Because these blue irises which once admired him, now fuel the sadness within him. The air is hot on his skin. Tiny needles of flame that pierce the surface, breaking through to his blood. His back presses against the building behind them. Ava stands before him. Hair raises along his arms. She hates him. Right now, the girl he loves wishes him dead. Her hand grips his throat. Rais screams, but there's no pain. Blue flames swirl from her grasp and wrap around him. The fire sucks oxygen from the air.

He doesn't bother to fight back. These consequences are inevitable. *I deserve this*, he thinks as Ava's nails cut into his neck.

His gaze follows the curves of her face. He did this to her. Caused this wrath. Time will never turn back for him. She will always look at him like this. There's nothing he can do. No words to say. Nothing can ever make the body lying ten feet away come back to life.

"You are nothing to me," she says.

A wall of wind slams into Ava, throwing her back

into the grass. Rais slides against the brick and onto the ground. His fingers travel to his throat. His lungs beg to be filled with air, but he doesn't want to breathe. He would rather close his eyes and disappear.

Ava pushes off the grass and runs to Levites' side. She slips her arms around his corpse and they fade away into the Sonder.

Nina walks toward him, shouting concerns he can't hear. People flow down the steps of the library and begin investigating the scene. Their gazes all fall on him. He stares ahead, into the emptiness where those eyes once were. To the eyes that held anger, grief, and disgust. All for him.

Rais had no choice. Levites was going to kill Ava. Even if the boy didn't want to, the Society of the Collective would have made him. Because Ava would choose death before going against her people. She trusted Levites enough to let him get close to her. He could reach into her mind and shatter it if he wanted. Levites already took her memories and her mother. Rais refused to let him take her life. He had no choice but to take Levites' life instead.

Nonetheless, Ava will never forgive him. He saw it in her eyes. She loved Levites. When he and Ava were together, he could sense Levites in the back of her mind, lurking there. A terrible and intruding shadow that never left. Last night was the first time it was only the two of them. At least since her memories faded to dust, and Ava became attached to that troubled boy.

If only Ava remembered the time before her mother's death. When she only knew Rais, and each moment was theirs alone.

A tear slides across his stinging skin. Their shared kiss in the hallway last night makes him want to tear the whole city apart. All he can think of is the hatred in her ocean blue eyes. He caused that, and he deserved it. But he didn't take her memories. He's never done anything but protect Ava—maybe that's his greatest mistake.

Nina tugs on his shoulder, says something about him being idiotic, but his mind refuses to register her words. Rais reluctantly stands and wobbles against his weight. He pushes Nina aside and says something about going into the forest. The thoughts blur together. He doesn't need to understand what Nina says, because it's not important. He'd rather be far away from here or nowhere at all. A Society officer steps before him. Hard lines crease the man's forehead and around his lips. The officer yells, but it's only balmy air blowing on his face. Everything is silent. Rais blinks idly for a moment. The officer moves to slap him, and Rais grabs his wrist.

Nina is close behind him, watching. He can feel the worry seeping from her skin, but there's no reason for Nina to be worried. Rais is fine. He twists the officer's arm, and yanks down. The movement throws the man into the grass.

An officer with red hair runs at him. The world bends around him—blurred by city lights and car horns. He can't imagine how Ava ever liked this place. He'd hate to live here. The man he threw to the ground grabs Rais' ankle. Rais drops to his knee and his weight slams onto the officer. Rais stumbles back, narrowly avoiding the fist of another attacker. His mind slips into the Sonder, and the familiar haze envelops him.

Rais steps into the Plane of Verity and walks away from the library. He is steadier on his feet now. But for some reason, he can't feel. There is a faint clicking in the back of his mind. As if there's an internal timer counting down to his end. The regular sounds of the world diminish with its ticking.

His body hums and buzzes against the pressures within the Plane of Verity. He walks for a while — not sure what his destination is. Then there is a familiar call. The clicking speeds up slightly, and he pauses. He stands at the edge of an access point. A line of energy that flows to his destination. Rais grasps an old memory, and steps through into the snow.

Everything is silent.

He stands on a cliff's edge. A small village rests in the valley below. The night sky stretches across the horizon. It's dotted with small stars and flecks of snow that drift down from it.

A faint thrum vibrates through the desecrated village. The quiet rising and falling of sleeping soldiers' lungs. Ava's scream echoes through him still. She is so angry now.

The town is like a memory he's dusting off. The buildings are where he remembers them. Except now, they have holes in the roofs and broken windows. Like a vision from a dream, the burnt and charred buildings return to their former glory. The neighbors from his early childhood flood the streets. He alates from the cliff to the edge of the disembodied town.

He moves slowly through the broken streets and scorched pathways. He follows a vision of his parents holding him. They walk with him down the snowy road. His mother holds his tiny hand. His father reaches down and scratches his head. The action muses his locks and leaves them sticking up in various directions.

Rais follows the path his parents lead him down. They stop and turn to him, but their eyes look through him. The younger version of him looks at the remains of their home. The roof is caved in, and glass is melted onto what's left of the window frames. His childhood home is in tatters.

He sees through reality and into his memory. To what his home looked like when he was a child, big and colorful. Covered in green.

He doesn't remember much from the winter before his parents died. Only faint recollections. But he remembers the spring. The day fire seized this village and ripped life from its hearth.

Through the window of his home, there's a shadow of what he dreams his mother looked like. She sits in a rocking chair, huddling him in a blanket. She sings a sweet melody. The same song he used to whisper to himself to fall asleep. On the nights when he was lonely and nothing but a fumbling kid in a great manor. He used to pretend that it was her singing it to him. That his mother sat by his bedside, singing that beautiful song while brushing the hair from his face.

He steps away from the house. The cold pricks at him, trying to rise feeling from his numb body. It all falls flat in his mind.

A large oak tree stands at the backend of the village. The same tree he woke up tied to years prior. The place where a Goldryn soldier with dark hair and light eyes dug a blade into his flesh, then left him to bleed out at the base of the tree.

Rais reaches for the sleeping soldiers' minds. He pries into them and searches each individually. All are Goldryn soldiers in Wyntryn territory. Each of them have memories of hurting his people. He cracks his neck and loosens his arms at his sides.

Click. Click. Click. The timer is almost out.

His fingers tense as they wrap around invisible strings of energy. He focuses on those tendrils, sending the lines of energy to each soldier in the abandoned town. Right now, he doesn't care about the consequences. He has nothing left to lose.

The clicking in his mind is deafening now. It rings in his ears and shutters off his surroundings. He throws his morals out the door and lets the mountain of pain collapse. The years of loneliness and disappointment. Never being enough for himself. The terror of losing the only good thing in his life. The person it was all worth trying for.

He closes his eyes, then lets go. With the release, his electricity flows. Strands of lightning careen through the village and into the enemies who have terrorized his people for generations.

The clicking subsides. The timer runs out. Their breathing stops.

For so long Rais has let everything build inside of him. Into a flimsy tower of emotion. Now, when it's all crashing down, he can finally relax. It has come time for the caverns to crumble. For the perfectly built statues to fall apart. No longer will he let others dictate his life. Rather than waiting on the sidelines, he will take his own charge. Wyntryn has fallen and he will do anything to help it stand once more. He will go on stronger than before. Ready to destroy anyone who stands in his path. Wyntryn is all he has, and he will defend it until his last breath.

Chapter One

Ava

Silence. There's a sound to it. A hint. A small buzzing that spins through the particles of the air. When all is quiet, what remains is a faint ringing. A voice to the silence. It speaks to Ava at night. It speaks to her when she stares at her ceiling and watches those all too familiar particles blur together. Somewhere, out there, in the silence, there's a voice. A buzzing. Maybe it's the Sonder, reaching for her when her mind refuses to quiet. Maybe there's someone out there, searching for her.

It's a nice thought, that someone might care enough to look for her. To want her.

Her memories cry for Raiden. As if he is the only person that can quiet the silence. Maybe he is the only one who can stop the buzzing. But that can't be. Because Raiden killed Levi.

She will never forgive that. She can never forget that.

There is no silence now. Only the crashing of waves and the music of the City on the Sea.

"Excuse me, my lady?" A voice sounds from behind her.

"Yes?" She glances over her shoulder.

It's Aliras. Not some stranger prying into her personal space. He's tall, with tan skin like Nina's. His hair is dark as the night, and his eyes a vibrant blue that are cut by amber markings. He has a sword at his back, weapons at his sides, and wears the sigil of her sister. A dragon with three heads. How fitting. Her sister, a monster with three faces.

Willow's prophecy lays heavily upon her. It flutters through her mind like birds over the ocean, whips across the waves with the gusts that carry sand into the air. It's always on her mind. A threat stalking her. A basket of flowers flows up into the sky and scatters across the boardwalk.

Ava has enjoyed the Goldryn city. The village filled with life and the palace hanging over the sea are mesmerizing. Except she is no longer in Goldryn by choice. Her sister forces her to stay.

She began to suspect Stygian when Willow went to her chambers and gave her that note. The note that stopped the world from turning. The written words that gave voice to the prophecy she believed to be a fairytale. A dark whisper that sneaks behind her waking thoughts and torments her dreams. A horrible tale she desperately wishes to be a lie.

Ava closes her eyes against the bright sun and pushes the thoughts away. "Tell me why the second in command is my guard again?" she asks.

Aliras steps up beside her and leans against the railing. Stygian assigned Aliras as her guard during her second week in Goldryn. Ava had ventured out into the city alone and when she returned to the palace Aliras was waiting outside her chambers.

"She claims threats are rising in Wyntryn," he says. Aliras usually doesn't say much to her. He's careful with his words.

"Well, I can assure you Wyntryn poses no threat to me." Her hair billows behind her, and her skin tightens against the sharp wind.

The thought of her people being a threat to her is amusing. But also, terrifying. While she hides in this foreign city, anything could be happening at home.

She doesn't even know what she's doing here.

Aliras' disinterest in responding is apparent. Though she is curious about his silence. He holds himself with composure and a straightened spine. His mind is either blank or well protected.

"You're a mage?" she asks. He doesn't move to respond. She tries to push through the folds of his mind without making herself noticeable but makes no progress. "You are well guarded either way. I assume only an irregular can have a hold as strong on their mind as you do. And I doubt Stygian would place you so high in the ranks if you merely had a brain and some physical strength."

"You were trying to enter my mind?" he asks, looking down at her. His brows push together, and his mouth dips to a frown.

"I've noticed I'm quite good at that, but it seems I am incapable of hiding my thoughts." She watches his expression. He's looking at her—more than he has before. What changed?

"That is not a fault, my lady." His eyes study her. She narrows hers, and he grunts, averting his gaze. "I came to tell you that Her Highness has requested your presence in the throne room."

"She always wants me cooped up in there when it's the most glorious time to be outside. You report to her though, so should I keep my thoughts to myself?" Stygian didn't assign her a guard for protection. Her sister wants to know her every move. Aliras begins to walk away. Ava follows, keeping in step with him. Her bare shoulders are turning red, so it's best she heads back anyway.

"I work for her, but I am not an informant." It's his response every time she accuses him of being one.

Ava hates that Stygian gave her a guard, but she doesn't mind one that's not utterly devoted to her sister. Ava came to Goldryn for sanctuary, but she wasn't expecting it to become a prison.

"Can you tell me about my sister?" Ava asks. He doesn't acknowledge her. "I'm only asking because I know nothing about her, and she isn't the talking kind." *Neither are you.*

They walk along the edge of the city. Each windowsill and balcony overflows with plants and flowers. Ivy stretches across the walls and down to the stones of the road. Few villagers roam the streets during the day. Ava learned from the servants in the castle that they think it's too hot when the sun is out. So, the Goldryns adapted into nocturnal souls to avoid the heat. At this time of day, she's usually the only one on the streets. Everyone else is asleep.

Aliras quickens his pace, and she hurries to catch up. "Do you know what she's going to discuss with me?"

He continues to stare ahead at the cobblestone road that winds along the coast. There's a wharf to their right. A cage of brown and green lobsters sits in a tank of stagnant water. Her nose wrinkles. She hates the smell of fish in the heat. Fishermen are sprawled in wooden chairs with cloths over their faces to block the sun. Cups of ale hang loosely in their tired hands, letting liquid drip onto the dock.

She raises her brows. Of course, her sister chose the only guard who hates conversation.

The palace looms ahead of them. It hangs off the cliffside, tilting ever so slightly toward the ocean below. How easily its foundations could slip and the whole place would fall into the sea. Hordes of seagulls scatter as they walk onto the bridge. Their squawks startle a dosing guard by the front gate.

Aliras approaches the guard, then grabs onto the lapels of his uniform. He shoves the guard against a stone pillar. "Wake up! You're a soldier, not a child in need of a nap." He lets go of the man and knocks on the gate with the back of his hand. The doors swing inward. He glances at her, then back at the guard. She tilts her head. She's still trying to decipher him. She knows whatever is going on in his mind is not what he shows on the outside. It's the small glances and nervousness that give him away. As if he's embarrassed for his actions.

Aliras leads Ava through the courtyard and into the palace. The distance to the throne room is too short. She's passing Aliras and entering the haunted hall all too soon. Ava crosses the marbled floor to the dais where Stygian sits on her throne, her black dress pooled around her feet.

"Darling sister, you walk so slowly," she slurs. Broken glass is scattered around Stygian's feet. A hazy green aroma floats in the air.

"My apologies, I didn't know I needed to rush." Ava folds her arms across her ribs.

"Well, I have a request to make. I want an alliance with Wyntryn." Stygian's lips stretch into a thin smile. This isn't the first time she has asked this. In Stygian's drunken state, she's likely forgotten.

"I don't have the authority to make an alliance." It isn't the first time Ava's declined.

"Pity. I thought you were the queen." She throws her arm over the side of her throne dramatically.

Ava fights the urge to roll her eyes. "I am the heiress. Not a queen."

"Officially, of course. Even so, I want an agreement that when you appear before the Wyntryn diplomats, you will push for an alliance."

"Only on the word that your army is to never set foot on Wyntryn land without my permission," Ava counters.

She stands from her throne, swaying ever so slightly. "Yes, that is only fair."

"And that you will allow me to freely come and go as I please—"

"No."

"Excuse me?" Ava asks. A bite in her tone.

Stygian squares her shoulders and softens her voice. "I need you to stay here. For now."

Ava tightens her hands into fists. Aliras speaks into her mind. *Listen to her. If you fight back now, she will lose her temper.* Ava stiffens.

She tries to conceal her reaction the best she can. "That's fine. There's nowhere I need to be. If you will excuse me, I would like to retire to my chambers." She has to force formalities. If leaving now wouldn't start a war, then she'd already be gone.

Stygian tilts her head in contemplation. "Very well. We will discuss this later."

Ava spins on her heel and walks from the room. Her jaw clenches and the skin by her ears tightens. As soon as the doors close behind her, she groans. It's her own fault she's in this situation. Aliras coughs and Ava glares back at him. No one should enter anyone's mind without making themselves known.

"You are right. I would like to apologize," he says.

There he goes again, intruding on her thoughts. "Didn't even notice you were listening." Sarcasm drips from her voice.

"I've noticed I am quite good at that, too. From now on, I will give you your privacy. Although it is hard not to catch waves of your thoughts."

"Right." Ava wishes she could pull her thoughts in and build walls to keep people out. But since Saira helped her break down those walls, rebuilding has been impossible. He trained her mind into vulnerability.

Aliras gestures to the stairwell that leads to her chambers. "Did you notice she was a bit taken by aromas?"

Is he trying his hand at small talk? Ava stalks to the staircase leading to the other side of the palace. "Yes," she says over her shoulder. Stygian was slurring her words, but she does that often. Ava studies the hard lines on Aliras' face. He's young, but his eyes are tired. Little scars trail across his hands and neck. It's rare to meet anyone without scars. Stygian gave Willow hers. It's only a matter of time before Ava gets the same treatment.

Ava was close to losing her temper back there, but Aliras stopped her. "Thank you, for warning me," she says.

"Not a problem, my lady." Why does he keep calling her that? It's the only thing that really annoys her about him. He talks to her like a princess instead of a normal person.

Ava reaches the doors to her chambers and gazes

over Aliras again. She glances away from him and asks, "Would you mind finding Willow for me?"

Aliras walks away without a response. He must have better things to do.

Not long after Aliras leaves, Willow knocks on her door. Ava wasn't sure Aliras had heard her. She lets Willow in, then goes to the windowsill. Warm air blows in, filling the room with a salty aroma. Ava curls her legs underneath herself on the cushioned bench.

Willow sits next to her, leaning back against the sandstone. Her lavender hair shifts with the breeze. "Aliras told me about Stygian."

Ava can only imagine what Aliras told Willow about Stygian. Besides being a menace, the most recent actions of her sister involved killing a palace guard. A guard who was working as a spy for Eieran Hynrule and tried to reach out to Ava. His message made it to her door but was found by Aliras.

"Why do you stay?" Ava asks instead. Willow enjoys oversharing things from her own life, so it's never difficult to avert Willow's attention.

"Well, after Stygian captured me and made her deal with Alys, I negotiated my own. Instead of returning to Wyntryn, a place that is not my home, I stayed. I became the Eventyrian representative at the Goldryn court."

Alys, the mother Ava lost, and the one she can barely remember. "Couldn't you have returned to Eventyr if you went back to Wyntryn?" Ava asks. A buoy bell chimes below. It floats near the rocky coast that lines this side of the palace.

"Yes, but I didn't want to go back. My father would marry me off to the first royal man he found. And the one I loved, married another. She was no longer an option, never was, really. But she was the only one I would want to marry. And as a representative at court, I must report to the Queen twice a year. So, you see, twice a year I get to see her rather than never at all."

"Does she love you?" Ava asks, despite it not being her business.

"In my dreams she does."

Ava glances at her. "Can you tell me about her?" Willow is a good distraction because Ava can't talk about her past. She only has small snippets of memory. Images with no correlation.

Willow smiles at the ocean below. "She is beautiful. On the outside she is perfect. Deep within her is a soul of kindness—seeking relief from burdens placed upon her. She has a talent for fighting and arguing. It sounds distasteful, but the way she fights, the way she spins her words, it's graceful. But underneath that beauty, she is plagued by nightmares."

"Nightmares?"

"Yes. Of the worst kind. There is a monster of darkness in her dreams. Both waking and sleeping—it never leaves her."

Ava places her hand on Willow's. "We all have our nightmares. Mine are so real that I don't dream them. I face them in my memories."

Willow's eyes go glassy. "Mine are of the past as well." She raises her chin against the salty breeze. "A few years after my brother was born, a plague took my mother. Exactly ten years later, the same sickness took my brother. My father calls it the curse of the Crystal Lakes. He claims it is because he refused to give medicine to a dying woman he found in the woods. He thought by letting her into our home to administer the medicine, she would get my mother sick. And yet, my mother still got ill and died." She takes a burdened breath. "In my nightmares, I am alone on the shore of the lake right outside my family home. The same dark monster that plagues my past love's dreams fills the sky above me. It reaches down and kisses me on the cheek. I begin to fade away. I hold my hand up to the sun, and it is so clear, that I can see right through it. Then, as I lose sight of my hand, I wake up." Willow holds her hand out before the sun now. She twists her fingers in the air, then her arm falls to her lap. Willow sighs.

"That's horrible."

"It is horrid, isn't it? The truth is death will come no matter what the cause or what the time. So, if I die due to this curse, it will be inevitable. At least it will take me home to my brother and mother. I can walk with them into eternity."

"For a long time, I wished for death. But then I met—" Ava catches herself. She shouldn't think of him. Truthfully, she never met him, she always knew him. That doesn't matter now. "But I realized there's a lot more to live for than what I've lost. And hey, even if this curse is real, you should live what life you have to the fullest. Why settle for only seeing this girl twice a year? One day, you won't ever be able to see her again."

Willow pulls her lips between her teeth, but eventually releases the strain and looks at Ava. "She is in love with another."

It takes Ava some time to find the right words to say. "Then maybe it's time to move on. I have never seen you leave this place, so why don't you come with me to Wyntryn when I return home? Live what life you have to the fullest."

"I'd love that. But what of you?"

"Hm?"

"I know you didn't love that boy in the same way you fell for Rais. Why are you risking what time you have with him?"

Ava's eyelids flutter, and she fists her freehand. "He killed Levi."

"I hear you. But you know Rais. He would not take someone's life without reason. I imagine what he did in that moment was out of fear for you."

"Even so—"

"Tell me, in Rebynrock, how many lives did you take with your fire?" Willow asks.

Ava scoffs, then averts her gaze. "I was protecting my people." Ava would not kill anyone on purpose. Commander Damon threw a knife into her cousin, what was she supposed to do? Let him do the same to her?

"And Rais was protecting you," Willow retorts.

Ava sits back, pulling her hand from Willow's. "How can I face him after all that I've done?"

"If he genuinely cares for you, and you truly care for him, you will find forgiveness in one another. You may be staying here, but it does not mean that you've turned against your homeland."

"I don't mean that. I mean my past. I'm not who I thought I was. It's like my identity was torn away from me when Levi told me that I ... I plotted against my mother. And that note—" The note Willow gave her, the one that prophesized her demise. She blinks away the tears. "I can barely think about it. If Raiden knew, I'd never be able to face him."

"Ava, you must look forward. You can't keep blaming yourself for your past. Especially when you can't even remember it. Start anew, fight for your right. For your people. For Rais. Find the current that you want to follow, and swim with it. Deep down you know what's best for yourself, but sitting around in Goldryn, riddled with grief, will not help you move on."

"You sound like my mother." Ava laughs, wiping a tear from underneath her eye. "I read a journal entry by her that sounded like that."

Willow's cheeks lift, creasing the skin beneath her eyes. "She always was good with words. I probably got the phrase from her."

Ava nods futilely—her eyes on the ocean. The water is far below them. Blues that are ever deep and ever wide.

When Willow first met her in Goldryn, she left Ava with a note. Simple curves of ink on parchment. Ink that sealed her fate. That same day Willow told her about the prophecy of the two sisters.

The prophecy foretells that when one sister kills their creator, a great power will consume her. If the sisters don't destroy each other with that power, then they will destroy the Sonder.

Ava sees the words in her mind like a nightmare. *The deaths around you have been influenced by your own actions. Your mother had to choose one daughter to ascend to the throne; she did not choose you. You killed your creator. Now your sister will take your head.*

She pushes off the window seat, then runs to the bathroom. She falls to her knees. The stone is hard and sends an ache through her thighs. Beyond the bathroom, she can hear a faint ringing, the sound of silence. She curls her fingers against her palms and tries to breathe. The ringing grows louder. She gulps down the sickness.

I killed my mother, and now my sister will kill me.

Chapter Two

Raiden

Since losing Ava, everyone says his eyes shine a little less. His electricity doesn't have the same spark. His skin is duller, and his mind emptier. Even the ethereal city he stands in is unimpressive in his mind. Rais walks through the streets as though he has seen them too many times, despite only being here once before.

He talks to the guards outside the palace without using prose or mind games. That would take far more energy than he has.

When the guards tell him to wait outside, he slumps against the railing of the stairs and waits. While everything else has fallen flatter, his patience has grown. With that, his need for isolation expands.

He hasn't recovered from the night of the rising moon ball. Rais released heaps of energy in his home village, Pheyais, that night. He killed an entire squadron of Goldryn soldiers on a whim, but it didn't help. When he closes his eyes, he still sees Ava. Her hand grasping his throat, and his world setting on fire.

These days everything is a blur. He recognizes time

passing, but it's as if he isn't here — simply a viewer watching everything happen around him.

"Sparrow Hynrule, the Queen is ready for you," the guard calls to him, and Rais trudges up the steps. "How do you know Exceail?"

Rais looks up at the palace carved from glistening metals. Multicolored glass spreads colored light across the surface. His gaze bends to the guard at his side. A young boy forced into the military. The guard already has a scar stretching across his forehead. He wears the region's colors of black and red. The sword at his side is too big for his small frame. Why would Eventyr put such pressure on someone so young? The Society of the Collective does the same. Both Grymyr and Eventyr are grand kingdoms that force innocents and children into making decisions they never wished to make. No one should be forced into military servitude. Though, Wyntryn lacks an army because they don't force people to join.

Rais gulps. *Exceail*, the kid asked him about Exceail. "I traveled with him once," Rais says.

The guard nods. "I only ask because he is a very private man. He committed treason against the kingdom, and yet they still allow him to live here in Eventyr. He's a General. Can you believe that?"

Rais wants to warn the boy to keep his mouth shut, but it's not his place. "It is possible that everyone's done things they regret," he says. Rais should know.

Exceail walks up to them. His eyes are honey brown. A shade barely lighter than his skin. He wears an all-black uniform. "Raiden." The general bows his head with a smile.

"Thank you for getting me an audience with Queen Kalenti."

The young guard leaves his side to return to his post, and Exceail steps up to him. He reaches out his fist. Rais bumps it with his own. "It's my pleasure. I rarely see a familiar face that doesn't hate me, so I am glad I can help you." Exceail grins and gestures toward the palace. They enter the extravagant hallway that circles the entire main floor of the palace.

"I have gained enemies of my own." Rais forces a laugh.

"That explains the dullness. I was expecting to be shocked by those golden irises again."

There goes another, commenting on his apparent change. Rais wants to stay the way he was before, but he is struggling to find himself. For so long, Ava was a part of him. Now he has to learn to be strong for himself. To learn to find something to live for, that isn't Ava or fulfilling the requests of the dead. Though he is in Eventyr now, to fulfill the requests of his late queen, Alys.

He follows the simplistic lines and sharpness of the palace's interior with his eyes. Women wearing large gowns and vibrant jewelry pass by in groups. Along with men in clean tuxes and complex shoulder coverings. A sculpted snake wraps around the upper body of a man passing by. A lion roars on the shoulder of another. Rais is out of place here. His jacket is simple, embroidered with the ancient language and markings of the Sparrow. He has his protector pin on the left lapel. His hair's brushed back neatly, and he wears a twisting dragon on his ear to represent his people. His boots are worn, and his pantlegs uneven.

Exceail stays quiet at his side as they make their way to the throne room. Rais tries to focus his mind on why he's here. To retrieve the talisman Queen Kalenti has.

Exceail stops and Rais looks at the large opening to their right. The doorway opens to a balcony overlooking the throne room. Rais follows Exceail into the doorway and down a wide staircase. The stairs lead into a magnificent ballroom, with a floor of glimmering black marble. The red-haired queen sits upon her throne. Exceail steps up to her side and watches as Rais kneels before her.

"Your Highness," Rais greets.

"I recognize you." Bright hair frames Kalenti's light and defined face. Her eyes are of obsidian—darker than the night sky. The last time he saw the Eventyr Queen she had light green eyes. They blended in with the trees of the Eventyr forests. The change must be caused by her power of darkness or the golden amulet around her neck.

"I am surprised," Rais says. It has been years since he met her. Much has happened since then. He barely looks like the boy he once was.

Dark clouds spin around her throne. She lets out a tired sigh and flicks the darkness away with her finger. It evaporates into the air, revealing her forest green dress. "You were part of Alys' party when she burned down my forest. A boy then, but still complicit. What makes you think I will trust you now?"

"I do not expect you to, Your Highness. Although I know you have put your faith in Stygian, who was also with us that day." Rais stands to face her, squaring his shoulders.

"She was, but she proved to be of use to me. Now, what is it you want?" She speaks coldly. As if whatever light was once in her has been snuffed out.

"I am seeking use of your talisman," he says.

"You don't even know what it is, do you?" Kalenti asks.

An odd assumption to make. She should know the talismans come from Wyntryn. As the Sparrow, he should be more familiar with them than anyone else. "It is a dragon's scale. A power amplifier." She watches him silently. "I need it because Wyntryn is uninhabitable. The Wyntryn people are spread across the two continents. I want to bring them home."

The hidden cities are home to thousands of Wyntryns, but the visible land is deserted. There are only outskirt towns left. The ones left barely survive under the protection of mages. Besides, Kalenti has no clue that there are three thriving cities under cover of rock.

"Why ask for the scale? Why not me or my troops?" she asks.

"Asking for that is to put a burden on your region and take you away from your people. With the scale, I will be able to rid Wyntryn of our enemies and then return it to you."

"Hm, but why you? I know you are not born of Wyntryn blood. Stygian told me once your mother and her sister immigrated from Aysand. Why help people to whom you owe nothing?"

"You are correct. Even my father was a foreigner. I indeed owe them nothing, nevertheless, they deserve to live in their homes. Not in refugee camps across the Gana ta Itzaale. Not hidden away from the villages they grew up in. I am the Sparrow of Wyntryn, and I will fight for those people until my last breath."

"That is admirable." She stands and walks to him. Evil creeps beneath her skin—a prisoner inside of her. One she buried long ago. "What of this heiress I have heard so much about? Does she not have the power to kill those beasts from Grymyr?"

He shouldn't tell another region about their politics, but he came here for the talisman. He's only going to get it if he's honest. "Our heiress has suffered many great losses. She is still in contact with her distant cousin, Anya Petrichor. But she resides in Goldryn now."

"Then you truly are here because you have nowhere else to turn?" She runs her finger along his shoulder. "Your soul has enough darkness to withstand the burden. Do not let it overtake you. Promise me that?"

"I promise."

She reaches behind her neck and unhooks her necklace. "Look down."

Rais tilts his head down. She pulls the necklace around him and clasps it behind his neck. It has a golden amulet. An amulet big enough to conceal a dragon's scale. Rais looks up, meeting her dark eyes.

"Be careful Raiden Hynrule." His heart pauses in his chest. "The scale is unstable. If you are not careful you may cause more harm than the beasts already in Wyntryn. Keep it close to you. Never give it to anyone, never show it to anyone, never let anyone know you have it." Her eyes narrow. "And if the scale does not return to me after your mission is complete, I will gladly send my troops to Wyntryn to finish what those Atane started."

"Thank you, Your Highness. It will be back in your hands as soon as my people are safe." Rais says it in earnest, but nerves trickle down his spine. He pushes the necklace below his tunic and coat. Nina already knows he's here for the talisman. It will be impossible to keep it from her, but he can hide it from everyone else.

"You may call me Kalenti. And you should know, I hid this power from Alys when you were here all those years ago. I owe this to your lands, to your people. My selfishness allowed those beasts to takeover and brought war to my lands. Hopefully, this will make up for my mistakes in the past." Rais bows and then turns to walk away, but her voice cuts through the air. "Wait."

He looks back to the queen. "Yes?"

Her face becomes shaded with worry. "Do not alate home. It will reveal the scale to the Sonder, which will become a beacon to anyone seeking this power. You may board a ship in the royal docks south of Aysand. My commandant Exceail is leaving with a band of troops for the coast in a few hours. You can travel with them. There's a ship leaving for the Dragon Isles in a few days. Safe travels, Sparrow Hynrule."

Rais bows to her one last time. "You are more than deserving of Alys' forgiveness, Kalenti. If she were still here, she would show nothing but gratitude for Eventyr."

The Queen nods to him. The talisman against his chest sets his nerves aflame. He takes a deep breath, then retreats up the stairs and into the hallway. A woman in a floor length gown watches him as she walks by. Rais avoids eye contact and leans back against the wall. Once Exceail gets out here he can get away from these prying eyes.

Beyond the window, the city blends with his visions of the torn-up villages across his homeland. Their largest civilization, Metarock, is nothing in comparison to the grandeur of Eventyr's capital. Skyscrapers touch the clouds here. Metal bridges connect buildings. Ivy and trees grow from the crevices of structures. On the streets of the city are sidewalks of moving stone. They carry people across the city without them having to take a single step. Grymyr is technologically advanced like Eventyr, but the regulars in the city are not efficient in this way. Pollution covers the skies of Grymyr. There's always construction and loud noises. Eventyr is busy but quiet. It's serenity at its finest. A kingdom lined with silk and bathed in magic.

The General steps into the hall. "Beautiful, isn't it?" Exceail runs his fingers through his dense curls.

"It's quite a different world from what I'm used to," Rais says.

"I must say, I am incredibly surprised she gave you that. She has held onto it for years."

"She had it when Alys came looking for it, didn't she?" Rais asks. In the throne room, Kalenti was referring to a trip Alys, Stygian, and Rais took many years ago. It was before Stygian stole the taaffeite talisman from Alys and ran to her father in Goldryn. They came to Eventyr in search of the dragon's scale. Instead, they found Willow and burned one of Eventyr's forests to the ground.

Exceail nods. "Yes." It's odd to think Kalenti had it this whole time and Alys never made another attempt to get it.

"When do we leave?" Rais asks.

"Soon. I can send a guard with you to the stables if you'd like. You can meet the others traveling with us. I have some business to attend to first."

"That would be great, thanks."

"Make sure no one knows you have that," Exceail reiterates Kalenti's warning. Rais isn't planning to tell anyone either way, but he appreciates their efforts to protect him. They have no reason to put their faith in him. He's thankful for their trust.

With his hands on yet another talisman, the arrow safe at the Wyntryn manor, Rais is ready for the battles to come. Wyntryn may not have a Queen, but they can withstand a fight. Right now, in Wyntryn, Eieran and Anya are gathering forces and leading them to the training camps outside the Wyntryn manor.

Between the talismans, an army, and their allies in the Isles, Wyntryn stands a chance. Rais will help them fight back against Stygian and the creatures that lurk across the Wyntryn countryside. Luckily, after Levites' death and the killing of one of their highest-standing commanders in Rebynrock, the Society has backed off. They might still attack, but at the very least it gave them time to gather their forces. The Society might be afraid of them. A shocking possibility, but if he didn't trust Ava, he'd be terrified of her too.

When it comes time for war, Goldryn will be caught off guard. Which allows enough room for their forces to rise and destroy the threats that have been plaguing them since Stygian became queen.

An Eventyr guard leads Rais out to the gardens. Flowers of all colors are planted in swirling designs between large hedges. The hedges open to the stables and wide pastures. Rais searches the grounds for his hooded friend. He sensed her traveling away from one of the city pubs and toward the palace when he was leaving the throne room. He can tell she is near, but he hasn't seen her yet.

Rais tugs the copper chain dangling from the inside of his cloak. He hooks it at his shoulder and pulls the cloth close around him. It's loose enough to maneuver in but keeps the cool breeze from reaching him.

At the edge of the courtyard, two guards try to wrangle a kicking shadow. As he gets nearer, the shadow becomes a blue cloak, auburn hair, and agile movements. A dagger glimmers at her hip—a Wyntryn blade. These guards aren't very attentive, they completely missed the dagger. Hopefully, she isn't mindless enough to use it.

"Hey!" he shouts to the soldiers. One is tall and broad with a long blonde braid, and the other stout with a small face. They glare at him as he approaches. The tall one holds his writhing friend by the collarbone. "What are you doing with her?" he asks.

"We found her scaling the palace walls." The blonde woman spits at his feet. Rais heaves a sigh. He doesn't have time to haggle with the palace guard.

"Gods Nina." He looks to the guards in distress. "I'm sure it's a misunderstanding. She's with me."

"And who are you?" she asks.

"Sparrow Hynrule, tenth protector of Wyntryn. We are traveling with General Exceail this afternoon." Rais looks around him for the guard who was accompanying him, but he's disappeared.

"Sure, you are." The guard pulls metal cuffs from her belt and locks them around Nina's wrists. She shoves Nina to the other guard, a man with a permanent scowl, and steps up to Rais. He's barely shorter but holds his ground. Nina bares her teeth at the woman. He catches Nina's gaze. Her eyes are bright with fury. He can tell she's fighting the urge to argue with her capturers. She has argued with everyone they've met in Eventyr so far.

"Let me go get the guard who brought me here to the stables, he can tell you himself," Rais suggests.

The woman narrows her eyes. She swings her hand back and grasps her long sword. Rais jumps out of the way of the falling blade. "I can sense you lying to me," she mutters.

She grips the blade with steady hands. Rais raises his hands in defense. "I promise you I'm telling the truth. I have no ill will."

The guard swings her sword at his left arm. He drops his shoulder back and grabs the sword at his side. He cuts through the air and stops the guard's blade. She pushes against him, but he holds firm. Rais doesn't want to make any offensive moves, so she can't use any baseless accusations against him.

She prances back and strikes again. Metal clashing rings true. The guards may be too daft to check a prisoner for weapons or listen to a foreign diplomat, but this one's certainly good with a sword.

"Drop your weapon soldier!" Exceail's voice travels across the yard. The guard loosens her grip and lets the blade fall to the grass. Exceail runs down the stairs of the palace, trotting to where they stand. Rais sheathes his sword as Exceail walks up to them. "Explain this," he snaps at the guard.

She squares her shoulders. "We found this woman climbing over the palace walls. This man tried to defend her and gave me reason to believe they were both a danger to the palace."

Rais scoffs. Exceail juts his finger at her. "This woman is a representative of Wyntryn, and this man is the tenth protector of the Wyntryn crown. You have disrespected them and their region. Actions like this can start wars. Take those cuffs off her and return to your posts. I will deal with you both later."

"I don't take orders from a traitor." The woman spins on her heel.

Exceail grabs her by the shoulder and turns her around. He throws an uppercut that knocks her backward. Blood spews from a cut on her chin. "I am your General, soldier. Undermine me again and I will lock you in the dungeons myself."

The guard spits blood into the grass. "Pity she didn't marry you and make you king."

Exceail slams his boot into her side. She rolls over, coughing into the grass. Exceail turns to the other guard, and he hurriedly hands over the key. Exceail bends down beside Nina and uncuffs her. With a flick, Exceail flings the key into the dirt.

Nina shakes her hands. Her nose twitches as she turns to Rais. "If someone else touches me, I will throw them over the gods damned wall."

"Were you seriously climbing the wall?" Rais asks. He gazes over the towering chunks of stacked metal. It's an art piece unto itself. Trees and flower beds line each side of the wall. Obsidian blanketed with a soft rainbow. Easy climb, but she probably stuck out like a sore thumb.

"No. I'm not dense. I was asking to get entry through the south-end gate. That woman shoved me away, so I pushed her back with some wind and she got all snarky," Nina says. Rais shakes his head. Clearly, they both were in the wrong. At least Nina wasn't trying to hop the fence of the most powerful region in Kanaleigh.

"Don't mind the guards," Exceail says. "We require all well-abled citizens to support the kingdom in some way for at least two years. We end up getting a lot of recruits into the palace guard. Most of them didn't go through any schooling." He cracks his neck, then stalks off toward the stables. "Come on, we have a long way to travel before sundown."

Rais pushes Nina's shoulder, and she glares at him.

"I got it," he says, tapping his chest.

Her mouth quirks up at the side. "One step closer to freedom."

Chapter Three

Ava

Ava pulls her arm back and lets the arrow fly. It spins through the air in a clean line, and snags near the bottom of the target. She tilts her head. With a sigh, she slings the bow over her shoulder and walks to the target. The outer deck it's on overlooks the palace docks below. Where a ship with three large masts passes by, traveling out into the expanse of blue. She pulls the arrow out and holds it loosely at her side.

Ava returns to the same distance as before and swings the bow back around. She grips it steadily and notches the arrow in place. She lifts her elbow and hooks her fingers onto the cord.

"You're not going to get anywhere close to that target," Aliras says, walking out onto the deck.

"I'm ignoring you." She narrows her eyes, focusing on the bullseye.

"If you were, then pretend I didn't say anything. See what happens when you shoot." He's so arrogant.

She shifts her stance. Ava pulls the arrow back and aims for the center of the target. When she releases the arrow, it flies right past the target and into the ocean below.

"Would've never guessed that would happen." Correction, arrogant and sarcastic. "May I try?"

She reluctantly throws her arm out toward him with the bow in hand. He grabs it from her and snatches an arrow from her back. She avoids his eyes and steps out of his way.

Aliras separates his feet and turns his chest to the side. Barely taking a second to aim, he before releases the arrow. It twirls in a perfect line into the bullseye. He passes the bow back, then goes to lean against the railing.

"Thanks for rubbing it in my face." She wipes sweat from her brow. Even in the shade, the Goldryn sun turns the air to fire. Summers here must be a nightmare.

Aliras crosses his arms. "When you get good enough you could turn that into a serious weapon. I'm sure fire arrows are not fun on the receiving end."

"Why would I ever need to do that?" she asks.

"A war seems more likely each day."

Ava rolls her eyes. "And who's fault is that?"

"Both regions are at fault."

"What has Wyntryn ever done to provoke Goldryn?" Ava asks.

"Exist." He pushes off the column and turns away from her. "Your Highness." He bows at the hip.

"I'm not a queen—"

"Sister, I'd like to talk to you. Aliras, would you excuse us?" Stygian steps out onto the terrace. Aliras exits into the hallway, holding Ava's gaze as he goes. Stygian steps in front of Ava, blocking her view of him. "I need you to do something for me."

"And what might that be?" Ava asks.

"I want access to your mind."

Ava smiles. Is she kidding? Ava wishes her sister

was, but Stygian doesn't make jokes. Ava shakes her head and looks out at the ocean. "No."

"What do you mean, no?"

"I think it's time I go home. If you want Wyntryn as an ally, I need to speak to the other protectors. I am still an heiress. I can help you politically, but I will not give you access to my mind."

Stygian's eyes narrow. Her expression changes as she stalks toward Ava. She holds her hand out. Ava keeps her gaze on the ocean. "You will listen to your queen."

Stygian wraps her energy around Ava's mind. Her teeth clench against the pain. Her sister's claws dig into her mind, like needles slicing through her. Ava bites back the urge to cry out. This is the same attack Saira has used on her many times before. Ava can steady herself. She's survived worse.

"You will listen to your queen," Stygian repeats.

"You are not my queen." Ava fights her sister's hold. Ava pulls on the energy around her, focusing it on Stygian.

Her sister's anger only rises. Heat billows around them in waves, turning the air a hazy purple and blue. "Guards!" Stygian shouts. Ava gasps as the claws retract from her mind. "Take her."

Two soldiers rush in, purple uniforms waving in the ocean breeze. They grasp Ava's upper arms and yank her hands behind her. They grip her wrists, pulling the skin tight.

"Is this how you treat your family?" Ava stills. Only her knees shake, begging to buckle beneath her. "You don't get your way, so you result to violence?"

"Darling, I don't want to hurt you." Her tone is grossly kind. A dark smile stretches across Stygian's lips.

She flicks her wrist, and the guards drag Ava into the palace.

Ava catches Aliras' surprised gaze as they pass him in the hall. His eyes widen and he runs past to the terrace. Ava plants her feet beneath her and yanks away from the guards. "Your Highness, what is the meaning of this?" Aliras shouts from down the hall.

"Aliras dear, she is to stay in her chambers unless I allow her to leave. If you break these orders, I will place a charm on the threshold and replace you with someone else. You know who will die if that happens."

The soldiers catch her with little effort and pull her back. "Let go of me," she grits out. Ava manages to free one arm. There's a clack as her knee hits the floor. It's hard to gain her balance back when they pull against her. She kicks her legs out, but it's useless. She could use her fire, but that will only enrage her sister more. The guards pull her back up and throw her ahead of them. In doing so they release her wrists.

There's no point in fighting this. Ava will find a way out later. She hugs her stomach. One guard grasps her shoulder and pushes her down the hall.

Aliras grabs the guard pushing her, then punches him in the chest. The soldier slams into the wall. "I'll take it from here." He moves past the other soldier and walks silently beside her.

They turn down the hallway leading to her chambers. "I never should have come here," Ava admits.

"There are benefits to being here," he says.

"I would rather get back to Wyntryn and try to fix the mess I made." Her head pulses and her hands shake at her sides.

"Mess?" he asks.

"I abandoned my region when they needed me most. I haven't done anything to help them. If anything, I've provoked a war." Her heart stutters in her chest.

"You thought coming here was a clever idea?"

She glances at him. His dark hair sways with his steady strides. She lets her shoulders loosen and fall forward. "Someone I trusted killed my closest friend. I had nowhere to go but here. I had just met my sister, or at least learned she was my sister."

"If you claim to have trusted them, why run?" Aliras asks.

Ava pauses. Her gaze bores into the sandstone floor. "No explanation would have brought my friend back to life." For three months, Levi was all she knew. She was in that apartment in Grymyr alone with no memories. Now she has some, but even now, Levi is still prevalent in her mind. Raiden had no right to take Levi's life. Sure, Ava would love to know why he did it, but Levi's gone and that won't ever change.

Aliras shrugs. "Everyone has their reasons. I watched my friends alate back from Rebynrock. Heard their screams. Waited for friends to return, who never made it back." She flinches, digging her nails into her palms.

It seems everyone is wise enough to consider Raiden's reasoning, but her. It may be the lack of memories, but she feels so foolish sometimes. As if everyone is far ahead and she's desperately trying to catch up. She sighs. "It's useless now anyway. Even if I were to ask, I can't. I'm stuck in this palace now, aren't I?"

"If you think so," Aliras says.

Ava is quiet until she reaches her chambers. She opens her door and turns to Aliras. "What does my sister hold against you?"

Light hits his irises, turning them into pools of blue with strokes of honey.

"Why do you ask?" Aliras crosses his arms.

The words don't come out at first, but they eventually form on her tongue. "I can sense your hatred for her, yet you stay." She doesn't mention that she overheard Stygian threaten to kill someone dear to him. That is not for her to know.

He looks past her, then narrows his eyes.

"Right..." Ava closes the door between them. She knows it has nothing to do with her, but she figured he might want to talk about it.

She goes to the desk in the corner of her room. She sits down and pulls out a pack of parchment. This won't be the first letter she's written to her cousin Anya, but if she escapes Goldryn soon, it may be her last.

She has been sending and receiving letters from Anya for weeks now via the servant who brings her dinner. The woman revealed her Wyntryn heritage to Ava on her second night in Goldryn. Ava learned that the woman was from a small village along the western coast. Her village was ravaged by Atane and the woman, Eris, was never able to find the hidden cities. So she made her way to Goldryn. Here she was kidnapped by Goldryn guards. When she was eventually released, the only job she could get as a foreigner was a servant's position here in the palace.

Ava sent her first letter through Eris when she learned of Stygian's threats to Raiden. Stygian told Raiden she would deliver Nina and Willow's heads to him if he didn't bring her the arrow talisman. Ava was able to convince Stygian to trade Raiden's life with an ancient artifact from the manor. She chose to reach out to Anya, and her cousin helped get the artifact to Goldryn. Ava isn't sure why the object has any power over Stygian. It's a small figurine covered in markings of the ancient language. Maybe Stygian had no interest in killing Raiden, she just wanted to put up a fight. Now she's stuck in this room for the same reason. Stygian wants control, and so does Ava.

The only issue is that Ava's at risk of something Stygian isn't—guilt.

Her mind melds with the wispy firelight that hugs her skin. She's curled up on the soft velvet couch in the Wyntryn manor, her face turned to the embers of the burning fire. The familiar smells of her time there, jasmine, and sweet cinnamon soak into her memory. She had loved the warmth of this place.

The door whispers quiet mumblings as it opens and closes. His soft voice travels out into the air. "I thought I would find you here." He sits down beside her and shifts his arm over the back of the couch. She moves to him, nestling against his chest. He wraps his arms around her. "She doesn't mean any of it, you know."

"My mother is very calculated. She never makes mistakes," Ava says. Her eyes sting from the aftermath of crying. She was crying because of an argument with her mother. Though, she can't remember what it was about. The world blurs in her mind as if in a dream.

"I know. Do you want to tell me about it?" he asks.

She twists her face against him, keeping it hidden from view. "She told me that my father needs to be taken out of the picture. She's going to kill him, Rais." That's who this is. She's lying against Raiden. She runs her hand along his bare arm. Her sobs have faded away now, but there is still a steady rumbling in her chest that rises up her throat.

"I—" he begins to say.

"You didn't know." She moves her face from the curves of his chest to face the fire. "I know you overheard some of it. But um … Goldryn and Grymyr have formed an alliance. The Society has begun shattering any irregular mind that does not fall within the borders of their agreement. Mother said the Society is going to move on Wyntryn by the end of the week. She's taking me back to Grymyr. To stay with my father under our hidden identities until the threat passes. But as soon as his protection is no longer needed, I think she's going to kill him." Ava's voice breaks and a light sob escapes. "I tried to convince her not to, but she wouldn't listen."

Raiden tightens his arms around her. "You may not be able to stand against her on your own, but there are other ways to fight back. You will find a way to save your father."

She upturns her face to him, catching the gold of his eyes. "Will you help me?"

"Always, but now that I'm the Sparrow, no one can know. I could be killed for treason if your mother knows I helped you."

"I don't know what I'd do without you," she mumbles.

The memory is breached by another, and Levi's empty eyes stare at her from the carpet. Blood pools beneath the couch, and Ava pushes from Raiden. "You don't understand. He was lying to you," Raiden says.

She looks to him. Her mage's jacket morphs into

the dark blue dress she was wearing that night. "You are the one lying! All of you …" The words force themselves through her mouth. "Well guess what, Raiden?" He reaches for her arm, but she moves away. "I don't trust you." The room blurs into the attic of the warped library. "You are nothing to me," she says, repeating words she's spoken before. Rage rifles through her and she reaches for his throat.

A knock sounds in the distance. Raiden fades away. There's another knock. She opens her eyes, breaking from the dream. A groan escapes her lips, and she rubs her forehead. She lifts herself up and leans against her elbows. Her quilt is crumpled at her feet and her pillow is on the floor. The memory recedes to the back of her mind as she balances herself in reality. Ava has to stop dreaming of Raiden. She gets waking nightmares of Levi's death, of her mother's death, but sometimes her dreams are of kind memories. Ava doesn't deserve those short moments of happiness. And Raiden doesn't deserve forgiveness.

She glances around the small room. The breeze from the ocean flows in, lacing the air with a salty tang. She slides off the bed, goes to the door, and opens it a crack.

Aliras leans against the opposite wall, his hands in his pockets. He opens his eyes and looks at her. She's suddenly aware of her bare legs and crumpled nightgown. Ava cuts her gaze away from Aliras to the maid who holds a tray of food, Eris. She pushes the door open for her.

Ava goes across the room to her desk and grabs the letter she wrote earlier. She slips the letter into Eris' pocket. Eris places the tray of food on Ava's bed. There's a letter underneath the bowl of soup. Ava whispers, "Thanks." Eris bows her head and leaves, closing the door behind her.

She sits on the bed and pulls the envelope open. The letter is in Anya's handwriting, as expected.

My Winter Drogon, the Society has been breached by our forces. They have agreed to back down and will not seek vengeance for the death of Levites or the officers in Rebynrock. We ask that you find a way to warn us of the Queen's plans. We hear she has discovered more than twenty of her soldiers murdered north of the border, in the village of Pheyais. Be wary of her terror. Sincerely, your Pheyani.

Ava goes to her open window and lights a fire in her hand. She burns the letter and watches the ashes spindle down into the ocean. Her cousin uses the name Pheyani because she is the air below Ava's wings. The air that keeps Ava in flight despite their dire circumstances.

Without their real names, Stygian wouldn't know who to target if she were to discover the letters. If she did, Ava would willingly take the blame. Though she has distanced herself from her lands and her people, she is still their heiress. She will protect them in any way she can. Even if that means risking her life.

Chapter Four

"Let's pick up the pace, we don't have much light left," Exceail calls from the front of their pack.

They left the capital of Eventyr hours ago. The sun now dips into the western horizon, its rays cascading across the hills. Rais travels with Exceail, along with four other mages. He and Nina fit into the group surprisingly well. He's found that these mages are much different than the guards who tried to arrest Nina. The four of them make casual jokes and even direct snarky comments at Exceail. Despite him being their superior, Exceail responds with the same bluntness—easily falling into the laughter and chatter of his soldiers.

"Our pace is only slow because your horse's gait is more askew than Grymyr's architecture," Nina remarks. The youngest mage, Myer, cackles loud enough to scare away the cicadas. Exceail glares back at the boy. Myer averts his gaze and coughs away the laugh.

"My horse back at home is quite the charmer," Rais says.

Nina rolls her eyes. "If only charisma were enough

to survive."

Exceail tugs on his reins, slowing his horse. "It is when you're as handsome as I, that survival is never an issue." His tone is stiff, exposing it as a stale joke.

"Oh, you wish," Nina chides.

Rais chuckles to himself. The other mages have to hide their shaking chests and breathy laughs. It's a good thing he went on this trip. For a while there, he was worried that he'd never laugh again. Nina and this band of buffoons have washed that worry away. Ahead, colors shoot across the blades of grass. A kaleidoscope of pink and orange cut through bright blue.

Wind whistles through the trees. A steady ebb and flow of energy travels through the lightly forested area. Rais settles back in the saddle, leading the horse into a walk. The others trot on ahead, but something pulls him back. He glances across the forest to a dark opening within the trees. The darkness spindles across the grass and rises toward him. *Raiden*, it whispers. The energy reaches out. A tendril rises from the grass and wraps around his chest. The amulet burns against his sternum. Rais turns from the webs of energy and presses the horse to move faster. The tendril that wrapped around him slithers back into the forest. He travels away from the beckoning darkness. His heart thundering against his ribs.

Rais wants to rip the talisman from his neck and chuck it into the darkness. If only he could save Wyntryn another way.

He catches up to the rest of the group and maneuvers his way to Exceail's side. Through the Sonder, he sends a trickle of his mind to Exceail—an invitation to speak with him. As soon as Exceail recognizes the question, his walls drop. Rais sends a thought. *Are there any side effects to wielding the talisman?*

What did you see? Exceail asks in turn.

I felt something calling to me. A darkness.

I wouldn't worry about it. Exceail pushes Rais from his mind, shutting his mental shields. Rais pulls on the reins, falling back with the other soldiers. That conversation ended quite abruptly. Exceail knows something.

Rais shakes his discomfort away and stares ahead at the setting sun. In Rebynrock, Ava noticed the arrow had altered his mind. She said it was changing him. Possibly the scale has similar effects, but ones that attack his physical reality. He knows there are few who can handle the influx of energy talismans provide. The minds sealed within the talismans have their own personalities and they must align with their possessor. If a soul doesn't approve of its possessor, it could destroy them. Rais hopes he can handle it. Even Kalenti Alberona had her struggles maintaining the abilities of the talisman. With her powers of decay and darkness, the talisman caused her to lose control of her deadly abilities. Six years ago, she was responsible for creating a crater of destruction within the central city. It was before she became queen, and her own parents imprisoned her for her actions. Rais turned thirteen that year. It is only a matter of time until he discovers if the talisman will tarnish his own soul as it has tarnished hers.

As the sun sets, Exceail slows their travel. They stop at a clearing in the forest to set up camp. Not long ago Rais saw a village in the distance. They could have stayed at an inn there, but Exceail must prefer the isolation of the forest.

Rais secures his horse to a fallen tree. Nina does the same, then turns to him. "Hey, I'm going to find some logs for a fire. Want to come?"

"No, I think I'll stay here for now," he says. Nina studies him curiously before walking away.

Myer, a short boy with coily hair and a thin frame, begins to set up tents at the edge of the clearing. Rais walks over and helps unfold the canvas. He asks, "How long have you been a soldier? You look young."

Myer's dark eyes flick to him. "You look young to be a Sparrow."

Rais' mouth lifts into a smile. "You are not wrong."

Rais grasps an extendable pole and slides it underneath the tent. He holds it in place as Myer works around him. The boy turns to him. "I joined the army when Gladlyn attacked the kingdom. My father was a royal mage at the time, and I wanted to help protect my sisters."

He moves out from underneath the canvas and pushes stakes in place along the edges of the tent. He follows Myer across the clearing. They unfold another canvas, then begin to set it up. "Why are you traveling to the western coast?" Rais asks.

Myer shrugs. "They needed mages with fire abilities along the coastal camps. So I didn't have much choice in the matter."

"Your energy manifests into fire?" In the western continent, the only fire wielders are those with direct blood ties to the Wyntryn's. He hadn't realized those same abilities existed elsewhere.

"Right, it's pretty rare where you're from." Myer secures the last stake, then stands, stretching his arms above him. "Why are you traveling with us, Sparrow Hynrule?"

Rais glances over to Nina. She drops an armful of logs before Exceail, then plops herself on the ground. "I needed Queen Kalenti's help. My region is on the verge of war."

"Did she help?"

"Yes, more than I deserved," Rais says.

After setting up the three tents, Rais walks over to Nina. He leaves Myer to set up the last tent with the help of another Eventyr mage, Kat.

Nina sends a gust of wind toward him, ruffling his hair. He looks down at her, and her smile drops. "Are you still letting her bother you?"

Rais moves his gaze to the forest floor. It's covered in pine needles, leaves, and small patches of grass. He doesn't want thoughts of Ava to plague him, but they do anyway. Sometimes they're memories of when they were happy. Other times her hand burns his throat. All he wants to do is get back to her. To hold her close and beg for forgiveness. He wants their past to fade away so that they can escape their demons together. Rais fights for his words, but nothing escapes him.

"I'm sure she's safe in Goldryn," Nina says. He shakes his head. No Wyntryn is safe in Goldryn. "I highly doubt Stygian would do anything drastic. She knows we have the arrow. And after Rebynrock, I'm sure she is suspicious of what else we are hiding within the mountains. She won't risk her own downfall." She shifts her arms behind her.

"I disagree," he says. "Stygian almost killed Alys the summer she left for Goldryn. If she is willing to risk the wrath of Wyntryn when the region is strong, she will risk it when the region is weak. Plus, she has no care for family ties. Ava will not dare harm her sister, but Stygian has no limits." Rais will believe Ava's safe when he sees it with his own eyes.

"Hmph." Nina pushes off the ground. "I suppose

you'll figure that out when you get back to Wyntryn." Rais watches her move to the fireside. Nina bends to her knee and accepts the food offered to her by a light-haired woman. Rais thinks her name is Jenny, but he could be wrong. Rais pushes from the ground, then strolls out into the forest.

As the sky darkens, stars begin to shine through the covering of trees. He slips along an invisible pathway, escaping the murmuring of his traveling companions. He reaches a place far enough away for the Sonder to be quiet. Where all he can hear are the chirping of crickets. Rais looks up to the sky.

"We will find our way back to each other," he says into the empty air. "We always do." He adds the last part to reassure himself.

The world whispers in response. The talisman that hangs against his chest sinks into him. The soul residing there, slipping into his mind, and twisting its way in. Rais doesn't fight the feeling—he lets it dig into him. He needs the energy. Needs the power it can provide. He will accept the consequences if it helps him save Wyntryn and bring Ava home. More than anything else in the world, he needs her.

He drops to his knees. His stomach flips, driving bile up his throat at the thought of Ava's hand around his throat. The smell of burning flesh in the air. Levites' still body lying in a pool of red. The rage in her eyes.

Despite all that, his passion and care for her have never subsided. He's angry and hurt, but not enough to hate her. He could never hate her. She is everything to him. Even though he is nothing to her.

Rais returns to the camp later that night. Everyone is asleep in the tents except for Exceail. He sits on a log by the fire. Rais takes a seat by him, resting his forearms on his thighs.

"Don't sleep much?" Exceail asks.

"No. My mind never seems to turn off."

Exceail's lips tug upward. "I'm the same way. Kalenti is like that too, but she has other reasons for avoiding sleep."

"Myer told me he's traveling to the coast because they need fire mages. Why are you going there?" Rais asks.

"There's an uprising of one of the units there. Normally I'd alate, but Myer and Nolan, our fire mages, don't have that ability."

"What will you use fire for?"

"You ask a lot of questions beyond your position." His voice is level and not accusatory as the words suggest. "You see, people fear fire. The presence of fire mages is threat enough to end an uprising. But if it doesn't, the power comes in handy for other purposes."

The muscles in Rais' jaw feather at what Exceail implies.

"What will you use that gift for?" Exceail asks, his voice low and swallowed by the noises of the forest.

Rais is in no place to judge Exceail for his choices. He will use this ancient power to save Wyntryn no matter what it takes. No matter the extent of the destruction. He will not stop until his people are free. Until every Atane is destroyed, and their borders are safe from Goldryn and the Society. If the Petrichors have succeeded in their endeavors, the Society shouldn't be much of a problem to them now. But he doesn't tell Exceail that. He says, "To stop the war."

"I hope it works then. Kalenti is beginning to part ways with Goldryn. Stygian hasn't kept her promise. But if you return that to her as she requested, you will have the greatest region in Kanaleigh as your ally."

His words are strong. Exceail would never tell him that unless he honestly believed it. Rais glances at him. "I will make sure it gets back to her."

Exceail gives him a curt nod. He stretches his tattooed arms above his head and rises from the log. "I suppose I will try to get some rest. You should too. We have a long day ahead of us."

Ava is in Goldryn, but no one knows what she does there. Rais hopes she returns to Wyntryn to claim her throne, to save her people, but he fears she won't. The prophecy never predicted the sisters would come together. It prophesized their demise—their rivalry. It said if they don't destroy each other, then they will destroy the Sonder.

Imperceptible tendrils of darkness escape the talisman and slither across his skin.

Rais won't find any rest tonight.

Chapter Five

Willow

"Do you feel it?" Willow asks. She holds out her hands, feeling the breeze run through her fingers. The air is tainted with salt and honeysuckle. If she shifts to the left, she can catch a northern breeze that carries pine and snow. The City on the Sea has air currents from all across the western shore running through it. A person only has to know where to look.

"Feel what?" the guard asks. He stands at the gate of the city, like a cat, ready to pounce if she gives him a reason to. All these guards are that way. They don't like an Eventyrian living amongst them. Especially not one with more freedom than them.

"There is electricity in the air. Very soon this city will be—" Her gaze catches on a bird flying toward them. "Goddesses save me. What a peculiar creature." Willow steps past the gate, and the guard narrows his eyes. She reaches her hand out to the bird—a sparrow. It lands on her finger with steady grace. Its rounded body is covered in intricate feathers that ruffle with its small movements. The bird's beady black eyes turn to her. She smiles at it.

"You are a special thing, mister sparrow."

A spindle of purple fire flies past Willow's cheek and engulfs the small creature. She gasps and wrenches her hand back from the fire. She watches in horror as the burning bird falls to the stones of the bridge. Tears burn in her eyes from the horrid smell that fills the air. If only she could save it.

"Willow, I expected your audience an hour ago," Stygian says.

She turns to the Queen. "I am not obligated to listen to you."

"Ah, but you are. If it were not for me —"

"If it were not for me, Syn, you would not have an alliance with Eventyr. You have burned many bridges that I have rebuilt for you." It is not often Willow has the need to defend herself, but this is less of a defense and more of a correction. She will not be treated as a pawn in Stygian's game. Stygian locks her gaze with Willow. The Queen's cheeks flush red and she opens her mouth to respond. Stygian hates being corrected. Hates being talked over even more. Before Stygian can make her smart response, with a delicacy Willow says, "You did not have to murder the sparrow. He did nothing wrong."

"If only it were a different sparrow that I killed." Stygian smiles contently. "Come now darling, I need to discuss my sister with you."

Willow doesn't doubt she would kill Rais, but she has no reason to. Stygian does nothing without reason, even if the reason is obscure and nonsensical.

Willow looks longingly over her shoulder as she follows the Queen. She was going to gather herbs from a vendor in the city. Instead, she gets to watch the train of Stygian's purple dress. Black stripes run down the length of the gown and a crown of black flowers rests in her hair. An elegant woman with a dismantled mind.

Afternoon sunlight pours through the high windows of the throne room, causing the tiles to glisten. Stygian doesn't go to her throne. Rather she turns to Willow and gestures for the guards to leave.

A chill travels along the back of her neck. Willow moves her hands to the small of her back. She doesn't fear Stygian, but that doesn't mean she trusts her either. The scars on Willow's palms and feet are proof that Stygian wouldn't hesitate to cause her harm. It isn't the pain that Willow fears, because she can outlast pain. What scares her is what Stygian is planning to do with Ava. Willow cannot stand the pain of others — of those she cares about. She nearly broke when she watched Kalenti Alberona slowly fall to madness. She would have stayed if given the chance, but Kalenti made her leave. Chose Exceail, the boy who saved her from the streets, and trained her into a huntress. Willow left Eventyr right as Kalenti returned to the palace to face the wrath of her wicked mother. It wasn't long before Kalenti's father, the King, passed the throne down to her.

"I've discovered letters have been arriving for my sister." Willow turns her attention to Stygian. Her words are precise, calculated. "They are given to her in secret. Delivered by one of the maids bringing her dinner. This is … unacceptable. You are close to her, what punishment would stop this madness?"

These letters must be coming from Wyntryn. From the protectors. She is the heiress after all. "She is her own person. Why would she be punished for letters she receives?"

Stygian's brows dip and her lip twitches. "You see,

she is defying me."

"What is to say these letters are not to negotiate an alliance with Wyntryn, on your behalf?" Willow asks. She is grasping at nothing, but there may be some truth to her lies.

"I have read one, and it is informing my sister of Wyntryn's affairs. It has nothing to do with an alliance. Although it would be smart of her to consider approaching them about it."

Willow twists the ring on her middle finger. She has to keep Stygian calm or at least off Ava's scent. Ava is not the most truthful person, but she is young. With her memories gone, who's to say if she is capable of reasonable thinking. "How can she approach the protectors of Wyntryn if she is being kept in Goldryn?"

"She is not," Stygian practically shouts.

"You assigned your personal assassin to her as a protector. You cannot say that was with good intentions. Last I heard his instructions were to report her every move to you. Are you planning to have him kill her if she turns against you?"

"He is my most trusted soldier. I have placed a lot of trust in you as well. Yet you are leading me to think you would defend Ava before defending me. Do not undermine me. You may be a royal in Eventyr, but here, I could easily return you to the underwater dungeons at any time." Stygian walks toward her, stopping inches from where Willow stands. She places her pointer finger below Willow's chin, lifting her face. "Now, what would be a reasonable reaction to what she has done?"

"Not allowing her to leave the palace, would certainly make her think better of working against you. She finds happiness out in the city." She keeps her gaze steady with Stygian's, but Willow can see right into her mind. The Queen is bold to touch her. To allow her access. "Ah, but you've already done that. Haven't you?" An image flashes in her mind. "Why ask for my advice, Syn? You killed that maid and dropped her in the Cataclyse ravine. What was her name, Eris?" Stygian drops all unwanted things in the Cataclyse ravine. It's a dreadful place that's a quarter mile from Iyer City. Most Goldryn's avoid it like the plague. Stygian retracts her hand from Willow. She has no interest in Ava's safety. Stygian only seeks control. Willow can see the dark thoughts which have sunken their claws into the Queen. The poor woman is so similar to her sister. She must never have a moment of peace in her own mind.

Stygian turns her back to Willow. "Leave."

Willow is careful not to move too quickly. There's no reason to raise further suspicion. She finds her way out of the palace and past the gates. Nina is in the city, so that's where Willow will go. Anywhere is better than the palace. There is only so much she can take of Stygian. After seeing into her mind, Willow has little room to sympathize with the Queen. Nina will be a breath of reason. Nina has sharp words, but her presence allows Willow to relax. If only a little.

She goes to the Fallen Anchor pub—the one Nina lives above. The sign outside flickers, its surrounding flowers wilted and crumpled. Willow enters hesitantly, and to her surprise, the pub is empty. Normally the location is filled with drunken irregulars swaying to piercing melodies. Those with power, irregulars, don't know what to do with it, whereas the regulars tend to despise the humans with access to the Sonder. It keeps most regulars in the north end of the city. Oddly enough, there's more crime there. Regulars can't access the Sonder—Willow's found that makes them hungry for chaos.

"Willow, is it?" Max asks. She has broad shoulders and a cold expression.

"Yes, is Nina here?"

Max raises her brows. "Hasn't been in weeks."

Her heart sinks. "Do you know where she's gone then?"

"Never told me. I suppose she's off somewhere up in Wyntryn. She always talks of it anyway."

Willow nods. "I appreciate the help. Would you let me know when she comes back?"

Max spins a mug in her hands. "I'll tell her to go find you."

The floorboards creak and a group of boards lift from the floor on a hinge. Someone pushes the hatch. It swings open, hitting the floor with a clack. In the empty space is a set of stairs winding beneath the pub. The man who opened the hatch locks eyes with her. Max huffs. "You shouldn't have come here," the man says.

He hops out of the hole in the floor. The man walks toward her. Before she can move out of the way, he grasps her wrists. Rather than struggling free, she intrudes his mind. She forces his mind to shut down. His grip loosens, and she pulls herself free. "You should not touch a person without their permission," Willow says. The man crumples to the floor. The veins in his neck strain and he grasps at the ground. She must have not done that right—he's not supposed to be in that much pain. His nails drag against the wood. It's not often she makes mistakes like this. Willow turns her gaze to Max. "Tell me, what's beneath this pub?"

"Nothing you have to worry about." Max grips the edge of the counter. An act to steady her anger, but Willow can see the rage rise in the creases of Max's face.

"I will choose to worry then." Willow goes to the stairwell and steps down. She can hear a faint murmur coming from the bottom of the stairs. Willow glances at Max, but she doesn't move to follow Willow. "I am not the Queen's pet you know. I have no obligations to her," she says. Max's nose twitches—she must not believe her.

The stairs creak beneath her, and the voices stop. Willow descends the steps. The room is quaint, but it appears to be connected to a tunnel that stretches into darkness. In the center of the room, chairs circle a table covered with a map. Four pairs of eyes look at her.

"What is this?" she asks.

One of them gulps. Another lifts her chin. "First, who are you?"

"Willow Evergryn. I assume one of you may know where I can find Nina?" Willow presses her palms to her airy dress and smooths out nonexistent wrinkles.

The same woman contemplates her response for a moment. "We do. Did she send you here?"

"No. Your"—she looks to the stairwell—"friend, revealed the staircase to me by chance. I am not here to expose whatever this is, but I am curious to know what it is."

The woman looks to the other three people sitting around the table. She stands. "This is the Drogon Insurgency. We are working together to stop the fourth resurgence of the Great War."

Willow's vision blurs. "Unfortunately, war is inevitable. As the flowers bloom in the north, the dragon will rise, and the ocean will open its depths to entrap an evil," she says.

The only regular at the table stands. He's unusually

tall with deep brown eyes. "Are you one of those fortune tellers? Because all they speak are lies." That's what everyone thinks of her. But she only lies when protecting the truth.

"No, sir, I only share what I see. The energies of Kanaleigh give me visions, but I have no control over them. I do not give fortunes. I speak truths," Willow says. The woman laughs. She quickly covers her mouth with her hand. Willow tilts her head. So peculiar these people are. Based on their accents and features, they appear to be from various regions. "Do you have a member from Eventyr?" They shake their heads. "Wonderful, I would like to join this … Drogon Insurgency. I would think having a royal on your team could provide you with more resources."

The man's brows dip. "We do not need more members."

The nymph speaks up, likely from Aysand by the looks of her. "I think we should let her join us. There are only six of us, including Nina." She has scaly skin and iridescent eyes. Her hair is long, and her ears are pointed. Willow has always been fascinated by nymphs. There aren't many in Eastern Eventyr or Goldryn. The Aysand nymphs often inhabit cities built right off the coast. All nymphs can breathe underwater, but water nymphs are the only ones who typically live in the seas. Their bodies are capable of morphing into sea creatures.

The regular rolls his eyes. "Zada, we have been doing just fine with six."

"What do you need?" Willow asks.

"Access to ships. It would allow us to help those who want to flee. We also need the five talismans of Wyntryn," Zada says. Her ears flicker.

"My father is the high lord of the Crystal Lakes. He

can get you ships, and I can help set up access points into Eventyr," Willow offers. Maybe she's jumping into this too soon, but Stygian has no regard for anyone who doesn't worship her. She's held onto her belief in Stygian's goodness for far too long. Clearly, there is no saving whatever soul is left inside. She is a bomb ready to explode, and if Willow has any chance of saving those near Stygian, this group may be the only way.

The woman who spoke before smiles. "We would be grateful for your help."

An irregular man at the table with long dark hair stares at the woman in disbelief. "You are kidding, right? Yes, we need help, but we don't even know this girl, Jess."

Jess takes a deep breath. "If you are going to speak to me like that, keep my name out of your mouth, Archer." She turns to Willow. "Can you prove you can get those ships?"

"Do you trust Nina?" Willow asks. The four of them nod. "Then you can trust me."

"You live in the palace, don't you?" Jess asks. Willow looks down at herself. She is wearing a finely made dress and heels. An Eventyr circlet stretches across her forehead, with an amethyst centered just above the bridge of her nose. She looks the part of a palace dweller.

They may not trust Willow, but she is not a friend to Stygian. The least she can do is fight against the coming war. Even if it is inevitable, maybe she can do something to bring it to a quick end. "I may live in the palace, but I do not support Stygian or her endeavors," she says.

"Well, Willow, we meet here once a week. On the only day the pub's closed. I'm Jess, that's Archer, Zada, and" — she points to the regular — "that's Kael. You've met Nina. And lastly, there's that fella upstairs you mentioned.

Though, I'll let him introduce himself."

Willow turns to the man leaning against the wall at the bottom of the stairs. "Name's Sean. And you could've asked for me to let go of you. Didn't have to try to destroy my conscience."

"You are fine. I wasn't trying to destroy anything," Willow says. She had every reason to defend herself. As far as she knew, he was attacking her. "It's nice to meet all of you. Though I must ask why you need the talismans. They are not easy to come by, and three of them are possessed by quite powerful mages."

Zada leans forward. "We need them to place a barrier between the regions."

"You want to amplify a barrier charm?" Willow asks.

Archer smirks. "The people in power are mages, and their power comes from their access to energy. So, we cut off their source, and what do they have then? Some decent swordsmen?"

The plan is quite genius. By taking away the energy, they take away the ability of the kingdoms to destroy one another. Though, getting their hands on all the talismans is no easy feat. They also have to find someone who can handle the possession of all five talismans at once.

No matter what it takes, the war must be stopped. Otherwise, Wyntryn will not be the only region abandoned by its people. The entire continent could be destroyed by the rage of the warring kingdoms.

Chapter Six

Ava

Her skin is damp to the touch. The humidity is an endless annoyance. Ava leans her head against the windowsill, relaxing into the warm breeze. To another, she looks at peace, but in her mind screams ricochet around her skull. Her own screams.

Every time she blinks, she sees headlights shine, and her mother falls to the ground. When she stands too quickly, she sees Levi falling through the window. Each time these demons attack, she hears herself scream. As her mother and Levi's minds fade into mist. She feels the sticky blood on her hands and the tears rolling down her face.

At night when she can't sleep, she stares out at the sea and whispers her troubles to her friend. The friend who will never hear them. The friend she will only see again when death takes her.

The constant circling of memories never ends. They break into her reality and all she can do is stare, feel, and hope it passes soon. She is at fault for her mother's death, and now she's doomed to suffer these waking horrors.

History will never change, but she can choose what path to take now.

Ava flinches as a finger taps her shoulder. Willow stands to her right. When did she enter the room?

"I would like you to go into the city with me tonight," Willow says. A gleeful smile on her rounded face. Wide-legged pants flow around Willow's feet. A blouse of sage green hugs her chest.

"What for?" Ava asks–her mind still far from reality despite her efforts to escape the memories.

"Tonight, the sky will be clear, so you can see all the stars. This is the best night to experience the city!" Willow takes Ava's hand, but her face drops instantly. "Oh my—"

Ava always forgets to hide her mind from Willow. Not that she could if she tried.

Willow's eyes narrow at the thoughts that spin from Ava's troubled mind. "I never realized it was like this," she whispers. Willow's fingers tighten around her hand. "Ava, I am so sorry that you experience this."

Ava shakes her head, pulling herself from Willow. "Don't worry about me." She breaks away from the topic by saying, "And Willow, I can't go into the city either way. I'm stuck in this room."

"Right… I apologize. I forgot."

Willow walks away, but Ava doesn't hear the door open. She turns to find Willow running her fingers through her lavender hair. "What is it?" Ava asks.

"Your sister listens to me. I could get you out for the night."

"If you can, then I guess I'll go." Going into the city would be nice. This room is becoming too familiar. She swears it gets smaller each day.

"I'll be back at sundown," Willow says.

Sunset is hours away, and Ava has nothing to do till then. Her head burns with vicious thoughts. But it's her burden to bear, and Willow already has enough of her own. So, she has no one to talk to. Only she and the guard who has no choice but to be here.

Ava goes to her door and cracks it. Aliras doesn't seem to notice. His face is chiseled and his stance intrepid. He wears a uniform, unlike any other Goldryn soldier. Fitted black leather overlayed with purple metal. The cloak has the Goldryn sigil stitched in silver on the back of his right shoulder. She leans against the doorframe, watching him. There's nothing better to do. Her shoulder slips and the door swings, causing the hinges to groan.

His gaze flicks to her. "See something you like?" he asks.

She turns away from him and retreats into her room. That comment doesn't warrant a response.

Ava falls back on her bed and stares up at the ceiling. Chunks of turquoise shine as evening rays hit sandstone.

"I know the feeling," Aliras says. She sits up. The brooding soldier wants to talk—that's new. He leans against her doorframe, studying her prison of lackluster furniture. She should have slammed the door in his face.

An image of Levi flashes in her mind, and she feels his blood on her hands. She wills the memories away. Aliras' gaze spikes prickles along her skin. He can distract her. Ava forces herself to meet his eyes. "What feeling?" she asks.

Levi falls in front of her. Why won't the images dissipate? The memory plays out before her. Levi's body lies between her and Aliras. Her stomach flips.

Aliras steps inside. "When you can't escape the thoughts. The guilt. The sad—"

"You don't know me, so don't act like you do," she says. Blood pools on the floor. It stretches toward her feet. Headlights flash, and ringing fills her ears.

Aliras bends down before her. His knees in the blood, but there's not really blood. Her mind is making fun of her. "When you feel like you're drowning, you can talk to me. Sometimes you need help to breach the surface."

Ava wants to reach out and grab his shoulder. She wants to touch another person. A living person. To feel the warmth of someone near her. Her heart is cold, and her memories are nightmares. Even the kind memories of Raiden burn through her. She can't find happiness in those memories. Not when Levi flashes in her mind. Not when she's supposed to hate Raiden.

Aliras stands up and leaves. The door clicks shut.

She wants to tell Aliras everything. To confide in him the darkness that spirals through her. But she can't get too comfortable with a Goldryn soldier. Especially one known to be the right hand of the Queen. He could too easily report her secrets to her sister. She can't risk her region over an exhausted mind.

She's left to whisper the words to the stars at night. Which she does. Though there is only so much relief she can provide herself.

The night Levi died, she slept on the window seat. She fell asleep talking to the stars. She told herself then, that if she ever needed her best friend, she would talk to him through the night sky.

The afterlife may not exist. Levi could be nothing at all now, but she doesn't care. She still talks to him in the stars. She can't help it. She relied on Levi's support for so long, and without it, she's lonely. Alone and forsaken.

That must be how Rais feels. *No, Raiden.* Calling him Raiden keeps the thoughts of him at arm's length. His nickname is too personal. He killed Levi. He doesn't deserve candor.

Ava runs her hands through her hair as she bends before the bed. She leans her forehead against the mattress and grasps the quilt between her fingers.

A low sob rakes through her. She gasps with each heavy breath. She still misses her past. Misses her mother. She especially misses her best friend. And whether she wants to or not, she desperately misses Rais. Raiden. Gods. She has no self-control. She sobs into the quilt. The rage and hatred that burns through her soul is nothing compared to how she really feels for that foolish golden-eyed boy.

But he killed her best friend without a second thought. How can she ever forgive that? Yet, deep inside, she knows she already has.

She can admit that to herself, but nothing will make the dark thoughts go away. They're always circling her. A vulture waiting for its prey to finally give up so that it can sweep in for the kill. And she is, so, so close to falling victim to it. It has been closing in on her for as long as she can remember. Patiently waiting.

Ava pulls herself from her thoughts and looks to the mirror on the wall. In her reflection, she sees hard lines. It's been more than a month since Levi's death, and she can see the toll it has taken on her. If not his death, then the toll of living under her sister's roof. Her collarbones are more prominent and there are dark circles below her eyes. She's not underweight, but she looks sickly. She needs to take better care of herself, mentally and physically.

Orange and pink stretch across the room. Beyond her window, the sun dips below the horizon. Has she been crying for that long? Maybe she had mistaken what time it was when Willow was here. Without her tracker from Grymyr, it's hard to judge the time. Evidently when you're magic — an irregular — you should just know things. Well, she doesn't simply know those things.

Ava goes to the armoire by the window and pulls the sunflower yellow dress out. The material is soft — likely silk layered with chiffon. She goes to the bathroom and slips out of her clothes.

Once on, the yellow dress hugs her ribs comfortably and flows into looser waves around her legs. Unlike the dresses from Wyntryn, this one doesn't have any sleeves, only thin straps of ribbon that tie at the tops of her shoulders.

She pulls her hair into a ponytail and the shorter strands fall loose around her face. Ava sighs, glancing away from her reflection. She slides on her most comfortable sandals and lays back on her bed, waiting for Willow.

Her vision glazes over as she stares up at the ceiling, watching the particles fade together. She used to waste so much time doing that in Grymyr. There's something so fascinating about focusing on one thing and watching how your brain melds it together.

Not long after, her door swings open. Everything is graceful with Willow. She struts in with a delicate smile. "You look beautiful."

"Thanks," Ava says with little effort.

Willow grasps her wrist and tugs. "Come on!" Her pale eyes don't darken as they did before when she touched Ava. After watching Willow for the past few weeks, Ava has gathered that she can enter minds undetected through touch. She hasn't yet been able to figure out whether Willow chooses to enter the mind or not. Because it always affects her differently. Sometimes, there's no reaction. Other times she flinches or takes a step back in surprise. They are usually subtle reactions, but noticeable enough.

Ava lifts herself from the bed and lets Willow pull her through the palace. Ava notices that somewhere along the way, Aliras begins following behind. She slips into the Sonder, pushing past the hazy blue and into the outskirts of his mind. *Stalking me now?*

She glances back at him just as a faint smile crosses his lips. Aliras enters her mind, taunting. *Always, my lady.*

Ava rolls her eyes. A small part of the snake coiled around her heart breaks off, giving enough release to allow not for happiness, but at least a little amusement.

They trail out of the palace and onto the bridge that connects to the city. Waves crash against the dense sand below and then fade into a fizzle. The sea foam is effervescent. In the city, lights begin to flicker on. Darkness slowly consumes the land. As soon as the stars awaken, the city bursts to life. People pour from their homes, into the streets. They trickle to the market and city squares. Welcoming music rattles from across the bridge.

Ava watches with amazement. The remaining cities in Wyntryn could never compare to this. These people aren't fearful of falling into the hands of an enemy. They aren't scared of hunger or riddled with the grief of losing a loved one. They are simply … living. Being able to enjoy life is such a luxury.

When they enter the city, Ava freezes. "This is what I was talking about Ava, can't you feel it?" Willow asks. People push around them as Willow and Aliras wait for Ava to stop staring at the buildings and people. Aliras' hand grazes her arm, and she looks at him. He points down the street. The square at the end is filled with life. Magical sounds rattle from brass and string instruments. People dance and spin, filling the Sonder with sizzling energy. A power that soaks into her bones.

"Yes, I think I can," Ava says.

A girl in a sky-blue dress runs past them, barefoot and grinning ear to ear. Ava takes off in the same direction. Willow and Aliras are right behind. Ava swerves around people until she is within the square of sandstone buildings. Flora and ivy cover the walls and women and men wear crowns of flowers atop their heads.

Willow takes Ava's hand and pulls her into the group of dancing people. Ava can't remember ever doing these dances before, but she falls right into step. The same as when she rode that horse for what she thought was the first time, and her body knew exactly what to do.

The music swells around them, and Ava spins with Willow. Their clothes flow out around them. Hair falls from her ponytail and into her face as she dances but looking disheveled is the least of her concerns.

A hand grabs hers. Aliras. He gestures to the edge of the square. Ava holds her ground, not wanting to break from the energy. Aliras tugs against her, and she reluctantly follows. What does she have to lose? A few moments of dancing?

Aliras leads her from the throng of people. His irises reflect the warm lights that hang across the area. He places a crown of blue flowers on her hair. She smiles up at him, brushing her fingers against the soft petals and smooth green leaves. He's a lot nicer than his cold exterior.

Ava gets a wicked thought and grabs onto her guard's hand. While she's free from her prison, she might as well enjoy herself. Ava pulls him back into the crowd. *Dance with me*, she speaks through the Sonder.

Aliras shakes his head, but she grabs his other hand as the music picks up tempo. He falls into step with her and spins her with the sounds. *He actually dances.*

Aliras' brows dip. "Of course, I dance. I am a Goldryn after all."

Her cheeks burn. It would be smart to keep a hold of her thoughts. Especially around him, because who knows where her mind might wander, Though keeping control is practically impossible. She's lost in the breath of the city. The vibrance of the colors. The soaring of the music. The night air is warm against her skin. Her troubles far behind. For once it's as if they may never catch up. The grief and torment were drained out by the energy in this place.

As the music slows into a quieter, wistful tune, Aliras pulls her close to him. One hand settles at the center of her back. The other against her arm. She notices her own hands against the black fabric of his shirt. He's not wearing his armor. How did she not notice this before? Anxiety prickles up her spine. But she doesn't pull away. She is afraid of breaking the spell that the city has cast upon her, but her stomach flutters. This is wrong. It's not Aliras she's supposed to dance with. It was always supposed to be Raiden, but that can never happen. Not now.

A muscle feathers between Aliras' brows. "Thank you for ... this," he says, quiet enough that only she can hear.

"I could say the same to you," she says, forcing Raiden from her mind.

He dips his head to her in acknowledgment. "You may not realize but being assigned as your guard has saved me in a lot of ways."

"Will you tell me about it sometime?" she asks.

"It would be best if you return home before that moment arrives."

Her brows push together. She isn't sure if that's meant as a warning or not. She studies his peculiar irises rather than overthink it. His eyes fade from blue to brown. Like Nina's whose eyes are amber with speckles of another color.

The night passes too quickly.

Willow takes her to the market before the sun rises. There they go through many tents full of goods from across the two continents. As the sun presses past the horizon, Ava's back in the palace. In her chambers, lying in bed, staring off through her open window at the sunrise.

Her mind is quiet now. Only the faint ringing of silence fills her ears.

Chapter Seven

Raiden

Nina lifts her hand into the breeze. "What if the ship capsizes?" she asks. Rais shrugs. Voyages across the sea are rarely deadly. Nina simply hates anything she doesn't understand and sailing happens to be one of those things.

Up ahead, the ocean sparkles in the afternoon sun. After days of riding, it's finally within reach. Across the horizon are ships of various sizes, with large masts and flags from across the two continents. An expanse of rolling hills separates them from the marina. They're not far from their destination now.

Nina turns abruptly on her saddle and the horse fidgets beneath her. "Is keeping that ugly piece of jewelry hidden worth the seasickness?"

"Rather than cost Wyntryn its chance of survival? Yes," he says. Rais has never been on a ship before. He's seen one up close, but because he can alate he's never had a reason to board one.

Nina chuckles. "No, Wyntryn will survive either way. It's whether you want to win a war or not. A war that hasn't even begun." Her hood is pulled over her hair. The air is cold here, but it's nothing compared to Wyntryn's below-freezing temperatures. Warm weather should be arriving soon.

"I disagree. I will not reveal it until necessary," Rais says. He'll do as Kalenti advised. Keep the talisman close and avoid using the Sonder.

"Hmph. Let's hope the ride to the Dragon Isles doesn't kill us."

"You are ridiculous."

The edges of her mouth curve up. "It's my job to keep you on your toes."

"Is it? I thought your job is to annoy me."

She waves her hand at him. "Am I doing a good job, Sparrow Hynrule? Or should I spook your horse for you?"

"Do not even think—"

A gust of wind rushes around the hooves of his horse. The mare rears and lets out a sharp whinny. He tightens his grip on the reins. The leather rips against his skin, and he shifts back on the saddle. Nina's laughter echoes around him. The horse's front hooves clash into the grass and a pang shoots up Rais' spine. He pulls the reins to the right and leads the horse in a small circle to calm her down.

He rolls his eyes at Nina, and they join the rest of their group at the bottom of the hill. "Was that entertaining for you?" he asks.

Nina nods. "If only I had one of those image recorders from Grymyr. Then I could share it with Eieran."

"How upsetting," he says coldly. Regardless of his tone, he does share some of Nina's amusement. He likes talking to her. Their interactions are enough to keep him from spiraling. Especially when there's growing darkness nipping at the edges of his mind.

They continue their ride through the foothills. Birds cross the sky in flocks as clouds scurry after them. The blues are shaded with dark gray, and the ocean swells grow larger in the distance. A subtle chill crosses the lands. It is not the best time to board a ship.

Only feet ahead of them now is a large wooden fence stretching around a cove. Exceail leads the pack of them through an open gate and into the small village surrounding the beach and docks. The streets are dry, but the humidity signals a coming rain. People rush around the village, dragging tarps over market stands and hustling mounds of fish into buildings.

Exceail signals to his soldiers, and they dismount their horses. "Go to the stables, and I'll meet you in a moment. Tomorrow, we head to the village north of here." If they're traveling north, then this uprising must be along the Aysand border.

Myer waves to him before walking down the path with the other soldiers. Rais waves back. The boy sends a thought to the outskirts of his mind. *Good luck.*

Exceail, Nina, and Rais continue along the dirt street to the edge of the docks. There they dismount and pass the horses over to a woman with scaly skin. She appears to be one of the rarer irregulars—a nymph. A bloodline that is less humanlike, and more like the aquatic creatures they fused their blood with.

Rais unhooks his bag and holds it at his side. He bows his head to the woman. "Thank you."

She blinks idly, but smiles, if only a little. In Eventyr, certain irregulars aren't treated equally. It may be rare that this nymph is ever acknowledged. All Rais did was say thank you, but that's more than she's used to.

Exceail grabs Rais' bag from his hand. "The ship you will be boarding is this way. Your captain used to be one of my officers." Exceail points to a dirty old ship. Its masts sit at a slight angle and barnacles crawl up the side.

Rais and Nina walk with the General to the end of the dock. Before them is a large ship with the name, *Ta Drogon Gana*, painted across the port side. "To the dragon realm," Rais says aloud.

"This ship was built before the second Great War on your continent," Exceail explains. "When the two Kings of Eventyr were at war with each other a century ago, this vessel was used to transport refugees to the Dragon Isles. It's quite the artifact for both regions."

Nina's eyes widen. "It still floats?" Rais shakes his head. The ship is floating fine.

"It has been restored many times," Exceail says. Nina raises her eyebrows. Exceail sighs. "It is perfectly safe. This same route has run for ages, and your captain is trustworthy, as I said before."

"It's not as if we have a choice, I suppose," Rais says.

Nina shakes her head and jumps onto the plank leaned against the ship. Exceail looks to Rais. "Make sure you bring that back," he says.

Rais' muscles tense. "I told you I will. I trust we will have the support of Eventyr when it is returned?"

Exceail smirks. "Ah, brother, I cannot promise you that. Trust Kalenti. She has given you a key to saving your people."

"Which I am sure she does not do lightly," Rais says. Exceail tosses Rais' bag onto the deck. Rais grits his teeth. At least there's nothing valuable in there. His hand goes to his heart, where he feels the outline of the talisman underneath his shirt. Nina gestures for him to follow her, so he steps onto the plank. It wobbles underneath his weight. He continues across, then jumps down next to his bag.

"Hey, Raiden!" Exceail calls from the dock. Rais turns to him. "Safe travels into the Gana ta Itzaale." *The Realm of Darkness.* It's the name for the waters that separate the two continents, but it is not often one hears it aloud. It's called the Realm of Darkness, because one of the ancient goddesses, Itzal, is said to have called these waters her home.

"Good luck with your endeavors as well, General!" Rais calls back.

He is excited to return to Wyntryn. He prefers the air there. Eventyr is… different. It isn't bad in any way, it's just not home. Home is at the manor with—he shakes the thought of her away. He still has a mark on his neck from her hand. She has made him her enemy, and Rais may never escape that.

"Hopefully I can be in Goldryn in three days. I didn't realize we'd be here for so long," Nina says. When he doesn't respond, Nina elbows him. "I'm going to go yell at the captain for fun." Nina saunters off to a group of deckhands gathered at the bow. Rais doesn't even bother to go after her.

He isn't sure what she's planning to do in Goldryn. Nina is close to Willow, always has been. But they are never in harmony. Nonetheless, Nina may be heading to Goldryn for a reason not at all associated with Willow or Ava. If Nina were in a rush, she wouldn't have come to Eventyr with him. There's no reason she can't alate back anyway. It's only Rais who's tied to a talisman.

"Boys, want to let me know why I am the only woman aboard this vessel, with the exception of the forest nymph you've imprisoned below deck?" Nina asks the crew.

The forest nymphs hail from a tribe of irregulars in Wyntryn. They are far and few between these days. Those who are alive often keep to themselves. Irregulars are persecuted enough in regular territories, like Grymyr, but it is worse for the more peculiar bloodlines. Those people often have no safety in any region they go to. There are populations of night nymphs below the city of Metarock, and many water nymphs in the Isles, but elsewhere, they find homes far from civilizations. Many use ancient charms to hide their villages. Kanaleigh can be quite dangerous for those who are different.

There's an opening nearby leading down into the ship. He leaves Nina behind to investigate what he can. He passes through the thin passageways of bending wood and hanging lights. One room is full of barrels and stores of food. The next is for the crew to store their belongings and sleep. Canvas hangs between columns so that they can swing with the ship's movements. Rais goes to the next doorway, but it's locked.

He slips his mind into the Sonder and listens to the quiet thoughts that filter from the ship's crew. There's one mind that's unique and nearby. It seems the forest nymph is sequestered beyond the locked door.

I can feel you there, Sparrow. Rais' title is thought with disdain.

Can you tell me your name? Rais sends back.

Their mind is quiet for a moment, then the voice breaks through. *My name is Bryn, and no, I am not as your companion assumed me to be.*

What do you mean? he asks.

I am not a she. My bloodline does not define ourselves by physical means, but by our mind's image.

I apologize for our misinterpretations, Bryn. Might I ask why you are a prisoner?

Steps approach the door. Their breath somehow seeps through the wood and tickles Rais' skin. *The crew of this ship is regular, and they despise me more than they despise you. I am a prize to their Queens, but the fools do not realize their Queens do not imprison nymphs.*

Are you from Eventyr?

Bryn's nails click against the wood. *I am Wyntryn. My family lived in the Brockade forest before the Atane came.*

Rais doesn't speak through his mind this time. "Then I will not leave you in the Isles. When we get off this ship, you should come to Wyntryn with me."

Bryn clicks their tongue, and their mind disappears from the Sonder.

"What are you doing down here?"

Rais turns to the voice. A burly man covered in tattoos stares him down. Rais forces a smile. "I was looking for a place to leave my bag. I am Sparrow Hynrule."

The man grabs the bag from him and steps back until he is in range to throw it into the sleeping quarters. His bag thumps to the ground somewhere he cannot see. "You will find it when you need it. Stay away from that door, kid, we don't need any trouble."

Rais furrows his brows. "I am not a kid. I am a diplomat, an ally to the Dragon Isles."

"That's not what you look like," the man says.

"What's your name?"

"I am the first mate of this ship, Sparrow Hynrule. I do not have to tell you a thing." The man points to the stairs. "You stay where we can see you on deck."

Rais raises his hands and moves past the man. He goes through the passageways, then climbs the steps in a few strides. On deck, the crew move in all directions readying to leave port. Nina catches sight of him and jogs over. "They're all imbeciles," she says.

"Are they?" he asks. She shrugs and he looks off to the horizon. By the looks of the vessel, this is a fast ship, but it will be a while before they are home. Their route takes them to the Dragon Isles, which is long out of the way, but it is safer than docking in Goldryn. The Fynger Isles are even closer, but their King despises Eventyr. He wouldn't allow an Eventyr ship within sight. Their journey may be long, but it will be safe.

Rais is familiar with the Dragon Isles' Queens—Natalia and Mica Erminia. They saw Alys as not only a mentor but a friend.

"I brought cards," Nina says. Rais keeps his eyes on the ocean. The sky is darkening, but it doesn't seem real. It's not turning to night, because it's far too early for that. Rather it looks like storm clouds growing from a singular point. They call to him, harnessing the buzzing that already rings in the back of his mind. "Or I can play solitaire." Nina exaggerates a sigh.

One day he won't feel this way. There must be a point before his own death that he finds happiness. At least he hopes there will be. Because it seems there is a permanent downward spiral, that's dragging him along. He's riding on the edge of oblivion. Always praying for a hand to reach out and stop him.

"Raiden Hynrule, always so serious," Nina says. She leans the small of her back against the railing. "Are you contemplating your existence?" He glares at her.

Time never stops long enough for him to think clearly. This coming darkness is certainly not going to show him mercy either. He will have to hold on tight and hope he survives the fall.

"Of course, you are." Nina gives him a grin.

The sky is darker than obsidian. Wide swells rock the ship, crashing against the side and spraying the deck. Tsunami force winds rip through the air. Rais wipes salt from his eyes. The rain is heavy and terribly cold. If the storm gets any worse, the whole boat might fall apart. Most of the crew is sleeping now, but Rais couldn't fall asleep. Not with the ship practically turning over in this storm.

They've been at sea for eight days. During the day-time, the two air mages stand at the back of the ship and push them at great speeds. At night they keep pace with the ocean and natural wind. Rais imagines they aren't far from the Isles now. Past the heavy fog a silhouette of a peninsula appears in the distance.

Lightning streaks across the sky. It lights up the deck, and Rais catches sight of Nina. She climbs the stairs to the deck and walks his way, reaching her arms out for balance.

She grasps onto the railing next to him. "This doesn't seem normal."

"No. It's not," he says. His eyes stay on the horizon. It's blurred by an unusual cloud. It looks like the darkness he saw in the Eventyr forest. If he didn't know any better, he'd say it was following him. His mind is playing tricks on him. It's nothing more than that. He's just tired. There's no telling what's causing it, but he's positive it isn't real.

"What are you looking at?" Nina asks. Energy rumbles against his chest, writhing within the talisman.

He breaks away from the gathering darkness. "I thought I saw something."

Light flashes behind them, then wood splinters. Chunks of deck fly into the air. Rais puts an arm over Nina. "We should get below deck!" he shouts over the roaring wind.

Nina shakes her head, water splattering off the end of her nose with the motion. "We need to wake everyone up!" she yells.

Lightning strikes the deck again, and someone screams. Water pours through the holes in the ship. The world turns with the waves.

Nina runs to the hatch leading below deck with Rais right behind her. A bolt of lightning lands beside him and throws him across the floor. Blackness fills his vision when his head hits a barrel. He blindly rolls onto his stomach and lifts himself to his knees. The ocean rocks the ship—violent swells that challenge the integrity of the wood. His head burns and he's soaked to the bone. He forces himself to his feet, keeping his arms outstretched at his sides. He slips across the deck as he runs for the stairs.

There's a pull from his mind and body as if he's manifesting his lightning, but he's not. Energy pools through his fingertips into the world. The talisman thrums. His mind quakes. His hand finds the wall. *Damp wood. Dark skies. Breathe.*

Rais looks down the stairwell. He needs to get everyone off this ship. He skips steps between strides. Thunder booms above. Nina is screaming at the crew. Rais runs to the end of the hall. "Are you there?" he asks, raising his voice above the sounds.

Yes, Bryn says through his mind.

Pain shoots through his shoulder. He spins to see the first mate with a bat in hand. "I told you to stay away from there," the man says.

"No."

The bat swings down at him. Rais dodges to the side, and the bat lodges into the floorboards. While the man tries to yank it free, Rais turns and slams his heel into the man's knee. The first mate's leg buckles beneath him.

"We need to get off this ship! Not fight as it sinks," Rais shouts, his voice barely breaking through the sound of the storm.

A large boom comes from the deck and water begins pouring into the hallway. It's quickly followed by a crash that has the first mate sprinting up to the main deck. It sounds like one of the masts fell, but he can't tell from down here.

Rais looks around and finds a broom. He lifts his knee and slams the middle of the broom on his thigh. It breaks in half. Rais jams the broken end between the door and the frame to pry it open. The door swings out. "Come on, the ship is sinking!" he shouts.

Their face comes into view in the faded light. Bryn has wide brown eyes and an upturned nose. Their dark hair cuts off at the shoulders, and a green gem hangs from one of their pointed ears. Bryn scrunches their brows together. "Well, what are we waiting for?" they ask.

"I need to get to something." Rais runs into the sleeping quarters. He spots his bag, then goes to it, ripping it open. Clothes are replacable, but there's one thing he can't leave behind. He grabs onto a notebook, then shoves it into his waistband.

"We need to go," Bryn says.

"I know, let's go."

Rais follows the nymph through the passageways and up onto the deck. Across the ship, Nina holds onto the railing. She stares back at Rais. Terror sweeps off her as heavily as the wind blows.

He crosses the deck to get to her, and Bryn looks between them. "Do either of you possess the ability to control water?"

They shake their heads. Nina glances at Rais. "I can use wind to propel us across the water, but we will have to be close together for it to work. We also need to be far enough away from the ship to avoid its suction."

Rais fumbles for the talisman with his fingers, but what can he do with it to fight the elements? He holds onto Nina's gaze. He will only use it if necessary. If they can survive this without it, then he prefers to keep it concealed.

The ship shakes beneath them, and Nina swings her feet over the railing. She hangs over the ocean. "Jump, and swim. Try to stay close to me. Once we make it far enough, I'll get us the rest of the way," she shouts above the storm.

Bryn does as Nina did and swings their legs over, holding onto the railing. Rais moves to do the same, but the boat wrenches the other way, and he loses his grip on the railing. "Jump!" he yells.

Nina reluctantly pulls herself and Bryn into the ocean. Rais' feet slip on the deck, and he slides across the wood to the other side. Another strike of lightning cuts through the ship. Rais holds his breath as he's dragged under the water.

Chapter Eight

Ava

Ava puts her boots on, then goes to the door. She tries to walk past Aliras, but he stops her with his arm. "You can't leave."

She pushes against him. "Are you serious? I was in the city with you the other night. You didn't seem to care then."

He smiles. Ridiculous. All she wants is to be anywhere but in here. She's not dumb enough to run. Ava curls her fingers into fists. Aliras leans his forearm on the doorframe. "If you run, I will stop you." She never would've guessed that.

"Are you messing with me?" she asks.

He puts his free hand to his heart. "I would never, my lady."

She frowns and punches his chest. Aliras purses his lips. He's trying not to laugh. Which only irks her more.

Ava steps back into her room. There must be another way to get past him. She looks out the window longingly "I can't believe I got myself locked up in here." She talks to herself, playing the sympathy card. "I walked into enemy territory without knowing a single thing about Stygian. I assumed because she's my sister, that she wouldn't turn against me. That's probably why no one told me about her because they knew I'd get myself trapped." She turns to him. His eyes narrow, unamused.

She's so tired of being in this room, alone. She could be even more dramatic to get Aliras to let her out, but he doesn't seem inclined to listen.

Wetness grows beneath her nose. She touches it with her finger. Red stains her skin.

"Are you okay?" he asks.

She stares at the blood and her vision clouds. "What the hell?"

Ava's head tilts back. Pain shoots through her skull as she collapses to her knees and the world bends to blue. Water surrounds her, flowing against her hair and skin. It slickens against her, and she hears a voice careening through the silence. *Ava?* She stares into the deep blue water, searching for him. His golden eyes are the first things to fill her vision, and then she sees him sinking below her. His hand reaches out to her. There's no way this is real. It can't be, but he's there, sinking.

Chapter Nine

Raiden

The water chills him to the bone. He tries to fight to the surface, but the force of the ship sinking keeps him under. Water slips into his mouth, burning through him.

There's a shadow above him, and he feels Ava's mind reaching out to him in the Sonder. He grabs onto her with his mind. *Ava?*

Her shadow swims down to him. He reaches out his arm. She says something to him, but he can't read the words on her lips. No, he can, she's screaming his name.

Ava. I need you, he calls out. She's not really here. That's impossible. But maybe she can hear him. *I am near the Dragon Isles, but I cannot breathe. I have the dragon scale. If I do not make it. You have to come for it.*

A hand grabs his arm and pulls him through the ocean. Water burns in his lungs. The darkness takes him.

Chapter Ten

Ava

She gasps as her vision clears. Before she could hear his whole message, his voice faded away. She coughs as if water has filled her lungs. Aliras is holding her. She's leaned against his chest on the floor. An ache wrenches through her skull.

What if this was another hallucination? It felt so real, but she has no way of proving it. If it was real, then Raiden could be drowning out there. Somewhere near the Dragon Isles. She has to go to him. Even if she's too late, she has to try.

"Who's Raiden?" Aliras asks. It doesn't matter if Aliras knows who he is. She has to leave now.

Raiden knows she wants to be miles from him. He wouldn't have sent her this vision unless he was in real danger. This wasn't a figment of her imagination. "I need to get to the Dragon Isles." Ava moves away from him. "Now."

"What just happened?" he asks.

Ava grabs the dagger Raiden gave her from the third drawer of the dresser. She hid it here as soon as she arrived in Goldryn. With her luck, she thought it was best to keep it nearby. "Raiden."

"What is that supposed to mean?"

She opens her window and slides one leg out. She grasps the top of the window frame and sits against the sill. "Are you coming?"

Aliras runs to her. "We can't alate in the city."

"There's water below us, idiot."

He shakes his head at her. "The water is shallow around the palace."

"Not here. I saw a ship go through here. A ship that large needs enough leeway to pass through, meaning we have enough room to not hit the bottom."

He holds his hands out to her. "There's no way I'm letting you jump."

"I know." Ava smiles.

Aliras moves close to her. "Give me a chance to talk to Stygian. I might be able to negotiate on your behalf."

"Aliras." He steps closer to her—probably afraid she's going to slip off the windowsill at any moment. "I don't have time for that."

His eyes narrow. She grabs onto his scabbard's strap. He begins to back away, but she yanks him toward her. Then she pushes herself from the window, pulling Aliras with her.

Gravity pulls her down and she slips into open air. The fall jolts to a stop when Aliras grasps the windowsill. Ava hangs from his strap. This is her only way out of here. It has to work. She releases her hold on him. Aliras grabs her wrist, but she slips from his grip.

The air is warm. She closes her eyes as she falls. Hands grasp her upper arms. She opens her eyes to see Aliras pulling her to him as they spin through the air. The surface of the ocean hits them like a rock, then they sink beneath the surface.

Her body stings—the impact shaking through her bones.

She holds her breath and fights against the pulling water. Aliras keeps a hold of her and swims upward. He lets go once they breach the surface. "You are insane," he says, exasperated. They swim to the beach underneath the palace's shadow. She drags herself onto the sand and closes her eyelids for a moment.

He spits water from his mouth. "What were you thinking?" Seagulls squawk nearby, drowning out the sound of his voice.

Ava pushes onto her knees. Her waterlogged body curses her. She forces herself up onto her feet. Seashells crunch below her weight. "There's someone I need to save, and I don't care what I have to do to save him."

"You could have killed us both!"

"Are we dead?" Ava crosses her arms and forces a look of bravery. Inside she is shivering, and her body is crying with sharp pains.

"My lady, I beg that you return to the palace." Aliras only followed her to drag her back. Here she was hoping he wanted to escape too.

"I told you, I have someplace to be. It's not my fault you're Stygian's pet." She stalks off through the sand, her clothes drenched and uncomfortable. At least she's out of that room. "Now are you coming with me or not?"

"I am not her pet!" he yells.

She spins on her heel. "Then stop acting like it." She stalks off toward the staircase leading up into the city.

He runs to her side. "Let's at least get dry clothes from the armory first. We will have to be quick though. It won't take Stygian long to notice you aren't in your chambers."

She does want to get into dry clothes. What she doesn't want is to get dragged straight to Stygian because she was dumb enough to trust Aliras.

Time stands between her and Rais. She has to get to the Isles as soon as possible, and she can't alate there on her own. According to her faulty memory, she's never been there before. Aliras has. She sighs and gestures for him to lead the way.

Aliras guides her across the empty beach to a palace entrance by the docks. Soldiers cover the area. "I'm going to shield our presence from them. Try to move quietly," he says.

He swirls his fingers in the air, and her world blurs over with a haze. Aliras stays on the balls of his feet, moving quietly toward the docks. Ava follows behind him, slowing her breathing to help keep them hidden. Aliras opens the door with his key. He drops their mental shields once they're inside.

Whatever that was, she needs to learn how to do it.

A Goldryn soldier stands in the hallway. His mouth opens and he bends his brows. Ava backs behind Aliras. She doesn't know what to do. The soldier watches her. Recognizes her. Aliras raises his hand to the guard. Aliras better have a plan. The soldier bends his brows. "I'm returning her to her chambers, Jak," Aliras says. Jak pulls the sword from his back. "Seriously?"

Aliras unhooks the chakram from his belt—two arced blades whose handles fit together to make a circle. Jak runs at him, rising his own blade. Aliras shoves her to the side. She is perfectly capable of defending herself. Before she can draw fire into her palm, Aliras slices the man's throat. Blood splatters across them. Ava wipes it from her face, staring at Aliras in shock. He didn't think twice about going for the killing blow.

Aliras glances her way. Shame burns in the air around him. "He would have gone to Stygian." Ava is at a loss for words. He's willing to kill to protect her, but what if he decides she's not worth protecting? Despite her unnerve, she goes with him to the armory. She can't get to the Dragon Isles by herself.

Aliras shuts the door behind them. Weapons and armor hang across the walls in the dimly lit room. In the center is a staircase leading beneath sea level. The underwater dungeons.

"Come on," Aliras says over his shoulder. He's already descending the steps.

She quickly follows. Her clothes are ice against her skin. It will be a relief to pull them off. The lower chambers of the armory are humid and even colder than above. Aliras points to a room to her right, and she slips inside. Aliras continues down the hall. The room is empty except for some weapons hanging along the back wall.

There's a quiet clack of boots on stone. Rhythmic footsteps. They continue to recede until hinges creak and the sound fades. Minutes later the door opens, and Aliras drops folded clothes on the floor. "You can change into these," he says. There's a clatter from above and a series of shouts. Aliras slowly shuts the door. "I'll turn around, but you need to change now. They'll be able to get in at any moment. We need to be fast." He picks up one of the stacks of clothes and passes it to her.

Ava nods and takes them from him. She pulls her belt off, dropping the dagger with it to the ground. She tentatively pulls her clothing off, uncomfortably aware of

Aliras doing the same only feet away. Her bare skin stings against the air. She notices red splotches covering her body from the impact of the water. Ava slips on the fitted pants and loose shirt. "You couldn't find any boots?" she asks. He doesn't answer. She forces her feet back into her wet socks and boots, tying them as quickly as she can. She slides her belt back on and pulls a sword from the wall.

"Good call," he says.

She spins to him. "You weren't watching, were you?"

"No. I only heard the sword," he assures her. He's already changed the rest of his clothes, but his shirt is still wet. She should have asked if he was changed before turning around. Aliras lifts his shirt over his head. A tattoo curves across his ribs, but it disappears below his waistband. She turns her back to him, keeping her gaze on the mossy wall. "But you were watching," he says.

Her cheeks burn. "Not on purpose."

"You can pretend I believe you if that makes you feel better."

Footsteps rush down the stairs outside the room. Someone calls out that the door is closed. "Follow my lead," he whispers. Ava steadies the blade in her hand and looks to the door. He gives her a reassuring nod. As if it could make her feel any better about this situation. Ava moves against the wall, out of sight of the doorway. Aliras pulls the door open, and a guard rushes into the room. Aliras slices the blade across the back of the man's legs. A gut-wrenching scream escapes the man's lips.

Aliras runs out the door with Ava in tow. They fly up the stairs. She didn't dare look to see how many are behind them. It's better she doesn't know.

The guards from below shout to them, following

closely behind. Maybe four based on the shouting, but she isn't sure. One grabs her calf, and she falls onto the steps. She pushes her knee against the stone, then spins, slicing the sword across the guard's chest. He falls backward, knocking down the guards behind him. Aliras grabs her wrist and pulls her up. The sword slips from her grip. She doesn't turn back to get it. Hopefully, she won't need it. They sprint up the last few stairs into the armory.

In the hallway, Aliras slams the door behind them. He pulls a painting off the wall and jams it beneath the door's handle.

Willow's mind fills Ava's. Her accented voice floats through her thoughts. Take your first left and open the gate to the sewers.

Ava grabs onto Aliras' shirt. "This way." She leads him down the hallway as instructed. After the first left, they run to the end of the hall, then she yanks open the metal grate on the floor. It's either the sewers or make more of a ruckus running straight out of the palace.

Ava jumps down into the tunnel, plunging into darkness. Shallow water splashes onto her legs and squelches beneath her boots. Aliras drops down beside her and pulls the grate closed. "Did he hurt you?" Aliras asks.

"The guard only grabbed my leg. I'm fine."

She can't see his face, but she can imagine it's painted with a scowl.

They trudge through the sewage water. At the first fork in the path, a figure steps out from the left tunnel. Aliras steps in front of her. Ava pushes him aside and raises her hand, setting a ball of energy aflame. Lavender hair and pale eyes. "You'll need this," Willow says. Oddly, Willow is calm here. As if the sewers are broadly lit and not stinking of rotting animals. She holds out Ava's mage coat—embroidered with her sigil of twin dragons.

Ava takes it and slides it over her arms. Its warmth instantly spreads through her. It has been a long time since she last wore it. "How did you know where I was?" Ava asks.

"I went to check on you, and you weren't in your chambers. When I began following your mind, I overheard someone reporting a dead guard outside the armory. I figured you two are quite reckless and might have found yourselves trying to escape. Then I followed your mind to the armory. You are both quite ... predictable." Her eyes slowly move to the ceiling of the sewer. "We need to get going. The guards are undoubtedly going straight to Stygian." So much for leaving quietly.

Aliras and Ava follow Willow through the sewers. After ten minutes of wandering in the dark, they reach an opening in the ceiling. A ladder on the wall leads up to a grate. Willow climbs up first and pushes the grate away. Aliras offers Ava a leg up. It's a kind gesture, but Ava is taller than Willow. The first rail of the ladder is not difficult to reach. Ava lifts herself up onto the ladder and climbs out onto the street. Aliras scales the ladder next. He gets out of the sewer and slides the grate back in place.

The alleyway is small. Some windows above them have clothing lines hanging from wall to wall. There's a pungent smell of fish, so they must be near the wharf or marina. Willow leads them down the alley, but Ava notices Aliras isn't following them. She turns back to him. "Aren't you coming?"

"I can't."

"Why?" Ava asks.

"Stygian knows where my nephew lives. I'm all that kid has ... I can't put him at risk. I was going with you because I couldn't leave you by yourself, but Willow's here now."

Ava doesn't know what to say. She wants Aliras to go with her. Sure, she can search for Raiden on her own, but it will be more difficult.

"Might I cut in?" Willow strides past Ava. "You should go with her. I'll tell Stygian you went after Ava to bring her back to Goldryn. She will see it as a more than reasonable reaction. And do not fret over your nephew. I am setting up an escape plan for him, as you requested."

Aliras lets out a shaky breath. "Fine. I will be back as soon as I can."

Willow bows her head to them. "You two do not deserve to be puppeteered by Stygian. I will send message if anything changes here. Be safe."

"You don't deserve it either," Ava says.

Willow opens her mouth to respond but holds her tongue. Ava doesn't turn away from her. "Go," Willow whispers.

A featherlike touch brushes Ava's arm, and she looks at Aliras. "I thought we were in a rush," he says.

She told Willow they'd leave Goldryn together. If Ava leaves now, she may never come back. It seems wrong to go, but Aliras is right—they must hurry. Raiden needs her. Ava will have to come back for Willow.

They leave Willow behind and run through the streets. It doesn't take long for them to reach the city gates. The guards didn't see them escape, so they're likely still searching the palace.

Outside the city, Aliras offers his hand to her, and she takes it. She focuses on the vision sent to her by Raiden. The deep blue ocean. Aliras adds to it with his own image of the Dragon Isles coast. They step into the Plane of Verity

and blue energy appears in the world around them.
Hang on, Rais.

Chapter Eleven

Willow

The doorknob is warm to the touch. Willow stares at the carvings in the door. Flames that twist together. The longer she stalls here, the angrier Stygian will be. Aliras and Ava have fled the city. Willow prays Stygian doesn't know.

She can't keep putting this off. Willow tentatively pulls the door open, only to see slate gray eyes staring her down. Was she standing there this whole time? Stygian's lips twitch up. "You adore making me wait."

"My apologies." Willow lowers her gaze to the paper in the Queen's hands.

Stygian invaded Willow's mind not long ago to call her up here. Willow grimaces, she despises the lick of Stygian's thoughts. They're sharp and ravage with a fiery burn. She prefers the peace of having a guard drag her here. Anything is better than having her mind invaded.

Stygian shoves the paper at her. This can't be anything good. Willow gulps a shallow breath and grabs the paper. It's signed by Kalenti Alberona, the Queen of Eventyr. She doesn't want to read this, let alone think of her home. Her throat tightens, and she passes the letter back. Willow steps away from Stygian's burning gaze and goes to the window. She watches the steady ocean waves crash on the beach below.

It's possible Stygian has no idea that Ava's escaped the city, but Willow finds that unlikely. Stygian likes things to fester before using them against someone. That must be what's happening now. Stygian's attempting to distract Willow with a letter so that she can attack her later with accusations.

"You didn't read it," Stygian says. As if Willow didn't already know that.

Stygian finds enjoyment in cruelty. Whether it's filling Willow's mind with threats or making her feel useless. "Do I need to get my knife?" Stygian asks.

The small scars scattered across her palms sting at the very thought. In the back of her mind, Stygian's cold stare lurks. The memory of Stygian holding Willow's wrist. The searing pain as the tip of the knife dug into her flesh and slowly spun while Stygian berated her with questions. It kept happening until Willow finally gave in. Until she gave up what fight she had left.

"Well?" Stygian asks.

She unclenches her fists. There are red indents left from her nails. "No, Syn. You do not need to get your knife. Tell me what the letter says?"

Stygian picks up the hem of her dress and struts over to her. She flicks her wrist in front of her. The paper flattens with the movement. "My Goldryn Queen, the ocean has kept a distance between us. With time you have lost your senses. You once comforted me when I was at my lowest, locked away in the dungeons by my mother's hand. We made an alliance when your mother did the same to you. Now, you have fallen from your throne. You act out of spite and not in vengeance for your people. I have received an offer from a young Wyntryn protector, and in the best interest of my people, I must end our alliance. I hope you learn that power is not success. You deserve happiness, friend, not your own destruction." Stygian crumples the paper in her hand. She throws it to the ground, then Stygian's hand slams against Willow's shoulder.

She falters backward. Kalenti has made a grave mistake. There is no world where Stygian won't overreact when insulted. Willow has been fighting back recently and now she will pay for it. A terrifying possibility, but Willow can take the pain. She has before, and she will again. As long as it stops Stygian from hurting others.

"You are loyal to me." Stygian seethes. She seems to grow in height as she looks down at Willow.

It's hard to believe she ever defended this woman. There's never been a good reason to defend Stygian. Only Willow's own sympathetic mind. This queen has never deserved it. Though after a while the pain Stygian caused only raised Willow's tolerance. Which isn't a good thing, but it allowed her to survive. If it kept hurting as horribly as it did at first, then she would have never kept her sanity.

"I am loyal to you," Willow whispers. A blatant lie. Willow isn't loyal to anyone. She doesn't really know where she's trying to go in life. Survival is the instinct that guides her.

"Then you better convince Kalenti Alberona that Wyntryn deserves to burn. That alliance is mine," Stygian says, so calm that from a distance one might guess this is a kind interaction.

"I can't just talk to her."

Stygian raises her hand and slaps. Willow's head is

thrown to the side, and she stumbles to the floor. There's a ringing in her ear, and she cowers away from Stygian. "You will go to Eventyr, and if I do not get my alliance back, then I will have to ensure your loyalty again."

Stygian will send Willow back to the dungeons. She will have her interrogated and tortured until she is satisfied with Willow's state of mind. "I will go to Eventyr," Willow says.

The Queen smiles and grasps Willow's forearm. Stygian pulls her up and caresses her cheek. "You are too kind, darling."

Willow pulls her arms across her stomach and leaves the room. She walks steadily through the corridors until she reaches an alcove with a view of the ocean. She leans against the sandstone and slides to the floor. Her heart thuds against her sternum and she lets out a low sob. "You are fine. Plenty fine," she reassures herself. Her hand slides to her cheek and she sucks in numerous breaths.

She pushes off the ground and stares out at the waves. If only she could slip beneath them and sink to the ocean floor. Live amongst the ocean creatures. Happiness is out there. Anywhere but here.

A guard leads a palomino horse from the stables. He holds the mare steady as Willow drags her finger along the horse's haunches, to make sure she doesn't spook it, around to the mounting block. She steps onto the stool, then hooks her foot in the stirrup. With a push, she swings her leg over and settles into the saddle. The guard pulls the reins over the horse's neck, and Willow taps the horse's ribs with her heels.

The only positive takeaway from all this is that Willow didn't see any sign of Ava's escape in Stygian's mind. Stygian may genuinely be unaware. After Willow watched Aliras and Ava leave, she intercepted as many guards as she could. But she didn't believe her efforts were successful.

She rides through the streets to the edge of the city. At the outer gate, Willow dismounts the mare and hands the reins to a Goldryn guard. She distances herself from the city and calls upon the energy surrounding her. Willow steps into the Plane of Verity, picturing her destination. The world is hazy as she walks, searching for the right tendril of energy to follow. When she feels the tug, she grasps onto it and slips through, her body and mind flowing with Kanaleigh.

The central city of Eventyr forms around her as her weight settles into reality.

With her eyes closed, Willow lifts her face into the sun. The air here is lovely. Dry and fresh, like sitting in a forest surrounded by old oaks.

The dark palace shimmers in the sunlight. A massive staircase rises before her with a line of pillars covering the face of the palace. At each column of metal, two guards stand post. Her gaze catches on a bird flying ahead, but she doesn't have time to greet it as she'd like to. The precious bird is dark blue with speckles of pink—a rare Eventyr species. She's home. Willow gathers her skirts in her hands and runs up the steps.

A woman with a shaved head stands in front of the doors to the palace. "Name?" she asks.

"Lady Willow Evergryn of the Crystal Lakes. I would like an audience with Her Highness, on behalf of Queen Stygian Liones." The words sound foreign on her tongue. She had to adjust to her thicker Eventyrian accent. It's faded more than she would have liked since living on the western continent. What would her father think of her? Losing her accent and wearing Goldryn clothes.

The woman gives a curt nod. "Welcome Lady Evergryn, you may follow me."

She is led through the all too familiar palace. From the wide windows to the chandeliers — this place is truly of Eventyr. Crafted with slick metals and sharp textures. As ancient as their accents and as familiar as her family home.

Her father's residence encompasses a substantial portion of the Crystal Lakes territory. She hasn't visited him in a long time, and if she's truthful to herself, she's scared to. Not because he may marry her off to some dull, good-statured man, but because she hasn't been home since her brother's funeral. She doesn't want to relive that pain.

The woman takes her into the throne room and past a line of citizens waiting to speak with Kalenti. The guard takes a deep bow.

There she is. Soft curls of bright red frame her sharp face and dark eyes. Kalenti notices her before she even acknowledges the guard. Kalenti stands and steps down from the dais. Everyone in the line falls to their knee, but Kalenti doesn't glance their way.

"Lady Willow," she says. Her freckles scatter as her cheeks lift.

Willow gulps. Being here, before her, is a stark reminder of the feelings she once had. Willow moves to bow, but Kalenti catches her hand. She pulls it to her lips and presses a kiss to her skin. A vision of Kalenti kissing her lover, the one she chose instead of Willow, shoots through her mind. "*Cyures Tyral,*" Willow mumbles to herself.

Kalenti laughs at her curse, unaware of the reason Willow said it. Kalenti turns to the guard who led Willow here. "Thank you for bringing her here. Tell the people I will hold audience again in an hour." Kalenti's eyes meet Willow's. "Come now, let's go somewhere more private."

They go to a small room attached to the extravagant ballroom. There's a black marble desk in the center. Two red couches sit against opposite walls. Kalenti takes a seat on the one to the left. She leans against the arm of the couch and rests her hand along the back. Willow sits down next to her and stares at her knees. If she holds Kalenti's gaze in this secluded room, she won't be able to control herself.

"You are here because of the letter?" Kalenti asks.

Willow tugs on the inside of her lip. "Stygian didn't take it well."

Kalenti laughs. "Ah, I wish I could've seen her face. I liked her at first, but there's a significant difference between acting for purpose and acting for power. That's where we differ."

Willow lifts her head to look at the desk. There's nothing on it. This must be an unused room.

"Did she do that to you?" Kalenti asks.

"Hm?" she hums nervously.

"The bruising on your face."

Willow's hand shoots to her cheekbone. It hurts to touch. How did it bruise so quickly? "Oh, that, it's nothing."

"You need to come home, Willow. If Stygian is hurting you, I will not allow you to be there any longer." Kalenti sits up and reaches out to Willow. Kalenti must have forgotten about Willow's ability to see into someone's mind when she touches them. Willow shifts away from

Kalenti and returns her gaze to the floor. "I know what happened to you when Stygian first took you. I helped you then, and I can help you again. I would kill for you. Ask, and it will be done."

"I am fine. I need to stay in Goldryn. War is on the horizon, and it will not be long before Wyntryn and Goldryn rip each other apart. I only ask for you to convince Stygian that you are on her side. At least for now." This is her chance to propose her own deal.

"I will not lie to her," Kalenti says.

"I'm not asking you to. Let me lie for you. If you care for my wellbeing, this will protect me for now. I can return to Eventyr as soon as the people I care for are safe."

"The Wyntryn Sparrow visited me recently. I gifted Wyntryn with a great possession, but I suppose I haven't committed myself to their side yet. Do what you need to do to keep yourself safe, but I don't want Stygian trying to get ships from me anymore. Her people can barely sail a ship bigger than a tree stump."

"About that..." Willow says. Kalenti squares her shoulders. "With the coming war, there are many people at risk in Goldryn. Stygian has threatened many lives, and I am working with a group who are trying to get those threatened out of the city safely. I only need a ship or two."

"If you are bringing them to Eventyr they require more than a ship or two. That's food, shelter, and clothing. That is a great request."

"I know. I would never ask if it wasn't important. You could help me save hundreds of innocent people," Willow explains. She closes her eyes for a moment. Not wanting to meet Kalenti's gaze. "If Stygian asks about the ships, I'll tell her they are gifts from you to reestablish your alliance. Then I'll send refugees back on them. She won't be any the wiser."

Kalenti's brows bend inward. "That is greater than you telling a fable to protect yourself. I would have to send Eventyr resources to Goldryn for that to be convincing."

"Please. It will only be this once." Willow can put up a façade for Stygian, but she can't fail to keep her promises. She has to get Aliras' nephew to safety and help the Drogon Insurgency save countless others.

Kalenti purses her lips, sighs, then says, "Two of my fastest ships. I'll send over some textiles that recently arrived from the Southern Dunes. They'll port at the south end of the city in three days. They leave by dawn the next day, so you will have to be quick. Keep your lies to a minimum. They are a reflection of me."

"Yes, of course. I cannot thank you enough," Willow says.

"Staging the death of that fire-breathing tyrant would be a lot easier, you know." Kalenti brushes the tips of her fingers along Willow's jaw. Willow sees through to her thoughts. *I would do anything to repay my debt to you. If only I never let you leave for that manor. Stygian never would have sunk her claws into you.*

Willow stands and backs away to the door. "I have to go. Thank you, Kal, you don't owe a debt to me. This … this gift means everything. I'll make sure my lies are short and believable."

Kalenti's lips part. Willow pulls herself into the Plane of Verity before she can hear what Kalenti says. Some things are better left unsaid.

Chapter Twelve

Aliras releases her hand as they step through the Plane of Verity and into the streets of the city. The streets are deserted except for a few fishermen and stragglers. The people of the Isles never stay in one place for too long, leaving many cities empty for a few months a year. Not long ago the King of the Dragon Isles was overthrown by his daughter, Queen Natalia Erminia. She is rumored to be nothing but caring, but her actions do not reflect her public persona. Though Ava can't judge Natalia for overthrowing her father. According to Levi, she attempted the same thing.

"Do you know where we're going?" Aliras asks. There are docks off to the right and a ramshackle city to the left. "I-I have no clue."

"Hm." He starts toward the boardwalk and she picks up her pace to keep up. The wooden path lines the edge of the beach.

A woman emerges from the water. Her hair is short, and her skin separates into small scales around her scalp. The scales spread down her neck and shimmer in the sunlight. Behind her, a man with the same likeness steps out. These people are not… human. At least not in the way Ava is familiar with. She glances at Aliras, but he's not even phased by them.

Aliras follows her eye line. "They are water nymphs, a form of irregular," he says.

"I thought all irregulars were the same." There's still so much she doesn't know.

"No. Those who do not come from the main bloodlines or were not brought back to life by them changed in other ways. The rarer bloodlines were made by what the main bloodlines consider failed fusions. Where the people did not retain their human likeness and became more animalistic. Despite their looks and abilities being different, they are just as human as anyone else. Their hearts and minds are the same as any other person. They are irregulars."

"How have I never known of this?" Ava asks herself.

"You lost your memories, my lady. It is a miracle you know anything."

Harsh, but true. The memories that do return aren't very helpful. "I suppose you're right. Can we go to the docks?" There might be someone there who knows about any ships sinking near the coast.

Aliras motions toward an area farther along the waterline. It's a rustic city with tall wooden structures. Past the buildings, ship masts rise into the skyline.

They go to the docks, and Ava scans the horizon. There are no boats out at sea, but even if there were, she doesn't know what to look for. She came here on a whim. She doesn't even know if the vision was real. Raiden could have fallen off the ship or been pushed off. All she knows is he is, or was, in danger … and he needs her.

A woman jumps off a ship to their left. Ava goes to her. "Excuse me, I am wondering if you might know if any ships were supposed to dock today?"

Someone on the same ship drops a crate down to the woman. She catches it and sets it down. "Do you know the captain's name?" the woman asks.

"No, but I am looking for a Raiden Hynrule. He's the tenth protector of Wyntryn."

"Don't know him. You can head over to Neil. He's in the pub right over there." She points to a ramshackle building with a large neon sign. "If he doesn't know, then they're dead or imprisoned."

Ava steps away. "Thanks." She and Aliras go to the pub.

Inside there are a few stray people having an afternoon drink. One person is fast asleep on a bench by the door. Ava goes up to the bar. "Hey, I need to talk to Neil."

"That'd be me, hun." The bartender's cheeks are sunken in, and dirt's smeared across his jaw.

Aliras slips his fingers over his chakram. Neil grins. "No need to be hasty, son. What's it you need?"

"I'm looking for a passenger whose ship might have been scheduled to dock today. His name is Raiden Hynrule."

"Ah, that young Wyntryn protector? He's quite the trouble that one. His ship went down in a storm, along with the crew. The Queens are bent out of shape over 'em. It's likely he's no longer in the city. That is if he survived the waters."

"Could you point me in the direction of the palace then?"

Neil laughs at her. A golden tooth shines through

his smile. "You're a funny one. No one gets an audience with the Queens by walking through the gates."

"I do," Ava says.

"And why's that little one?"

Aliras steps forward. Ava places her hand against his upper arm. Through the Sonder, she can feel his rage. Whether he likes it or not, she can handle this herself. "Because I am Ava Beckett Wyntryn."

Neil's mouth gapes, then he chuckles away the false surprise. "No. You're kidding, aren't you? We don't like liars here, hun. You think I'm going to believe a snarky thing like you is an heiress?" Ava raises her chin. The Dragon Isles are not leaving a good first impression on her. "You can find your way out now." Neil juts his finger at the door.

Aliras steps toward him. "If you wish to keep your life, you will not say another word."

Neil chuckles and raises his hands. "I mean no harm, but she is just a child. No?"

Aliras grabs the collar of Neil's shirt and drags him over the bar. He pushes him to the ground and puts his boot on Neil's neck. "Would you like to try that again?" Aliras asks.

Neil's face has turned a cherry red. He keeps his hands raised and fervently shakes his head.

Aliras pushes down before moving his foot away. "Have a nice day."

Ava stares down at Neil, then turns away. Insane. Aliras is insane. He always goes straight to violence. There are other ways to deal with problems. "You don't have to defend me, Aliras. If I had a problem with him, I would've said something myself."

"Well, I had a problem with him."

"Obviously," Ava says under her breath. He grunts and scrunches his brows together. "You're in quite the mood today."

His expression softens and he holds the door open for her. She steps through, eyeing him warily. Aliras lets go of the door and follows her out. "Aliras."

"Yes?" he asks.

"I will not let anything happen to your nephew. I'd shoot an arrow into anyone who tries to hurt him, even my sister."

"With your aim?" he asks with a smirk.

Ava frowns. "I would've practiced more if I hadn't been locked up in my chambers. Also, just so you know, I have hit the target before. You happened to walk onto the terrace when I had a bad shot."

"Four in a row actually," he says.

"Of course, you were watching." She glares at him.

He side-eyes her, then purses his lips together to stop him from smiling. He clears his throat. "What was your vision?"

"Of Raiden?" she asks. Aliras nods. There's not much to say about it. At least nothing he'd understand, but she can try to explain. She pushes stray hair, still damp, behind her ear. "My vision went dark, and I was in the ocean. I heard his voice, and I searched for him. He was below me, sinking. He reached out for me and told me he needed me and he was in the Dragon Isles. I may hate him, but how could I say no? He'd come looking for me if our roles were reversed."

"Do you trust me?" he asks. An odd thing to ask. Ava fidgets with the edge of her tucked-in shirt.

"Yeah, I suppose I do." She has only known him for a brief time, but he's protected her so far. He's risking his own family to be here with her.

"Then you should know I wear a different Goldryn uniform because I am not a soldier. I am not exactly Stygian's right hand either. She only tells people to protect my identity. Willow is more of a right hand, actually. I'm … her assassin. Not by choice, but I've never turned down one of her requests." Ava stills. An assassin. He stops and faces her.

"So, you… kill people for her? Anyone she asks?" He nods. "Why are you telling me this?" she asks, her voice deathly quiet. Did Stygian order him to kill her?

"I'm telling you because Queen Natalia already knows this. I don't want you caught off guard. I am also telling you because your Sparrow killed one person. I have killed countless, and you can still find trust in me."

She isn't so sure about trusting him now. Aliras hasn't done anything to her. The difference between him and Raiden is that Raiden didn't only kill one person. He killed Levi. Aliras' eyes study her. A feeling of fear flickers into the Sonder. His fear. "If she asked you to kill me, would you?" Ava asks tentatively.

"Before I knew you, yes. I would never dare hurt you now. Not only because of the heart inside you, but because you would never hurt me," he says.

He's telling her this because he doesn't want to lie to her. His fear is not caused by what she suspected. Aliras is afraid of her pushing him away. He needs someone as much as she does. All the tensity in her body gives way. "I never said I wouldn't hurt you," she points out with a smile.

"Yes, but I don't believe you will."

They keep walking through the streets until the castle walls tower above them. The structure's made of gray stone. It's boxy and neither warm nor inviting. Guards do not stand along the outskirts or at the bridge, so Aliras and Ava walk into the castle with no trouble.

Tall pines and evergreens cover the courtyard. A low growl escapes from the dense trees.

Ava glances at Aliras, but he stares ahead. She follows his gaze to a large creature that struts across the stone. It keeps low to the ground, and its speckled fur lifts with anticipation. Aliras slowly unhooks his curved blades as the beast nears. It's only feet away now. A deep growl ripples from its scarred throat, and its haunches lift, readying it to pounce on its prey.

"*Ay fin mayta!*" A voice commands.

The creature of white and blue lifts itself from its position and turns to its commander. It glides to the woman and pushes its head against her thigh. The woman's black hair floats around her rounded frame. She wears a crown of emerald green and intricate fighting leathers. "Is that you Aliras?" she asks.

"It is, Mica. I know it's a lot to ask, but we need a place to stay for the night," Aliras says. Ava tenses, she's not here to sleep. She's here to find out what happened to Raiden. Aliras lowers his voice to explain to her. "The queens will not tell you anything until they've asked their own questions. They like to put on a show."

Ava bows her head to Queen Mica. "I am Ava Beckett Wyntryn."

Mica juts her chin to Aliras. "I figured. Syn sends her Aliras here all the time. It's about time she sends her sister." Mica runs her fingers through the fur of the snow leopard. It practically purrs at her touch. She spins on her heel and walks across the courtyard. The cat at her heels.

"I do not like liars," Ava says. Even if they are to

stay the night, they should have told Mica why they are here. For Raiden, nothing else.

Aliras bows his head to her. "I don't either, my lady. Mica is a regular, and her wife is very protective. If we have to stay the night to find out the truth, then we will. Sometimes it takes a lot of convincing to get an answer." Ava has no intentions of staying here longer than necessary, but Aliras is free to do as he wishes.

She follows Aliras into the castle. Mica's not far ahead of them. Ava doesn't know much about the queens, but she knows it's rare in Kanaleigh for a regular to be in power. Grymyr is the only region entirely run by them. Regulars make up the majority of the populations on the two continents, but the irregulars seem to always find themselves in power.

Mica takes them to a sitting room with floral furniture and a large fireplace. The window offers a view past the castle to the ocean. Statues of leopards sit in the corners of the room—what she assumes to be statures. A woman with blonde hair pulled into a bun sits on one of the dull couches. She spins a golden crown between her fingertips while looking out the window. She sets the crown aside as the leopard runs up to her. She lets it sniff her hand then points her finger above its head. It sits, then slides onto its belly.

"Stygian has sent her sister to see us," Mica says. Queen Natalia lifts her chin. "Thank you for coming heiress, but we have nothing to negotiate. We're allied with Alys Wyntryn and only Alys. She was the only trustworthy irregular in all of Kanaleigh."

She must have not known Ava's mother very well. Ava steps past Aliras and bows to Natalia. "I was not sent here by my sister."

"Then why is her assassin here?" Natalia asks. They must have faith in Aliras. They know he's an assassin but still allow him into their home.

"Aliras helped me escape Goldryn. I did not want to have an alliance with Goldryn either, but in my case, it got me imprisoned," Ava says.

Natalia smiles softly. "Then, might I ask why you are here?" Mica sits down beside Natalia. The two queens contrast with each other. Mica has a wide frame, dark skin, and straight hair. Natalia is thin, pale, and has curled tendrils that frame her face. Even their clothing is opposite, fighting leathers versus a corseted dress.

"The tenth protector of Wyntryn, Raiden Hynrule, was or is, in danger," Ava says. For all she knows, he could be floating in the sea out there. Full of salt water. Her heart burns and Ava forces her fear away. She shouldn't care. "He sent me a vision this morning. I came here to find him."

Mica leans forward, pressing her elbows against her thighs. "Did your vision show you the destruction of one of our sacred vessels?"

Ava gulps. All she knows is that Raiden was drowning, and he reached out to her. She set aside their differences for his sake, but she did not know about anything he might have done.

Natalia narrows her eyes, studying her like a prize pony she might buy. Ava shifts beneath the stare. The queens have a right to be upset. They don't know her and evidently one of her own destroyed something of theirs, but that doesn't settle her unease. Natalia speaks slowly. "Sparrow Hynrule was aboard Ta Drogon Gana, a ship with great value to us. This ship was destroyed off our coast this morning by an isolated thunderstorm. Every irregular in this city could feel the energy wafting off that storm. We lost the entire crew."

"I am sorry for your loss, Your Highnesses, but do you know what happened to Sparrow Hynrule?" Ava asks.

Natalia releases a small sigh. "Your sister sent Aliras to us once a moon to ask for our talisman." This is what Aliras meant. The queens will do anything to avoid her questions. All of their answers are indirect and honestly, confusing. "I eventually reached out to Sparrow Hynrule with the location of said talisman. I trusted him, and I imagine many others have as well. From my understanding, Queen Kalenti has power liked to that of a talisman. After Sparrow Hynrule visited Queen Kalenti, he decided to travel back by ship, rather than alate. We both know he is a very capable mage and can alate as if it is nothing." She snaps her fingers, then leans back and stares at Ava. The talisman never belonged to Natalia. All five talismans were created by the sacrifice of Wyntryn souls on Wyntryn land.

"Are you accusing him of something?" Ava asks.

"He manifests lightning, yes?"

Ava opens her mouth to speak, but Mica lifts her hand, silencing her. "Your sworn protector was seen on a beach on the outskirts of the city. He has broken our alliance by destroying one of our sacred ships and murdering almost two dozen of our people. If you wish to be held in our graces, Lady Wyntryn, you will take care of this issue."

Aliras shifts so that his arm lightly touches hers. A small offering of comfort. "What action would make up for his offenses?" Aliras asks.

Natalia glances at her wife. "I would argue a death for a death, but I am not a tyrant. You are not yet queen, so a protector's actions are not within your control, yet. If you want to prove to us that you are as trustworthy as your mother, then send him to us. He will receive one punishment for each life he stripped from this world." Ava can hate Raiden, but she would never send him off to be tortured. "What if I can prove the storm was not caused by him?" she asks.

Natalia lifts her chin. "There is nothing you could possibly show me to alter what I already know." A challenge Ava will gladly conquer.

"What if I could keep my sister away from the Isles?" It's a long shot, but Wyntryn only has the Isles. If Raiden did take Queen Kalenti's talisman, then Eventyr will be after her region. She has to keep what alliances she does have.

"Go on," Natalia says.

"Stygian wants an alliance with Wyntryn. I will allow her into my region's borders, on the condition that she stays far away from the Isles."

Mica and Natalia look at each other. Mica nods, then Natalia smiles. "I heard about Rebynrock. If you are willing to protect my people with that same *feya*, we will protect you as well." Ava tries to hide her sigh of relief.

Mica stands and offers her hand to Aliras. He places his fist on her palm. "With all due respect, Aliras, I hope this alliance means I never have to see your face again."

Aliras chuckles. "I'll make sure to stay far away." What an odd relationship they have. It seems friendly, but they clearly don't enjoy having him here.

Natalia bows her head to Ava. "Try not to start a war with your sister. I would hate to send my precious wolves into battle."

"If it ever comes to that, I promise it will be for a

good reason," Ava says.

Mica pulls her hand from Aliras'. "There's always a good reason to kill that Itzallas."

Natalia clasps her hands together. "Now, do you need a place to stay for the night?" Ava raises her brows. Her interrogation has quickly switched to kind formalities. It's likely she will never understand this world of politics. "No thank you. It's best I get back to Goldryn before my sister decides to invade Wyntryn." With Ava's luck, it's possible that Stygian has already done something reckless. "I am grateful to have met you, Queen Natalia and Queen Mica. Your willingness to continue this alliance brings me great relief."

Natalia hums. "I am intrigued by you, Lady Wyntryn. I am curious to see how you do as queen. I have heard your people already call you such, so I trust you have earned their approval."

Ava isn't sure what to think of that, but she supposes it's meant as a compliment. Especially because Natalia already held this opinion of her but forced Ava to prove herself.

She and Aliras will search the city one more time before leaving, but maybe Raiden is better off left alone. If he really did cause a storm and sink that ship, then he never needed her help. He's probably off gallivanting somewhere with a talisman in hand. That is if her vision wasn't anything but a vivid daydream.

Chapter Thirteen

Willow fights through the Plane of Verity and stumbles out into the grass. She coughs up phlegm, then wipes her mouth with the back of her hand. Alating such a distance twice in less than an hour has ravaged her system. Head spinning, she tries to steady herself on her knees. There's no time for this.

She forces herself onto her feet and stalks through the city streets.

The seaside market is quiet in the afternoon. There are only two merchants with open tents. One's a fisherman. A tray of water filled with clams and mussels sits on his stand. Fish hang from the poles of the tent. Beside him, a merchant sells imported goods. The table looks to be covered in rock salts and spices, but Willow doesn't get close enough to get a good look. Willow strolls past the merchants and continues down a side street leading to the pub.

Willow has gone from the sewers to Eventyr, and back to the City on the Sea. The sun fades on the horizon, but she is nowhere near the end of her day. She must speak to the Drogon Insurgency and then face Stygian. "Goddesses give me strength," she whispers.

Neon green flashes in the pub's sign. Willow watches the erratic flicker. Her eyelids are heavy and there's a tight pain growing in her chest. She breaks from the trance and enters the pub. Max isn't behind the bar, and the hatch to the hidden room is shut.

Willow bends down above the hatch and runs her fingertips along the wood. She recognizes this energy. One of the insurgency members is nearby.

No sounds come from below, but the energy sizzles as if the hatch was recently closed. She moves her hands along the wood until she finds the nearly invisible crease. The floorboards resist her pulls. A slight creak sounds from below — an idling presence close by.

The energy of another mind circles her. It tries to delve into her mind. "It's Willow," she says. Wood groans and Willow backs away from the hatch. The floorboards are lifted from below. There's a clack as the hatch is thrown open.

Archer leans against the opening and crosses his arms. "Did you get us those ships?"

"Is that all I'm good for?" Willow asks. She pushes her hair behind her shoulder. The question is simple, not asked out of anger, but people have been using her lately. She's always been a trophy to someone, but it's taken her a while to become aware of it. Alys used her as a chip to cash in for an alliance with Eventyr. Then Stygian did the same. She doesn't think the Drogon Insurgency has the same malicious intents for her skills or connections, but she must remain cautious. There's a limit to how much pain a person can endure.

"No. But I don't trust you," Archer says. His dark hair is slicked back, and he wears a tight-fitted shirt.

"Yet." Willow leans back onto her heels.

"We'll see."

"Are you the only one here?" Willow asks.

"No, Zada is downstairs."

Kalenti only gave Willow three days. Not nearly enough time to gather all the people who are in danger, but it will have to do. "Can I speak to you both?" she asks. Archer shrugs. Then recedes down the steps.

Willow slides across to the edge and stands up on the stairs. She follows Archer down into the hidden room. Zada stands over the table. It's covered with papers that she frantically moves around. "What's up?" Zada asks, not bothering to look up from her work.

Willow rubs her thumb across the palm of her other hand. "I have spoken to Kalenti Alberona. Two Eventyr ships will be arriving in three days at the south end of the city. They will leave at dawn on the next day."

Zada pauses and looks up. She isn't facing Willow, but her shoulders push back, and her neck tenses. "That's soon."

"It is our only opportunity. I also have a request for someone I need out of the city."

Zada turns now and leans the back of her thighs against the table. Willow takes a breath. She's not under scrutiny here and she's doing them a favor, but the possibility of their judgment terrifies her. "There's a boy, the nephew of one of Stygian's guards. This guard does not support Stygian, but he has no choice. She threatens this boy's life to keep the guard in line. I would like to make sure there's a spot on one of the ships for him."

"Who?" Zada asks.

"The guard is Aliras. I can bring his nephew to the ships myself."

Zada glances at Archer. "We have hundreds of people who will want a spot on one of those ships."

"I know. That's why I'm asking for a favor."

Archer steps up to Zada. "It's just one kid."

"And that one kid would be taking the spot of another," Zada says.

"Willow is the only reason anyone will have an opportunity to flee Goldryn," Archer says. "These people are poor, they cannot pay their way. We are lucky Willow was even willing to go to her queen for this." He's defending her for some reason. Odd since he has consistently been harsh.

"Fine. We're a democracy, so I get it—two against one. Make sure he gets there in time." Zada turns back to her work.

Despite her nerves, Willow wasn't expecting a response like that from Zada. From anyone really. Willow's gaze falls to the ground, and she backs into the steps. Her ankle hits the wood before she can stop herself.

She nods to no one and goes up the stairs. Her hand pushes the hatch closed on her way out, but Archer stops it with his hand. He climbs out and Willow turns to him.

"Sorry about her. She is thankful, but there's a lot on her mind. We're all thankful, even though not everyone knows yet. So, thank you for doing this."

She bites the inside of her cheek. "I didn't do it for any of you. I did it for the people that deserve better. I know too many people who have been trapped by Stygian. You hear people say the Goldryn people adore her and respect her, but I do not see it. I see the threats, the patrols of guards, and Stygian's desperation for power. She is trying to prove to the world that she's powerful, but in turn, fails to see her recklessness."

"You are very insightful," Archer says. His sincerity causes her to back away. Part of her was expecting it to be accompanied by a laugh or hint of sarcasm.

His eyes travel across her. He opens his mouth, and Willow turns. She gets to the door as quickly as she can. "See you in three days," she says.

Willow isn't leaving in a hurry because she wants to get away from Archer. It has more to do with the way his eyes traveled across her body. She doesn't like being looked at that way. Willow doesn't wear revealing dresses to invite gazes. She wears them because they give her the confidence she lacks on her own. Archer's words may have been sincere, but his gaze was not. She wishes nothing more than to run back to the palace and hide in her chambers. But Stygian will be waiting for her, and there's no avoiding that. She should have never protected the one who has scarred her and forced her to cower in fear.

Willow was once friends with Stygian. Then she was taken and tortured by her. Now she has sympathized with her enemy and given Stygian easy access to her heart. Who's to say Stygian won't rip it out?

The streets fill with activity as the moon rises. She steps around loose cobblestones. Up ahead is the bridge leading to the cliffside palace. The entire place is littered with guards. Stygian must know of Ava's disappearance.

Willow keeps her head down as she walks to the bridge. She tugs on the edges of her neckline to cover her chest. A headache blossoms behind her eyes. The day's events have left her exhausted and frustrated. Her cheekbone throbs and her feet hurt from wearing heels. At least she'll sleep well tonight.

The dead sparrow still lies on the edge of the bridge. Flies scatter as she walks past, and her heart thuds against her ribcage.

The prospect of Stygian's wrath burns through her. "Be brave," she says to herself.

A pain splices through her mind. She grasps the railing and falls to her knees. White light fills her vision. *When the flowers bloom in the north, the dragon will rise, and its heart will be consumed by fire,* a voice whispers to her.

Her sight slowly returns. The guards stare at her, but none show concern. She reaches out for the railing and pulls herself up. Her headache is even worse than before. She rubs her knuckle against her temple, then lifts her foot to unstrap her heeled boot. When both shoes hang loosely from her fingers, she walks barefoot to the courtyard

The guards' eyes follow her. The air stills. Stygian stands in the center of the courtyard. Willow's shoes slip from her fingers and clatter against the ground. The smell of ash is in the air.

"You better have news, or I will burn you at the stake." Stygian's stature is steady, and her eyes burn with fire. *Would she really burn me alive?* In all honesty, Willow doesn't know the answer to that question. Stygian is unpredictable.

Willow gulps. "You have your alliance back and as a sign of good faith, Her Highness Kalenti is sending two ships full of imported goods from the Southern Dunes." Stygian narrows her eyes when Willow refers to the Eventyr Queen as Her Highness.

Kalenti may not know this, but the goods from the Southern Dunes are powerful in Stygian's mind. Because despite Stygian's best efforts, she has yet to build an alliance with the Outpost Cities. It is extremely difficult for anyone not allied with the Southern Dunes to trade with them. "Good girl," Stygian says.

Nerves buzz through Willow.

She bends down to grab her shoes. They catch fire. Willow jumps back and stares at Stygian. Purple fire pulses in her peripheral. The starch smell of it fills her nostrils. "I am not done with you," Stygian says. The Queen flicks her finger, and the fire goes out. "Ava has escaped the city, but you already know that." Willow's lungs are empty, and her face drains of blood. Stygian chuckles. "Did you think no one would recognize you? That no one would know you helped her?"

Willow draws on what confidence she has left. No one saw them. Stygian is testing her. "I knew she left yes, but I did not help her. Ava is her own person. She only left to solidify her alliance with you." Willow grasps the lie. It's too easy to do—to make up words and thoughts that aren't real. The truth is fragile and easily shattered by sweet lies. "You have been sending Aliras to the Dragon Isles for months. The Queens reached out to Ava. She was planning to tell you of course, but you trapped her in her chambers. She told me she was going to the Dragon Isles to solidify an alliance for you. I asked Aliras to go with her, for safety reasons. They asked me to distract you."

"Distract me?"

Goddesses, why did I say that? Willow nods slightly. She must sell her story. "Yes. I should have told you, but I knew Ava was going to advocate for both Goldryn and Wyntryn before the Queens. I was supposed to distract you until they returned. That way it could be a surprise… a gift, for you."

"I am supposed to believe this?" Stygian asks. Willow doesn't even know what to say. She doesn't often lie and has no clue how to defend something with no footing in reality. "For your safety, let's hope she returns soon then. When do my gifts from Kalenti arrive?"

"In three days."

"Well darling, I'll let you get some rest. Do not test me again. I do not have time for petty matters." Stygian spins on her heel and stalks off into the palace.

Willow is walking a dangerous line between life and death. If she can't follow through on these lies, then she may never see the light of day again.

Chapter Fourteen

Raiden

Water pours from Rais' mouth as he coughs. He could use herbal tea. Nina is bent over him with the heels of her hands pressed against his sternum. Rais reaches for his neck, for the talisman, but his fingers only graze salt and sand. Rais dry heaves. His lungs burn. Around him is only beach and ocean, nothing for miles in all directions.

"Thank the gods. I thought we'd lost you!" Nina pulls him into her arms.

His mind is blurry, but he remembers sinking into the ocean. Then being pulled into the suction of the ship, but after that, there's nothing. He pulls away from Nina. He tries to lift himself, but weakness prevails. He catches himself in the sand and moves to his knees. At least he's alive.

He's face to face with Bryn. They smile, and he notices the flecks of sand-colored freckles across their cheekbones. "How did I make it ashore?" he asks. His throat is sore and his voice is scratchy.

"I dragged your sorry arse through miles of ocean, is how. Right now, we are on one of the southern shores of the Dragon Isles." Nina stands and reaches her hand out to Rais. She opens her fingers to reveal the necklace. "This fell off. Anyway, I have to get to Goldryn. Will you be fine without me?"

Rais takes the necklace and pulls it over his neck, dropping the amulet beneath his soaked shirt. "Do what you must. Bryn seems trustworthy enough." He glances at the doe-eyed nymph.

"I've never hurt a soul," they say. Rais raises his brows. "I do not lie, Raiden. I specialize in healing energy."

"So, you won't kill me," he says dryly.

Nina pats his head. "You'll be fine, Rais. Just get to the manor and save our home."

"Because that's not difficult."

"It's not," Nina says. She disappears into a blue mist, and Rais falls to his back. The sand shifts around him and tickles his skin. Simply having this talisman in his possession is one of the most stressful things in the world. Let alone finding his way to the manor through territory he's never traveled.

What's worse is Ava might be at the manor. He isn't excited or nervous to see her. He's terrified. He's hurt. Worst of all, he hurt her. She would be completely right to never forgive him.

Ava may feel differently if she knew the truth about her supposed best friend. Levites was the one to take her memories. As all energy works, nothing can truly be destroyed. With Levites' death, her memories should return. Not only the ones Levites let slip by when he felt guilty but all of them. It could take minutes or months. Even years for them all to return.

Rais' only chance of forgiveness is if Ava remembers. At least he thinks that's his only chance.

"Do you need a hand?" Bryn asks.

"Give me a moment." He stares at his closed eyelids, watching swirls of blue and red. It would be helpful if the sand wasn't so comfortable. He has someplace to be, and it's not here.

He sighs and lifts himself from the ground. His knees almost buckle beneath him as he stands. Rais brushes the sand from his clothes and drags himself across the beach. Bryn trots up to his side and slows their pace to match his.

Rais has never traveled to the Isles before. Even if he had, he still wouldn't know where they are. There isn't a town or city anywhere near them. Only miles and miles of forest beyond the beach, and at the end of the trees the mountains stretch their jagged peaks into the sky.

"How did Nina figure out where we are?" he asks.

They study the treeline, running their finger along an invisible path in the air. "It took us a long time to get to shore, but on the way here we passed an outlying island that your Nina recognized as Fynger Isles' territory and we are north of there now," Bryn explains.

Even with that knowledge, it leaves a lot of room for error. They could be farther north or south than Nina estimated. Though based on the position of the mountains in accordance with the beach and sun, he figures the manor is at least a five-day ride southwest of here. If only they could find someone willing to let them take two horses. The trek wouldn't be so bad if not for the mountains they have to cross, and the heavy northern snow.

Rais eyes Bryn warily. "Give me one reason to trust you."

They tilt their head, staring at something Rais can't

see. "I can tell you the truth."

"And what's that?"

"I was outside of the refugee camp in Eastern Eventyr when I was captured by those Eventyr regulars. They caught me hunting monsters," Bryn says.

"A monster hunter?" He can't help but laugh. The rapid air causes his chest to strain, and he wheezes.

Bryn doesn't even react to him. "Monsters like the Atane that took my tribe from me. Genetically modified beasts that terrorize innocent people. There are creatures like that in Eventyr. I was hunting them, and training to better fight hordes of Atane."

"Sorry for laughing. I thought you meant creatures that don't exist. Fairytales," he says. Bryn purses their lips, a hard line forming above their brow. "Look, I know what it's like to want to get vengeance. I have spent years training so that I can stop what happened to my home village from ever happening to another. Except what happened wasn't caused by a monster. It was a person who did it. I was never able to exact justice. I eventually learned that not everything is black and white. We all have our faults. We all make terrible mistakes."

"Do not compare your story with mine. We are not alike. I did not make a terrible mistake. I was captured because I'm a nymph. Regulars do not see me as human. I only want to get home and save what family I might have left."

"Then let's get to Wyntryn. We both have monsters to face. Let's help each other."

They trudge across the beach and into the forest. For hours they walk across fallen pine needles and overgrown plants. There's darkness gathered in the distance that never fades away or gets any closer. Rais sees it withering out there, waiting for him. He can hear it buzzing in his mind when he and Bryn don't talk. Every time they turn, and he thinks he'll get away from it, the darkness appears again. Close enough to imagine the touch of it on his skin, but far enough away to remain a mystery.

He slides his fingers across the amulet beneath his shirt. His clothes are dry now, but there's a chill in his bones. When they stop for the night, he hopes the darkness will keep its distance. He's not strong enough to survive its touch.

Chapter Fifteen

Ava

She's a shadow in the trees, pressing herself against the rough bark. The gates to the City on the Sea are twenty feet away. A clearing of grass between her and two Goldryn guards. There's one guard who keeps looking into the trees. She swears the guard can see her, but it's probably her nerves getting to her. Ava doesn't know why she's nervous. She isn't scared of being imprisoned or stuck in an alliance with Goldryn. There's something else that scares her, but she can't quite put her finger on it.

Aliras emerges from the trees to her right. "Doesn't seem like she's done anything in your absence," he says.

"That's odd." Ava and Aliras are sneaking into the city because they fear Stygian's wrath. They can't walk into the palace and expect to have a level conversation with Stygian.

"It is. We might as well take our chances and walk right in. She's not going to arrest you in the streets. There are too many eyes."

"What if we draw her out? Force her to listen to me in the streets?" Ava asks. If she can negotiate with Stygian before her sister can act on anger, then she may be able to avoid imprisonment, again. Even if she does get trapped by her sister, it's not as if escape is impossible.

"How exactly, do you plan to do that?" Aliras asks.

"I figured you would know. You're her assassin." Ava doesn't look at him as she says it. When Natalia pointed it out in the Dragon Isles, it unsettled him. His position isn't something he's proud of.

"Right. Let's try to cause a disruption."

"Take something of hers?" Ava asks. The wind whistles through the trees.

A storm must have swept through while they were gone because the wind is colder now. Aliras reaches his hand out and catches a leaf blowing by. "I meant to get through the gates," he says. Ava smirks, she knew that, but Ava doesn't want to stay on her sister's good side. Aliras studies her. "If she feels her power is at risk, she will do anything to protect it."

"How do you take someone's power?" Energy cannot be created nor destroyed. It is always flowing through Kanaleigh. It is in the oceans and the trees. Irregulars can see it visibly on the Plane of Verity—a place where they walk amongst it. The Wyntryn talismans are special because there are no limits. They allow someone to have access to all energy within their reach. If a talisman is taken from its possessor, then the possessor loses power. They are left with whatever abilities they were born with or brought back to life with.

"She has the taaffeite talisman," Aliras says. There he goes again, reading her thoughts. At least that's the only explanation for the coincidence. Nevertheless, the taaffeite talisman would be a great way to cause a disruption.

"It's that necklace she wears sometimes, the pale

crystal?" she asks.

"I believe so," Aliras says.

She sucks air through her teeth. Stygian's had it this whole time. No wonder Raiden was so serious about gathering the other talismans. They barely stand a chance against Stygian and her army. But if Stygian has a talisman, their chances of surviving a battle are even less. If they could take it from her, Wyntryn might survive. "You know, I've always wanted to stage a heist."

Aliras looks at her with a smug smile. "Can you use one of those mind tricks to knock the guards out?"

"I've only seen others do it." Truthfully, she saw Raiden do it once. No one else.

Two guards lean against the sandstone entrance. One yawns and the other tosses a rock between his hands. "I'll figure it out," she reassures herself.

The energy of the Sonder slips around her. She opens her mind to the flurry of blue. She's not worried about the drowsy guard, so she focuses on the other one. The guard's defenses are easy to break through. She speaks into the man's thoughts, trying to mirror his inner voice. *There's something in the trees. I need to go investigate it, quietly.*

The guard blinks in their direction. Aliras tenses and glances at her in confusion. The red-haired guard pushes off the wall and meanders to them. His companion doesn't seem to notice.

Ava speaks into Aliras' mind. *Grab him.*

The guard steps near the trees—only feet away from them now. As soon as he moves through the undergrowth and out of sight, Aliras pulls him behind a tree. Aliras' hand wraps over his mouth, and Ava presses her fingers to the man's temples. She hushes his mind and lulls him into sleep. It's not a smooth pull or a sleep that will last, but it's the best she can do.

Aliras leans the soldier against a tree. The other guard falls in and out of sleep at the city gate. Ava easily slips into his mind. She tugs on his drowsiness until he slumps down the wall. His head falls to the side, and his body softly hits the ground. That wasn't as difficult as she was expecting.

Beyond the gate, a passerby glances at the fallen guard. It's a woman with two swords strapped to her back. She moves up to the guard and places her fingers on the soft of his neck. The woman studies the tree line.

"My turn." Aliras' voice is a quiet rumble. He leaves the cover of trees, and the woman grabs one of her swords.

She cracks her neck and springs across the grass. Aliras crosses his arms before his chest and swipes them down. Slices of wind cut through the air, slamming into the woman. She's thrown backward but easily gets back on her feet. She spins her sword around her. Aliras flicks his finger and the wind spins around her blade. It pulls it from her hand and throws it across the grass. She reaches for the other sword. Aliras pushes his wind around that one as well, sending it flying. It hits the city wall and clatters to the ground.

The woman raises her fists, and Aliras moves to her. She catches him with a few hits, but it isn't long before Aliras elbows her neck and she's thrown to the ground. The woman gasps for air. Aliras unhooks his chakram and walks toward the steely warrior. Oh, gods, he's not going to kill her, is he? As Aliras gets closer she gets more unsure. Ava runs through the trees, then falls to her knees by the woman's side. Ava places her fingers on the woman's temples and presses her mind to sleep. This trick comes in handy.

"I had it taken care of."

Ava shakes her head. "I don't want to kill anyone."

He raises his chin. "I am not the killer you perceive me to be."

"Then what were you going to do to her?"

Aliras holds his response. She isn't sure how she sees Aliras. He defends her and they are both trying to protect those they care about. But that doesn't change who Aliras is. He's her sister's assassin. A skilled mage that does Stygian's dirty work. Under threat or not, Aliras is not innocent.

And neither am I.

"We should find a place to rest for the night," Aliras says.

They don't have time for sleep. Ava doesn't want to see her sister, but she's going to have to deal with this eventually. There's no trusting Stygian anymore. Ava is an heiress, Natalia reminded her of that. She needs to focus on Wyntryn, not wallow in self-pity. What she needs, is that talisman.

"If we are quick, we can be back in Wyntryn before midnight," she says.

He shakes his head. "It's too dangerous. We need time to plan. We have no idea what we're going to be walking into. It's better to figure it out in the morning."

She wants to argue with him, but she can't deny her drowsiness. She could use some sleep. Plus, she'd rather not infiltrate the palace now... or ever.

They travel through the city under the cover of terraces and alleyways until they come upon a staircase. The shadowed stairway takes them down into the southside port. Small ships bob in the water.

A gust of wind knocks ships into the docks with asynchronous thuds. Aliras leads her through a dark alley to a wooden shack of a home. It's parallel with others like it. The homes sit on wooden beams and water runs underneath them. Aliras goes across a wooden plank leading to the entrance of the house. She hesitantly steps onto it. The plank wobbles beneath her and she hurries across.

Aliras knocks on the door. The sun casts a low glow across the water, leaving much of the city in shadow. The door to the home opens and a woman waves them inside. The woman has elongated ears and high cheekbones.

"My lady, this is Zada. An old friend of mine," Aliras says.

Zada smiles and offers Ava her hand. Hopefully, this old friend isn't an assassin too. Ava places her fist in Zada's palm. "Nice to meet you. Now, Aliras, what's going on?" Zada asks.

"Ava and I have just come back from the Isles, and I'm not exactly on good terms with Stygian right now. We need a place to stay for the night."

"Well, you're welcome here. I have some leftover dinner. You two can get some food and rest." Zada takes them to the kitchen and points to the table in the corner. The chair teeters back and forth when Ava sits down. The kitchen is like the outside of the home — rickety, but somehow holding together. "Oh, and Aliras, I need to speak with you about the —"

Zada and Aliras turn to her. Ava's eyes widen and she looks down at her lap. She doesn't belong here. Not in Goldryn or this stranger's home. Aliras says, "Don't worry. Her beliefs align with ours."

Zada sets dishes on the table and takes a seat. While she talks, Ava piles food on her plate. Slices of an orange fish, chunks of green and yellow fruit. "I know you are not officially a member of the Insurgency, but you should know a woman named Willow has recently joined our ranks. The boys weren't so happy about it."

Ava listens carefully. This is the first she's heard about anything like this. The more she knows about the politics in Goldryn, the better she can help her people.

"Sean and Kael are magatines. Archer isn't any better. You should never listen to a word they say," Aliras mutters.

"Oh, I'm aware. She's a lady of Eventyr, you know. We accepted her offer because she's getting us ships for refugees and hopefully an audience with Queen Kalenti if we ever need one. Plus, she's aligned with Wyntryn and Goldryn. I'd say we're lucky to have her on our side. Oh, and you should know she requested a spot for your nephew on one of the ships." Zada smirks and leans forward in her chair. "I acted like I was against it. I don't want her thinking she runs the place." Zada leans back in her chair, revealing more of her nymph-like features to the overhead light

"Do you know who I am?" Ava asks. Zada mentioned the importance of Willow's allegiances with Wyntryn, but wouldn't that be trivial if the heiress was sitting at her table?

"You're Ava." Zada doesn't bother to look her way.

"Ava Wyntryn," she corrects.

Zada stills. Her eyes go from Aliras to Ava and back. She pushes from the table and stands. "Aliras! You damned fool. You bring the gods-damned Queen of Wyntryn into my disgusting home and don't even bother to tell me? We have a reputation to protect here!"

Aliras' cheek is full of fish. He keeps chewing and

rubs a piece of food off his lip. Zada scoffs. Aliras swallows and leans his elbows on the table. "There is no reputation. No one knows about the Insurgency. And the few who do could care less about reputation."

Zada forces a smile. "I apologize for my behavior and home."

Ava clears her throat uncomfortably. "Your home is nice, and I've seen worse behavior. Don't worry about it."

The nymph seems put off by her response. Zada sits back down and stares at the food. Probably worrying if it's good enough for an heiress. Ava doesn't mind; she can find comfort anywhere and she'll eat almost anything. Unless it's scallops. She despises scallops. Stygian served scallops at a dinner she hosted. Likely to win Ava over with conversation and Goldryn cuisine, but the scallops had a horrific texture. Ava shudders at the memory.

They spend an hour talking about the Drogon Insurgency and its plans. Evidently, two Eventyrian ships are arriving soon and it's all because of Willow. Anyone who has told Zada and her group they're in danger are going to board those ships—including Aliras' nephew. That poor boy must be terrified to leave his home, but at least he will be safe.

News of this insurgency has only solidified Ava's disliking for her sister. She knows Stygian is cruel and dangerous, but Stygian's people seem to respect her. Possibly they only act that way out of fear.

Stygian has kept her people loyal by threatening their families, friends, and their lives. Aliras' case is not an isolated incident. It is happening to hundreds, if not thousands of people within these city walls.

Her sister may have reasons for what she does but

treating people like this is vile. Willow's hands should have been proof enough. Ava felt them herself. She should have always known Stygian couldn't be trusted. It was right in front of her this whole time.

The scars aren't in any of Ava's memories from the manor. Which means Stygian or someone here in Goldryn did that to her. Ava shakes the thoughts from her mind and asks where she can sleep. Zada points her to the stairs.

There are two rooms upstairs. One is clearly Zada's. The other room is smaller, its walls covered in a dull green wallpaper. The bed is small and layered in soft quilts. There's a vanity in the corner next to a window that overlooks the docks.

Aliras knocks on the open door. He hesitantly steps inside the small room—his tall figure fills the space. She gestures to the bed, and he sits down. "I'm sorry Stygian has put you in this position. I'm sorry we couldn't find your brethren in the Isles and that—"

"There is no need to apologize," Ava says. She sits down beside him. "None of that is your fault."

Aliras grabs her hand. For a moment she wants to yank it away. He rubs his thumb across her skin. Which is not a normal thing to do. Not something she's used to. Her breath hitches and her chest burns. He has kind, tormented eyes. She sucks in another shaky breath. There's a hole in her mind where memories are supposed to be. She misses her childhood, even though she can't piece it together. "Are you okay?" he asks. She's not okay. Not even fine. This is not the hand she wants to hold. Not the person that makes her heart stutter and her knees wobble. It's only Aliras.

"I—" Rais' face fills her mind. She sees them jump off the cliff together. She hears his laugh and feels his gaze on her neck. The way the very hairs on her skin raised at his touch. She remembers his lips on hers and his kind voice. His golden eyes and whitish hair. His crooked mouth and hooded eyes. She pulls her hand from Aliras'. Her fingers press against her sternum. "I can't stand another second away from him."

"Away from who?" he asks, oblivious to the visions that soaked into her mind. The ever-flowing desire to run into her enemy's arms and kiss him like they only have seconds left on this plane of existence. Is he even her enemy? Gods. She doesn't know. He is her enemy… in a way. She's supposed to hate him—to despise the very thought of him, but she doesn't. Why do her thoughts of him have to be so overwhelmingly addictive? She's addicted to the memory of his touch. His careful choice of words. His desperation to protect her with every ounce of his being.

"Rais." She looks up at the speckled ceiling of her room. "I miss that damned idiot." Aliras laughs, so loud it practically shatters the buzzing of thoughts in the back of her mind. "What?" she asks.

"You are so blind to yourself."

"What do you mean?"

Aliras leans back. His weight shifts to his hands. "You say you hate him, but he is always in your thoughts. The noise of him in your mind is so loud I could hear it from a mile away. And you just now realize it, don't you?"

She scoffs. "I can't forgive him for what he's done."

"Why?"

"He killed my best friend."

Aliras smiles. Why does he think this is something to smile about? "My lady, your best friend was a member of the Society. I would not put it past one of those fools to have nefarious intentions. There is likely more to this story than you know."

"That's what Willow said, but what if it's not true? What if Rais killed Levi out of cold blood, and I forgive him? That would be so wrong. So, so, wrong."

She's been calling him Rais. Not Raiden. Why is she allowing herself to let go of Levi? She's not supposed to feel like this.

"Even if that's true — do you think you could avoid him for the rest of your life?"

No. She could never avoid him, but she's going to have to. Despite her feelings, Rais killed Levi. Rais almost ruined her alliance with the Isles. And Rais is a distraction. An unrelenting and dangerous distraction. The ringing grows in the back of her mind. She blinks idly, trying to fight against it. The sound is unyielding. Ava's throat tightens. "You should find your nephew. Make sure he's okay. Willow lied to Stygian for me … who's to say if Stygian believed her."

Aliras stands. He keeps his gaze on her for a moment. "I have been working for a queen who has burdened me, abused me, and threatened those I love. If you will have me, Ava Beckett Wyntryn, it would be a pleasure to protect you and your people for what time I have left in this world."

"Thank you for trusting me, Aliras."

"No, thank you for trusting me," he says. He keeps his eyes on her for a moment before leaving and carefully shutting the door behind him.

She leans back on the mattress and pulls a quilt over her arms. There's a sudden chill in the air, and she closes her eyes against the sound of her thoughts, but nothing can stop them. Not even jumping into an icy sea.

Chapter Sixteen

Willow

People sway against her, forcing her to fight through the crowd. Aromas of sweet cream and Goldryn flora fill the air. Each aroma has its own magical effect. Sweet cream dulls the senses and flora makes one feel like air. Willow's favorite, not shockingly, is lavender. It causes the mind to mend with nature. A connection to life itself — amplifying the energy already felt as an irregular.

The Fallen Anchor is a small pub, so it must have taken a miracle to pack all of these people in here. It's just after dawn, so everyone should be dispersing soon. Willow has yet to see any sign of Aliras or Ava in the city.

She was hoping they might be here. Aliras knows this pub is safe from prying eyes. Nina and Max have done well to keep it that way.

Soft laughter travels from the far corner. A waitress holds out a pale green aroma to Willow, but she declines.

A rhythmic dripping of water is nearby. Willow focuses on the small splashes. Her feet carry her to the source, a table nestled against the wall. There, a sodden Nina sits curled up in a chair. Her braids are undone and her eyelids heavy with exhaustion. There is no way she was in Wyntryn, but where else could she have come from? Water drips from Nina's clothes to the floorboards. It's unsettling to see her like this, submitting herself to vulnerability. Something scared her into this, and Nina does not scare easily.

Willow falls into the chair next to Nina and pulls her into her arms. Whatever it is, Willow's here now. What world lay between them has dwindled into a sliver of space. That doesn't make the small distance left become anything less than a ravine. The last time they talked, really talked, was two months ago. A few days before Ava set Rebynrock aflame. Nina leans onto her, closing the gap, resting her temple against Willow's shoulder. Water seeps through the thin chiffon of Willow's dress. Blue ripples at the corners of her vision. Willow shuts her eyes and opens herself to the images that flood into view.

In Nina's thoughts, the ocean rips back and forth. It throws her and another into a rough current. Water engulfs her mouth and travels into her lungs. Nina gasps, over and over, fighting the salty water. Nina watches Rais from a distance sink into the dark waters. She frantically swims through the violent swells. A shadow of him shimmers below. The only light is from the moon which barely escapes the clouds. Nina dives and grasps his hand, but his weight drags them both down. A vacuum forms above and sucks them to the surface. A forest nymph swims to her. They grasp onto the collar of Rais' jacket and together they fight the waves. Nina creates a channel of air beneath them. Then she pushes air behind them, gliding them toward a hazy shore in the distance. The vision fades and is replaced by a flurry of panic. Nina's pressing on Rais' chest. Nina swears at him, begging him to stay with her.

Rais coughs up water, and the vision dissipates.

Willow holds on tight, letting Nina's emotions filter through her. It was Rais that scared her. Nina thought she was losing her closest friend. That's why she hasn't even bothered to go upstairs for a change of clothes, resigning to curling into this chair. Willow supposes being down here is better than being alone.

"You knew I was here?" Nina whispers.

Willow tries to remove herself from Nina's mind. "No." She brushes her fingers across Nina's tangled curls. "Fate must be on our side. I came to speak with the Drogon Insurgency."

Nina lifts her head from Willow's chest. Their eyes meet. Irises like coffee with a spoonful of milk. "You what?" She asks, her voice dimmed from its usual bite.

"I came to find you not long ago and happened upon the group. I offered my assistance," Willow explains.

"Not surprising." Nina's jaw clenches and she moves back to her seat—the space between them a chasm. Willow is being shut out, again. Nina's features dip and she leans against the table. "I thought you were on Stygian's side."

"I am on the side that protects innocent lives. I am an Eventyrian, through and through. I will never side with anyone unless I have to."

Nina raises her chin. "They let you help them?"

"Why wouldn't they?" Willow folds her hands on her lap.

Nina smiles in a tense and unsettling way. "You are the reason Rebynrock was under siege."

"How do the politics of two regions fall to me? I am not a queen of either. I do not make decisions for their rulers." Even as she says it, her heart burns with the residue of her guilt. "Nina?"

"What?"

"What happened to Rais?"

"He's fine. Just waterlogged, I guess. He'll be back in Wyntryn soon." Nina pushes her palms against the table and kicks the chair back with her heel. Her hand grasps Willow's. "Come on."

Willow stills. She meets Nina's eyes. If only they had never left that manor. Every day since then, they have fallen further away from each other. Even if they were only friends then, it was better than nothing.

Willow could tell Nina had feelings for her before Nina recognized them herself. Nina's always liked her, but it took Willow a long time to detach herself from the enigma that is Kalenti Alberona. Not that Kalenti ever gave her the time of day or treated her the way Nina does. Well, did. They haven't been close like that for months.

Nina tugs on her hand. Willow could pull away, but she'd rather follow Nina, up those stairs and to the second floor. There's no point dwelling on what has already passed. She's here now and Nina needs her. So, she stands and follows.

The door creaks shut behind her. Sunlight shines through the window onto the center of a blue and gold rug. Nina likely placed it there on purpose. It perfectly highlights the room.

Nina goes to her wardrobe and pulls clothes from it. She sets them on the bed and glances warily at Willow before turning away and gently pulling off her drenched clothes. Willow keeps her gaze on the floorboards. Not that she hasn't seen Nina before.

She has something to say but can't locate the words. Nerves spiral through her. There's a plethora of thoughts she wants to speak aloud, but now that she can, her mind is blank. The bed creaks. Willow looks up at Nina, who now sits on a crumpled quilt. Willow can always say them another time—when her world doesn't feel like it's crumbling. "About the Drogon Insurgency," Willow says.

Nina lifts her head. "What about it?"

"I have already gotten them the help they require." A bird lands on the windowsill. She moves to the window and places her fingers on the glass. Willow taps her nail against the pane and the bird tilts his head. "I went to Eventyr yesterday." Nina fidgets. Willow bends down to meet the little eyes of the bird. Facing the bird is better than facing Nina—who knows who's in Eventyr. "Kalenti ended her alliance with Goldryn. Stygian sent me there to fix it. I didn't, but Stygian thinks I did. While I was there, I negotiated with … her to take in some refugees from Goldryn."

"You did?" Nina asks. The bird's cedar feathers ruffle in the breeze.

"Ships are arriving in two days." It's soon. Willow's relieved it's happening, but it's surreal. She's caused so much harm, pulled many strings, and now she is finally helping people. Empathy's a tug of war within her. She needs to learn when to back off—when to stop helping those who have fallen too far. Stygian dived straight into the darkness. Not bothering to look back. Willow followed her out of fear and sympathy, but she looked back. And when she did, everything went dark. She's been fighting for the light since. It's in Willow, she's a good person.

Nina moves to her and kneels on the floor. "I'm sorry for how I treated you when Stygian attacked Rebynrock. I know you never intended for that to happen. I get angry and take it out on whoever is closest."

Willow slowly turns from the bird. It's not often Nina makes the first move. They've apologized many times, for many things, but it's always Willow who brings it up first. "I am responsible though. Stygian may have done it with or without my input, but I still feel horrible. Watching those soldiers alating home, burned alive, was like feeling my heart and lungs ripped from my chest," she says. Her fingers push against her sternum, hitting her corseted top.

"Don't." Nina holds her palms out to Willow.

Willow stares down at them. Her palms are lighter than the rest of her skin. The creases are smooth — not scarred or damaged.

"Don't think that way. Not anymore."

"I could've sworn you hated me after that. Are you sure you want to push it aside?" Willow asks.

"I want us to trust each other again. And … um. I trust you with my thoughts." Nina's gaze bores into her.

"We are on different sides of a war." Willow may be against Stygian's actions, but she's still working to support her. Although she's tried to help Wyntryn, she has not done enough. She doesn't want it to be that way but turning against Stygian is terrifying. There's no saying what Stygian may do if she were to openly defy her. Willow can say she's neutral, but because she lives in Goldryn, in the palace, that would be a lie. Stygian controls her.

"You are helping the Drogon Insurgency now, so it doesn't matter what side you are or aren't on," Nina says, seeing a perspective Willow's blinded herself to. "The group's only desire is to save those caught in the crossfires. Zada is from Aysand, Archer's from the Isles, Kael's from the Southern Dunes, Jess is from Goldryn, Sean's from Grymyr, and I'm from Wyntryn. Now, we have you, from

Eventyr. We are from everywhere and nowhere."

She notes that Nina leaves out Max. For some reason, she assumed the pub owner was a part of their group.

"It's not only our allegiances." Willow sucks in a breath. "It's more than that."

Nina pulls her hands back, closing them into fists.

"What happened between us…"

Nina scoffs. "What happened was that you abandoned me. After you gained Stygian's trust you sent me that letter. I gave up everything to come to Goldryn. I faked going on a mission just to be here. I worked so hard to afford this apartment. All so we could be together. Then you stopped showing up and when you did … you were distracted. Distant. What did I do?"

"Nothing," Willow whispers.

"Then why?" There's a desperation in her voice. A sadness chills the room.

Willow twists the rings on her fingers. She stares down at her hands. Stares at anything but Nina. "I… was ashamed. Not of you. Never you. I was ashamed to have any loyalty to Stygian. I became so tolerant and comfortable around her that I started calling her Syn. She wanted to—" Willow covers her face with her hands. "She made me feel awful and other times she made me respect her. You deserve someone better than me. You deserve someone who will follow you to the ends of this world."

Nina pulls Willow's hands from her face. Their thoughts mingle together. "You are always enough for me," Nina says.

There was a time when there was no question if they were enough for each other. Never a second thought. They were all that mattered. There was no danger on the horizon. When Willow had visions, they were about menial things. Not prophecies of how entire regions may collapse. If only their relationship could be simple. She could be happy living a life of small pleasures.

"Nina?"

"Yes?" she hums.

"When this is all over... I want you to come to Eventyr with me. I can tell my father the truth. Tell him that the only person I will marry is you. We can live at the Crystal Lakes. Our greatest worry will be the decision of what to eat for dinner. No wars. No responsibilities. Only us."

Nina's lips quirk up. "I'd like that." Nina shifts her back to the wall and pulls Willow to her. Willow leans her head against Nina's shoulder, finally relaxing. A breath of cool air on a hot summer's day. Her mind wanders away from this place.

Willow left a note for Ava, telling her of the prophecy she envisioned before Alys Wyntryn's death. That note was a warning to Ava, based on how Willow interpreted the prophecy. What she still contemplates now, is how her newest vision fits into the original prophecy. They both appeared to her in the same way. Her vision was filled with a white light after seeing the carcass of a bird. Both were so specific, there is no way they are not connected.

There will be two sisters who rise from the north. Through killing their creator, one will rise more powerful than before. They will either be each other's savior or destroyer of the Sonder.

When the flowers bloom in the north, the dragon will rise, and its heart will be consumed by fire.

Chapter Seventeen

Ava

Ava and Aliras run through the streets, duck into alleyways, and dodge people returning to their homes. The sun sneaks up the horizon, creating a watercolor sky of orange and pink.

Aliras slows and drops to his knee. He pulls up a sewage grate and looks up at her. "Is there not a cleaner way into the palace?" she asks.

"Not without detection."

Ava lets out a snort of disgust as she sits on the ground and hangs her legs into the opening. She braces her hands on the edge of the aperture and lowers herself down. Her feet hit the bottom and brown water sloshes onto her. The smell is more rancid than she remembers.

Their plan is not complex because they had nowhere near enough time to plan a heist. Their success relies on improvisation and luck. The goal is to get that talisman and run. Well, that's all they could agree on. Ava wanted to distract Stygian while Aliras searched for the talisman. Aliras wanted to kill Stygian.

This morning Zada left at the same time as them.

She said there was a meeting with the Drogon Insurgency she couldn't miss. Ava promised she'd help them in any way she could, but with Wyntryn's deficiency in resources, there isn't much she can do.

Aliras hops down into the sewer after her. His face is shrouded in darkness. Likely, he's not even fazed by the stench down here. "You know, I can't wait to see her face when you succeed," Aliras says. Definitely not fazed by it.

"I'm pretty sure if we see her, then our plan would've failed," Ava says.

"A plan can only fail if you have one." He walks ahead of her and glances down the different sewage pathways.

"Is it crazy to suggest we make one?" she asks.

Aliras takes the path that continues straight ahead. "Stygian doesn't wear it all the time. The talisman is what keeps us from alating from the city, because of that, the crystal never leaves the palace," he says.

Ava drags her feet through the muck. Of course, it's tied to her sister's energy, her power. She tries to stay near the edge, but the water still sloshes up her calves. It reeks. A smell like rotting flesh. "Can you get me to her chambers? I've never been there before."

He gives her a curt nod and takes a left.

They continue to go through the maze of tunnels, shooting ideas back and forth between each other. Her hands shake the whole time, and it takes a great deal of effort not to trip on the loose stones. If only there were a better way to get into the palace undetected.

Iron bars block the tunnel, stopping them from continuing forward. Aliras turns to her. For the first time, she can feel his fear. Not because of the dead end, but because this is becoming all too real. She's scared too, but she doesn't want to admit it.

"I have to tell you something before we do this because there's a small chance we won't be leaving this palace," he says. Another secret. With it, there's always another lie.

"Don't say that. We aren't going to die." She pushes her hand on her hip, bracing herself for whatever he has to say.

His jaw tightens. "I know you haven't forgiven your Sparrow yet, but you should know something about him. Well, I suppose it's more about me." Ava shifts her feet, begging her muscles to stop quivering. "The scar he has…" The one that slices from his cheekbone to the base of his neck? "… I was the one who caused it." Ava wants it to be a lie, but Rais did tell her it was a Goldryn soldier. He helped them kill off Atane along the Wyntryn and Goldryn border, but the Goldryns began to raid the village. When Rais tried to stop them, they attacked. Tied him to a tree and left him to die. Aliras left him to die.

"What?" Her chest burns. "You did that?"

"It was a long time ago, and —"

"A year ago," Ava corrects. How could he do something so cruel? She would be disgusted if Aliras did that to any random person, but this is Rais. She knows how much that scarred him. It's more than a physical mark, it's a memory. A trauma of being betrayed and falling close to death. One he faces every time he looks in the mirror. Why does she trust so easily? Aliras is an assassin for goodness' sake.

"I had to tell you. Because I know you care about him despite what he's done. And I didn't want to lie to you. You don't deserve that."

"Do you think he deserved to be tied to a tree after helping your soldiers? Do you think he deserved to be carved like a fish and left to die?"

She shouldn't be this angry about it. Levi didn't deserve to be cut and thrown from that window. Her anger isn't only about Aliras' actions. She's horrified by this world and its people. She's angry at herself for setting Rebynrock on fire. Terrified of what she's capable of — she has done things as horrible as Rais and Aliras. Maybe even as cruel as Stygian.

No one is honorable or evil. Morality is a spectrum. A blur of many colors. It's like the Sonder, hazy and dark. Sometimes there is light in people and sometimes they're darker than night. They are all trying their best to survive, and sometimes they make horrific mistakes.

Aliras leans against the grate. It creaks with his weight.

Her hand slips off her hip and hangs at her side. This may be the dumbest thing she's ever done. She shakes her head. "Okay."

"Okay?" he asks.

She sighs. "Let's get this over with."

In the dim light, she can see his raised brows and wide eyes. His emotions slip into the Sonder — nervousness, guilt, and a little surprise. She gestures for him to move off the bars. She can't be angry at him — her hands are blood red too. There's a darkness in all of them and it only takes a small push to be released.

Willow unlocked this grate before, so they didn't have to worry about it then. Neither of them have a key now. Ava wraps her fingers around the metal bars. She pulls on the energy around her and focuses it into the metal. The water on the bars evaporates into steam and the metal turns to liquid in her hands. It pools into the water at her feet. She carefully steps over the molten metal as it sizzles and resolidifies in the greenish water.

Ava recognizes the ledge up ahead and the dark stones of the palace. This is certainly the same sewage tunnel Willow led them down. She goes to the circle of metal in the ceiling and pushes against it. It gives way, and she shoves it aside. Ava pushes onto her tiptoes and places her hands on the ledge. She lifts herself onto the floor. Once her feet are below her, she stands.

Since leaving Grymyr all those months ago she's found a strength within herself. In her body and mind. It still surprises her how much she's capable of. If she hadn't lost her memories maybe it would feel normal.

"Where are her chambers?" Ava asks.

"Don't you want me to go with you?" he asks.

She shakes her head. "Can you keep watch instead?"

She's vulnerable here, so this will be a true testament for Aliras. She needs to know if he meant what he said at Zada's. He said he wanted to follow her instead of Stygian. This improvised heist of theirs will prove whether he means that or not. Despite his actions, she kind of likes him. She sees a fire in him like her own. He may be an assassin, but he acts with good intentions. Isn't that all anyone can do? Do their best to protect the ones they love. If she were in his position, she would do anything to protect her nephew too. Even if it meant going against her beliefs. Even if it meant killing.

Aliras opens his mouth to argue, but he sighs instead. "If you go through the throne room, there's a staircase on the left wing. You go up two flights of stairs. The door will be on a hallway to your right. I think it's the room to the left."

She turns to Aliras. The blue in his irises blends with the brown. "Are you prepared to go against her?" Ava almost says her sister's name, but she's afraid Stygian will overhear somehow. Ava doesn't doubt her sister has ears all over the palace.

"For you, yes." His voice is clear. He doesn't stumble over the words.

"Good."

Ava checks for the dagger strapped to her thigh. She would use her fire before the dagger, but there's nothing wrong with a backup plan.

They go through the hallway and wait at the bottom of the steps. There's a thump of boots from above. A soldier trots down the stairs. When he sees them, he stops and reaches for his sword. Ava takes a breath, then alights a blaze in her hand. The soldier's eyes go wide. She backs away from the stairs and the soldier follows her into the hallway, his sword raised in shaky hands. Good. She's not the only one who's nervous.

There's a crack as Aliras' elbow connects with the man's temple. Violent, but it will do. Ava meets Aliras' eyes as the soldier collapses to the floor. She breaks their gaze and runs past to the steps. The more guards they encounter the more chaos will ensue. There's a very small chance they get out of here with that talisman. Aliras follows her up the steps. At the top, a double door blocks their path. She cracks it open and peers down the corridor. There isn't anyone nearby.

She pushes the door open, and Aliras catches it with his hand before it hits the wall.

It doesn't take long to get to the other end of the hall. They climb the steps to a terrace that overlooks the courtyard. It's flooded with soldiers. The bridge and roads leading to the palace have soldiers stationed every few feet. This would've been a disaster if they didn't use the sewers.

"Hey, you got this," Aliras says from behind her. She nods. It will be fine. Whether they get the talisman or not, they will be fine.

Ava tugs herself into the Sonder. Using the Plane of Verity, she can see the patterns of energy. The different hues of blue allow her to see the remnants of minds. It's a skill she knew Rais used frequently, but she'd never tested it herself.

Deep blue blossoms ahead in the Sonder. The color stirs within waves of energy and spirals up the stairs. Ava hurries after it, listening intently to the sounds of the hollow palace. Aliras' steps are heavy behind her. But he keeps a distance.

At the top of the stairs, the darker hue fades. Across the hall, a door swings shut. Aliras' mind curls outside of her own. She doesn't fight him off. His voice sounds in her mind. *I'll follow their trail. Go to the talisman.*

She doesn't pause to reply and hurries down the hall. She stays on the balls of her feet to quiet her boots on the stone. Sunlight pours through the windows as the sun rises. Stygian better be far from her chambers. Her sister usually goes to sleep at noon, so Ava should have plenty of time to get in and out before then.

Ava reaches the large doors of the throne room. She doesn't know the layout well enough to find another way around. There is only through. If her sister is beyond these doors, then there is only down. A dungeon cell and a lock without a key. At least that's what she imagines will happen. It's unlikely Stygian would trust her enough to keep her in a normal room. Not after her dive into the ocean.

She places her ear against the door. There's no sound from the other side. *Please don't let me die.* She pulls the door open and steps inside. The throne stands alone on the dais. All the tiles are shiny and unmarked by shoes. Dark purple banners adorned with a three-headed dragon sway loosely in an invisible wind. She's alone … for now.

Ava crosses to the left side of the dais. Through an open arch, a wide staircase. She goes up the steps, listening for anyone nearby. There's nothing but the sound of her boots hitting sandstone. The staircase leads to a hall with numerous doors on either side. At the end is a spiral staircase.

She takes the staircase up to the next floor—to the hallway Aliras mentioned. There's one door on either side. He said it was the hallway to her right, the doorway on the left? There's light coming from underneath the doorframe of the door on her right. It must be that one. She twists the handle and the door swings outward. As if a phantom wind is forcing it open. She grips the handle as it pulls her out, and her feet slip off the edge. This is no room. It's a false doorway.

Her arm jerks with her weight. She grabs the handle with her other hand. This is a trap for people like her. People trying to steal what isn't theirs. Her heart lurches and panic seizes her gut. Below her is a stone deck with chairs laid out for sunbathing. How is she supposed to get out of this? It's not safe to alate when her feet aren't on solid ground. She could try jumping, but she would never be able to clear the deck below or the jagged rocks that line the edge of the water. "Aliras!" she screams.

Ava pumps her legs, trying desperately to get back in the hallway. One of her hands slips and she screeches. "Aliras, help!" Wherever he is, he can't hear her. She must survive this on her own.

She pumps her legs again and grasps the edge of the doorway. The muscles in her fingers tighten and fight against her. Wind pushes the door in and she's able to swing her foot up onto the floor. She pushes her boot into a crevice in the sandstone bricks and pulls the door toward her. With a fateful yank, her knee is in the hall and she lifts her other leg in. Ava shimmies herself further into the hallway.

Now she just has to let go. Her stomach is on the floor, so there's no way she'd fall, but it's still terrifying when all she can see is the drop below. Ava takes a dreaded risk and lets go of the handle. She grabs onto the cool stone below the doorway and slides herself inside. The stone grounds her. Its cold touch seeps through her. She pushes herself further into the hallway. The door swings idly in the wind, and she wraps her arms around her legs. Nauseated and scared to death, but safe.

She's seen herself die through Levi's eyes, but it's different than being mere seconds from it. Not even close to seeing it through her own eyes. It can't compare to the horrid feeling in her gut. The knowledge that if her grip slipped, she'd fall to that terrace below and splatter like a fly on a windshield. She gags. Why does that door even exist? Is Stygian not scared of accidentally opening it herself? This place is insane. The sooner she finds that talisman, the quicker she can get out of here. Hopefully, it's anywhere but hanging from her sister's neck.

Ava draws her mind back into the Sonder and listens for Aliras but she can't detect him. She leaves the door swinging and goes to the other side of the hall. There's no sign of energy moving inside, so she pushes open the door.

The room glimmers. From the white tiles to the

crystal columns. An entire wall made of glass opens to a large balcony. There's an arch to the left that reveals a four-poster bed with maroon bedding. To the right are two doors. With any luck, they won't lead to open air.

She goes to the bedroom and searches for a jewelry box of some kind. Where else would someone keep a necklace? The jewelry boxes Stygian does own have no pinkish talisman in them. Not even something resembling the crystal. She ends up going through every room before giving up. There's not even a sign of it in the Sonder. Where else could it be? Shoved in a box somewhere? Hidden in an underwater cavern? She should've known this plan was too good to be true. Stygian would never put the talisman somewhere Ava could find it.

Ava sits on one of the sofas and closes her eyes. She should be in Wyntryn. With the family who cares about her. Anya and Aran are there. She could spend this time getting to know them, rather than trying to fight a war that hasn't even begun. Then there's Rais. He could be dead at the bottom of the ocean, and she wouldn't know any better. She never even gave him a chance to explain himself.

She leans her head into her hands.

"Looking for something?" Stygian's voice snakes from behind.

She snaps her head up and meets her sister's gray eyes. Stygian's hand is wrapped around the back of Aliras' neck. She shoves Aliras to his knees. Did he tell Stygian she was here? She thought he was on her side. Was his honesty a ploy to gain her trust?

"Darling sister, I thought better of you." The talisman hangs around Stygian's throat. She lets go of Aliras, then taps the taaffeite crystal. "You could have asked to borrow it. Sisters are supposed to share, aren't they?"

Ava bites her tongue.

"Now, for attempting to take what is mine, I will take what is yours," Stygian says.

"And what is that?"

"Your darling Sparrow, of course."

"You're a disgusting person," Ava whispers. The words come before she can stop them. There is an intrinsic force within her attached to Rais. A force always wanting him, searching for him. A desire that defeats any hatred she tries to hold onto. So, when she hears Stygian's threat, she lets that slip out. Against her better judgment, she can't help but want to protect him.

"I am not evil." Stygian laughs—a quiet menacing laugh. Stygian clasps her hands together. "I am not disgusting."

"You kill people to stay in power," Ava says. "You threaten people, trap them so that you can get what you want. Is that not evil?"

Stygian stills and seems to contemplate this. "Goldryn is all I have. Without this crown, I am nothing. I do what it takes to survive, and I do what it takes to keep my people safe."

"But you don't keep your people safe."

Stygian smiles. It's as if a shadow crosses her features, hugging her with anger and darkness. "You killed my people in Rebynrock. Those that returned had severe burns and many will never walk again."

"I had to free Rebynrock."

"I never entrapped anyone but you in Rebynrock," Stygian says. "I was there to protect the people and get what I wanted from the Society of the Collective. So really, you were only freeing yourself." That can't be true.

"What about Aliras? You keep him in line by threatening his nephew. At your core, you are cruel." She feels Aliras' gaze on her.

His voice slips into her mind. *She knew we were in the city. We never stood a chance.*

At least he didn't turn against her. A small victory.

Stygian clenches her jaw. "Is it wrong to be in control? Is it wrong to ensure my survival, my reign? Wouldn't you do the same?"

Ava does want to be in control. She doesn't want others to make decisions for her. She wants to make them so that she knows what to expect. So that she knows what to do next. But does the need for control make someone bad? Isn't it, at its core, a defense mechanism?

No one is inherently evil but they can become that way. Ava was crafted, led down a path of misfortune that forced her to develop a need for control because so many horrible things happened that she couldn't stop. It's the same for Stygian. If Ava can understand her sister, she can predict her actions. At least for now, Ava understands her. Enough to take a risk. Perhaps, Stygian isn't evil. Perhaps, like Ava, she has been guided by many unfortunate events. Nonetheless, Ava knows what she must do. She is not guilty about the decision, because it is necessary.

"Your thoughts have changed, sister." Stygian tilts her head, studying Ava. "Willow said you wanted an alliance, but you came here for a talisman. What is it you want now?"

She doesn't support her sister or agree with her actions, but she made a promise to the Dragon Isles' queens. If she can't get the talisman by force, then she can negotiate the alliance Stygian's been begging for. "I will work with you. We both need things from each other. If you give me the taaffeite talisman, then I will give you what you need.

You want power and land. I have both. As you said, sisters are supposed to share."

The words sting Ava's throat. She hates everything she says, but it is time she stopped relying on others to save her. An hour ago, she was seconds from death. No one was there to save her. How's she to know if anyone will be there next time? She must be selfish. Risking the safety of Wyntryn to get her hands on the talisman is selfish. But it'd what she must do.

A wicked smile crosses Stygian's face. "Give me the Sparrow, and I'll give you the talisman."

"No," Ava says. Almost too fast. She gulps. "Unfortunately, Raiden has put himself in a predicament. It would be impossible for me to send him here. Is there something else?"

"A Petrichor," Stygian says.

"They are our family."

"So?"

Ava steps around the sofa. Aliras watches her closely, then his voice appears in her mind. She keeps her gaze steady on Stygian. She wants to feel powerful. She doesn't need real power. An illusion is enough, as long as she believes people see her as better than themselves.

Ava drops to her knee. If it's power Stygian wants, then it's power she will get. "What about my loyalty?" Ava asks.

"Prove it to me."

Ava reaches for the dagger on her thigh. She holds her hand out to Stygian and pulls the blade across her palm. "Is my blood enough?"

Stygian unclasps the talisman, then tosses the pink crystal to her. Ava catches it with her good hand. Stygian bends down before her, then brushes the hair off Ava's face. "You better get to Wyntryn. I'd very much like to have all your protectors kneeling before me. I know you need their permission to solidify this alliance since you are only an heiress. So, get their permission. As soon as that crown is upon your head, you and I are going to take Eventyr for ourselves. Imagine how the world will see us then. The prophecy says when we come together, the Sonder will end. People are terrified of us, Ava. It is because they aren't us and they will never be good enough."

Chapter Eighteen

Raiden

A rumble sounds behind Rais. He sits up and peers through the trees. A carriage led by two horses is rolling this way.

Rais woke up an hour ago when the sun cast its rays through the pines. Bryn is still fast asleep on a bed of pine needles. He's been leaning against a tree and watching birds fly through the branches above. They chirp to each other and take turns diving for prey in the underbrush.

He looks through the pines and watches the carriage speed around a tight path. There doesn't appear to be much cargo aboard. Just a small man steering the horses. Rais runs toward it, waving his arms.

The driver scoffs at him and rolls right on past. Rais wants to yell at the man, but it'd be no use. The large wheels crush through the undergrowth. At least it's creating a path they can follow.

By the end of yesterday, they had made it to the base of the mountains. There is a valley that stretches for at least a mile on the other side. But to get there, they'll have to either go around or find a path through the mountain.

Wyntryn miners have dug many cavernous routes through the Wyntryn mountains. He and Bryn haven't been following a mapped route, so it's likely they won't find a tunnel through the mountains nearby. The only issue is he doesn't know where this region ends and where Wyntryn begins. There's no line in the dirt that says, 'This is the border.' But there's a chance this carriage is going toward a safe route.

Foliage rustles behind him. He turns to see Bryn walking sluggishly. They rub the sleep from their eyes. The noise of the carriage must have woken them up.

He runs his hand through his hair. This part of the mountain range juts into the lower portion of the Dragon Isles territory. Yesterday they traveled from the coastline, a few miles past Dire Town where the Queens live, to the edge of Dire Lake, then continued south from there.

Bryn kneels in the dirt with their hands cupped over a green sprout. The sprout quickly grows into a flower, which blossoms into a small fruit. They pluck it from the stem and pop it into their mouth.

"I think Wyntryn land picks up a few miles past the start of this mountain range," he says. Bryn blinks up at him. "I can get us to Rebynrock without a map. It will take a while to make it there. Especially without horses. That carriage may be following a route into Wyntryn. We could try tracking it."

"Are you sure it's impossible to alate?" Bryn asks.

The talisman sizzles across his skin in response. "I can alate, but it would not be smart."

"I saw the necklace. What's wrong with people knowing you have a talisman?"

Rais bites his lip. Bryn must have figured it out on their own or they're making a wild guess. Honestly, Rais doesn't care if they know. Bryn feels familiar enough to him, like a person he's met before. "It is a matter of protection. We have no idea who is looking for talismans right now. It could bring dangerous people to Wyntryn borders and put my people at more risk than they already are."

"They wouldn't see it as a threat?" they ask.

"I would imagine if someone wanted the talisman, its power would not be a deterrent."

"What is the point in waiting to reveal it to the Sonder then?" Bryn asks. "You have taken it for a reason. If that reason isn't to destroy it, then it must be to harness it. You will expose it to your enemies eventually." Bryn is awfully invested in the talisman. Maybe he shouldn't have confirmed their suspicions.

"Because it will put people in danger. I will not use it unless necessary," he says.

Bryn lifts their fingers to his sternum and slides them down so that they rest over the amulet. He flinches away from their touch. Their forwardness makes him uncomfortable. He doesn't like people getting this close to him. "What if you could disguise it?" Bryn asks.

"How?" Rais grabs their wrist and pushes it away.

"That storm that overtook the Dragon Isle's ship. It wasn't caused naturally."

He steps around them. "It seemed perfectly natural to me."

"The storm was isolated. It followed us to shore." Is Bryn saying he caused it? That is impossible. He would have known. "Nina and I don't have power like yours. You create friction in the air, lightning, electricity. The air will quake with you if you ask. This... amulet commands you to quake. It tells the air without your permission. You see darkness, yes?" Bryn doesn't wait for him to respond. He has no clue how they have learned all of this. "I watched your eyes all day yesterday. I saw how you stared into nothing last night. The more you give yourself to the dark-ness—the soul inside that talisman—the more control it has over you."

This can't be true. How can something control him without him knowing? "What does this have to do with disguising the talisman?" he snaps.

They don't seem to notice the harshness of his tone. "Create a storm with your own power, make it as real as any other. We will alate from one end of the storm to the other. Completely under cover of a natural event that is normally high in energy. No one will think twice about a powerful thunderstorm. You can even claim it's the same storm that took down our ship, and it's traveled over the mountains."

"Then magically disappeared?" Rais steps away from them. He hates to admit it, but Bryn does have a point. He could disguise the talisman that way. But he's never consciously created a storm of that magnitude. He easily draws upon bolts of lighting and the electricity in the air, but he's never created a phenomenon like this. How would he know how to stop it? Wouldn't it be impos-sible to draw all that energy back into himself? He would have to release it back into Kanaleigh. Which would cause a disruption in the natural flow of energy.

"You have no reason to trust me Raiden, but I trust you. If you can cover enough of the mountains to get us to Rebynrock, then we can take numerous days off our trav-els."

There's no way he could summon that much en-ergy. Even if it was life or death. The storm will have to stretch across the entirety of the mountain range. Rebyn-rock is all the way on the other side. He will have to use the talisman.

If there is a chance of this working, then he should try. If Alys were alive and sent him to Eventyr, she'd want him back with that talisman as soon as possible. There are Atane flooding the mountains between here and Rebynrock. This means if his calculations are even a little too short, they could be alating into a herd of them. If he doesn't do this, then they'd have to travel through those hordes on foot.

If they can scale the mountain closest to them, then he can get a better vantage point. That way when he tries to create the storm, he will know how far they can go. They only have one shot. He only has so much power within him. The energy in this territory is raw and unused, but that will only get him so far.

He must make the thunderstorm appear natural. The prospect makes his head spin.

"Okay. We need to scale this mountain. If we can find a ledge high enough that will let me see across the mountains, then I might be able to do this." Rais picks up his sword and dagger. He straps them on, then heads toward the mountain. Bryn follows close behind.

The mountain has a slow incline. It will be a while before they hit the jagged rocks and precarious pathways.

"Why are the talismans so important?" Bryn asks.

He glances at them. "Everyone wants power in this world. Those in power do not care about the people's rights or what will keep the people alive. They are selfish and ignore the issues. These rulers could care less about the choice or life of a singular person. Stygian is one of those rulers, and it won't be long until she tries to take over Wyntryn. We are a large region with a small number of people. These talismans allow us to expand our abilities.

We can turn a single soldier into an army."

Bryn's gaze stays ahead, looking past the mountain looming above them. "My mother used to tell our tribe stories of the crystals mined from the mountains. About the arrow made of unique metal and a scale that had fallen from a dragon. She said the souls isolated inside the objects are vengeful and wicked. The souls latch onto you and twist your mind. They force you to become as vengeful and wicked as them. Why take such a huge risk to further a government that is already corrupt?" Bryn's voice is light, but the words are dreary. Clouds travel across the sky from the coast, shuttering the sun.

"Wyntryn is not corrupt," Rais says.

"Then you are as blind as your enemy."

His jaw tightens. He keeps moving up the mountain at a steady pace, but he can't ignore Bryn's words. He is ignorant. Bias of his home. Ava may become a better ruler than Alys, but that doesn't eradicate corruption. The word, ruler, is unsettling on its own. To have a person or group of people control the lives of a population seems… wrong. But without that, wouldn't the world fall to pieces? At least he assumes it would. There seems to be no perfect way to live as a society.

Rais believes in protecting the individual's right to live how they wish to live. In Wyntryn there are no laws set in stone. There is respect between the people and the protectors who reign over each area of the region. There hasn't been an uprising from the people in nearly a century. The people in Wyntryn respect one another enough to set their own qualms aside and protect each other. They know survival is a shared fight and turning against one another will only lead to a horrific end.

But as Bryn said, Wyntryn is not without corruption. Alys was a ruthless leader. She often acted out of line to get what she desired. She never asked for the opinions of her protectors before making a decision. This created quarrel after quarrel within the legions of their government. Those arguments never spread beyond the manor, but that doesn't mean her actions within the barriers of protection were excusable.

Even Rais has done wrong. He's allowed himself to take the lives of others.

They reach the mountain's peak by midday. This cloudy sky can be used to his advantage.

"Can you find a line of energy that will take us to Rebynrock?" he asks. Bryn nods. "Okay, when I grab your hand, you'll have to pull me through with you. I don't know how long I can maintain the storm."

He bends his knee to the ground. His fingers dig into the dirt, and he slips into the hazy blue of the Sonder. There's an excess of energy in this area. Not many people live here, so the energy remains unused by irregulars.

Rais pulls on the energy. It flies through him in a flurry. His eyes close against a growing pressure in his mind. He reaches one hand above him and draws upon the electricity already buzzing through the air. The wind picks up and carries a strong current across the mountains. He pulls bolts of lightning from the clouds, and they strike the rocky ground. His body is a vessel for the energy to travel through. It moves from the mountain and into the air with steady grace. The world thrums around them. The clouds erupt into rain on their own, and he reaches for Bryn's hand.

He sends out bolts of lighting and stretches the storm as far as he can. His own energy dwindles within him. Bryn finds a point on the Plane of Verity and pulls them through.

They fall into the snow. There's a light rain here, and booms of thunder ring through the sky. A bolt of lightning falls near them, causing the compact snow to erupt. It should terrify Rais, but relief washes through him. This is his world, lightning, and snow. Here his energy mingles through the land, strikes the ground, and sends flurries of snowflakes into the air. He lets go of his hold on the energy. Some of it careens back through him and the rest soaks back into Kanaleigh. The atmosphere shimmers with energy. His energy.

He pulls his knees beneath him and breathes heavily into the melting snow. It's not as cold here as it was when he last visited Rebynrock. He's missed the winter weather. It won't be long until spring comes, and he'll have to wait months for the snow to return. Sometimes he doesn't even wear a jacket because he's in love with the prickling of cold on his skin. The chills that shake his bones. The slight chatter of his teeth. It's probably because he's lived in Wyntryn his whole life, but the white landscape is alluring. He likes to think he'd love it no matter where he grew up.

Fingers grab his shoulder. "Are you all right?" Bryn asks. Their soft voice is polarizing. Its calm breaks through the ringing in his mind. His thoughts are a never-ending storm that keeps him from rest.

Rais lifts himself from the snow. He blows a breath that shakes off the snow stuck to his lips. "I will be."

Even with the talisman, creating that storm drained him. He tried to use as little of the talisman's power as possible, though creating a storm of this magnitude would be unfeasible without its help. Or so he guesses. He's never tried before.

He stumbles back to his feet, but his legs give way.

What a horrible feeling. His body is useless to him now. Sleep would be fantastic, but he can't sleep in the snow. Maybe he just needs to sit here for a while.

"Is there anything I can do?" Bryn asks.

He stares out at Mount Rebyn. It stretches far above them, covering the horizon. "Give me a moment. The storm is still pulling energy from me."

Thunder booms from above, sending shivers through the ground. Rais isn't quite sure how to stop it. He knows it's not natural— he created it. So why hasn't it gone away?

He moves a leg up and leans his arms against his knee. Darkness wraps around him. It beckons him to keep pouring energy into the world. Bryn is on edge beside him. They watch him as if he might collapse at any moment. Unfortunately, that is not out of the question. He presses his weight forward and tries to stand again. Pain presses through every inch of his body. Exhaustion and depriva-tion consume him. He should have gotten more sleep last night. If he can make it to the entrance of the mountain, then he can get into the tunnels. There, Bryn can find help.

His muscles don't give up on him this time. He finds balance on his feet and takes a few steps. Bryn of-fers their arm, and he holds onto them. He tries not to put too much weight on Bryn. They slowly make their way through the pine trees and to the overhanging rock that hides Rebynrock's entrance.

The tunnels are dark. A steady drip of water echoes through the mountain. Somewhere an animal cries. There's even the clop of horse hooves, but they're far away. He can't tell which direction the horses are going. Hopefully, they are coming this way and will find them in the tunnel. Then they can drag Rais into the city, drop him at an inn, and he can sleep for eternity.

Bryn shakes him. His eyes open, and he stumbles forward a few steps. "Stay awake. We are so close." Is he so tired his eyes closed without him realizing it? He didn't get much sleep last night or the night before. And the other day he practically drowned.

His shoulder hits the cavern wall, and he lets himself collapse. It doesn't hurt and it's better than standing. "I'll be right back. I'm going to find help. Just—just stay awake. Please." He thinks he sees Bryn walking away, but they're a blur. His brain is fuzzy.

Ava's voice whispers in his ear. She bends down before him and grazes his cheek with her fingertips. "I'm sorry I was gone for so long. Ms. Brella stopped me in the hallway, and I was stuck talking to her. My mother yelled at me last time I made an excuse to get out of a conversation with her, so I had to wait until the end of the story."

Rais laughs, but it's not really him laughing. Is this a memory? He can't tell. "She is a good person, but I swear she enjoys watching us suffer through her stories," Rais says.

"Stories we've heard a million times!" She passes him a biscuit and sits down next to him.

Her head leans against his shoulder, and she yawns. "Do you ever think about the future?"

"Sometimes." He brushes loose hair behind her ear. This is a dream, isn't it? "I like living in Wyntryn, but I would like to travel someday. Maybe the Sparrow will take me with him on his missions. I have been to Eventyr, Grymyr, and Goldryn, but there are so many other places in Kanaleigh."

"Hmm. That sounds nice. I'd like to travel too, but I don't think my mother will ever let me out of her sight. The idea of being queen someday scares me. Not only knowing that to become queen my mother has to die, but that I'll have to be queen. I don't want that. I want freedom. I don't want to be responsible for the lives of so many people."

"We could run away together," he says. "You won't have to be queen and I could stop training to be the sparrow. Maybe we could live in Aysand. Nina's parents took her there last year, and she said it was amazing."
Ava grabs his hand. She rubs his palm mindlessly. "Aysand it is."

He leans his head against hers. If only she was here with him, and he wasn't dreaming of a time that has long passed. He'll never go to Aysand with her. Fate has a different plan for their lives.

Chapter Nineteen

"You're right, Stygian. There's no one like us, and that's probably for the best." Ava tightens her grip on the taaffeite crystal. It doesn't pulsate energy like the arrow. There's no power lurking within it. It is not a talisman at all. It's a fake.

Aliras slowly stands and steps behind Stygian. Ava holds her sister's gaze. Stygian tilts her head. "Are you not pleased with what graciousness I have given you?"

Ava smiles. "I cannot thank you enough. You've shown me the truth. I have never been surer of what path I'm supposed to take."

"It's because we are meant to work alongside each other. To be the source of fire that changes Kanaleigh forever. We will destroy the Sonder, and no one will ever be able to challenge our reign. Mother will watch from the skies and realize how wrong she had been. About the both of us. We have always been better than her—" Stygian collapses onto the floor.

Ava gulps. Knocking Stygian out might have not been the smartest choice, but it will allow them to flee the city. Stygian will be on the warpath now. Unless she forgets this entire dilemma. Which would take a miracle.

"I cannot tell you how long I've wanted to do that," Aliras says.

"What do we do now?" she asks.

"We could look for the real talisman, but I think our better option would be to run." He recognized it as a fake too. Aliras must have seen the real talisman before.

"Do you think I should have stuck to the alliance?"

He shrugs. "Too late for that."

"Can you help me pick her up?" Ava grabs Stygian's ankles, and Aliras hooks his arms under Stygian's. They lift her and carry her into her bedroom. She looks peaceful there, asleep. Not so terrifying. There has to be a way to fix this. To avoid her sister's wrath. Ava taps her fingers against her thigh. She doesn't need a miracle. "What if I were to alter her memories?" Aliras frowns. "I'm serious. I could make her think she sent us to Wyntryn. It would buy us some time."

"Messing with people's minds is a dangerous game," he warns. Aliras says that as if she doesn't know. If anyone knows the danger of tarnishing memories it's Ava. Her memories are still broken and twisted. At this point, they always will be.

He grabs her wrist and she narrows her eyes. "Aliras, if we leave now, she'll know you knocked her out. Your nephew is still in this city. She would go after him, then us. Do you trust me?"

"Yes."

That's all the assurance she needs.

Ava climbs onto the bed and places her fingers against her sister's temples. She slips into the Sonder. Her sister's walls are weak when she's asleep. Ava easily breaks into Stygian's mind and delves into her thoughts. She finds her way into Stygian's most recent memories and focuses on their conversation. Instead of having Stygian pass out, Ava begins to construct a false reality. She has Stygian tell her and Aliras to leave for Wyntryn immediately and to not report back until the alliance with Goldryn has been approved by the protectors. When Ava and Aliras leave, Stygian goes to lie down. Ava plays the conversation over with the new addition. Once she's sure Stygian's memory has been altered, she detaches from Stygian's mind.

Ava pulls her fingers from her sister's temples, then slides off the bed. "Ready?"

Aliras gestures to the door. "After you."

They make their way out of the palace and through the City on the Sea. Outside the gates, Ava sends Aliras a vision of the Wyntryn manor. Together they alate into the snowy landscape.

People stream in and out of the manor. The pastures are full of horses grazing and the air is full of chatter. She barely recognizes the once lonesome fortress. When Ava was here before, it was only her and Rais. No one else existed in the world but them. Now, mages practice their abilities, and soldiers spar in the fields.

"You grew up here?" Aliras asks.

"That's what people tell me."

Hopefully, her people don't hate her for abandoning them. It's been over a month now. The few letters she's traded with Anya aren't nearly enough to make up for the distance. The Wyntryn people may have named her their queen, but she hasn't been here for a long time. There's no way of telling how they feel about her now.

"Ava? What are you doing here?" Anya holds her skirts up and runs across the snowy field. Grass springs up from the blanket of white, and the trees glimmer with melted snow. Spring is on its way. Her cousin's dark hair is tied up in a bun, and her long green gown collects a snow-drift behind her feet.

"It was a last-minute change of plans," Ava says. The last thing Anya expects is for Ava to be here. She's shocked herself too, but it was a mistake to go to Goldryn. That decision was based on anger. She's not as angry any-more … just empty.

Anya slows before them. "Who's this?"

"Aliras." He bows to her.

"Nice to meet you," Anya says.

Before she introduces herself, Ava pulls her aside. "I need to speak with you and the other protectors. Are any of them here?" There's time for her and Anya to re-connect later, but she needs to move quickly. There's no way of knowing how long Stygian's memories will remain altered.

"We are all here. Everyone except Rais, though he should be on his way back from Eventyr—" Anya's ex-pression changes. "Never mind him, let me introduce you to the others."

Aliras nudges her arm. His voice enters her mind. *Are you sure it's okay that I'm here?*

If they make you leave, then I'll leave with you, she sends back.

Anya leads them into the manor and through the foyer. They go into the left wing. Through a door off the hallway is a massive ballroom with doors that open to the outside. She's dreamed of this ballroom before. It flashed in her memories, but she never thought about where it was.

"You can stay here, I'll go find the others," Anya

says before leaving.

A man who looks to be in his thirties sets down a book and walks over to them. He has shoulder-length blond hair and green eyes. He towers over her with a scowl. "Osidias Donsen, eighth protector of Wyntryn." He drops to a knee before her.

"Diplomat of the Western Coast," Ava murmurs to herself.

He gives her a nod and stands. "It is good to see you again, Ava. None of us imagined your mother leaving for the stars so soon. We are here to help you. Every step of the way."

"Thank you. That means a lot to me. I should have been here these past few months, not in Goldryn." Her eyes catch on the pin he wears. The pin she's seen Anya and Eieran wearing too. It's a golden dragon holding a sword between its wings.

"Do not regret the past," he says, gesturing to her with a hand. "It will tarnish your perception of the future. All we can do is try to make better decisions as we move forward."

"Are all of the protectors so annoyingly wise?" Ava asks. She grits her teeth. She didn't mean to say that aloud. It's like she never learned basic manners.

Osidias' face stays stern, but then his cheeks lift, and he laughs. It's shockingly loud. Ava lets out a nervous, breathy laugh. Osidias' face drops to a scowl again, and he sighs. "They're here."

She can't help but think about how odd this man is. His laugh seemed genuine though. Which is what's so odd.

Anya and three others walk into the ballroom. Ava recognizes Eieran Hynrule. He has a new tattoo that swirls up his neck. His long white hair and brown eyes are the same. The others are familiar, but she can't place their names for the life of her.

Anya loops her arm through Ava's. "These are the protectors. What's left anyway. You've met Eieran and Osidias. This is Hyacin Moore, the sixth protector." Her cousin points to the man with a shaved head. He's tall and wears a cloak that hangs to his feet. It's beige with swirls of darker brown that mirror the tones of his skin. Anya points out the next protector. "Genevia Cross, the fifth protector." Genevia is the shortest in the room. She has hooded brown eyes and straight black hair. She wears fitted leather armor and a scarf that wraps around her neck and shoulders. "My father, Aran, has been filling in as the seventh protector, but he's at Mount Meta at the moment. The ninth position is not filled, and Ra—" she stops herself. "The tenth protector has been filling in duties of the second, as your mother requested."

Ava doesn't mind if she hears or talks about Rais. Anya doesn't have to be so careful around her. She's not made of glass. It's only seeing Rais that she both dreads and desires. If it's even possible to feel those at the same time.

She pulls her arm from Anya's, then steps back to face everyone. "Well, thank you all for meeting with me. I haven't been here, and I should have been. I have been working to protect Wyntryn. I went to the Dragon Isles a few days ago and solidified our alliance with Queen Mica and Queen Natalia. They are not only loyal to my mother's reign, but mine, if you are to have me. I have also worked out an alliance with my sister." Ava glances to Aliras. "Truthfully, Stygian lied to me. Tried to give me a fake talisman, so that I would agree to an alliance with her." Ava reaches into the pocket of her slacks and pulls out the taaf-feite necklace. "Aliras here, knocked Stygian out. I altered her memories to believe that she sent Aliras and me here. I do not know how long she will believe the lie I've given her, so we will have to be careful."

Nerves spindle within her. She still wears her mucky clothes and dirt clings to her skin. She doesn't belong in this room, standing before these honorable people. She has excused all her actions by saying they were for the good of Wyntryn, but some of them were more selfish than she cares to admit.

Ava takes a breath. All five protectors stare at her. Even Aliras can't remove his gaze, but he's not looking at the fake talisman like everyone else, he's looking at her. "My sister may believe we have an alliance, but I don't think she'll keep it intact—she threatened Raiden's life." Anya's joyful expression drops, and she takes a step toward Ava. "Stygian wants access to our borders. She wants to force the prophecy. Wants to work with me to take down the Sonder. That is not what I want. I am here to serve Wyntryn. To save our people. If that means putting on a façade for my sister, so be it. To get what I thought was a real talisman, I had to promise her my loyalty. So, we will have to be careful with what steps we take. If she asks me to do something, and I don't, we could be risking immediate war."

Genevia walks up to her. She drops to her knee. "Wyntryn survives because Wyntryn is one. I support your decision and will do whatever you ask of me, within reason of course." Genevia winks.

Ava offers her hand to Genevia. "Thank you."

Hyacin drops to his knee. Then Eieran and Osidias. Even Anya bows to her. Ava isn't sure if this is a tradition or not, but it makes her jaw tense and her heart warm. She may not remember these people, but they remember her. They support her.

She wants to ask them what this means, but she's supposed to know. There are so many things that she has to relearn. She has a past that's turned into a faded film. A reel that only shows her short, damaged snippets.

Eieran stands and walks to her. "We all agree to your coronation. Stygian knows to have a true alliance you cannot decide that yourself. If you are prepared to take on the responsibility, the burdens, the pain of our people, and the joy of getting to lead this region, then we will travel with you to Metarock."

"Why Metarock?" she asks quietly.

Eieran gives her a sympathetic smile. It stings, though she understands. He says, "Every queen and king has been coronated in Metarock. It was the first hidden city to be built. Before it was a city, it was..." He glances at Anya. "... a stronghold for our most precious resources. It is tradition for coronations to take place there."

"I'm sorry I cannot remember everything. I am trying my best." Ava's still not used to the humiliation of not knowing. No one means to make her feel this way, but she can't help it.

"We know," Anya says.

The protectors stand. "Is there anything I can do to help here?" Ava asks.

Genevia chuckles. "There is plenty to do. If you leave Anya to plan your coronation we can show you around. We have been recruiting mages from across Wyntryn and from the interregional refugee camps..." Genevia goes on about what the protectors are doing here at the manor, from the training methods they're using to the names of the horses in the stables.

No one asks about Aliras always being one step behind her. Some people give him looks or whisper as they pass by, but the protectors don't seem to care.

Genevia introduces her to the mages and asks Ava her opinion on what they're planning. It's all so… real. And she's had nothing to do with it until now.

She hopes she can prove herself to Wyntryn. To these people. She cannot fail them.

It isn't until the end of the day that she finally makes it to her room. Anya offered Ava her mother's chambers, but she would never be able to stay there. It's not like Rebynrock. Her mother lived here—in those rooms. It took some convincing, but she was able to get the room she stayed in the last time she was here. The room on the second floor, only a few doors away from the study at the end of the hall. Aliras got a room in the other wing of the manor—which he was not happy about. Ava wouldn't be surprised if he stands watch outside her door.

Being by herself isn't as comforting as she wants it to be. It forces her to sit in silence. Horrible, crippling silence. She rolls over on the bed and grabs the comforter. There's a scream building up inside of her, but she can't release it. Not here where everyone could hear. She closes her eyes and lets the tears fall. Silent sobs rake through her.

She misses Levi's comfort. The apartment she lived in with her father. She hates that he left her. Hates that her mother had to die. She despises herself for plotting to kill her mother. What sane person would do such a thing? She should not be a queen. She doesn't deserve the trust of the protectors. If Rais knew, he'd be disgusted. But he never has to know.

Ava slides off her bed. She takes the comforter and

wraps it around her shoulders. She rubs the tears from her cheeks. There are no footsteps or voices in the hallway, so she opens the door and rushes down to the end. The study still smells like dust and ashes.

Ava goes to the sofa and sits down, tucking her legs below her. She slips into the Sonder and lets out a spindle of energy. The logs in the fireplace catch flame.

The fire crackles and spits out embers. The sound is a welcome relief. It quiets the silence — if only for a little while.

Chapter Twenty

Willow

The hit sends a loud clap through her skull. Willow falls on her hip, and a shockwave of pain spreads through her. She's exhausted from trying to hold onto any respect for Stygian. There is nothing left in her to give. Stygian will not have control over her anymore.

Stygian grabs her forearm and yanks her onto her knees. The Queen bends down before her. Stygian's breath blows against Willow's forehead. It's hot, and Willow can't stop the tears from falling. She's being treated as less than human. She deserves more than this. Willow stayed in Goldryn because her father wouldn't respect her sexuality or choices. Now she's living with someone worse. There must be a better life out there. A thought she's had far too many times in the last few days.

"You only share your opinion when I ask for it." Stygian spits on her.

Willow grimaces. She pulls her arms around her ribcage. Willow had commented on Ava and Aliras disappearing. It triggered something inside the Queen.

Stygian grabs her forearm again, twisting the skin

with her grip. "Do not—"

Willow yanks her arm free and slams her hand against Stygian's chest. The Queen falters back. "You do not tell me what I can and cannot do." Willow seethes. She pushes Stygian, forcing her to fall backward. Willow pushes her weight onto Stygian and enters her mind.

I have more power than you, Syn. Kanaleigh breathes through me. The goddesses speak to me. If I ask, I can see your future. I can tell you when your sister will slide a blade through your heart. Do not touch me again, or I will speed up time and you can see your end before you've even had a chance to fight back.

Willow stands and struts out of the room. Violence is not something she enjoys, but she will not allow herself to be touched like that again. She chooses who gets to lay their hands on her body. Anyone who abuses her will not get away with it. Not any longer.

Her hands have been torn to shreds, her mind tortured, and her sanity broken. Willow has power and she will not let it become useless.

She runs to her chambers and pulls a trunk from her closet. It doesn't take long to gather her clothes. She grabs the photo of her brother and leaves the rest of her belongings. Most of them are herbs and aromas she's been experimenting with in her free time, nothing significant.

Willow tests the Sonder. With the taaffeite talisman supposedly gone, Stygian isn't strong enough to maintain the charms placed on the city. People still cannot alate into the city, but it's broken enough to allow her to alate within it. If Stygian still has the talisman, then this is all just for show. She holds onto the trunk and pushes herself into the Plane of Verity.

There are few lines of energy not blocked by Stygian's hold. She catches onto one that will take her to the market street. She pictures the abandoned buildings and blistering sun. Willow steps through onto wobbly stones. The wind billows against her. It's difficult to alate with items. Somehow, she manages to get the trunk through. She lifts one side of it and drags it with her down the street. The pub isn't far from here.

At the Fallen Anchor pub, she drops her trunk inside by the door. There are a few stragglers inside and some chairs are turned on their sides. She swerves through the tables and up the stairs. Nina sits up in bed. Her book falls to the quilt. "What are you doing here?"

Willow chooses who gets to touch her. She is in control. Not Stygian, not Kalenti, and certainly not Alys. No one has power over her.

There's only one person she wants. Willow goes to Nina and reaches her hand out. Nina takes it—her touch sends heat through her. A blaze burns through her chest and spreads through her nerves. Willow runs her other hand up Nina's waist. "You're bold today," Nina whispers.

Willow tugs Nina closer. She presses her mouth against Nina's. Her lips are soft and warm. Heat twists between them. Willow pushes her hand from Nina's waist to her upper back. The two of them are like fire and ice. Opposites that perfectly fit together. She graces Nina's neck, then slides her fingers through Nina's dense curls.

Nails graze Willow's cheek. She leans into Nina's touch. Desperate for it. There's no malice here. No risk of pain. Willow has made so many mistakes. Nina pulls from her. "Are you sure you want this again?"

Her chest pushes against Nina's with each quick breath. "It never should have ended."

"What changed?"

"I'm tired of other people trying to make decisions for me. I want to do what's right for me … and that's with you. I stopped myself because I was scared. I was pushing my feelings for you onto an old crush. I never really loved Kalenti, I was infatuated with her. Nina… the thought of losing you is more terrifying than the world falling apart." Willow rubs Nina's arm. "I want you. Always you."

Nina shakes her head, her cheeks flushed. "I am opinionated, but I'll never tell you what to do. You are enough as you are." They share a smile, then Nina narrows her eyes. "You need food. Come with me."

Nina grabs her hand and pulls her across the room, then down the stairs. "Max! I need some pancakes!"

Willow blushes fiercely. Pancakes are what she used to request for breakfast at the manor. Nina used to make fun of her for it. After all this time, Nina remembers.

They sit at the bar, and Max comes out of her room. She picks up a knife and chucks it into the wall. Willow's eyes widen and she shimmies closer to Nina.

"I was trying to sleep," Max yells.

Nina grins. "Uh-huh."

"Make your own damn pancakes," Max says before going back into her room and slamming the door shut.

"But you're already awake!" Nina calls after her. Her eyes catch on Willow's trunk at the door. "Hey, is that yours?" Nina tilts her head, then frowns. "What did she do to you?"

"Nothing, I just don't want to live there anymore." She's not completely lying. Willow would rather be anywhere but in that palace. This city is unsafe too, but it's better. Especially since Nina's here. And Willow can't leave Goldryn, not yet. She has to see the prophecy work itself out.

"You're lying. What did that fire-breathing wench do to you?"

"She was being herself. Threatening me and such," Willow says.

"And such?" Nina seethes.

"I dealt with it on my own. I can defend myself." Her side aches and Willow remembers her fall. There's still the residue of a bruise on her cheek. Soon a matching one will stain her hip.

"I know you can, but I still want to rip her limb from limb."

"That's a little drastic."

Nina grits her teeth. "She deserves worse." Willow smiles. "What?" Nina's fists clench at her sides, and her nose is all wrinkled.

"You're cute when you're angry."

Nina purses her lips.

Willow laughs, and Nina scowls. It's nice to finally relax. She's been living on the edge of a cliff. Constantly watching where she steps and trying to balance as rain pours down on her.

It's been a long time since Willow shared a laugh with Nina, but it was worth the wait. She's missed her smile. Her laugh. Her voice. The way Nina's left brow twitches when something aggravates her.

One day Stygian will get what she deserves. She'll be forced to her knees and have to beg for forgiveness. The image warms Willow's heart. She even hopes Stygian gets the peace her mind has always longed for. But getting peace does not mean she gets to avoid consequences. One day someone will succeed in dragging her down and putting Stygian in her place. Tonight will be the first piece in a puzzle to dismantle her reign.

The boards creak beneath them. A mass of bodies cloaked by night. They all carry their most important belongings and hold onto the hands of their loved ones. Willow holds onto Zachary's small hand. He's only eight. She promised Aliras she'd take care of him. If he gets to Eventyr, Willow's father will be waiting for him. Her father may be conservative, but he's a good person. His intentions to force Willow to marry are out of his fear for her. He wants to make sure she's taken care of. What he doesn't realize is that she can take care of herself.

When this war is over she can visit him and Zachary with Aliras and Nina. She can introduce her father to them. Her father would like Nina, but it may confuse him if he knew what Nina is to Willow.

Zachary tightens his grip on her hand. "I'm scared," he whispers.

"Do you trust your Uncle Aliras?" she asks. He nods fervently. "Then you can trust me. My father is going to take care of you for a few months. Aliras is going to come to get you as soon as Goldyrn is safe."

Zachary doesn't respond, but she can hear his thoughts. He's terrified. Images of his worst fears fly through his mind—from storms turning the ship over to pirates. He creates images of them being attacked before boarding the ship.

She rubs her thumb on the top of his hand. "Will you let me enter your mind?" she asks. Little does the kid know she already has a painted view of it.

He nods again. She sends images of the Crystal

Lakes to him. Visions of her and her little brother running across the sandy beaches and splashing in the water. She shows him images of her father laughing and reading to them. She continues this until they make it to the docks.

Archer is at the head of the group. He begins to help people board the ship. Kael helps the crew move luggage onto the ship from another ramp.

Willow and Zachary make it to the main ramp. She bends down and kisses his forehead. "Be optimistic. Eventyr has creatures you've never even heard of before. This is a great opportunity for you. My father will meet you when you arrive. He will make sure you're safe. If you're scared while on board, think of Aliras. Think of the good things in your life. Cherish the happy moments."

His eyes are wide, and a tear slips down his cheek. She wipes it away with her sleeve. "Be brave, young soldier."

Archer takes Zachary's hand and leads him onto the ship. Eventyr is in peacetime. All these people are going to be safe. She hopes.

Someone bumps into her. Willow backs away to leave room for the others to board. A purposeful tap on her shoulder has her spinning. Zada has a nervous smile. "Thank you for this," Zada says, gesturing to the ships. "If anything should happen in the coming weeks, we know these people won't be harmed."

"Even this is not enough," Willow says. Stygian is on the verge of giving up any ties she has to morality. As soon as Stygian lets go, there is no hope for her. She will set the world on fire to get what she wants. No matter how irrational her desires may be.

Willow pushes past Zada to cross the dock. Latifolias bloom by the edge of the water. She hops down onto the sand and kneels before some. Her fingers brush against the pink flowers. If these are blooming now, it won't be long before Wyntryn wakes from winter.

When the flowers bloom in the north, the fire will come. It will consume and ravage the darkness spreading through the land.

Willow hopes it spreads to the City on the Sea and goes searching through the corridors of the palace. It's time for the darkness to burn.

Chapter Twenty-One

Raiden

"Sparrow Hynrule! Are you awake in there?" a familiar voice calls.

The mattress is a rock beneath him. Rais rolls onto his side. His muscles quiver with the movement, but at least he can move. The room is small. He's been here before, but this isn't Rebynrock. A small window shows a view of rooftops covered with a thin layer of snow. Hazy light refracts through the glass and scatters through the room.

"Sparrow Hynrule?"

He grumbles and swings his legs over the side of the bed. "Yeah, I'm awake," he says. An ache pangs in his head and he rubs his temple. Being awake is not something he wants to be. This is the first time in a while he's gotten real sleep. The kind where he's so drenched in sleep, that the dreams feel real. When he reaches for them now, they dissipate in his touch.

The door swings open and Nadia walks in, the innkeeper. She still has a sword far too large for her small frame. Her hair is intricately braided back, with loose tendrils that hang against her back. "Thank our ancestors you're okay. You looked worse than the heiress did when you were brought in here."

She must be talking about the state Ava was in after Saira attacked her in the manor. That feels like lifetimes ago now. Rais runs his hand up his chest. His fingers hit the amulet and he breathes a sigh of relief. The talisman is far more important than his health.

Nadia stands idly in the doorway. "Is there a reason you came in here?" he asks, pushing off the bed onto his feet. Surprisingly his knees don't buckle beneath him. Maybe he should make a habit of sleeping. It really does help.

"I wanted to check on you is all," Nadia says.

Rais goes to the window. This is the town outside of Rebynrock. Which explains why Nadia is in here. She probably lives in the inn.

He pulls his jacket on and slips his feet into his boots. "I'm fine," he says, tying the laces on his boots. "Can you tell me where Bryn went?" There's an unusually long silence. "The forest nymph."

"They left not that long ago. Headed toward the stables … or maybe it was the forest? I can check for you."

"No. I'll find them." Rais straps on his sword. He's been rushing to get home, but nothing is waiting for him at the manor. He's tired of always being on the move, always fighting against threats that never go away, but he'll never stop. Time will keep moving, and he'll keep running to catch up.

The boards creak beneath him. He passes Nadia but pauses before entering the hallway. "We're training mages at the Wyntryn Manor. It's a day's ride west of here if you follow the border. We could use all the soldiers we can get." Nadia gives him a nod, but he doesn't expect her to join them. She has a village to protect. That's at least what she told him two months ago.

Rais continues down the hallway and into the stairwell. His hand grips the railing as he descends. Muscles all over his body twitch in ways that make him cautious. He's not exactly sore. It's the exhaustion that has torn away his physical stability.

The outside air is strikingly cold compared to the inn's warmth. Rais smiles into the frosty air. There's not much time left to enjoy this dry cold. Soon heat will sweep through and lavender blossoms will cover the countryside. Rais strolls through the village, scouring over every nook and cranny he can see from the road. He would search for Bryn in the Sonder, but that storm would have been for nothing if he did that now. Well, not nothing, he supposes he learned he's capable of a lot more than he thought.

Ava better watch out, because he might take down a whole city of enemies on his own next time. Warmth spreads to his cheeks, then falls straight away. Replaced with the memory that Ava despises him.

There's a shadow in the trees. He squints his eyes to get a better view, brown hair, hands traveling across random plants — undoubtedly Bryn.

Rais watches them for a moment, before heading to the stables. He trades his spare dagger, the one hidden in his boot, with the stable hand for two horses. The pommel of the weapon is embedded with raw crystals mined from the mountains. It's worth its weight in gold and could've bought him far more than two horses.

The two horses are chestnut, one with a star between its eyes, the other with three white socks on its legs. He leads them into the forest.

Bryn has their fingers pressed into the dirt. They glance at him as he walks up. "I can feel the forest, she is… weeping," Bryn says. He wonders if it's caused by the influx of energy in this area. When he released his hold on the storm, that energy broke through the natural flow. It oversaturated this land.

"You can feel it?" he asks.

Their body practically shimmers with energy. "You can't feel your element?"

"I can, but it feels the same as the Sonder does."

"Ah, that is because electricity—lightning, is the sister to Kanaleigh's energy waves. Might I ask how you, of all people, are the Sparrow?" "You certainly are not the first to wonder that." Rais was never meant to be the sparrow at this age. Yet here he is, trying his best to be wise with barely eighteen years of experience.

Bryn pulls their hands from the ground and stands. He can see elk-like features in Bryn now. As if being close to the forest has ignited that part of them and strengthened their connection to Kanaleigh's sacred energy. Deer-like fur contours their face, stretches down their arms, and speckles their ankles. Their eyes are large and round, they have a small, upturned nose, and their ears are long and pointed. An earring twists through holes in their ear, ending in a shiny green gem.

The forest nymphs of Wyntryn fused with that of the great elks. Many forest nymphs can morph their bones into that of their animal cousin, but Rais has never seen it firsthand. Bryn lifts their chin. A quiet curiosity has her eyes wide and mouth parted.

He tries to jog his memory. "Alys Wyntryn chose me to be trained into the position after an incident. She saw great power in me and chose me as the successor. I was not supposed to become the sparrow for many years, but my predecessor was killed by the Society when I was only fifteen. The next year, I was made the sparrow before I had even finished my training."

"This incident you speak of … that wouldn't happen to be the storm cloud that was said to cover the entirety of Wyntryn? I remember seeing it five years ago. My parents said it was created by a talisman, but it wasn't, was it?"

Rais remembers it clearly. That day he was consumed by his power. It's why he is so careful not to store too much energy at once. Why he enters the Sonder so frequently, because if he didn't, that energy would continue to build and build inside of him until he… explodes. That's what happened that day. He didn't know he had to release the energy. While training outside the manor, one of the other kids accidentally cut Ava with their blade. Rais was so consumed by his mind, his own emotions, that he completely lost control. Luckily, he did not harm anyone, but he could have. And that possibility terrifies him.

"There was no talisman," he says.

Bryn's lips quirk up. "You must truly be something then. I have never heard of someone with power like that. Queen Kalenti can extend her energy that far, but I believe she did have a talisman in her possession. The one you now have?" Bryn doesn't even try to be subtle.

Even without a talisman, Rais could have sustained the storm from yesterday for longer if he hadn't nearly drowned the day before. It also took a lot of energy to alate to Eventyr, so he was already running on empty. He tried not to use the talisman to help him since the point was to hide its power, not utilize it.

Bryn's suspicions of him being the cause of their

ship sinking sends chills down his spine. He's been seeing the darkness in the distance and has felt something … other pulling on his energy. There's no telling what else the talisman could be doing that he can't sense. Like the arrow talisman, it could be changing his very aura.

He's lost control before and it's bound to happen again. Alys didn't consider that when she pulled him under her wing. She saw him as a weapon to be molded rather than a ticking time bomb.

He holds Bryn's gaze for an uncomfortable moment, then cuts it away to the trees. "Why is the forest weeping?"

"She has been drained of life. Us forest nymphs once protected her, but we have been driven out by the Atane. Along with all her other inhabitants." Bryn's features droop. They have sympathy for the forest itself, for the animals and people.

"Well, let's get going," Rais says. "The manor is near."

He lifts his foot into the stirrup, then pushes off the ground. Rais slides into the saddle and shifts the reins between his fingers. Bryn mounts the other chestnut. They lead the ponies through the trees. Bryn's lips are pressed together, and their brows twitch as if they want to ask more questions.

Rais speaks up for them. "You can pry if you wish."

Bryn runs their fingers through the air. Rais swears the tree branches move with them, but it could be the wind. "Who is she?" Bryn asks.

"Hm?"

"The one always on your mind."

"Ava Wyntryn."

Bryn's breath escapes in a quiet laugh. "The

Queen."

"The heiress," he corrects. Bryn studies the forest. "Why? Are you judging me?"

"Oh, I wouldn't dare. It simply surprises me is all."

"I have known her since we were little. She is… my person. And I am hers. But I did something, unforgivable. She left the region just to get away from me."

"Ah, so you love her."

Rais doesn't answer. But he does … love her that is. How could he not?

They continue through the forest until sundown. It stays quiet the whole way. Birds don't chirp and insects don't crawl. He never once sees a creature. Not even an Atane. The darkness still withers in the distance, but it's closer now. The tendrils slip across the melted snow, sneaking closer and closer, raising the hair on his skin.

They break through the tree line as stars begin to dot the sky. Finally, he is here. Home. The manor looks the same as always. Aged and lonely in a clearing full of snow.

At the door, Rais pauses, but then he opens it. Inside people meander through the manor. It is different than before. Full of the life it was missing.

Rais recognizes Erka as he walks into the foyer. His gaze catches on Rais and he smiles. "Golden Sparrow! You're finally back."

All the chandeliers are on and all the candles are lit. Sounds travel through the air. Numerous voices filled with laughter. This is what he's always wanted. What he has been waiting for since Alys Wyntryn's death. There's no more dust layered on the furniture and thick in the air.

"Good to see you." Rais offers his palm to Erka in greeting.

Erka looks around them. "Ava is here," he says. His heartbeat quickens. "What?"

Bryn places their hand on his arm. They look to Erka, then back to him. "Nothing is unforgivable," they say.

Rais forces a smile. It would be nice if Ava believed that too. Bryn has never seen Ava's rage before. The burns on his throat are healed now, but the memory hasn't gone away. Once Ava Wyntryn's been crossed, there is no way of getting back on her good side.

He asks Erka, "Where is she?" It's better to confront her now, than wait for someone to tell her he's here.

Erka points up the stairs. "In the office, I think. Last I heard, the protectors were having a meeting up there."

Rais climbs the steps. Bryn follows silently behind. He should tell Bryn to wait downstairs, but he likes their presence. Bryn has a softness in their soul. A kindness that spreads into the air around them. It's comforting.

The door to the office is the only thing that stands between him and facing his fears. She's right there. Close enough to touch. Though she's not alone in there. He closes his eyes and takes a breath. "Can you wait out here, Bryn?" Bryn steps aside and leans against the wall. Rais' hand stills on the doorknob. His eyes burn at the thought of seeing her.

He opens the door and steps inside. The protectors sit in chairs that face the desk by the window.

"Cousin?" Eieran stands from his chair.

Ava sits behind Alys' desk. She meets his gaze for a moment, and he almost sees forgiveness in her. He's wrong, because as soon as he thinks that, her forehead creases, and fire sparks from within. Heat consumes the room. A man with dark hair stands beside her. He places his hand against her arm and says something Rais cannot hear. The heat fades away.

That man… Rais recognizes him. The dual eyes of brown and blue. He's the Goldryn soldier who pulled that knife across his cheek and neck. The one who gave him his scar. What in the world is she doing with him? Of all the Goldryn's she could've befriended.

"What are you doing here, Raiden?" Ava asks. *Raiden.* He hates when she calls him that.

"I brought…" Kalenti's warning slips into his mind. *Keep it close to you. Never give it to anyone, never show it to anyone, never let anyone know you have it.* If he tells Ava, the talisman will never make it back to Eventyr. That would bring more danger to Wyntryn. "Sorry, I meant to bring back the Queen of Eventyr's talisman. I do not have it with me now."

"So, you sunk our ally's ship for nothing?" she asks.

"What are you—" Rais begins to say.

Everyone is watching him. Anya, Hyacin, Osidias, Genevia, and his cousin all stare. These people he knows so well look at him like a danger. A threat.

Ava leans forward. "Queen Natalia told me that lightning destroyed one of their ships. The ship that you were aboard. Now here you are, without the talisman. You almost singlehandedly dismantled our only alliance. Along with killing a Society commander's son. You alone have caused enough damage to start a war." Not any Society commander's son. The one that stole her memories.

Rais looks at his cousin—Eieran has a sympathetic smile. Something is happening here. They aren't looking at him like he's a threat. His stomach drops. What is Ava about to do?

"Do not look to Eieran for help, Raiden. It is my decision and my decision alone."

"What decision?" he asks. His hands are shaking. He tries to hold them still, but it only makes it worse.

"I am stripping you of your title and your duties. You are no longer the Sparrow of Wyntryn. You are free to travel the world. Take it as a blessing that you are not being thrown in a cell for the harm you've caused this region."

His heart stops. Is she serious? Rais has built his entire identity around his position. Without it, what is he? Without Ava, without Wyntryn, he has nothing. He is nothing.

"Ava, perhaps you should take a moment to think about this?" Anya isn't making a suggestion.

"There is nothing to think about," Ava says. A bite in her tone.

He can't argue his place or plead with her. Rais can't change her mind. No matter what he does, she will not listen. He reaches for the lapel of his jacket and unhooks the protector's pin. It falls from his fingers before he can pass it to someone. He stares at it on the carpet. Such a simple thing, but it means the world to him.

"Cousin, you should go to your room. I'll find you after our meeting," Eieran says. Rais hadn't even realized Eieran stepped toward him or that Eieran's hand is on his shoulder.

Rais steps back and fumbles for the doorknob. He goes out into the hall and stumbles across to the other side. He catches himself against the wall and presses his forehead against it. His hand goes to the amulet on the center of his chest. Its power settles his nerves.

Bryn presses their hand against his back. They begin to hum a melody.

"How do you know that song?" he asks quietly.

"I heard it in your dreams last night. I apologize, I didn't mean to overhear."

He pushes off the wall. "You have no reason to apologize." Rais walks down the hall to his room.

Everything is wrong. Horribly wrong. He was never meant to hurt Wyntryn, gods, he didn't even realize he was. What if he did cause the storm that sunk the ship? He didn't do it knowingly, but his mind has been… off recently. Bryn suggested he started it too. How can he create something so menacing without even knowing?

There has been darkness nibbling at him, watching him.

What he can't shake is how she looked at him — like he was a stranger. An intruder in their midst. Then she destroyed him. So easily ripped away his identity. Without Ava, without being the Sparrow, who is he? Rais can't answer that question. At least not yet. He has wrapped his entire identity around those facts, and now, he is scarcely a person at all.

Chapter Twenty-Two

Ava

"What have you done?" Anya says through gritted teeth.

"Only what was necessary."

Hyacin raises his brows. His arms are crossed, and he leans against one of the bookshelves.

Eieran glares at Ava. "You should have given him a chance to explain himself." There's nothing for her to explain.

"None of you stopped me," Ava says. She must act like this was a decision she wanted to make. If Stygian does destroy Wyntryn, then Ava doesn't want Rais involved in the slaughter. If he's not the sparrow, then the Queens of the Dragon Isles can't act their revenge on him. Stygian will get nothing out of capturing him. This is the only way to save him. She can't forgive Rais for killing Levi, but that doesn't stop her from caring. Right now, she has to hate him. It shouldn't be too difficult.

"I seriously hope you take some time to think about your future decisions." Anya shakes her head and stalks to the door.

"I know I'm new to this, but my only goal is to protect Wyntryn. I can't allow anyone to threaten this region." Ava's hands press against the top of the desk. She doesn't like the way she sounds or the way she's acting. But it's necessary, isn't it?

Hyacin steps between them. "Why don't I give you a tour of what we've set up here? Your uh … guard can come along." Genevia gave her a tour yesterday, but if this gets her mind off Rais, then she doesn't care.

"Yes, that would be great," Ava says. It's dark outside now, there's chatter in the hallways and loud noises downstairs. The training must have moved inside.

Anya steps aside, and Ava follows Hyacin out. As the door shuts behind Aliras, Hyacin turns to her. "Do you know how the tenth protector is chosen?"

Ava tenses. "No, I don't remember." A door closes at the end of the hall. Ava looks longingly at it. That's his room.

Hyacin leads them to the stairs. "The sparrow is a coveted role. It is often chosen by the queen and then they're trained by the current sparrow. It is not like the other protector positions, as it doesn't come with land or any grand titles. A sparrow is not a lord or a lady, they are simply a trusted advisor. They're chosen with many factors in mind. A sparrow must have the ability to handle a substantial amount of energy. They must be kindhearted, selfless, and devoted to their region. The most important factor is their loyalty to the queen. Besides the second protector, who we do not have, the sparrow is the closest role to the queen."

Ava pushes her shoulders back and stares ahead.

"Your mother chose Rais, not only for his abilities or traits but because of his devotion to you. No matter what, you can trust his actions to not be without reason. Perhaps, you should talk to him."

Why is everyone telling her the same thing? She gets it, he wouldn't kill Levi without reason. Even so, Levi didn't deserve to die. Enemy or not.

Aliras watches Ava silently. She tries to ignore them both. She made her decision to keep Stygian's claws out of Rais. They may not know that, but she's not obligated to explain herself to anyone.

Hyacin must realize she won't pursue this conversation, so he begins the tour. "We have been using the training rooms to work with our inexperienced irregulars. Though the real magic is happening outside." He holds himself with well-mannered confidence.

They go out the back of the manor. To her surprise, there are pairs of regulars and irregulars sparring across the field. They've lit torches and stuck them into the snow. It's given them enough light to keep practicing. She figured they would be inside by now.

"We have been alternating fighting techniques with the soldiers. Before Rais went to Eventyr, he was teaching them how to shut down people's minds without harming them. Anya's been filling in for him, so I suppose she can continue that." There's judgment behind his words, but Ava doesn't let him see her flinch.

"Hopefully, we don't need to train for much longer," she says. "During my time in Goldryn, I've been discussing an alliance with my sister." Ava told the protectors the truth about what she did to her sister, but she mentions the falsified alliance to Hyacin because she hopes Stygian will believe the memories Ava gave her. Ava doesn't want to send these people to war. Most of them will not return home.

"Stygian does not make alliances unless she gets something in return. What is worth losing?" Hyacin asks.

Ava gulps. "You seem to have little faith in me."

"With all due respect, the last time I spoke to you, you were nothing but a child. You still are a child, except one with no memory of your years of training."

Aliras' hand slips to his belt—a position that would allow him to easily unhook his chakram. Ava smiles at Hyacin. "With all due respect, I have no memory of you having authority over me. Possibly we can both learn from each other, but I have no ill intentions. You can trust that I would give my life for this region and its people."

"I've already approved your coronation. You have nothing to prove to me."

Is it possible for the protectors to rescind their approval? If so, at least she didn't visibly offend Hyacin, because this could have gone in a completely different direction. "Thank you, Hyacin. I look forward to working with you." Hyacin bows his head to her before walking away. Ava keeps a smile on her face, but as soon as he's at a safe distance her face drops.

"I thought you missed that damned idiot?" Aliras asks.

"Right." She forgot she admitted that to Aliras. She does miss Rais, but what she wants doesn't matter anymore. She crosses her arms over her stomach. "I'll have to hate him for a little while longer."

"My lady, I think you're making a mistake."

"You do not have to keep calling me that." Ava glances at him.

He shrugs. "What should I call you then?"

"Something else. My lady seems too formal."

"I'll have to come up with a nickname for you."

"How do you shorten a three-letter name?" she asks.

"No clue. You will have to do something really dumb, and then I'll use that," he teases.

"Please don't do that." She doesn't want to be light-hearted right now. She feels incapable of laughing.

They reenter the manor, and Ava leaves Aliras to find her cousin. She doesn't like the idea of Anya being angry with her. She knows stripping Rais of his title was extreme, but it might save his life.

Ava goes through the entire manor before giving up.

She goes back to her room to find Anya sitting on her bed. Anya lifts her chin. "I've been sitting here, trying to figure out what to say to you. I have nothing, Ava. Nothing can describe how... disappointed I am."

Ava may not remember everything, but her cousin sounds like Alys. Her mother was fond of telling her how disappointed she was. Sometimes over the littlest things.

"I wish I could tell you why," Ava says.

"What? That he killed Levites? Do you know anything about that boy beyond what he told you? Levites could have been manipulating you all those months. I have never known Rais to kill without reason. If that's your excuse, because he killed Levites, then you should feel really guilty right now." Anya is dripping with rage, but she keeps her hands relaxed in her lap.

"I can't tell you."

"Why?"

Ava gulps. "It's for his safety."

"His safety?" Anya stands. "Rais is safer with us. Especially when our ancestors can protect him, but you taking his title, possibly revoking his oath, removes him from them. He is now more vulnerable than ever before."

"He sunk that ship—"

"He would never do that. I don't care that you lost your memories. If you know anything about Rais, you know he hates taking lives. He drowns himself in guilt over the smallest of things. Do you want to know what he did after you almost killed him?"

Ava shakes her head. She doesn't want to know. She was angry. Horribly angry. She never meant to hurt him like that, but she did—at that moment. She is as bad as Saira, isn't she? Nearly killing someone out of pure unrequited rage.

"Rais went to his home village that night. He slaughtered an entire squadron of Goldryn soldiers. Thank the gods my Eieran was able to find Rais and cover it up. He staged the slaughter as an attack by Atane. But you must understand Ava… You have power over Rais. He is deeply in love with you. Whether he tells you or not, he would kill anyone who ever dared touch you. You acting this way will cause him to lose control of himself. He has abilities none of us quite understand. They consume him. If he lets go, they can cause him to do truly horrible things." A chill runs down Ava's spine. She can't remember who, but someone told her Rais is capable of great destruction. But it isn't him killing the Goldryn squadron that shocks her, it's that Anya says he loves her. She supposes she knew this, but it's weird to hear it. Especially from Anya rather than Rais, or a memory of him.

Anya continues, "There was a storm when you two were younger. It covered the entire region. It was caused by Rais. That is why he was chosen as the sparrow. Without his role, without you, he will make his own path. And it will not lead to anything good." Anya breaks her stare and storms to the door. Her hand strays on the doorknob, then she turns back to Ava.

Ava's gaze bores into the floor. She's abandoned Rais, but he chose this when he killed Levi. She owes him nothing. He is strong, and she trusts he'll be able to figure this out on his own. Her stomach turns at the thought. No one deserves to be alone and she's singlehandedly ripped everything from Rais. It's too late to go back on her decision now. It would look worse for her if she suddenly decided her reasons for taking away his title were no longer valid.

"Your coronation will be at the end of this week," Anya says, breaking the silence. "We are leaving for Metarock in three days. I reckon you resolve your differences with Rais. If Stygian attacks, we will not survive without his power." She closes the door and Ava listens to her footsteps disappear down the hall.

Anya spoke to her like she was a child. Ava has been acting like one, but she doesn't know any better. She's grasping at whatever makes sense, and there's very little of that these days. How will she ever lead an entire region? She can barely make decisions for herself.

How hard would it be to talk to him? Willow, Anya, and Aliras have each told her she needs to let him explain himself. So, maybe she should let him. Though he probably wants nothing to do with her after what she's done. Ava grabs the door handle. This is a bad idea. He's going to close the door in her face. Laugh at her. No, he wouldn't laugh at her. He'd give her a sympathetic look and apologize. Maybe she doesn't know him as well as she thinks she does.

In her mind, she sees him in her father's apartment reciting their shared memory. His lips press against hers and everything else fades away. Nothing else matters. But those are old feelings. A day that has long passed.

She goes back and forth between what could and couldn't happen until finally, she opens the door. The halls are bustling with activity. She steadies her breathing and goes to the third floor. She finds the door to his room and presses her hand to the wood. There's a voice inside she doesn't recognize. She places her ear to the door. "Do you want me to stay with you?" The voice is quiet and has a clear Wyntryn accent.

"Please," Rais says. He sounds as if he can barely breathe.

Ava backs away from the door. She can't do this. If she can't forgive him, then she can't expect him to do the same for her. She retreats to her room and curls up on her bed. This day can't end soon enough.

Chapter Twenty-Three

Raiden

Water droplets cling to his skin. Humid air from the storm has breached the manor's walls. Rais meant to leave yesterday. He's been hiding out in his rooms, avoiding watchful eyes. Each gaze burns through him. If only this wretched storm would pass.

It began yesterday afternoon and has only grown. Even with spring around the corner, sleet showers across the surrounding land. The wind is strong and lightning falls like tributaries—branching and spindling in the sky. If he tries to leave, the storm will not subside. Wherever he goes, it will follow, and he has no clue how to stop it. At least here in the manor people are safe and the stables were repaired while he was in Eventyr. There's no real danger. Only Rais is at risk of losing control. He can't ask for help. He must stop it on his own. Otherwise, he will have to reveal the talisman that hangs against his chest. The talisman that controls the energy flowing through him.

Whoever resides inside the talisman is strong. An angry soul with a vengeance. Rais has tried to beat the darkness, to cast it aside, but it doesn't want to go. It beckons him on. Slowly dragging bits of his mind under its shadow. Maybe it's best he's no longer the sparrow.

A shadow stretches across the carpet—a hand shape bent over his desk chair. Someone else is in the room.

"Now that we are both proven to be murderers, I must say, I have acquired a new understanding of you," a voice whispers in his ear. One he recognizes but doesn't wish to hear.

"What is that supposed to mean?" Rais turns to face Saira.

An empty smile rests on the man's face. His eyes are even duller than before. As if the green fades away as his mind delves deeper into madness. "Ah, you want me to say I respect you?"

"I do not care what you think of me," Rais says. No one respects him anymore, not even himself. He's almost as emotionless as Saira. The thought forces a breathy laugh from him. He is losing his mind.

Saira's mouth opens a bit, then closes. His arms limp at his side. "I think you should … care."

Rais raises his brows. "Why is that?"

Saira's head falls to an odd angle. Strands of hair shift across his forehead with the movement. "You are losing control, and I am an expert at reeling in madness."

"I do not need your help." He does need help, but he can't accept it from Saira.

"Mm. I think you do. This storm is not caused by your power alone. I put the arrow talisman in that metal dragon, where you found it because I could not wield its glory. Though, you can, and you have. But this is not the arrow. The soul in the arrow likes you. This one does not." Saira's words burrow into him. Rais is desperate, but he knows he shouldn't accept the offer. It's best if they stay away from each other. "My brother was too innocent for this world. The Society crumpled him up and tossed him away. He wouldn't have lasted long anyway—"

"I'm sorry about Levites." Rais gulps. He didn't like Levites, but that's not reason enough to kill someone. He certainly didn't want to hurt Ava, but he did.

Rais stopped himself from killing Saira in the library because he knew there was a greater evil beyond him. Someone else pulls the strings. Yet he killed Levites all the same. Killed the brother that truly did have an ounce of goodness left in him.

"No need to apologize. I hold nothing against you." Saira's lips thin and he steps closer to Rais. "I will help you if you help me."

It's a horrible idea, but Rais wants to get out of this place. He wants to pack his bags and run. As far and as fast as he can. "How can I help you?" His conscience seizes him, taunting him for even considering Saira's offer. Though part of him, the part being corroded by the talisman begs him to take it. Rather, it insists.

Saira pokes his finger against Rais' chest. He holds as still as possible. Saira's finger barely missed the amulet enclosing the dragon scale. "You"—he turns his finger to himself and taps his chest—"will take me to Metarock. Your heiress will have her coronation there. As it has always been for Wyntryn coronations."

"Why?"

Saira blinks idly at him for several seconds. "The dragon of course."

"There are no dragons left on the Western Continent. Alate yourself to Eventyr if that's what you're looking for," Rais says.

"No. No," Saira says slowly. "The great winter

dragon resides in the mountain, doesn't he? The one said to live a thousand years. The one that the scale was plucked from to create the talisman. The last dragon."

Rais will not confirm Saira's interests or indulge in them. But he will take him to Metarock if only to escape the gathering storm. Even if Wyntryn still had dragons, there would be more than one. They are not solitary creatures. When dragons did roam the skies, they were used as vessels for manifesting elements. If a dragon chose its person, that person would be able to manifest their energy into the dragon's breath. That's why Ava's family is so dangerous. They rode dragons in the Great Wars. Utilizing dragons as vessels for energy, they could burn whole cities with little effort. That was until Grymyr created a weapon that killed dragons and plucked them from the sky, taking many direct Wyntryn descendants down with them.

Thunder booms outside. The ringing in the back of his mind grows. It's loud enough to silence the storm. Rais hits his fist against his bed frame. *Fine.* "I'll take you to Metarock." It may risk the safety of the city, but it's not as if Rais is obligated to his oath any longer. If all goes well, Saira won't even make it to Metarock. Rais only has to escape this storm and then block away Saira's memory of coming to the manor. He'll be careful.

"Wonderful. Now, you must let the darkness consume your mind."

"What?" Rais snaps.

"The only way to beat a ravaging soul is to bow to it. If you let the power take over you if only for a moment, you show it respect. Then, instead of fighting back, you accept the power it offers and take control. Never turn away from the darkness, brother."

Brother. *What a joke.* "I will not give up control."

Saira smiles. "So be it. The storm will never end."

Rais pauses. He looks out the window to the stables outside. To the fence being torn apart by his energy. This storm is caused by him and he has no control over it. There must be another way. "Sai—"

The door opens. "Who are you talking to?" Bryn asks.

I'll wait for you in the stables. Be quick. Saira's voice seeps into his mind.

Rais looks at Bryn. "I'm just thinking aloud. Once this storm is over, we should get out of here."

"You want me to go with you?" they ask. He nods. "Good, because I'm just starting to like you." Bryn plops down on his bed and pulls an earring from their pocket. Bryn has multiple holes along their elongated ear. They weave the chain through the piercings. At the end, a green gem hangs down and catches the light.

"You didn't like me before?" he asks.

Bryn turns their face away. Their pale freckles shift with their smile. "I didn't know anything about you. No one in their right mind is fond of someone upon first meeting them."

"I disagree," he says.

"Why's that?" They chew on a fingernail.

"I think I was at least a little fond of you when you clicked your tongue at me. I knew you would be trouble after that." Rais turns from Bryn's bright eyes to the storm brewing beyond the window.

Bryn doesn't say anything after that. They lean back on the bed and begin humming. The same melody they hummed before. The one his mother used to sing to him. The one he has sung to himself during many long nights. Bryn may not even realize they're doing it. They just are, and it's nice. It quiets the talisman's voice.

Rais watches a bolt of lightning cut the air before disappearing into the clouds. He closes his eyes and listens to the steady thrum deep in his mind. The buzzing that rings out to him, beckons him. He slips into the Sonder and opens the door. The storm appears natural, but when he looks closer, he can see imprints of his mind. To the naked eye, no one would guess a talisman is at its core. He can enter the Sonder now without worrying about a beacon going out. The energy waves look like a normal storm. Disguised as the natural movements of Kanaleigh and not the movements of his uncontrolled mind.

When he opens the door in his mind, darkness floods in. It pulses and wavers against him, but his physical self stays steady. He focuses on Bryn's humming to ground himself while his mind is consumed. The talisman floats through him. It soaks into his blood and seeps through to the Sonder. For a moment, the wind grows stronger outside. As soon as the quiet ringing subsides, Rais catches hold of the soul within him and claims the power as his own. He reaches out through the energy held by the talisman and places his mental holds on it. He grasps the lightning and settles the storm, blankets the Sonder with a sweep of his mind. Once he can feel all the energy within his hold, he draws it in.

It hurts at first, spindles through his bones. His stomach flips within him, and bile rises in his throat. He stands steady and focuses on the humming. On the words in his memories.

> *Silent bird, fly through the night.*
> *Open your mind to mine.*
> *Hear the call and follow the stars comforting our cries.*
> *The ones on our path light the way.*

Sweet, sweet ringing.
Silent bird, fly through the night.
On the wind, we rise.
Tame your heart and open your mind.
Sweet, sweet ringing.

When he opens his eyes, the storm is gone. The trees waver, and rain patters against the icy ground, but all is calm. Whatever is left of the storm is not caused by him or the talisman nestled against his chest.

Bryn stops humming and sits up. "How peculiar."

Rais glances at them. Their elongated ears quiver. "We should leave now before it picks up again," he says. Bryn slides off his bed. He pulls his favorite sword off the wall, then attaches daggers to his belt. He grabs two cloaks and tosses one to Bryn. "Need anything else?"

"Some food would be nice," they say.

"I suppose we can store some in a saddle bag. By the way, someone will be traveling with us."

Bryn raises their brows. "Who?"

"Saira. Though I'm not planning to let him travel all the way to Metarock with us," he says.

"Why Mount Meta?"

"That's where Saira wants to go, so we have to at least travel in that direction. I'd prefer to go anywhere else, but Metarock does seem nice. I almost bought an apartment there once."

Bryn smiles. "I wanted to move there when I was little, but my parents told me the people there would treat me as badly as regulars."

"I thought there was a population of nymphs beneath the city?"

"Mm. No, the night nymphs are different. People in the main city still dislike us forest dwellers."

"I hope they don't feel that way," Rais murmurs.

"As long as it allows people to stay in power, those seen as different will always be looked down upon." Bryn pulls the cloak around their shoulders.

Rais stares at them. If only Bryn could be the one to lead a region. They are conscious of their words and actions. He doubts Bryn would act rashly or purely on emotion. "I like that you are different. If every regular and irregular were the same, this would be a horribly boring place."

Bryn huffs in amusement. "I like that you're different too, Raiden. You don't have to fear telling me why that storm suddenly calmed. I do not judge others for what they cannot control."

He hums in response. Not wanting to say anything more. He doesn't have any reason to trust Bryn. It's only been a few days, and he wants to get to know them better before sharing such personal information. Though it seems they already know. They did help him disguise the last storm, but that one he created by choice. Bryn also took him to the village and made sure the healer got him rejuvenating herbs. Nonetheless, he's skeptical of their kindness. But possibly they're like him with nowhere to go.

Rais pulls the hood of his cloak up before he leaves his chambers. Anyone he passes will know who he is, but he wants to hide. What has happened hasn't soaked in yet, so there's no pain. Only a bitter taste in his mouth and a desire to run to Ava. An electrifying urge spirals down into his gut. He desperately wants to face her. Not to yell at her, but to hold her. If only for a single embrace. He is angry or at least he thinks he should be.

Whatever Ava's plans are, he has no control over what happens. He is standing in a sinking boat and the waves are crashing against him. So, no, he doesn't wish to be angry at her. He is hurt. She has torn his identity from him. And he is left to slowly lose control of himself. Rais will never stop thinking of her. Even as he's sinking. Even as storms crash down upon him.

"Are we leaving?" Bryn asks.

Rais pulls his hand from the doorframe. He's been frozen in place—staring out into the hallway. "Yes," he mumbles.

Bryn carefully steps past him. Their cloak sways with their strides. Rais closes the door and forces a step. Then another, until he is moving to the stairs. He doesn't look toward the office as he passes by, but he can feel Ava there. Her mind swirls in waves.

He passes by mages he recognizes on the stairs, but they avoid making eye contact. His fingers curl into his palms, and he keeps his breathing steady. The only thing keeping his legs moving is Bryn leading the way.

Once they're outside his muscles relax. "You can go back in and gather some food if you would like," he says.

Bryn shakes their head. "I will not make you stay here for another moment."

He almost smiles at that. Bryn has been a small light in this gathering darkness. He catches their gaze for a moment, but he cannot see through to their mind. It's nice because few people remain a mystery to him.

They trek across the icy ground to the stables. Saira stands in the center of the barn staring at a crack in the rooftop. Light rain showers him through the hole, but Saira either doesn't notice or care. "I've been waiting longer than I expected."

"You have no authority over me." Rais' tone is

mild, and his words empty. What authority does Rais even have over himself?

Rais goes to Oberyn and slides open the stall door. Bryn watches him quietly. He points to the tack room and without having to ask, Bryn moves to it. They bring him his saddle and bridle. How they knew it was his, Rais has no clue, but he doesn't care to think about it. Bryn just knows things. A chilling, but useful insightfulness.

"Do I get a horse?" Saira asks.

Rais looks up at him. Saira stands at the edge of the stall. He's an unsettling presence. "There is a stall on the other side. The plate on the front says, Robin. You can tack him up." The horse is one of the two he bartered for outside of Rebynrock. He gestures for Bryn to get the other chestnut, Indy.

The chestnuts, Robin and Indy, are likely not strong enough to make the trek through miles of heavy snow and rocky mountain trails. Oberyn is built for this. Her muscles are strong and pelt thick. Wide hooves that make traveling through snow a breeze. Rais hopes the other two horses can keep up and not keel over before they make it past the Brockade forest.

Once the horses are tacked up and ready, they lead them outside. There's a movement on one of the manor's balconies. Ava stands outside the study, staring down at him. He subtly slips the talisman off and hands it to Bryn with Oberyn's reins. Bryn hasn't tried to steal it yet, so he figures they can hold it for a moment.

Rais steps through the Sonder. The wispy blue hugs his skin as he alates into the study. Ava looks at him through the glass. She opens her mouth but doesn't let the words slip out. He opens the door, breaking the divide. Her eyes travel across him, moving from his legs to his neck, then meeting his gaze. There's no hatred in her eyes. Not like when she held a flame against his neck. Not like when she took his title. Yet they are still mountains and valleys apart.

"Why?" he asks in a breath.

She turns from him and the separation grows. He can't feel her emotions or see into her mind. This room is full of so many memories—ones she's oblivious to.

Rais shifts his weight to his other leg. "Sorry will never make up for what I did … and it was not my place to—" *kill him.*

Ava's demeanor changes and she squares her shoulders. "Do not expect forgiveness." She steps through the open door. Her arm brushes against him, and he swears she hesitates. Ava doesn't look back.

Chapter Twenty-Four

Ava

The railing is damp against her arms. That violent storm thankfully subsided hours ago, but it left a huge hole in the barn's roof. She shifts her arms so that they touch the drier spots of stone.

Raiden left as soon as the storm passed. She watched him from the balcony outside the study. It was him, that nymph, and Saira. She wishes she knew why he is traveling with them, but it's not her business anymore. It was her choice to push him even further away.

When he alated inside the study, and she was finally alone with him, she couldn't form a single thought. She has so much to say to him. So much to scream.

He stood so still there. Looked at her like if he breathed too hard, she would shatter. She wanted to jump into his arms. Wanted to yell at him for being so idiotic. She hates him and misses him. Her grief for Levi should be more prominent, but it's not. Guilt rakes through her for not missing her friend more. She never loved Levi, only the comfort he gave her, the breaks he gave her from grieving, but not him. It's horrible, but she can't force herself to feel any differently.

The door at the end of the hallway opens. Her Uncle Aran hovers there, holding the door with his hand. "You want to join me?" she asks.

He steps out, and the door swings shut behind him. "I wanted to talk to you about your mother. You are going to be a queen in a few days, and I thought you might like to hear more about her."

"I thought you were in Metarock," she says quietly.

He meanders toward her, curiously eyeing her. "I was. I came to bring some old books for the trainees. And to talk to you."

"Aran, can I ask you something first?" He dips his head. "How do you see me? You knew me as a child, and now you have to explain all of these things I should already know. It's like the entire world is looking down on me and I'm just trying to hold onto something so I don't fall."

"You have always had a fire in you. You may be more mature now, but your personality hasn't changed." He pauses and looks off into the trees. "I don't look down on you. I can't speak for everyone, but I respect you for remaining so strong in these trying times. Everywhere you turn something tries to knock you over, but you keep fighting. You, Ava Beckett Wyntryn, will be the queen we have all been waiting for."

"My mother didn't want me to be the heiress. She wanted that for Stygian. She saw something in me that wasn't good enough. She chose Stygian over me. Even when Stygian left for Goldryn. Even when according to Wyntryn law, I would be next in line. I have these memories of being so scared of not being enough for her. I remember studying until I passed out and trying to outperform everyone in my classes. Not for myself, but for her. And no matter what I did… I was never going to be enough."

His forehead creases and he taps his forefinger against the railing. "Your mother was not forgiving. When she latched onto something, it was hard for her to see from other perspectives. Stygian was her first child, and she saw herself in her. I think that's why she pushed that little girl so hard. Then she had you, the true heiress, not born out of wedlock. Everything changed then. Stygian became… different. No matter what, your claim to the throne was stronger than Stygian's. So Alys held standards for you that were unreachable. She loved you, Ava. Despite her anger and her flaws, I believe she did care for you. Some-times our minds cannot break free of their burdens, and it causes us to act in horrible ways. You were always good enough. Your mother wasn't capable of allowing herself to see that."

"Aran, do you think I should have given Raiden protection from the Isles and Goldryn instead of taking his title?" It seems her uncle will be the only one who can give her an honest response. She wants the guilt to go away, but it never will. Ava doesn't want to become her mother. So rooted in her anguish and torment that she hurts the peo-ple around her. She never wants to be so lost in her head that she forgets to ask for help.

"I think the only way for you to rule this region, is by trusting yourself. If you decide something and act on it, do not question it. If you are questioning yourself, then everyone else will too. Be confident and don't let anyone push you around. Though, I think in the future you should discuss such a matter with others before reaching your fi-nal decision. There are ten protectors for a reason. They are not only meant to protect the land but to council and support their queen. Just as you are meant to counsel and support them."

"I am not a queen yet," she whispers.

"Hm… well, if you have any questions, come find me. I will always be glad to help you."

There's a whistling in the trees and the branches sway in a shaky formation.

"Thanks," she says.

A flock of birds breaks the tree line and escapes to the skies. Their squawks echo around her.

Search those who search you. It's what both Anya and Ms. Ethelle told her. Maybe it was something her mother used to say. She's inclined to think it's directed at a particular person, but who would be searching for her? No, that's far too literal. She will have to give it time, and hopefully, the answer may reveal itself.

The sky is still cloudy and gray. Sunlight barely filters through. Not long ago she stood here next to Rais. Her first night back in the manor, he told her a story about them as kids. Back then, when they were young and imaginative, she was struggling. Not as severely and for more menial reasons, but she's always been tormented.

Some memories Ava's regained have exposed her mother's cruelty. Those recollections are often filled with the pressure of expectations and irrational anxieties. Has she ever been truly happy? Has anyone?

The only small moments of relief she's had are with Rais, but he chose to ruin that. He chose to kill Levi. Then she chose to leave him behind. Happiness may come in spurts, but it doesn't last long. A few laughs with Aliras and then it's back to whatever this is—attempting to be something she isn't. Aran believes in her, but is that enough to make up for seventeen years of lost memories? That time is gone. If she ever had a chance of remembering, it has to be long past by now.

Chapter Twenty-Five

The world is a blistering white. A colorless land interrupted by a dark figure in the distance. Cold prickles along her skin. She nears the shadow. It bends into something other. Wings flap by her ear, and a purple sparrow careens past her. It circles the amorphous shadow and lands on an outstretched hand.

The bird's head snaps to her. The shadow bends into the shape of a man. It lifts its free hand in the air. Points at her. *If the dragon rises in the north, the darkness will fall. The ocean will open and consume it. Stop it.* The voice turns into a screech. *Stop it. Stop it!*

The figure floats toward her. "Get away from me!" she shouts.

The darkness is inches away. *Stop it!* She stumbles back and presses her hands over her ears, but the sound is in her head.

Willow loses balance and falls through pearlescent grass. Her fingers push against soft fabric. Willow jolts upright and gasps for air. Sleep clings to her eyes and her head spins. She groans and forces herself to sit up. Why does she have to get these visions? The goddesses could have chosen anyone else.

The space beside her is empty. Nina's not here. She runs her fingers through her hair, finding something sticklike. She pulls it out of her hair. It's a feather. Small and brown. A sparrow feather. Willow looks around. The window is ajar, a breeze pulling in the scent of the sea. She slides off the bed, then pads to the window. There's no sign of a bird inside. She presses her fingers against the window's ledge, then slams it closed.

If her dream was at all real, she must find a way to stop the dragon from rising. Whatever that's supposed to mean.

Willow pulls on a flowy chiffon dress. It's a bit wrinkled, but all her clothes are.

She wishes she knew where Nina went, but she doesn't know much about Nina's schedule. She's only been staying here for a few days. Nina could be down in the pub or off on a walk. Willow ties her hair back with a ribbon. She supposes she'll have to go investigate herself.

Downstairs, the pub is empty. Outside, the streets are abandoned. She turns to go back inside, but a Goldryn guard comes out of nowhere and steps in front of her. "Willow Evergryn, Her Highness Stygian Liones has required your presence at the palace." Just her luck.

"Do I have a choice?" she asks.

"No."

He grabs her upper arm. Odd, she can't see into his mind. If she doesn't fight back, then she can go with this guard and learn why his thoughts are missing.

She allows the guard to tug her along.

They cross the bridge to the palace and go through the courtyard. The seagulls are quiet here. Even the ocean's waves are small and create nothing but a hush. Something is wrong.

Stygian has stationed more guards at the palace than usual. They stand so still anyone would think—wait—they aren't thinking. Willow yanks her arm from the guard and places it on the closest soldier. His mind fizzes in and out of consciousness. It's webbed and mangled. She caresses his cheek. "What has she done to you?"

Her escort grabs her arm again and pulls her away from the webbed mind. That soldier's mind is slowly shattering, getting worse with each passing second. It is a cruel state to live in. Stygian has betrayed so many people that she's resorted to creating mindless soldiers. Willow wouldn't be shocked if she passes Society members in these very halls.

The guard pulls her into the throne room and shoves her to her knees. There's an enraged cry from across the room. A hooded figure is tied to a chair. Willow knows that cloak—recognizes the embroidery. Nina. Stygian will pay for this. Willow yanks her arm from the guard and runs. She doesn't make it ten feet before Stygian steps in front of Nina and puts her hand out. Fire incircles Willow. She stills and pulls her skirts away from the flames.

"Why am I here, Syn?" She fists her hands at her sides.

Stygian clicks her tongue. "My, my, Willow. You are quite the liar. I thought you prided yourself on honesty and morals." The purple flames nip at her.

"What are you talking about?" Willow asks. Nina's dagger must've been thrown across the tile. It now lies on the floor far to her right.

"Darling, you have forgotten your own treachery. You never got Kalenti to agree to an alliance. You got her to agree to a lie. Two days ago, you sent two hundred of my people back to Eventyr on those ships. If I was a cruel person, I would have those ships sunk. Instead, I'll take my rage out on you. Unfortunately, Kalenti would never forgive me if I killed you, so I'll hurt someone you love instead."

"Please don't hurt her," Willow pleads. Sweat drips from her brow. The fire rises higher.

Stygian walks around the chair and lights a flame in her hand. She holds it close to Nina's throat. Nina cries out. A pang sears through her chest. Stygian can turn Willow's skin to shards, but she will not get away with touching Nina.

Stygian forces a look of distress. "What do you want me to do, Willow? You've betrayed me," her voice rises, echoing through the great hall.

"You don't want to hurt me because of the ships. You want something else from me. What is it?" Willow asks. She hates playing Stygian's games, but she doesn't have any choice. Nina scowls at Stygian, but her eyes betray her. They plead with Willow, revealing her fear. If only she was closer to Nina and Stygian and not walled off by these scorching flames.

"Ava promised her loyalty to me, but I know she was lying," Stygian says. Willow scoffs. The Queen says it as if she has always known about this grand lie. "I gave her a taaffeite crystal, but it's not the one she's looking for. I took down some of the barriers on the city to convince her otherwise. I know Ava trusted you. If you want me to let you and your little knife thrower go, then give me something that will let me have control over Ava." So, the breaches in this city's barrier are just a façade. Stygian thought she was tricking Ava. There's no taaffeite crystal around Stygian's neck now. That means it's still locked away in the queen's chambers. Hidden in a place Stygian assumes no one knows about.

The most amusing part of this is that there's nothing Stygian could do that would make Ava bow to her. Right now, it's not about Ava. It's Nina's life on the line. Willow squeezes her eyes shut. There has to be something she can say or do. "I can get you the dragon's scale or the entrance to a hidden city, but I don't—"

Stygian grabs Nina's wrist, and she screams. The fire melts through Nina's flesh. Willow wails—her heart lurching with Nina's pain. They need to get out of here.

"You know Ava better than me!" Willow digs her fingernails into her palms. Why won't this nightmare end? Stygian lets go of Nina. "You saw what happened in Rebynrock. You investigated the minds of many soldiers after the incident. Tell me what caused Ava to lose control."

Willow takes a moment to breathe. There was only one Goldryn soldier inside the fortress that survived when Ava lost control. Somehow, he escaped with his life. Willow watched the whole scene through the man's eyes. "Commander Damon threw a dagger at Anya Petrichor."

Stygian smiles. "Did he?"

Willow nods. "Ava would do anything to protect the ones she loves." It's something Stygian should already know, but she's been too selfish to notice.

"Do you know if she's altered someone's memories before?" Stygian asks.

"Not that I recall." Why would Stygian ask her that?

"Well, you see darling, I remember saying something, that I would never say," Stygian drawls. "I remember doing something, that I would never do. When I think about it, all these things connect back to my sister. She did… something to me."

"Why are you telling me this?"

Stygian drops the flames imprisoning Willow. She runs across the marble. Her foot slips. Pain shoots through her as her knee collides with the floor. Stygian wraps her fingers around Willow's chin. "Look into my mind and find the truth."

Willow blinks back tears. Stygian's mind rifles into hers. She closes her eyes and lets herself see.

Stygian stands in her chambers. She's saying something to Ava, who's on her knees before her. Blood drips from a slice in Ava's hand. From the corner of Stygian's vision, Aliras stands. Moments later, Stygian's vision blurs. The memory goes blank, but then it returns to the same scene. Stygian stands before Ava. Blood drips onto the floor. Stygian instructs Ava and Aliras to leave for Wyntryn right away.

Willow yanks herself from Stygian's grip. She catches herself with her hands. "Are you sure you want to know?" Willow asks.

"Tell me."

This could get Ava and Aliras executed, but if Willow doesn't tell her, Nina's life will be taken. Willow can't lose Nina. Not now, not ever. "Aliras knocked you out. Ava must have altered your memories shortly after."

Stygian steps back, and a smile stretches across her lips. "I'm through with you for now, but know you are on thin ice. I am not afraid of hurting you or your petulant Wyntryn."

Willow scrambles onto her feet and goes to Nina. "I'm so sorry."

Nina yanks against the ropes. Tears stain her skin.

Willow reaches to wipe them away, but Nina turns her face. "Just get me out of here," she says.

Stygian walks to the corner and says something to a guard. He leaves the throne room. Stygian watches Willow scramble for the dagger and then struggle to release Nina from the restraints. As soon as Nina's free, Willow steps into the Plane of Verity and alates them to the market street.

The streets are empty except for a stray dog that rummages through a fallen trash bin. Willow reaches for Nina but is pushed away.

"You should have let me die!" Nina shouts, crossing her arms against her stomach.

"You don't mean that."

"She's going to kill Ava. You know that right? She's going to hunt her down and slaughter her."

"No. No, she won't. Trust me, okay? I had to make sure you were safe. We will find a way to protect Ava. She's going to be fine."

Nina gapes at her. "You're delusional." She sits down on the road and shoves her face in her hands. Nina's left wrist is marred by a ring of red. "I ... hate her," Nina says. "I hate this horrible world we live in. Everything is politics and—" She chokes on a sob and leans her weight forward into her hands. "I can't—I can't do this anymore!"

Willow bends to her knees. She pulls Nina into a hug. Thankfully she's not pushed away this time. "I know, but we have to keep going. We have to hope that each day will get a little easier. You know, you're supposed to be the strong one."

Nina chuckles through her tears. "This won't happen again."

"Mhm." Willow lets go of her and stands. "At least

we know Ava doesn't have the taaffeite talisman. That will help us with what comes next. With the help of the Insurgency, we can find the talismans and stop this war. We will make sure Ava and all of Wyntryn are safe."

Willow wants to tell Nina about her visions, but she keeps them to herself. She doesn't want to rush the Drogon Insurgency's plans, but they don't have much time left. Willow has to stop the dragon from rising. The only way she knows how to do that is to gather the talismans. Unfortunately, they are scattered all across Kanaleigh. And winter is ending.

Soon the flowers will bloom, and this land will be covered in blood.

Chapter Twenty-Six

Raiden

The days are endless, dragging on like an injury that refuses to heal. Not that it's anything Rais isn't used to, but this journey has been dreadful.

The saddle pinches his tailbone and inner thighs. There's a constant tensing of his muscles as they move from a walk to a trot and the occasional canter. They've been on the path to Metarock for four days now. It has felt like weeks.

They stop every few hours to let the horses rest. Unfortunately, they don't get much rest themselves. That time is used to find food and tend to the horses. After a quick nap, they're back on the road.

Bryn's to his right, and Saira is a few feet ahead. Rais isn't sure why he's brought Saira along. This whole time he's been contemplating ways to leave the odd man behind. There are plenty of options, he could take away Saira's memories of the past few days. He could put a thought in his mind telling him to run off in the other direction or knock him out and leave him behind. All of it requires energy, and that's energy Rais can't risk using.

What's worse, Saira hasn't been a nuisance. He's helped them hunt and has shared stories while riding to keep them awake. Saira has been frustratingly decent. It makes Rais hate him more. The man remains expressionless, and his mind is still empty, but he isn't unbearable. If this is Saira's tactic for gaining Rais' trust, then he's pulling quite the convincing scheme.

"Raiden."

"Hm?"

"I've said your name three times now," Bryn says. "We are coming up on Mount Meta. Do you need us to stop again?" They're holding Oberyn's reins now. At some point, he let go and grabbed Oberyn's mane. He keeps having these moments of forgetfulness. When his mind completely blanks out, all he can see are his thoughts. He's sure it's nothing to get worked up about.

"No. I'm fine," he assures. Rais brushes Bryn away and grabs the reins.

"If being exhausted is fine, then yes, you are fine." Saira's tone is grotesquely bland.

Bryn was right about them being close. The mountain rises above them, covering the entire horizon. The valley they ride through has sparse vegetation. They pass a few trees, though the area is mostly clear. The mountains that rise on either side of them are too high in altitude to have trees. They're mainly rock-covered in snow. To the left of Mount Meta, there's a large shimmering lake, but that's the only identifiable factor of the hidden city.

In their travels, they have only come across a few Atane, but they were small enough to take down without using the Sonder. Coming up on Mount Meta they may not be so lucky. Atane are known to roam this area, drawn to the scent of irregulars. Metarock has the largest population of irregulars in Wyntryn.

"Saira, you wouldn't mind if I blindfolded you?" Rais asks, but Saira doesn't have a choice.

"I'd rather take you both out and find the entrance on my own," Saira says.

"Do you even know which mountain it is?"

Saira tilts his head.

It's obvious since the mountain is straight ahead, and Bryn practically gave its location away mere moments ago. Though this part of Wyntryn all looks the same. Gray rock and white snow. Some dead trees here and there. Nothing eye-catching.

Rais shouldn't even care if Saira sees Metarock. Wyntryn's protection isn't his responsibility anymore. Once he gets to the city, he's planning to take his assets out of the bank and buy an apartment. One that has its own walkway and a personal tunnel to a ledge for him to see the night sky. At least two bedrooms. He could finally get a dog. He's always wanted one.

What he desires is for this to be a dream. He'd like to open his eyes and be back at the manor. He wants to wear the protector's pin on his jacket and have Ava at his side. She doesn't need him, but he needs her. Desperately needs her. He can buy that apartment and get a dog, but that will never make him whole. Only his other half could make him whole again.

Bryn slows Oberyn. "Let's stop here. There are Atane up ahead."

Saira stops his horse. "Atane are no trouble. Why have we stopped for them?" Saira asks. Rais glances at Saira but doesn't bother to answer. Everyone dismounts and pulls the horses underneath an overhanging rock. Rais passes Saira a blindfold. Saira holds it before him with two fingers. He waggles the torn cloth in the air. "You seriously want me to put this on?" Rais swings the hilt of his dagger onto Saira's temple. Saira collapses to the ground. Rais bends down and pulls it over Saira's eyes—in case he wakes up before they get into the city.

"What was that for?" Bryn asks.

"He's a Society Commander. I don't want him going back to Grymyr and giving away the location of our biggest city."

Bryn shakes their head. "You still care for Ava, and she betrayed you."

"Yeah, well, I betrayed her too."

Rais could play the part of the vigilante, fighting to protect the people who told him they don't need his help. He has the dragon's scale now, and if he's honest, he likes the darkness. It scares him, but it makes him feel a way he's never felt before. The darkness is addictive.

Nonetheless, he still knocks Saira out. The morality within him wouldn't have let him do anything else. Rais hoists Saira over his shoulder and lays him over the saddle on Robin. He pulls off the amulet and hands it to Bryn. "I'm going to take care of the Atane. Can you stay here and watch him?"

Bryn narrows their eyes. "I've taken out a few Atane of my own. You forget I hunt monsters as a hobby."

"Then put that in the saddle bag. Saira should be out for a while," he says. Bryn drops it in the saddlebag on Oberyn.

Leaving the talisman here is a foolish idea. It's not that he doesn't know better, he does, but part of him wants the talisman gone. All he gains from it is a power he shouldn't tamper with and a demonic force tormenting him.

Bryn is already trudging through the snow toward mount Meta. He listens for Saira's mind in the Sonder, but the odd man is out cold. The talisman is fine here. Other than the hidden city there's no one within miles of this place.

He runs after Bryn—easily catching up with them.

The closer they get, the more Atane they see. The beasts roam the area in hordes. They're going to have to take out a lot to safely make it to the entrance.

Without the talisman's energy flowing through him, he is significantly weaker, but he'll be fine. This will not be the first time he overexerts himself. Rais takes the sword from his back. An Atane approaches. Its ears flicker, and it sniffs the air. The hooves of the creature crunch through the snow. It catches sight of him and rears on its hind legs. Rais raises his blade and moves toward it. "Slow and steady," Rais whispers into the crisp mountain air.

Energy gathers in the creature's gut and it pounces toward him. Rais lunges. He slams his blade into its chest and yanks it up. The animal yowls and falls back. Rais holds his sword steady. The creature writhes on the ground, fighting to get back on its feet. Rais swings his blade across the Atane's throat. Red snow flurries into the air as the beast crashes back onto its side. One last breath rushes out of its huge nostrils before it stills.

There's a roar from behind him. Rais spins around to see an Atane charge Bryn. Fire blazes from the Atane's mouth. The flames engulf the ground, rushing toward Bryn. Before he can do anything, huge vines rise from the ground. They wrap around the creature's stomach and squeeze. The vines grow thorns that dig into the creature's flesh. Bryn nears the Atane and slides a small knife into its throat. The vines disappear into the snow, then the Atane falls.

Bryn doesn't need his help after all.

He turns from Bryn as an Atane gallops toward him. This time he pulls a bolt of lightning from the sky and sends it crashing down into the creature. It's enough to stop the Atane's heart.

They repeat this with each Atane they face until the ground is littered with the animals. He wipes sweat from his brow, then they alate back to the horses. Rais grabs the amulet from Oberyn's saddle bag. He slips it around his neck. Rais mounts Robin, and Bryn gets on Indy. He must hold Saira steady as they ride to the base of Mount Meta. Oberyn keeps a steady pace behind him. It's almost unreal how well-behaved the horse is.

The entrance is not along the outskirts of the mountain like at Rebynrock. They have to ride the horses up the side. It's a small incline at first, but the closer they get, the steeper the path becomes.

Ahead of them, a part of the mountain is cracked in two. A huge slab juts to the side, but if you're not right by it, then it looks like any other ledge. Right near the opening, one can see it twist into a tunnel of darkness.

Rais leads Robin into the small space. Saira's legs drag against the rock on one side. The path leads down, then opens into a cavern. Three tunnels branch away from the entrance. He's been here before but has only taken one path. The other two are supposedly wide openings. At the bottom of the gaping holes are sharp stakes. An extra security measure, but Rais is certain many unknowing Wyntryns have fallen to their death here. Rais takes the path to the left. It leads them in a large arc that eventually opens to the city.

Metarock is built with numerous levels, and from

the tunnel's entrance, all five are in view. There are massive staircases carved into the rock that trail up the cavern walls. Across each level are walkways like in Rebynrock. The stone paths zigzag through the city's stacked buildings. There are no openings at the top of the cavern, although many tunnels lead to the outer edges of the mountain. Those tunnels only open to the backside. All the ledges are in areas that are near impossible to climb to. The only viable entrance is the one they came through. Rais clicks his tongue and Oberyn trots up beside him. He grabs the reins and holds his horse close.

He and Bryn lead the horses to the stables on the lowest level. Some ramps lead down to small pastures for the horses, the grass in is them grown by mages as are all the plants in the city.

Rais dismounts Robin. They walk the horses into the stable. No one here knows he's not the sparrow anymore, so he uses the title to get the horses fed and in stalls. Before letting them take the horses, he pulls Saira off. Saira groans when he hits the ground but doesn't wake up. Bryn helps Rais drag Saira outside the barn. They lean him against the barn wall, then Rais removes the blindfold.

A bruise has formed on the side of Saira's face. Rais didn't mean to hit him that hard. Bryn kneels beside Saira and places their fingers against his temples. At Bryn's touch, the bruise fades away.

Saira slowly opens his eyes, then blinks a few times. "That was incredibly unnecessary," he mumbles.

"I disagree." Rais grabs Saira's wrist and pulls him up.

"Where's the dragon?" Saira asks.

"There is no dragon." Rais walks off down the path to the main staircase, which crosses Metarock's manmade water source. It's a series of thin ravines that direct water to the plants grown on the west side of the lower level. This part of the city holds Metarock's agriculture. Since the mountains surrounding this area are unsafe and mostly barren, the people living here have created new ways of growing food. They also raise chickens, pigs, cows, and other animals within the mountain.

The main light source inside the mountain is from bioluminescent plants that grow along the walls. They shine neon blue and purple. Some light shines through the ledges and tunnels on the higher levels, but down here it's completely lit up by plants and isolated fires.

All fires and torches burn red. When Ava arrives their hue will change to blue. It is a technique crafted by their ancestors. A way of announcing a true-blooded Wyntryn's arrival. The fire turns to the color that the royal manifests.

"The city is beautiful," Bryn says. They walk in step with him. "I've read descriptions of the city in books, but to see it in person … it's like nothing I've seen before."

It is hard to encapsulate the whole city in one description because it's filled with so many overlapping cultures. It has the heart of Wyntryn, warmth, and equity. It features the qualities of the night nymphs that live beneath this very ground, but it has created a new lifestyle. No other city in Wyntryn is like this. Rebynrock is the closest, but even that city cannot compare. Metarock is five times the size.

They climb the stairs to the second level, and Rais leads Bryn and Saira to the bank. He's surprised he remembers the way.

The bank itself is a fortress. He leaves Bryn and Saira outside and goes in by himself. Inside, he's greeted and pointed to a bank teller. The man behind the glass asks him for his name and personal details. Eventually, he gets access to his funds. Most of it was left over by his parents, but as sparrow, he got some coin deposited to him each month. He takes out enough to pay for food and a few nights at an inn. An apartment will have to wait.

When he leaves the bank, Saira is gone.

"He told me he had to find something and that he'd make his way back to us. Then he disappeared," Bryn explains.

Rais doesn't even care enough to go after him. If Saira tries to go beneath the lowest level of the city, he'll be stopped or thrown out. Saira isn't his problem anyway.

"Let's find a place to sleep," Rais suggests.

They roam the busy streets for a while before settling for an inn that has two rooms available. Rais wanted to get three rooms, but Saira can sleep on the floor if he finds them.

While walking the streets, Rais overheard people talking about the heiress' coronation. It won't be long before she arrives. He will have to be careful to keep his distance.

Rais pulls off his cloak and jacket. He drops his weapons to the floor. This room is one of the nicer ones he's stayed in. The bed is long enough to accommodate his height and the pillows look like miniature clouds. He collapses onto the mattress. His eyes close and he sighs.

A scream ricochets through the city.

Rais jolts upright. He goes to his window and flips the latch open. The window pane swings outward. Below him in the street is the screaming woman.

"She killed them!" The woman falls to her knees and sobs. "Save us, sparrow, please! She's going to kill us

all!"
      "Killed who?" he shouts down to her.
      "Our protectors!" she wails.

Chapter Twenty-Seven

Ava

Ava pulls her mage's coat on. Today they're leaving for her coronation. Tomorrow morning, she will be a queen. She's been hearing people call her their queen for months now, but truly being the queen is different. It shouldn't be real, yet it is.

She leaves her room and goes up to her mother's old office. Ava's been wanting to speak with Anya for four days now but her cousin has been avoiding her.

Anya isn't in the office, Eieran is. He's holding a picture frame that was sitting on the desk. She's walked into another lesson from one of the protectors. All of them have been giving her random lectures and advice. Despite the helpful content, Ava dwells on how this proves they don't see her as an equal. She's a child to them. It will be a long time before she can escape that.

"Do you know where Anya is?" she asks.

Eieran looks at her. His eyes are much darker than Rais'. "No. Do you need something?"

"She's… upset with me. I imagine you are too."

Eieran sets the frame down. "Not at all. I did mentor you after all, and you have something in common with my little cousin."

"What's that?"

"No matter what you do, you've reasoned it out in your mind. You two are not irrational. I trust you had a good reason. Even if you won't tell me."

"Maybe I should though. I suppose the only person I didn't want to tell was Rais. If he knew, then he would find a way around it." She let his nickname slip. She pulls her lips between her teeth. Ava can't allow herself to give in to her desires. There are more important things she needs to focus on.

Eieran chuckles. He pulls a flask from his jacket and takes a swig. "Right again, little Wyntryn." He tucks the flask away. "I saw Anya this morning. She was talking to your Goldryn friend. Haven't seen her since."

Aliras? She hasn't seen him since dinner last night.

There's a knock on the door. Eieran walks past her and opens it.

"Finally. I got a message from Goldryn. Ava needs to see it, now." Genevia is on the other side of the door. Her gaze catches on Ava, and she shoves past Eieran. Genevia holds a letter out to her.

Ava takes the paper, then unfolds it. *Sister, I have taken it upon myself to prove the loyalty you promised me. I am hosting a family gathering at the palace. I hope you do not mind that I took my guard back. You won't be…*

The parchment drops to the floor.

"Eieran, have you seen my uncle since this morning?"

"No."

Genevia stares at her with wide eyes. "Wait, why…"

"Go to Metarock without me. I have to go to Goldryn," she says.

"What about your coronation?" Genevia asks.

"Don't worry, I'll be there. Eieran, give me a vision of Metarock. I'll need to alate there on my own."

Eieran hesitates for a moment then his mind slips around hers, and a vision of a large mountain appears. Its entrance is hidden by a ravine jutting through the mountain side. A silver lake nearby.

Ava pulls herself into the Sonder and alates to Goldryn. She could care less about her coronation. Anya and Aran need her.

She steps through the Plane of Verity and onto the bridge of the palace. Without acknowledging the guards, she stalks across the bridge to the main entrance. When they try to stop her, she enters their minds and commands them to stand aside. With power like Stygian's, there is no reason to keep the strongest soldiers at the gates. Her charms keep her protected more than any person could. It doesn't matter if the soldiers announce her presence or not, Stygian undoubtedly knows Ava is here.

She runs through the courtyard and into the halls made of sparkling sandstone and coral.

She senses Aliras' mind nearby and reaches out to him with her mind. He steps around the corner. His skin is ghostly. Drained of any life. His lips part as if he's going to say something, but instead he looks away, blinking back glassy tears. She narrows her eyes. "What did you—"

He lifts his hand, silencing her. Ava steps up to him. "Don't worry about me, my lady," Aliras says. She wasn't worrying. If he was the last person to see Anya and Aran, then he's the reason they're here.

"Where's Aran and Anya?"

"You need to leave," he insists.

"I'm not leaving without my family."

"She will kill you." His voice is deathly quiet.

"So be it. I would trade my life for my cousin and uncle. You have to take me to them."

"I wish I had that choice."

"Where are they?" she demands.

His jaw clenches as he glances around them. "The throne room."

Ava shoves past him and hurries up the steps. She twists around the main tower to the throne room. The doors are closed. Ava throws her energy into the doors, slamming them inward. Inside her uncle kneels before Stygian. He's being held down by two soldiers. Anya is six feet away from her father, her knees on the tile, and hands tied behind her back.

"Stop this, sister!" Ava shouts across the room.

Stygian meets her eyes and flashes a grin before waving her hand. The gesture could be flippant or graceful, but the result is anything but.

A long blade slices through Aran's neck. His head rolls. A cry builds in Ava's throat and she falls to her knees. Anya looks at her father and screams.

"Silence, girl," Stygian spits at their cousin.

Ava pushes off the ground and runs to Aran. She doesn't know what to do. His mind has faded, and she can't... she can't fix him. Ava touches her uncle's back with a shaky hand. There's nothing she can do. Ava looks at her sister. Flames spring to life in her hands. A force of energy slams into her chest and throws her across the tiles.

"Darling sister, it is about time you arrived. I've been patiently waiting," Stygian says. She steps over Aran and stands before her. "I have so much more in store for you."

"What is wrong with you?" Ava can't even process what's happened. Her energy buzzes and burns through her. Wrath rises in her with each passing second.

"You have disobeyed me, sister. That is what is wrong. Rather than supporting our alliance, you have been working behind my back. Sending letters in secret. Allying with the Isles and Eventyr. Altering my memories. It is petulant and rude. If I ignore those betrayals, there's still Rebynrock where you murdered my soldiers. For those crimes against Goldryn, you will face punishment. Our uncle and cousin are here to receive those punishments on your behalf." Stygian twists fire within her fingers.

"I thought we had a deal."

Stygian swishes her hand. "You never planned on being loyal to me. I can see it in your flawed and open mind. You despise me. So much, you would manipulate my memories when you of all people know the pain of having your memories tarnished."

"If you are going to kill our cousin, take me instead. Then there will be no one between you and the Wyntryn throne."

"No, that won't do." Stygian sighs. Ava pulls through the Sonder and attacks her sister's mind, slicing through it with one solid swipe. Stygian is barely fazed by the attack and throws her energy out, forcing Ava to crumple. "Seize her."

Ava's vulnerable here. Incapable in the presence of her sister. She can hear the ticks in her head as the events occur.

One second.

Ava stands, her eyes widen, and her gut falls. The ringing grows. Soldiers in purple grasp her wrists and yank her arms back. She falls again to her knees. Her shoulders wrench backward.

Five seconds.

Stygian stretches her arm out to a guard who hands her a blade. A weapon with a clean shine and long handle. Twisted metal that's carved to a sharp point. Stygian approaches Anya, and Ava's throat catches. She pushes herself forward, dragging the guards who hold her a few feet forward.

Her shoes slip on the tile.

A silence spreads through the room.

Ava shouts as she's dragged back.

Ten seconds.

Light from the windows beams down on her cousin's face. She turns her head to Ava. Her eyes glint with tears. For a reason Ava can't understand, her cousin smiles. Anya faces forward as Stygian swings the blade.

Twelve seconds.

Blood sprays, floating in the air like petals on the wind.

Ava stares at her sweet cousin as her body falls against the floor with a thud. Her blank eyes stare off into the distance. Ava doesn't pull against the guards. She relaxes on the floor and tears her gaze from her cousin. Stygian's blade drips with red. Ava's voice carries out with a steady hum. "And now your sister will take your head."

Willow was right. She warned her. Anya warned her—told her to search those who search you. Stygian sought her out and Ava followed. Now Anya is dead.

Ava rips her hands from the guards, slamming them backward with the force of her energy. The two guards catch fire. Blue flames consume their screams. With deadly calm, she stalks across the room. Ava faces Stygian. "How does it feel Stygian... to become the villain you always despised?"

Stygian's brows push down, and she pulls the sword back. It swings toward Ava.

Ava flicks her wrist, and the blade's thrown from Stygian's grasp. "How does it feel, sister? To be like our mother?" Stygian falters back a step. Her face stricken with unease. "Did you think I would simply lie down while you slung me around like your little doll?" Her voice is steady. Calm. "Did you think I would listen to your every word and treat you like a goddess?"

Ava smiles, looking around at the soldiers gathered in the room. Her eyes catch on Aliras. He stands by the doors, unphased by Ava's sudden change in aura. Ava whips back to her sister. "I refuse to yield to you any longer. I will not kneel at your feet and watch as you murder my people. I tried to be on your side, to understand you. The effort was worthless. In killing Anya and Aran Petrichor, our family, you have called for war. Stay alert, because when you think I am finally gone, you will find me standing before you, sliding a dagger into your heart. Recompense for the one you slid into my back."

Ava picks up her cousin in a swift movement and alates to Aliras at the end of the hall. She slips her hand around his. She sends him an image of a snowy landscape, Metarock, then pulls them into the Sonder with her.

Claws sink into the back of her shoulders and drag her out of the Sonder. She's thrown back and slams onto the marble. She skids across it, rolling and finally crumpling at the feet of her sister. Stygian grabs her jaw and pulls her into the air. In a fluid motion, Stygian rams energy into her and Ava flies backward. Pain rings through her skull as she hits the marble again.

"Stop!" Aliras screams from across the room,

Anya's body crumpled at his side.

Stygian looks down on Ava, a dark glint in her eyes. "You will not talk down to me and get away with it, you naïve little girl."

Ava gets her elbows underneath her and pushes up from the floor. She throws a wide blaze across the room, trapping the soldiers against the walls.

Stygian gathers her venomous fire in her hands. It glows lavender around her.

Ava gets to her feet. Her body screams with pain. She gathers energy in her hands and lets the fire spread through her. As Stygian throws fire at her, Ava retaliates in an explosion of power. It throttles her sister across the room and into the dais. Stygian gracefully stands, brushing invisible dust from her gown. She picks up the twisted sword from the ground and runs at Ava. This isn't a fight Ava wants to have. She wants to get out of here and bring Anya and Aran home to Wyntryn.

Stygian slashes the sword at Ava.

"Would you kill me too?" Ava shouts. She ducks to the right and slams fire into her sister.

Stygian consumes the fire with her energy, letting it dissipate into the air. Stygian's hair floats around her thin flame as she sucks the energy around them into herself. Stygian reaches her hand toward Ava's head and a bullet of energy flies into her skull. Ava's thrown into the air and slams into the doors. She can hear herself screaming against the pain of the hit, but she can't see her surroundings. Her vision is fading. Everything dims until there is only a steady ringing.

The familiar sound of silence.

Stygian penetrates her mind. *You will never have the opportunity to slide a dagger into my chest, dear sister. You will never get close enough, not even with those little talismans you seek.*

A force pulls Stygian from Ava's mind. A distant ringing slowly builds to a crescendo within her.

"I am getting you out of here," Aliras says.

Ava tightens her hand around Aliras'. He pulls them into the Sonder. They fall through the Plane of Verity and into soft snow. Aliras crouches beside her and lifts her. She leans against his bent knee.

"Condolences, my lady." He pushes away the hair that falls before her eyes. The depths of his amber and blue irises are filled with understanding. What a horrible thing to understand. Grief is a torment no one should have to suffer. Ava can't help but wonder what happened in the time she was separated from her soldier. Aliras has changed in that time—his face drawn and his mind drowning in dark thoughts.

Ava nods in thanks but can't form a response. He helps her stand. A mountain towers before them. Ava sags against Aliras, barely able to hold herself up on wobbly legs. "Where do I go?" he asks.

A dream takes over and instead of Aliras, she sees Rais. Golden eyes and a kind smile. She falls into the snow, her eyelids fluttering, blending reality with memory.

To her mind, it's not Aliras' arms that wrap around her and pull her up. *You are a menace, Ava Beckett,* Rais' voice slips through her mind. His electricity sparks in the air around them. She opens her eyes to meet the curves of his face. The jagged scar that twists up his jaw and the slight hood of his rounded eyes. His voice coats her mind once more. *You are going to be okay.*

As the darkness consumes her mind, she falls out of touch with her senses and into a shrouded sleep. Filled with visions of her uncle beheaded and her cousin falling to Stygian's blade over and over again. Those twelve final seconds of Anya's life plague her dreams.

The Hidden City

The Aftershock

Raiden

"Do you think she knows?" Rais asks. He stares off into the horizon. His back is against a tree. His legs are numb, buried in the snow.

The elk stares down at him. Its black eyes shine in the morning light. It tilts its head and sniffs Rais' hand. He lifts his arm and runs his fingers down the elk's smooth face. Tan freckles cover the dark brown creature. White reaches from its belly to its bottom lip. The antlers lift delicately above it, crafted with elegance.

"I love this girl, but she doesn't feel the same. Not anymore," he says to the elk. The animal blinks mindlessly. It lifts its head and looks to the cliffside covered in snow. Rais sits at the base of the tree. The place where he got his scar.

Last night he slit Levi's throat. Then in a rage, he killed a squadron of Goldryn soldiers who had infiltrated the Wyntryn border. He's nothing but empty inside. Tired and empty. "You don't care, do you?" he asks.

The creature sniffs the air. It begins to walk away from the disembodied town, toward the cliff. Rais pushes off the tree and stands. He follows the graceful animal. The elk stops and looks at him. Rais reaches out to touch its coat. His fingers barely grace the wooly texture before the world bends. He's pulled into the Plane of Verity and dropped somewhere deep in the forest.

The trees here are wide. Large redwoods reach hundreds of feet into the sky. There's not much snow here thanks to the branches covering the forest floor. That elk sent him to the Brockade forest.

He meanders through the trees until he comes across the ruins of an old manor. One much like the Wyntryn Manor, except this one, has nearly fallen to rubble. Rais steps onto the front stairs that open to a large stone porch. Columns broken in half, holding up nothing, frame it.

He crosses the stone and steps inside. In the center of the foyer is a large staircase. It branches off and leads to a third, but that part of the staircase has fallen to the ground. Rais hesitantly walks up the main staircase to the second floor. He's following a feeling. That elk wanted him to come here, to follow this feeling.

Rais crosses the hallway to the only room remaining intact. The window is shattered, but the walls remain standing. Faded wallpaper barely clings to the walls. The paper was torn to shreds. As if a bear was trapped inside once upon a time. Bookcases are toppled on one another. In the center is a table and four chairs. A leatherbound book sits in the center of the table covered in leaves. Well, what's left of one.

Ancient symbols are burned onto the leather cover and spine. He brushes off the layers of dust with his sleeve. Rais can make out the words *Ta Menani Mey Fin* — For when I'm gone.

He unwraps the leather tie, letting it dangle onto the table. He opens the cover and his suspicions are confirmed, it is a journal. *Alys Rosaline Wyntryn* is scrawled in red ink on the first page. The late queen loved her journals. She probably used a charm on that poor elk before she died. Planned to have it find him.

He flips through the pages of the journal, but there's only writing on one page. The rest are blank. He turns back to the writing and reads aloud, "If you have found this, know I have lied to you. Nevertheless, you need to retrieve the talismans. If you are who this book is bound for, then you can unspell these pages. On them are the answers you have been seeking."

He drops the journal onto the table. The locations of the dragon scale, the painite, and the tanzanite talismans could be on these pages. The truths to Alys' lies might be here too, but he doesn't want to know. Ignorance is a way to protect himself. If he knows, then he can't ignore it. Especially if Alys chose him to hold this information.

Rais opens the journal again and stares down at Alys' writing. It is time to learn the truth.

Chapter Twenty-Eight

Willow

Cool water soothes Willow's throat. Nina leans back against the bar with her eyes closed. It's a painfully hot day.

This week has wrung her out. A headache pulses against the back of her skull. If she had her herbs, she could ease the pain, but they are in the palace. The one place she's trying to avoid after what Stygian just pulled — kidnapping Nina and using her to get information out of Willow.

There's a clamor outside, and the pub door slams open. "The Queen killed two Wyntryn protectors!" Kael has his hands braced against his knees. He takes heavy breaths, his eyes wild.

Water splashes on her legs. Glass shatters. She looks to the shards at her feet, then up at wide-eyed Kael. "Who?" Nina asks.

Her hands shake. Her blood pulses to an unsteady song. Kael rubs the bridge of his nose. "I know one was the fourth protector, but I don't know their names." Nina covers her mouth. A sob echoes from her throat.

Willow knew Stygian was on edge, but to kill two protectors. She's utterly lost her mind. Willow presses her hand to Nina's back, but Nina pushes her away. "I am going to—"

"You aren't going to do anything," Willow whispers.

Nina's pupils dilate. "She killed Anya. I don't even know who the other person is. She could have killed Rais." Nina staggers outside.

Willow follows her. "Where are you going?"

"To Wyntryn."

She can't go to Wyntryn. Willow needs her here. The Drogon Insurgency needs her. Nina and Willow are supposed to get the taaffeite talisman from Stygian. They must do their part to stop this madness. To alter the fate of the war. "You can't go," Willow insists.

Wind picks up around them. "The work we're doing here is only making it worse. She almost killed me because of those ships. I am glad you want to be with me, but my people need me. If Rais is dead… I don't know what I'm going to do. He's my best friend. Don't you care?" Nina clenches her hands into fists.

"Of course, I care." The wind lashes against her. She leans into it to stay upright. "It's okay." Willow reaches for Nina's arm.

"No, it's not! I've been here in Goldryn avoiding my responsibilities. I've been sauntering around this pub and walking through the streets of my enemy, while Stygian's been plotting the deaths of my friends! I have to leave. The Drogon Insurgency is useless against these massive, powerful regions."

Willow understands her anger, but she can't leave. They can't leave. Willow wants Rais alive too. Where does it end? There will always be conflict and war. Willow doesn't care about any of it. She cares about Nina. They have been building a life here in Goldryn. Wyntryn treated her as badly as Goldryn has. Willow wants to destroy the talismans and whisk Nina away to the Crystal Lakes. Away from this wretched continent. But she can't escape until the talismans are destroyed. Only then can Nina be free from her ties to Wyntryn.

Nina steps toward her. "Are you coming with me?"

Stygian has listened to Willow before. She might listen to her now. Stygian is lonely. She has no one in her life who cares. If Willow never left, this wouldn't have happened. Those two protectors would still be alive. Nina wouldn't want to run away from her. Willow needs to go back. However dangerous it may be. She doesn't have to fake sympathy for the Queen, but she will have to pretend she isn't terrified of her. Nina is fine on her own. She always has been. This war is inevitable, but Willow can at least slow it down by stealing the taaffeite talisman. Then she'll be free.

She pulls her hand away from Nina's reach. "I have to stay." The wind slows.

Nina sucks air through her teeth. "Why am I surprised?" Nina shakes her head. "Good luck trying to fix that broken woman. Oh, and don't wait for me to go to Eventyr."

Blue energy sizzles around Nina, and she fades away.

Willow fights the dread clawing through her. She didn't have a choice. If she turns the tides of this war, she's saving her homeland the trouble of having to fight in it. Besides, Willow is the only one who has ever gained Stygian's trust. She can use that pull to take the talisman. If she's making a mistake, so be it. She's endured plenty of pain in her life, what's a little more?

Chapter Twenty-Nine

Ava

Ava dreamed it was Rais hoisting her up from the snow. Envisioned him whispering in her mind, *You are a menace, Ava Beckett.* She wishes it were real, that he held her. That he saved her in that horrible moment. But he didn't. She woke up in Metarock a few hours later with Aliras at her side.

He told her she passed out as soon as they alated. Aliras carried her to Metarock. Not her Golden Sparrow. Though, she supposes he'll never be that again. She has no clue how Aliras found his way into the mountain, but she's thankful he did.

The protectors stand around the room, waiting for her to speak up. To say anything. She wasn't made for this. She isn't a Queen… she can't be. She sits behind a desk, trying to come up with something to say. This room is full of strangers and they all look at her. As if she knows what to do next. She's barely a month from turning eighteen. That's not nearly enough time to learn how to lead a region or one facing war.

Anya and Aran aren't here as they should be. Ava

thought she'd have years with them. It hasn't been a week since Ava returned to Wyntryn. Finally, she had a chance to get to know her family. Now they're gone.

Fire crackles from the torches along the walls. The furniture is made of twisted wood. Each chair has a velvet cushion. Ava caresses the fuzzy material. It's soothing to watch it change from dark green to light green with her strokes. She should speak up. But what would she say? *Sorry I couldn't save your friends, my family. My apologies for leaving their bodies there. I was too busy fighting with my sister.*

It's a joke. Her entire life is a cruel joke written by their ancestors. Willow must have read the prophecy wrong. Ava is not powerful. She is not important or good. She is cruel. She is selfish and watches her family die. The timer counts down in her head again. She sees his head roll and her body fall. The blood pools around her hands and feet. If she couldn't save them, how can she save a region?

The door swings open. "Is it true?" Golden eyes bore into her. "Did Stygian really kill them?"

Eieran goes to him and holds a hand to his cousin's chest. "We are all grieving," Eieran murmurs.

"Ava, how could you let this happen? You just watched as Stygian murdered them?" Rais shouts. His eyes reflect the flames on the walls.

"She's my sister," Ava says. It's true Stygian is a cruel, terrible person, but Ava's lost everyone in her family. After Aran fell to that blade, Ava couldn't move. She wanted to believe Stygian wouldn't take Anya too. It was only after Anya was gone that Ava fought her sister. Even then, it felt wrong. She doesn't want to be alone.

"Did your sister care when she murdered Anya? Did she care when she murdered Aran? Your family, her family. Wyntryn survives because Wyntryn is one. You do not hold to that truth, Ava. All you do is act on emotion. If something doesn't go your way, you turn your back. There is no excuse. You chose to leave Wyntryn and go to Gold-ryn. You chose to—"

"I did not kill them!" Ava shouts. She didn't. It wasn't her fault. She was there, and she couldn't do anything. Maybe she could, but she didn't know how. All she knew was her family was dying. The walls were crumbling. They were falling and crashing into her, and she was hope-less. Lying on the ground and gasping for air while stones crushed her chest. She had to watch them die. Just like Levi and her mother. These torments will never end, will they? She is not a queen. She is simply a person. A person whose memories were stolen. She was thrown into a world she doesn't want to be in. She was told she was this, instructed to do that, manipulated to act, and for what? Wyntryn is still suffering. She is suffering. Wouldn't it have been bet-ter if she stayed in Grymyr? In that small, dull apartment, with Levi visiting each day and chastising her. She was in pain then too, but at least it wasn't guilt. Because guilt is a horrible beast tearing her apart day by day. And she can't do anything to stop it.

"What now, Ava?" Rais asks.

She stares at him. Tears are dried onto his skin. He's not angry at all. He's broken. She broke him. What is she supposed to do now? Abandon an already deserted region?

"No one is lying to you now. No one is telling you what to do. You must choose for yourself," he says. He's always reading her mind or maybe he simply knows her that well. Either way, she hates it. She hates Rais.

Eieran looks at her. His gaze as grossly sympathet-ic as the rest. Eieran is in pain too. He shared more than a friendship with Anya. How can he stay so calm? Why is she the only one who can't hold it together? "I do not blame you for what happened to the Petrichors," Eieran says. "Though it does beg the question of where your loyalties lie."

"With Wyntryn. Always with Wyntryn!" Ava cries out. She shoves her face into her hands. A sob shakes through her. "I couldn't do anything. I was too late. I walked in and the sword swung. Then... then my uncle was just gone! I tried to get to Anya, but I couldn't." Ava stands and throws her chair into the wall. The wood splinters. Broken pieces fall to the floor. "I cannot control everything! I'm sorry I failed you. But I can't—" She gasps. "I can't save everyone. They keep dying around me, and there's nothing I can do."

Her eyes find Rais. He stares back at her and the rage he came running in with is gone.

She wipes the tears from her face and straightens her jacket. "I'm sorry. My family was planning the coronation, so I'm not sure what happens next. But I don't think I can be your queen."

Rais speaks up, "I know I have no authority here, but Ava, Wyntryn needs a leader now. You couldn't save your family or your best friend, but you can save these people. They need you. If you become Queen nothing is stopping you from doing whatever it takes to stop Stygian."

Aliras steps up to her side. She forgot he was here. He places his hand on hers. "Stygian has been preparing to invade Wyntryn. This was her plan all along." It wouldn't shock her if Aliras knew about this. About what Stygian was planning to do to Aran and Anya. Ava hasn't had the chance to ask, but she needs to know. Somehow her family got to Goldryn, and it happened to be the same time Aliras went to.

"We don't need to make a show of it, but we should go forward with your coronation," Eieran says.

"Are you all right with this?" Hyacin asks.

Ava doesn't want this. She's spent every second she can remember grieving. People will always leave this world, but it doesn't mean she has to disappear with them. They're right. Wyntryn needs a queen now more than ever. "Okay."

Everyone leaves the room except for Aliras. He keeps his hand on hers, but he won't meet her eyes. "Hey," she whispers.

He continues to stare at the floor. "Ava."

"Look at me," she says. It's now or never.

He fights it, but eventually meets her gaze. "I— I can't be here for you."

"Yes, you can. I want you here." It's true, she does want him here. Even if he has a dark heart and blood on his hands.

He glances away. "No. It's not what you think. I brought the Petrichors to Goldryn." Her chest tightens. She'd already figured that was the case. "Stygian sent a guard who told me she was going to sink the ship my nephew was on if I didn't comply. I know it put your family at risk, but I had to protect my own."

She wouldn't want him to do anything else, but why does everyone choose to stab her in the back? He could have told her, warned her. Then she may have had a chance to stop Stygian. "Did you know she was going to execute them?"

"No. If I knew—"

"Aliras," she says. His eyes are glassy. Ava tightens her grip on his hand. She wants to be angry, but she would've done the same if their places were reversed. "You had to protect your family. I wish you would have told me before you went to Goldryn, but at least you're telling me now." His face is drawn and he averts his gaze. "There's something else. Isn't there?"

A tear slips down his cheek. "The ship made it to Eventyr, but my nephew did not."

"You need to go back to investigate, don't you?" she asks.

"I only know what Stygian has told me, but it could all be lies. I need to figure out the truth, and if my nephew is alive, then I need to make sure he's safe."

"You should do whatever it takes. If there's any chance your nephew's alive, then find him. I might have to face my fears and finally talk to Rais. He'll protect me when you can't." There is much left unsaid between her and Rais, but after losing Anya and Aran, she can't risk losing him too. He's all she has, and she's abandoned him. One of the last requests Anya made was for Ava to talk things through with Rais. It's finally time she does.

"I'll worry about you," Aliras mumbles.

Ava pulls him into a hug, nestling her cheek against his chest. "I'll worry about you too."

"Goodbye, my lady." He steps away.

She catches his arm before he enters the Sonder. "Aliras, wait." He meets her eyes with a solemn gaze. "Will you do one last favor for me?" He bows his head. "Bring my family home?"

"It would be my honor."

Chapter Thirty

Willow

It's time to face the monster that could tear everything away from her.

Soldiers line the hallways. Clad in gold armor with purple velvet draped over one shoulder. The hallway is dark and Willow can't see much past the kitchens. She's alated inside. Normally that would be a horrible idea, but she knows this palace like the back of her hand. There was a time when she alated into the open air and fell quite a distance, nearly breaking her leg. Magic is a dangerous tool.

The dress she wears is dark orange, with a slit that runs up her right leg. Underneath the skirt is a dagger tucked into her garter. Willow was trained to use a dagger at the manor, but she's never used it on anyone. If Stygian tries to touch her again, she finally will. Willow doesn't have to draw blood. She could always attack Stygian's mind. Though Willow would hate to do so. Physical wounds heal. A person must live with mental wounds. They never go away, not entirely. Mental wounds can plague people for decades. It can be what tarnishes the soul or strengthens it. Those who outlive their trauma often have the strongest minds.

What's odd about these soldiers is that they line the hallways near the kitchens. Stygian has never stationed them here before.

Willow waves her hand before one of the soldiers. Their eyes follow her hand, but it's as if their muscles are frozen. She places her hand on the soldier's shoulder. There's nothing but darkness within. Willow presses through their mind and searches for something, anything. Thoughts move through the back of their mind, but it's slow and webbed. A dark goo with speckles of purple fire.

Willow pulls her hand away. Stygian has been reckless before. Placing mind control charms on Goldryn soldiers is beyond that. Willow must be careful with her words. If she is to manipulate Stygian, she'll have to think clearly. Willow can't risk Stygian's wrath or her mind too might be shattered.

She walks past the mindless soldiers to the stairwell. It leads her through the main tower and to the throne room. The double doors are open and Anya's body lies on the tile. Willow's hand presses against her stomach. This kind woman didn't deserve such a fate. Willow didn't know Anya well, but she had met her on a few occasions. She can't imagine what Ava must be going through. It's as if the Itzal is walking in her shadow, plucking people from her life when she least expects it. A kismet more torturous than death.

Willow must hold her breath to walk past the body. She wants to take Anya's remains to Wyntryn, but she doesn't know where to go. Last she heard, no one resides at the manor. Willow gasps when she sees Aran. She closes her eyes tightly and runs blindly to the dais. Stygian isn't even trying to make a statement by leaving them here. She simply doesn't care and somehow that's worse. So much worse.

Willow is glad the other protector isn't Rais, though it doesn't make this situation any better. There are two dead Wyntryns in this room. The only relatives Stygian and Ava had left.

She makes her way to Stygian's chambers and knocks on the door. Stygian knows it's Willow. She would never let anyone get this close to her rooms without knowing. Willow still knocks, even though Stygian doesn't deserve the kindness.

After a minute passes, Willow opens it and steps inside. The door swishes shut behind her.

"You're here to ridicule me. Tell me I'm a horrible person, but in my defense—" Her defense. There's nothing Stygian could say to excuse her actions.

"I am not here for that," Willow says.

"Is that so?" Stygian sits on the couch staring out through the window.

"Are you hiding up here?" Willow asks. It isn't difficult for her to force a conversation. What's difficult is trying not to say something she'll regret.

Stygian combs through her hair with her fingers. She then twists the hair around her hand and lets it fall over her shoulder. "I have nothing to hide from."

Willow circles the couch and stands before Stygian. "You wanted Ava to trust you. That's why you let her and Rais keep the arrow. That's why you brought her here after that kid's death."

"Our mother was consumed by a need for power. I promised myself I would never be that way."

"Yet you are." *Rein it in, Willow. Not so blunt next*

time. Willow pushes the heels of her hands across her hips.

Stygian doesn't flinch at her words. "I am not a good person. I never will be." At least she can admit that.

"You told me once you strived for authority and power because it is the only way you can feel something." Willow doesn't dare sit on the couch. She has some power standing here, looking down on Stygian

"Why are you here?" she asks.

"You have no one else." It's true. Stygian has either driven away or killed every person who cared about her. Unfortunately, Willow still cares. Enough to stand here now, but not enough to stop her from reaching for the dagger beneath her dress.

Her fingers brush against the hilt. Stygian stands and points at the door. "Leave."

There's no way Stygian saw the weapon. If she did, then it would not be words telling Willow to leave, but something more painful. Willow gives Stygian a sad smile. "If you need me, I'll be in my rooms. No one should be alone in a time like this." The words leave a film on her tongue. Willow wants to follow Nina. She doesn't want to be here, but she is. She made this decision. She must see this flimsy plan through.

Stop the dragon and save its heart.

Chapter Thirty-One

Ava

Voices of a choir reverberate through the walls. The sounds bend and whirl like the flames of a fire. Ava stares into the mirror—past herself. Anya chose this dress for her. Blood red silk. Sleeves hang loose on her upper arms. Gold beads line the various seams.

The dress was left with a jewelry box. Her mother's initials, *ARW*, carved onto the lid. Alys Rosaline Wyntryn.

She breaks her gaze from the mirror and goes to the jewelry box. The hinges creak as it opens. She fiddles with the golden chains and rings inside. Ava chooses a necklace with a red gem and its matching bracelet. Then she tries on the various rings. Some fit and others don't.

There's a knock on the door. She's not ready for this. Never had been. Red isn't even her color. It makes her appear more regal than she feels.

Her chest still rattles from the crying, but she will be fine. All her attempts to remain positive have been futile. The only family she has left is her sister, and her sister wants her dead.

Ava opens the door, and Eieran offers his arm to

her. Eyeshadow masks the red rimming her eyes, but she can't hide the dark circles beneath them or the puffiness of her face. At least Eieran understands she can't talk right now. It's taking everything she has to remain upright. Ava places her hand in the crook of his elbow. She will be fine.

Eieran leads her through the fortress of Metarock. It's built into the highest level of this bioluminescent cavern. The hallways have wooden beams on the ceilings to keep broken rocks from falling. Twisted wood shapes flowers and rivers on the breams.

The hallway opens to a large space framed with columns of rock. Three steps lead up to the main floor where hundreds of people stand shoulder to shoulder. Her heels click on the stone, the sound echoing out into the silent cavern. Hyacin, Osidias, and Genevia kneel at the dais. At the end of the aisle is a throne of rock embedded with glimmering crystals. On the throne sits a golden crown with gems the same color as her dress. A burning red. This place reminds her of Rebynrock. Of walking through the crowds after sending the Goldryn and Society soldiers running. That day was the first time she felt like she could do this—be a queen.

Wyntryn mages she recognizes from the manor crowd around her as she continues down the aisle.

Ava lets go of Eieran's arm when they reach the platform. Eieran goes to kneel by the other three protectors and a woman with long graying hair steps before the throne. Ava searches the crowd for Rais, he must be here, but she can't find him in the crowd.

"As the *paaite* of Metarock, I, Helena Donsen will initiate the coronation of our heiress, Ava Beckett Wyntryn." Helena was once a protector. When she retired from the position, her child took her place. If Aran were alive, he would be the paaite, standing up there. Ava's jaw clenches. She has to keep herself together.

Helena steps in front of the protectors. She asks each of them if they approve of Ava's reign. They each swear a new oath to the ancestors, the land, and now her. Helena goes back to the dais and picks up the crown. She bows to Ava. "Ava Beckett Wyntryn, will you kneel for your people?" Helena asks. Ava picks up the skirts of her dress and moves to her knees. "Do you swear to the ancestors, to honor them, to open your mind to their guidance, and to protect the customs of our people?"

"Yes," Ava says. She presses her hands against her stomach. *You're okay. You're fine.*

"Do you swear to defend and protect the sacred lands of our people?"

"Yes." Wyntryn needs her. They need a Queen, and it's either her or Stygian. She can't step away from this now.

"Do you swear to defend and protect the Wyntryn people, and put their lives above your own?"

"Yes." She is not afraid to die. She's done it before. If that's what it takes to save this region, then so be it.

Helena places the crown on her head. Ava stands and goes to the throne. She sits down and Helena turns to the crowd. "*Mey chessya* Queen Ava!"

Ava can hear Anya yelling those same words from the temple in Rebynrock. Her heart picks up its pace and she swears under her breath.

"Queen Ava!" the crowd shouts.

From the lower levels of the cavern, she can hear the same praise shouted.

Within the crowd is a man with white hair. His skin burned red from the sun. She stares at him. He stares back with a sad smile. His voice slips into her mind. *I'm proud of you.*

Rais. He is here.

She stands from the throne. Eieran says something to her, but she ignores him. Rais turns from her and moves through the crowd. People reach their arms out to her, but she politely pushes past them.

She loses sight of him. Ava pushes her mind into the Sonder and searches for him amongst the other minds. There's a distinct feeling of him that she follows. She's only been in this city for a day and has no memory of where anything is. She follows his trail down the large staircase to the lower levels.

Ava ends up somewhere on the second level of the city. People shout at her from the windows of their homes. She barely notices the streets filled with people holding candles. Ava must get to Rais. There's an arrow inside her pointing to him. It tugs her along his path. She doesn't even know why she's so desperate to see him. Maybe it's because she wants him or because she hates him. She's yet to yell at him for his betrayals, but even so, she doesn't want to be angry. Not at him.

She finds herself outside an inn. When she goes inside there's no one at the desk. She follows the smudges of his mind in the Sonder. It takes her up a staircase, down a hall, and to a door. She hates Rais for killing Levi. For not coming for her in Goldryn, and for sinking that ship.

She wants to tear him apart, but she also longs for him. Every day she missed him. She can't help herself. He is a drug she can't ignore. She knocks.

It creaks open and Rais gazes down at her. That's all they do for several seconds — stare. But there's something inside of him that doesn't reflect the outside. He's angry.

"Rais—" His name catches in her throat.

"What do you want?"

"I… I came to…" She searches for the words. Tears build in her eyes as she gazes at him. Levi was never really a best friend or someone she loved. She loved that he took away her loneliness and forced her to break out of grief. It was nothing more than that. If it was, why has she stopped grieving so soon? Why did it stop hurting? Ava follows Rais' scar with her eyes. "I miss you."

"Am I supposed to fall to my knees for you?" His voice is empty, diminished.

Her breath hitches. "What?" She didn't expect it to go back to normal between them, but why is he being so harsh? He's the one who hurt her.

"You have strung me along for years. While we were together, you spent at least two summers with Levites. A boy you told me you loved. You pull me along and share memories with me. Tell me I'm your person, promise to never leave, then you disappear. Without a word. You didn't even let me explain."

"I just don't understand why you murdered him. You could hate him, hate me for all I care, but why kill him?" Why would he say all of this? He's never mentioned any of it before. Not that she'd remember if he had.

His eyes narrow. "Levi was given orders to assassinate you. He was the one who took your memories. Then he told me you were plotting to have your mother killed. I was angry and scared for you. I got protective—I couldn't control myself. I killed him because if I didn't, he would have killed you."

Levi took her memories. Her heart flutters in her chest and her legs seem to give way beneath her, but she remains standing—barely. "I've convinced myself that I can't forgive you … that I shouldn't. You betrayed me. How am I supposed to trust you?" she whispers. She's supposed to hate him, but it's not Rais in the wrong anymore, is it? Rais knows she worked with the Society against her mother. She can't defend herself or explain it. She doesn't even remember why she would do such a thing. She only knows what Levi told her. That her mother was going to kill her father, and that she went to him for help. How does that explain such a horrible, horrible thing?

"Don't you see what I mean? You came here, told me you missed me, and say you can never forgive me. Gods. You drive me crazy! You are so selfish. All you think about is how everything affects you. Have you ever once thought of someone other than yourself? It was okay at first because you didn't remember, you were grieving. You should know better by now. You are a queen, Ava." He runs his fingers through his hair.

"I—" She tries to find the words, but nothing comes.

"Even before your mother's death, you were this way. Promising me things, telling me I was your person, then leaving me behind. What hurts the most is that I cannot shake the image of you choking me. Of the hatred in your eyes that night. Then you were gone. I mean, you stripped me of my position! That title was my identity. The only consistent thing in my life is my duty, my oath to this region. You took it away without even asking me what happened. I didn't sink that ship. I didn't piss Stygian off. And I certainly do not deserve to be treated like a second thought. I have spent my whole life bowing to and protecting you. I defended you when I heard what you did to your mother. I don't need an explanation for it. Because

I trust you. You never give me a single second to explain myself before you shut me out. You can't keep doing this to me! You can't miss me. You can't treat me like this. It's confusing and it hurts. It's… selfish."

She never realized she had been treating him like this. Rais has always been there for her. But he's right. He bent to her will no matter what it was. In all her memories when he's opened up like this, she's shut him down or complained about one of her own burdens. She was so afraid of him knowing the horrible things she's done that she almost killed him the night of the ball. Fear has led her to push Rais away and to avoid confrontation.

But she has been there for him too. She's bandaged his wounds and sat by his side when he's needed it. "Why can't I be selfish?" she asks, surprising herself. "I didn't kill my mother. I thought about it, sure, but that was because she was going to kill my father. And the Society ended up killing me. They took my memories. Manipulated me. My sister promised she'd protect me, then locked me up like some misbehaving pet. Then she killed the only family I had left. I deserve to be selfish. Because I have to protect myself. The only person I can trust with my life is myself. If I am not in control, I don't know what will happen. If I am not in control, someone might manipulate me again or kill someone I care about. They might kill you." She takes a deep breath, trying to stop the growing headache and the tears begging to fall. "I had to take the Wyntryn crown and your title."

"You do not have to do anything." He practically spits the words.

Ava shoves him back. He barely budges. He claims she's selfish, but he's blind to what it's like to be her. She's been thrown into a world she never wanted to be a part of.

She passes the doorway and shoves him again. "You don't understand! I am angry. I am tired of being thrown around like a pawn in everyone else's game! Didn't you and Anya plan for her to make Damon angry in Rebynrock? Was it not you who knew I would tear myself apart to defend the ones I love? I have been broken, destroyed, and thrown to the ground. You can be angry at me. You can call me selfish, but I am only doing what it takes to survive." His back hits the wall and she pulls the dagger from her belt and presses it to his neck. "Do you trust me?"

His golden eyes stare at her in silent shock. "I have always trusted you." His skin presses against the blade as he says it.

"Then trust that I would not hurt you for my own gain. The Queens of the Dragon Isles wanted to torture you for sinking that ship. I traded your torture for the guarantee that I would make an alliance with my sister and stop her from going on their land. Then Stygian told me she wanted to take you. All I could picture was what she's done to Aliras and Willow, and I couldn't stand to imagine you being treated that way. So, I stripped you of your title so that Stygian couldn't get anything out of hurting you I put Wyntryn at risk by allying with Stygian. Even if that alliance doesn't stand anymore, I did that for you."

Rais pulls the dagger from her hand and tosses it to the floor. Her eyes follow it, watching it wobble to a stop. His gaze burns through her. Heat prickles across her skin and her heart pounds, a thudding that vibrates through her chest. He cups her jaw, and she lifts her chin to him. Their lips meet and all the anger fades away. Her headache recedes and she wraps her arm around his neck. Tingles spread through her body, warmth flooding her senses. This is what she's been desperately missing. Her other hand presses against his chest. He pushes from the wall and twists them so that her back is now against the stone.

Chapter Thirty-Two

Raiden

Rais never thought he'd be this close to Ava again. At the manor last week she felt miles away from him.

Ava's eyes meet his, and the ringing dissipates. He can hear her. See her in the Sonder. Feel the emotions move in the air around them. The talisman sizzles against his skin. Whatever is inside the dragon scale doesn't like her. She is somehow replacing the darkness, the soul within the talisman, with her energy. A fire that hugs against his skin.

He smiles, so subtle, yet filled with happiness he cannot fathom. There is no hatred in her eyes. No disgust. Only the desire they have both felt every second of every day. The want they've pressed so deep within themselves to stop from falling apart.

Red rushes into her cheeks. His own cheeks flush, and he tightens his hold on her. Rais hugs her against him and kisses her again. Electricity feathers in his chest as he leans into her. She brushes his cheek with her thumb and his heart skips a beat.

Rais smiles into the kiss, and he swears she laughs. Her breath is warm. Her lips chapped. His hand travels to her waist, and she breaks the kiss. Rais opens his eyes to her. That ocean of blue. Not engulfed by fury, but a memory. It seems to trickle against her mind and spread through her. She leans her head against the wall and lifts her fingers to his face. She traces the jagged line of his scar and shakes her head.

"What?" The word barely escapes his lips. If he speaks too loudly, he might ruin the moment. The ringing may return. Her mind may shut him out. Even worse, she may push him away and leave. Return to ignoring him, hating him. Gods. All he wanted was her forgiveness. Then he wanted to get away from her. He ran to Metarock, with Saira of all people, only to run right back into her.

She chases his worries away as her hand slips around the back of his neck. As she takes a deep breath and says, "You stopped the silence."

"What?" he asks again. His mind is breathless—wordless. He wasn't the only one hearing it.

"I've been hearing a ringing, faint, but always there," she says. "It's been calling to me since about a month after I arrived in Goldryn. I assumed it was the sound of silence, but now, I can't hear it."

It's almost a relief to hear he wasn't alone in that heavy silence. "I heard it too," he says. Her forehead creases and she opens her mouth to respond, but nothing comes out. Rais gulps. "It stopped as soon as I could feel, no, hear your mind again," he explains. He thought the ringing was from the talisman.

"You couldn't—" she pauses. She unconsciously taps her fingers against his neck. "I couldn't hear you either. At the manor, I thought you were doing it on purpose. I thought you were protecting yourself or doing it out of spite for what I did. Since... that night, I've only heard your mind once. It was when you were in the Isles."

"You saw me there?" he asks. He thought it had been a dream. Her reaching out to him in the ocean. Figured it was his mind creating a fantasy.

"Yes. It came to me like a vision. My nose started to bleed and I heard you call my name. Suddenly I was in the ocean above you and you were sinking."

"I saw you too, but I didn't think it was real."

She runs her fingers up his neck and into his short hair. "I pulled Aliras out the window with me after I got that vision. We fell into the ocean below the palace, and I convinced him to help me escape. We went to the Dragon Isles to find you." A breathy laugh escapes her.

"That's when you learned about the ship and met with the Queens?" He studies her face. The dryness of her skin. It wasn't dry before. Below her eyes is tainted skin. Stained a bluish color. She wears the blood-red dress from her coronation and the crown. It hid her exhaustion from a distance, but this close he can see the markings of her pain. He reads it in her mind too. On the outskirts that she can't control, he can sense the turmoil. "Are you okay?"

Ava's lips move between her teeth. She closes her eyes. Rais slides his hands to her back and pulls her into a hug. She doesn't make a sound but leans into him. He shifts his feet to support her weight. Her hair presses against the crook of his neck and Rais moves her to his bed. She shifts on the mattress and relaxes against him, her face turned to look at the floor. He brushes his hand in small circles on her back.

Rais can feel the anguish trickle through her. He holds her against him and begins to whisper the song from his childhood. The verses he thought he had forgotten. "As the clouds fade low into the snow the lighting strikes loud. Their whistles do blow. We have nowhere to go—but down. Underground. When the winter winds blow. We wait for you now. Till the fates decide"—he closes his eyes—"the end of this sound. The burning is nigh. As our fates decide. We must go down. Underground. When the winter winds blow the lightning strikes sound. We'll wait for you now, down underground." He has to force out the last words. The memory is consumed by whatever darkness lurks in the talisman on his chest.

Ava pushes off him. "Underground." She gets off the bed. Her hands go to her hips. "Anya, she ... she said there were weapons underneath Metarock. Like the tunnels, you told me about in Rebynrock. They're below us now, right?"

Rais nods. There are tunnels, but he's no longer a protector. As far as he knows he's not even a Wyntryn mage. He has no way of accessing them now. The guards would never let him through.

"Can you take me there?" she asks.

"Now?" He presses his hands onto the bed. She looks at him expectantly. "Look, I can't go down there."

"Why not?" she asks.

He stares at her. Doesn't want to tell her why. It will only make her remember what she's done. But he can't avoid that gaze. Her pain has completely washed away with this new curiosity. The energy sweeping off her is filled with excitement. He grimaces. "I am not the sparrow anymore."

Her smile drops. "Right." She twists the ring on her thumb. "I am the queen now ... they won't turn me away. Come on, I want to see it for myself."

He doesn't move to stand.

She reaches her hand out to him. "Come on." Her

voice is cheerful. Eerily cheerful.

Rais doesn't want to go down there. It seems wrong. He has no title, no connection to Wyntryn. Not even his lineage matters anymore. Eieran may be a protector, but even he can't return Rais' ancestral connection. Ava's decision stripped him of all ties he had to Wyntryn. Before he may have been angry enough to want her to feel his hurt. But she doesn't need anything else weighing her down. As she said, she's a queen now. She shouldn't waste her time with him or have to worry about his feelings. She has to avenge her cousin and uncle. Ava must save Wyntryn. That's no longer Rais' purpose.

Ava steps up to him. Her dress brushes against his knees. "We don't have time to waste. There's no avoiding war anymore. No alliances to be made. This is more serious than my wants or yours. I need to see what's below Metarock. What arsenal we have at our disposal."

"It is more than that. There is something down there. You may not remember, but it is dangerous. Something that causes more damage than an unaligned talisman. If you choose to go down there, you will not be able to hide it from your enemies. You do not have control over your mind. If Stygian finds out—"

She holds her forefinger against his lips. Her expression turns to stone. "Do not belittle me. I will do whatever it takes to protect my people. I refuse to allow any more lies in my life or any more deaths. You will take me to the tunnels. It is not a question."

Rais stands and looks down at her. "I only mean to protect you."

"I need to know what's happening in my region," she says.

He often forgets how much Ava doesn't know.

When she first returned to the manor after the accident he only thought of the basic things. The obvious memories she was missing. At the time he only felt his emotions for her. Only cared about being near her and helping her understand the world she had been missing. She lost her entire life, and that is so much more than it seems. Right now, Ava's life only consists of what she remembers. She has no clue how much is gone.

She has no memory of the dragon lurking below her. No recollection of the city below Metarock and the creature he is taking her to.

Chapter Thirty-Three

Each day is a new breath. A breath that casts out a bit of pain and replaces it with something new. Some days it's happiness. On other days it's more pain. Yesterday her lungs filled with terror and hatred. Today, they fill with hope. Underlying it all is grief. The storm that never subsides.

Ava paces across the small room. Rais left nearly an hour ago. He should have been back by now. She asked him to find her some clothes. Something that will blend in with everyone else. She wouldn't make it two feet into the city before someone recognized her in this current attire. It's odd to wait for Rais, but it's right. It's normal. This is how it should have always been. The separation from him was needed for her to see that. And if her memories never fully come back… she'll survive.

As Ava paces, she finds it difficult to breathe. Thoughts penetrate the fragile parts of her mind. Worries and concerns deafen her. It's nothing new. She's been drowning since the day her mother died, but she can see the surface now. Water shifts above. Clouds of grief cast shadows across her mind. The shadows try to stop her from escaping, but she's close. So close. Ava may never breach the waves, but she can't let that stop her. She has to hope for a better life. This one is filled with treacheries and sorrows, and she can make it better. With Rais, it's already improved. One day she won't even remember what it's like to grieve. What a wonderful life that will be.

She stops pacing when the door opens. Rais holds out a small stack of folded clothes. "The boots might be a little big."

"That's fine, thanks by the way." She takes the clothes from him and steps toward the bathroom door. Her dress is intricately tied behind her back and will be difficult to undo herself. "Can you untie the back for me?"

"Sure." His voice is soft and his gaze delicate.

She turns her back to him and his fingers begin to carefully unthread the ribbon. "I missed you too," he says, his voice deceptively mild. Little fires blossom beneath her skin where his fingers graze skin. The air is still. Frozen in the silence. Whatever ringing plagued the two of them, it's gone. Without it, the air is electric.

Ava holds the bodice of the dress up with one hand. Once it's unlaced nothing will be holding it up. He finishes unlacing the back and she turns to look at him. At those golden irises. She missed them, his eyes. The way he looks at her. As if she is the only thing that will quell the darkness.

He isn't shy about where he looks. Neither is she. There is no tsuris here—all their troubles are cast aside. In this moment she can forget again. All she wants to remember is him. That's all she's ever wanted. It was stifled by his betrayal, but that desire never disappeared.

Ava averts her gaze and goes into the bathroom.

Her fingers push the door closed. She sets the clothes down, but in turn, releases her hold on the dress. It catches on her hips for a moment before falling to the floor. The dress is a pool of blood around her feet. She gulps down sour saliva and steps out of the dress. Phantom blood sticks to her hands.

If only she could choose what memories to forget.

She pulls the new clothes on. They're simple, militaristic. A black button-down, with green cargo pants. The boots are a little big, but they're fine. She goes to the sink and splashes water on her face. Light reflects off the crown. In the mirror it's regal, but when she pulls it off her head and holds it in her hands, it's nothing. It has no power here, in this small room at the inn.

Ava picks up the dress and slides the crown onto her forearm. She goes back into Rais' room. She lays the garment on the bed and places the crown atop it.

"Ready?" he asks.

She forces a smile and nods. She's glad to be with him, but her body still sags against the death of the Petrichors. Hopefully, Aliras can do what she asked and bring their bodies home to Wyntryn. They deserve to rest peacefully in their homeland.

Her gaze follows the outline of Rais. She wants to familiarize herself with him. Because he's different now. His skin isn't as vibrant. His hair's unkempt. There's even a scar on top of his hand that she swears wasn't there before. The biggest difference is his mind. When she listens to it in the Sonder, it feels broken. His mind is not whole, and it's shrouded in energy she can't identify.

Ava pushes the strange realization aside and takes Rais' hand. Now is not the time to bother with personal worries. There's an armory below Metarock that could help them win a war.

They walk through the city toward the steps to the lowest level. She can't tell what time it is without a view of the sky. Her tracker has a clock in it, but she left that in Grymyr. After Levi died, she never went back for any of her belongings. A few weeks after the incident, she asked her sister if she could go to get them. Stygian told her instead to reach out to Grymyr, so Ava sent them a letter. Not even a week later she got a response from the Society of the Collective. In summary, they banned her from ever returning to Grymyr without invitation. Supposedly, she is a danger to their constructs of peace.

Which is fair. She did set a city block on fire. Then she killed one of their commanders and countless others. To top it off, Wyntryn's previous tenth protector murdered an officer at their headquarters. It's a miracle Grymyr didn't do more than ban her.

They travel down the staircase and to the cavern floor. The path takes them through rows of plants and fences containing various animals. There's so much she has to learn about Wyntryn. To think she's the Queen, and before yesterday she had no memory of this gorgeous city.

Past the fields and animals, there's a small set of steps that lead down to an alcove. In that alcove is a set of double doors. A Wyntryn guard stands on either side of the entrance. The doors have markings of the ancient language. Swirls and lines that interconnect to seal the area. It's like the pattern of symbols at the Warped Library. What is so dangerous that it needed to be sealed down here?

Ava releases Rais' hand and addresses the guards. "I'm Ava Beckett Wyntryn, I would like to pass through."

The guards instantaneously drop to one knee. "Your Highness, we apologize for not recognizing you right away. You may pass through." They stand and press their palms to the doors. "*Malla gana ta drogon fin. Mata mey chessya feya fin,*" they recite.

The doors creak and the carved symbols glow blue. Rock dust shakes onto them as the doors swing inward.

"Thank you," Ava says to the guards. She and Rais pass through. They walk into a tunnel with a steep decline. The ground isn't slippery, but she has to duck here and there to avoid stalactites.

They continue downward for some time until the tunnel opens into another cavern. The space is filled with misty blue fog. It looks like the world when she enters the Sonder. She waves her hand through the mist. It disappears for a moment before returning. Rais walks through the mist, so she follows. It begins to fade, and the silhouette of a city becomes visible. Tall buildings entirely made of rock stretch from the cavern's roof to the floor. Even more wild varieties of bioluminescent plants fill the space. Here they aren't only blue, but orange, purple, pink, and green. On the streets of this peculiar city walk irregulars.

These must be the night nymphs. Their ears elongated, and their skin tinted the neon colors of the plants. She can't tell if that's the real color of their skin or if it's face paint.

Rais nudges her. She turns her gaze from the city to him. "Those doors are sealed because there are people who hunt these nymphs. If Grymyr or Goldryn ever infiltrated the hidden cities, they wouldn't massacre the regulars. But if they were to see this city, they would want all these nymphs dead. So, we protect them. After the forest tribes fell to the Atane, we made a point to protect the other nymphs living in the region. Your mother loved this city. I think it's because it feels detached from the rest of the world. When you're here, it's so easy to forget about everything above," he says.

"I thought Metarock was the most beautiful place I'd ever been, but this is…"

"Beyond." He smiles down at her.

From the ledge they stand on, they have a full view of the city below. But how can this small world they're protecting be dangerous?

"On the way back, we can look through some of their shops. There's a creative district by the reflection pools and they have the most beautiful artwork." He points to the back of the city. Past the stone structures, a waterfall casts shimmery reflections on the cavern wall.

"Wait. Back from where?" she asks.

"This isn't what you asked to see. The arsenal is farther below."

How can there be all this and even more? Her ancestors had to mine for centuries to create a place of this magnitude. One could believe Rebynrock was created by miners. But if they saw Metarock, that lie would wash down the drain. Wyntryns are indeed miners, but those mines are not within this mountain.

Rais leads her along the ledge that skirts the edge of the city. They reenter the tunnels and continue the decline. Cold prickles across her skin. The farther they go, the colder it gets.

Once again, the tunnel opens to another cavern, but it's the size of a small room. There are barrels and crates along the walls and weapons in piles. Rais takes her through many more manmade rooms like that before they get to the doors. The symbols are identical to the ones the guards opened for them. Except these doors are ten times the size. She has to crane her neck to see the tops.

Rais places his palms against the stone. "Malla gana ta drogon fin. Mata mey chessya feya fin."

The symbols glow blue and the doors slowly move inward.

Behind the doors is only darkness. Ava lights a fire in her palm and holds it out before her. Air blows at her, and she lifts her hand. Two large eyes peer down at her. Its nostrils flare and the creature lifts its lips to bare its massive teeth.

The creature looks like it's sculpted from clay. With a reddish-white undertone and iridescent white scales. Ava's heard stories of dragons. In the book she read about her grandparents, it said her family used to ride dragons into battle. That they would use the creatures as vessels to manifest their fire. She never thought that dragons still existed today.

"This is Aathmika," Rais says. He steps up to the dragon, and Ava goes rigid. Rais opens his hand to the dragon, and it nuzzles his palm. "She is the last winter dragon. Her mate died three years ago. Alys found eggs in one of the caverns beneath Rebynrock, but they've never hatched."

"Are all the hidden cities built on dragon nests?" Ava asks.

Rais nods. "Yes. We say they were mines, but the actual mines are in different mountains. Alys told us her father chose the three hidden cities because the great dragons guarded them." He pulls his hand from the dragon's scales and walks back to her. "When I became the Sparrow, Eieran brought me down here. That's when I got to meet Aathmika. This dragon has been alive for a century now. She's been taken care of by your ancestors and in turn, she protects Wyntryn blood."

Ava can't tear her gaze from the pale creature. Its head is twice her height. She hesitantly moves toward it. "Aathmika," she whispers.

The dragon's scales shiver at its name. Ava keeps the flame lit in her hand. The creature lets out a low snarl. Ava lifts her other hand in the way Rais did. With her wrist and palm upturned. It's a vulnerable gesture. Aathmika's breath whistles through her nostrils. The dragon lifts her head and tilts it to watch Ava. Aathmika presses her face closer and sniffs her. Then she nuzzles Ava's palm. The scales are cold and rough. Not slick like they look. Ava watches the pupils of the dragon's eyes dilate.

Scales swish across the rock. It must be the dragon's tail. She can't see it because its body is shrouded in darkness. The dragon's breath blows across her arm. It's a unique sensation that creates goosebumps on her skin. Ava pulls on the Sonder, veiling the world in blue. If this creature is self-aware, then she should be able to communicate with it. It's worth the try, anyway. She reaches out for the dragon's mind. It's well guarded—as strong as Eieran's.

"Ava."

The dragon pulls from her hand and backs away.

"People are going to worry about where you are," he says.

She doesn't care. She'd rather be here. Far away from the crowds.

Ava closes her fist, and the fire dissipates. She reluctantly turns to Rais, and they leave the cavern. Ava speaks through the Sonder to the dragon. *I'll come to visit, Aathmika.* The creature won't understand her, but she's drawn to it. She wants the dragon to hear her. To know her.

She walks close to Rais. His hand hovers near hers.

She elbows him. He raises his brows and gives her a funny look. "You know, I'd rather be close to you than stay away forever. We both made mistakes. I lost Anya and Aran before really getting to know them." She didn't get to know them because she was in Goldryn. And she wouldn't know Aliras if she stayed in Wyntryn. There are so many what-ifs in her head. But she's been through this before. Nothing can change the past. But what she can do is not make the same mistakes again. "I refuse to stay away from you," she says. "I can't lose anyone else. Especially not you."

Rais moves his arm behind her and holds her waist. She leans into him. She's glad it's a long walk back to the city. Next to Rais, she's already home.

Chapter Thirty-Four

Raiden

Ava brushes her thumb along his jaw. "You and that nymph can move into the fortress on the upper level," she says. Rais can hear Bryn's response in his head. Being at the manor was uncomfortable for them both.

A farmer stares at them while filling a trough of water. "Their name is Bryn, and I'm not sure that's a good idea." Rais should be grateful for the offer, but he's not the sparrow anymore. He shouldn't be there. Rais doesn't want to face all the protectors again. He saw them yesterday, and none of them looked at him the same. Not even his cousin.

"Why not?" Her voice is quiet. Can't she guess why?

"No need to worry about it," he says. It would make her feel worse if he was honest. She pulls away from him and starts walking along the pathway to the stairs. Rais closes his eyes for a moment before following her. It's clear he's upset her, but he needs to protect himself. Right now he's not comfortable being in that environment. She should understand that or at least try to.

"I'm sorry for making you feel… alone." Her voice carries in front of her, but he can still hear. He infers she's talking about taking his title. Isolating him even more in an already lonely place.

"It's okay." Rais knows Ava can get lost in her torments, but he can't let himself get hurt. He puts too much on the line when it comes to her. She could easily destroy him without even knowing it. But for once, he spoke his peace. "Would you ever consider reinstating me?" he asks.

"I made this decision for a reason," she says, glancing over her shoulder. Rais isn't asking for that answer. That was never something he pondered over. "Aran told me to be confident in my choices. If I waver and begin to question my decisions, then so will everyone else. This is hard for you, I know, but you just need to wait for me."

Good thing she's not facing him because he can't hide his reaction. He never needed her protection from Stygian. All this has done is hurt him. If there's one thing he's learned this past year, it's patience. He can wait if that's what's necessary. Patience doesn't make the annoyance go away, it makes it survivable.

They walk quietly for a while. Halfway up the steps to the second level she turns to him. "You know, it's not okay. I hurt you. We need to be honest with each other. You shouldn't settle for something just because you don't want to disagree. Yes, you asked, but you're trying to hide how you feel about it." She sucks in a breath and sighs.

She has changed. For once she might be listening to him. "What's okay is you needing me to wait. It doesn't make it not hurt. I am angry about it, but I'm not angry at you."

"Can you tell me what happened that night … why you killed Levi? I want to let go of it. To move on."

"Every detail?" he asks.

"Please."

"You should sit down." Rais sits with his back against the cavern wall and Ava sits down next to him. It's a lot to say and he isn't entirely sure where to start.

"I, uh… followed Levites up to the attic that night. Saira was there. I hid from them and listened to their conversation. They were talking about you. I interrupted them because I had to know the truth about what they were planning. They told me if you didn't change allegiances to Grymyr, that Levites' orders were to execute you. As for Saira, he was training, or rather, manipulating your mind. He made it impossible for you to close your mind off — to put up walls." Rais keeps his head down and closes his eyes for a moment. "And um, I also learned that Levites took your memories. I was not thinking it then, but your memories can't simply disappear. The mind manipulation that's done to take them, doesn't remove them. It pushes them back into your unconscious. Now that Levites is gone, he has no control over them anymore. Right now, it's your mind stopping them from returning."

Ava stares at him with wide eyes. He averts his gaze. "They told me about you working with the Society and planning the death of your…" He stops and looks around them. It may not be safe to say it here. Even a crown of rubies can't protect her from the consequences of treason. "Ava, I got so angry. I could barely hear or think straight. At some point, I knocked Saira out, and then I heard my dagger hit the floor. Then your scream… I am so sorry. I should have never gone up to that attic."

Ava's fingernails scape against the stone in steady movements. The cavern is dark, but torches are lit along the staircase, casting blue light across them. "You were protecting me. I never even considered switching allegiances. They would have—Levi would have tried to kill me. And maybe part of you did it to get my memories back." She looks toward him, but her gaze seems to bore into the wall behind him. Her forehead creases as she processes it. "That whole time he was the one who took them. He pretended to help me search for a way to get them back. And that means every memory I got back before his death was triggered by him." She meets his eyes. "Do you think he had control over what memories were returned to me?"

"I've never messed with people's memories in that way, so I cannot say."

"The ones I did get back weren't exactly in his favor. So, I suppose he may have just been giving them to me out of sympathy." She seems to fight the thoughts. "He liked me because I was so different from everyone in the Society. I guess we both loved what we got from each other. Not the actual person."

Rais doesn't like hearing her talk about someone else that way. Especially not Levites, but there's no reason to be jealous. He wants her to choose him again. If she decides he isn't good enough for her, she's probably right, and he won't fight it.

He fumbles with the amulet beneath his shirt. "Ava, you need to know something else."

"Hm?" Her shoulders are slumped, and she chews on the edge of her lip.

Rais tugs on the chain of the necklace and pulls the amulet out. "I did get the talisman from Kalenti. If we return it to her after the war, she has nearly ensured an alliance with Wyntryn."

"What?" she snaps.

This is too much at once, he knows that. But keeping it from her any longer will lead them down the same path as before. He can't lose her. Ava can handle this. It's a lot, and it hurts, but she can handle it. He should have known that before. Maybe he would have told her about Stygian, the memories, the prophecy, everything.

Ava stares at him. Her face softens, and she rubs her forearm. "Why didn't you tell me?"

"I was hurt. You didn't even give me a moment to explain myself at the manor. So, I kept it. To protect it until it was needed. I figured I would join the fight whether you let me or not. Thought this would come in handy."

Ava nods. "One of the reasons I gave the protectors for taking your title away was that you were a threat to Wyntryn's alliances. You could have stopped me. Argued." She purses her lips, stopping herself from continuing. "Sorry, I just… I want to listen to you and hear you out. I think I get wrapped up in my own decisions and forget that listening is something I should do." Her cheeks lift into a sad, small smile. Rais moves to take the necklace off, but she pushes his hand back. "Keep it. It might come in handy."

He drops the amulet beneath his shirt.

"I should probably get back. I'm sure someone is up there looking for me." Ava gets up and jogs up the stairs. She pauses and looks down at him. "Can I get your key to the inn? I left some priceless jewels in there," she says lightheartedly.

Rais pulls the key from his pocket and tosses it up to her. She catches it. Before walking away, she chuckles and meets his eyes. "Can you believe dragons are real? Now that I wish I remembered!"

It's nice to see real happiness within her. Though he can't keep his focus on Ava forever. Rais needs to check on Bryn. They left the inn at the same time he left for the coronation, but he didn't get a chance to ask where they were going.

He roams the streets of the second level. Rais tries not to use the Sonder much so that the talisman doesn't leave a trace.

There's a stone building up the street that stretches to the ceiling. The bottom floor is held up by huge stone pillars that arc upward. The pillars look like stalagmites covered in glowing blue flowers. A bright green moth flutters in front of him. He watches it fly up toward the ceiling. Rais moves underneath the building and listens for Bryn's mind.

A small pressure on his arm causes him to spin around. "Nina?" He can't believe he didn't recognize her mind in the Sonder.

She lets out a gasp of relief and throws her arms around him. "I thought you were dead!"

Nina releases him and steps back. She paints a stern expression on her face and crosses her arms. Vulnerability makes Nina cringe, so it only ever lasts for a few seconds.

Rais grins. "How was Goldryn?" Behind her expression he can tell her heart is fluttering. The Sonder gives away so much when a person isn't actively trying to hide.

"Horrible. Stygian full-on lost her shit." Nina scrunches her nose and looks behind him. "I went to the manor, Rebynrock, and your home village before coming here. I thought you'd be avoiding Ava. Also, why is there a squadron of dead Goldryn soldiers in your village?"

He holds up a finger to signify each of his thoughts. "One, it is no longer my village. Two, that was me. It happened when I lost my mind. Three, Ava and I worked our stuff out, and —"

"I missed one of the arguments? I used to love watching you two bicker back and forth before suddenly not being angry at each other." Nina throws her hands up dramatically. He and Ava haven't changed much.

"That is beyond intrusive," Rais points out. Though he and Ava didn't exactly argue in private at the manor. There used to be so many people there that the roof was the only place they could be alone.

Nina shrugs. "Since I know you're going to ask, yes, I worked out my differences with Willow too. I wanted her to come with me to Wyntryn, but she chose Stygian over me, again."

"I'm sorry." Rais has witnessed Willow and Nina fall in love over the years. It took them a long time to finally see it in each other, but he supposes it was the same for him and Ava. The four of them have been friends for a long time. He's always been closest to Ava, but when she left in the summers, he became good friends with Nina and some of the other students at the manor.

"It's fine. I needed to make sure you were okay, and you are," Nina says.

"Not exactly. The Queens of the Dragon Isles blamed me for their ship sinking and Stygian threatened my life. When I arrived at the manor, Ava took away my title."

"You're kidding me." Nina practically growls.

Rais explains Ava's reasoning and fills in the events since last seeing Nina. He even admits he's been seeing an apparition of darkness. He tells her about Saira and the aftermath of Stygian's treacheries. They sit on the ground like they're still kids, sharing memories of the past and the people they've lost. Nina tells him she thinks he's lost his mind—he agrees.

Bryn. He completely forgot about finding them. Rais stands and turns to Nina. "Can you do me a favor and look for Bryn? I'm going to go check the inn. It's the one down the street from the bank."

"Sure. Let me know if you find them first. I don't want to be roaming the streets forever," Nina says.

"I'll let you know. Thanks."

He jogs through the streets to the inn. His room is a few floors up, but it doesn't take him long to get there.

"Do not touch me," someone says.

Rais turns down the next hallway. Ava has her red dress folded over her arm. Saira's leaning over her, whispering something into her ear. She flinches. A look of terror flashes across Ava's face. Saira's lips stretch into a smile.

Rais can't draw on his energy with the talisman on. His chest burns. He keeps his pace steady as he walks toward them. "Saira."

Saira whips toward him, but he keeps his hand pressed to the stone next to Ava's head. "Is there something wrong?" Saira asks.

"Get away from her."

"I was only congratulating Wyntryn's new Queen. I do owe her for taking care of my little brother," Saira slurs. Ava closes her eyes and turns her face from Saira.

Rais grabs Saira's shoulder and shoves him to the floor. "She said not to touch her. Do you need me to escort you back to Grymyr?"

"I asked around, and there is a dragon here. You lied to me. I want you to take me to it."

Saira didn't ask, he looked through Ava's thoughts. Rais is sure of it. He should have left Saira behind when he had the chance.

Rais grabs Saira's shirt and lifts him. Saira smiles

down at him. Some people never change, do they? Rais punches him, and Saira has to catch himself on the wall.

Ava puts her hand on Rais' chest and pushes him back. If it was anyone else pushing him away he'd fight back. She turns to their enemy. "Saira, what do you want with the dragon?"

"The last living dragon is the one that shed the scale made into a talisman. I'll let you know my plans once I get my hands on that dragon." Does he think the talisman is attached to the dragon? Saira must be extremely clueless. Though Rais supposes Saira hasn't seen what's inside of the amulet Rais wears.

"How about we make a deal?" Ava asks. Rais wants to stop her from offering anything to the man, but he wants to hear what she comes up with. Saira grins. There's blood on his teeth. "I'll take you to the dragon tomorrow if you sign an oath to Wyntryn."

Rais scoffs. She's kidding, right? Rais might have sympathy for Saira, but they can't trust him. Let alone have him on their side where he can access their plans.

"Why would I do that, Your Highness?"

"The Society stole your life. They forced you to kill your best friend. They are the reason your brother is dead," she says. Saira narrows his eyes and looks past her to Rais. Probably thinking, *You, Rais, killed my brother, not the Society.* "You should sign an oath to Wyntryn because we do not turn anyone into mindless soldiers. We protect each other. The Society would kill you if they knew you traveled here with a Wyntryn protector and let him live."

Rais gulps. He's not a protector anymore and how does she know Saira traveled with him?

"It is… intriguing," Saira says.

"Decide now. Sign an oath to Wyntryn or return to

Grymyr. Maybe when they imprison you this time, they won't ever let you out." Ava holds Saira's gaze.

"Where do I sign?"

"Go to the fifth level of the cavern tomorrow morning. You will sign the oath and I will personally take you to the dragon." This is ridiculous. She's negotiating with him. What could Saira have said to make her do that?

Saira backs away from them and enters his room. Rais doesn't even know what to think. He didn't think Saira would agree to it or that Ava would offer.

Ava turns to him. "Wouldn't you rather have him on our side?" She knows him too well.

"He's a powder keg bound to explode." He sighs. "Better that it happens to our enemies and not us."

"That's what I was thinking." Ava picks up her crown from the floor. "You should come with me tomorrow. I'd feel safer if I wasn't by myself. Plus, we still have to stop in that creative district."

"I'll think about it," he says.

Her brows push together as she walks past him. Nina and Bryn step to the side to let her pass.

"What was all this about?" Bryn asks.

At this point, they're inviting just about anyone down there. If Ava is going to trust Saira with Wyntryn's greatest secret. Then she won't mind if he brings a few trusted people of his own. "Do you two want to meet a dragon?" Nina rolls her eyes and Bryn tilts their head. "Good, we leave first thing tomorrow."

Chapter Thirty-Five

Ava

Genevia shoves Saira to his knees. His lips press into a thin smile. Saira's manipulated her, but she must take this risk. Otherwise, what he whispered in her ear may come true. That fate would be worse than death.

Ava holds her hand up to Genevia. "He's not a prisoner here. He has agreed to work on behalf of Wyntryn."

People say to keep your enemies close; she's doing exactly that. If he tries to betray her, then he already knows what will happen. Half of his face is lined with pink scar tissue. Part of his right eyebrow is permanently burnt off. Saira can pretend not to fear her, but she knows somewhere deep inside of him, he is terrified. No one can go through that torture and not be scared to relive it. She knows she can't. Last night she dreamed of being chained to Stygian's throne. She fought against the iron. Screamed at her sister to stop. But the sword still cut through Aran. Her sister still killed Anya. Then, Stygian turned the blade to Ava. It pressed into the dip of her throat. Ava woke up before it drew her blood. Before her sister could take her life.

Ava gestures for Saira to stand. "Are you willing to infiltrate the Society for us?" she asks.

"Yes." His voice is dull. He stands and brushes dust from his knees. His gaze flicks to hers. "Your lover killed my brother. You and I both lost Levi that day. I will work for you because my brother trusted you and he did not trust the Society of the Collective."

"You didn't protect Levi that day," she says. "In the attic. You let him die. If anything, it sounded to me, like you pushed Rais to kill him."

Saira's lips tug upward. "Yes. I suppose I did. You see, I didn't think he would do it. He had a blade to my throat once and did not kill me. Why I cannot know. I do know my mother is the reason I was in that attic. She tried to lock me up again and that's when I sought out Rais and the dragon."

"Why the dragon?"

Genevia steps behind Saira. A hand on her blade.

Saira looks past the stone pillars to the cavern wall. His eyes study it as if there's a phrase written there. She follows his gaze, but there's nothing. "When I escaped my mother's grasp, the Society called for my capture. There are people out there—my friends—who want me dead. I do not want to die. If I have a talisman, I can protect my-self."

The reason seems genuine enough. Saira doesn't know Rais has the talisman and she gains a lot from having a spy in the Society.

Ava pulls the dagger from her belt. She grabs his wrist and holds his arm out, keeping his palm facing up. She pushes his sleeve back. "Thank you for telling me. Relax your arm now, you don't want to lose too much blood."

Genevia keeps close to Saira. Ava places the blade

across the main crease in his palm. "Saira Grenier, do you swear to use the energy of Kanaleigh in defense of the Wyntryn ancestors, land, and me, your Queen?"

"Yes." There's almost emotion in his voice.

"With this oath, you swear to serve Wyntryn for the entirety of your life." She pulls the dagger across his skin and blood pools from the cut. The words come to her easily. A memory she should have never lost. "*Reyani fin* Wyntryn. Let your blood be one with the lands of our ancestors."

Saira fists his hand and tilts it so that blood drips onto the cavern floor. Genevia pulls a cloth from her pocket, then passes it to her. Ava wraps it around the cut on Saira's hand. "Wyntryn will protect you now," she tells him.

Saira holds her gaze. His features are eerily similar to Levi's. What would her old friend think of this? Of Saira becoming an oath-sworn mage of Wyntryn. He wouldn't believe it. If Levi had the chance to change sides, she wonders if he would do it. She wishes she had helped him escape.

The first few weeks after his death, she dreamed of Levi.

It was often the same dream. A replay of the night he died. But when Levi turns to walk back into the library, she grabs his hand. Pulls him into a hug. She asks him to leave the Society and come to Wyntryn with her. He tells her that he would love to. Then he disappears from her arms and falls from the window.

She always woke up screaming.

Ava didn't love him as he loved her, but she wishes she had saved him. Because he was her best friend. Sometimes she needs her best friend.

Saira coughs, and Ava snaps back to reality. She rubs a tear from beneath her eye. "I'll be back later, Genevia. I'm going down to the tunnels again today. Rais will be with me. If anything happens, please come get me."

Genevia bows her head. "Yes, my Queen."

Ava is only a day into being Queen, and she's already tired of it. She had a meeting with Eieran last night to plan a funeral for her cousin and uncle. Tonight, she has a meeting with the protectors. They have to make plans for the war. Eieran said she must decide whether to play offensive or defensive. She has no clue which will be best.

She told Stygian their alliance, although short, was over. Her sister could attack any day now and they'd have to scramble to protect themselves. She doesn't like the idea of waiting for something to happen. They could make the first move and choose where the battle happens. It seems like the logical option, but what if Stygian never attacks? It's an unlikely dream, but a favorable option.

Ava descends the stairs to the lower levels with Saira. It's weird to be near him. She doesn't trust him, but it's too late to change her mind.

At the bottom of the stairs, Rais stands next to the nymph, Bryn. They have short dark hair and tawny eyes. Nina's here too. She's sitting on the last step, opposite Rais.

Rais offers his hand to Ava when she reaches the bottom of the staircase. "Ava, this is Bryn. They have been traveling with me since I left Eventyr."

Bryn bows their head to Ava. "Your Highness." They look to Rais. "He saved me when the ship was sinking."

Ava bites the inside of her cheek. "He's always saving everyone, but himself."

Rais' smile drops. She hadn't meant it offensively.

"Let's get going," he says. "It's a long way down."

Water drips onto the tunnel floor in a steady rhythm. The sound echoes through the hollow mountain. Another set of footsteps adds to theirs. "Your Highness!"

She spins on her heel. Rais' hand brushes against her upper arm. He doesn't do it by accident. He's being protective. Genevia walks out of the shadows and presses her hand against her hip. Catching her breath she says, "I don't mean to intrude, but Stygian sent a message to the manor. One of our mages came to let us know."

"Do you know what it is?" Ava asks.

Genevia glances at Saira and then narrows her eyes. "The mage told me there were two letters. One from Grymyr and one from Eventyr, each confirming an alliance with Goldryn. They were sent with your… um… cousin and uncle. I was told they were dropped on the doorstep of the manor."

Bile rises in her throat. Dropped. Though their bodies have been returned, it is not in an honorable way. Used as a statement. Not respected as the people they were. Ava's hand covers her mouth, and she turns to the wall.

Breathe. Her lungs tighten and she closes her eyes. *Breathe. You are fine. I am fine.* Ava squeezes her eyelids before opening them again. She gulps and meets Genevia's sympathetic gaze. Why does everyone look at her like that?

"Thank you for telling me. Can you send the mages there a message?" she asks. Genevia nods. "Tell them to set a memorial fire, then bury their ashes in the plot past the ancestral fountain. I believe that plot is where my family rests." She can plan a memorial for after. It seems wrong to wait until she's back at the manor to have a burial. The sooner they're buried, the sooner they will join their ancestors.

Genevia bows her head. "Yes, I will have that done. Is there anything else?"

Rais told her yesterday on their way back through the tunnels about his trip from the manor to Metarock. He and Bryn killed at least a dozen Atane and left their bodies scattered out in the snow.

"I want the remains of the Atane outside of Metarock dropped off at the gates of the City on the Sea. If there aren't more than twenty of them already, send a few mages out to track down some more. If you need help alating their bodies, call on me and I'll gladly assist." She squeezes her fingers into a fist. She must stay strong. No more sympathetic gazes. If she gets them from the protectors, then her people will begin to see her that way too. They don't need a damaged Queen. They need a dragon that will fight for them until her last breath. Ava needs to be that. For her mother, for Wyntryn. For herself.

Genevia raises her brows. "Okay. It will be done."

Ava steps away from Genevia and Rais. She pushes past Nina and Saira and clutches her lower ribs. Pain flowers above her right eyebrow. Why does grief follow her? It hasn't left her since her mother's death. She hates the feeling and yet she doesn't know life without it. Every second is painful. If only there was an ocean nearby to jump into. Falling through open air, if only for a few seconds, is enough to shutter the pain from her conscience.

"My Queen," Bryn says. Ava stares ahead. "Listen to the mountain." When Ava doesn't acknowledge her, Bryn takes her hand and presses it flat on the wall. What happened to her being strong? She only lasted a minute before breaking down. She thought her pain was discreet, but it was visible enough for Bryn—a stranger—to notice. Bryn moves their hand next to Ava's. "The energy that birthed and brought us irregulars to life breathes through the very land we walk on. When you cannot breathe, all you must do is listen. The energy will find you and give you life."

Ava listens to the dripping of water. A rock falls somewhere up ahead and a bat flaps its wings. She keeps her eyes closed and lets her mind fall into the Sonder. Air blows through the rock and spreads through her body. *Aathmika*. Even this far away, she's sensing the steady breaths of Aathmika.

Energy pulses through the rock, and Ava pulls on it. Through her fingers and up her arm. It circulates through her blood and settles within her. The abhorrent feeling subsides.

She pulls her hand from the rock and meet's Bryn's gaze. Their eyes are obsidian in the darkness. Ava doesn't have to say thank you because Bryn appears to already know. Ava can see it in their subtle expression. It's not sympathetic or sad, but a shared understanding.

It's sickly that Bryn can understand the pain coursing through Ava's mind and body. No one should ever have to feel this pain. To understand the torment of losing so much.

They continue to traverse through the tunnels until they reach the large doors. Rais presses his hands against the stone and calls out in the ancient tongue. The doors open, and the dragon slithers away from the light, her scales and talons scraping against the stone.

"He's real," Saira says with a giggle.

She, Ava says to herself.

Saira runs into the darkness, and Aathmika bares her teeth. "Let me touch you." Saira splays his fingers before the dragon.

Aathmika slashes her claws and slices through Saira's hand. He screams and yells insults at the fiery beast. He runs to Ava, cursing her name. There's no reason to yell at her. He's the one who was acting like a fool. Light hits Saira's hand, revealing his middle finger which hangs unnaturally against his palm. His cut from her dagger has a parallel wound. Blood pools from his finger and palm down his forearm.

"You did this!" Saira shouts. His eyes are wild as he holds his injured hand close. Any sane person knows not to approach an animal like that. She did nothing. Oddly enough this might be the most emotion she's ever seen from Saira.

Bryn grasps Saira's wrist and holds it before them. "Let me help you." Energy spindles from their hand, creating vines that wrap around Saira's arm. From the vine blossoms a flower. It drops a yellow liquid onto the torn flesh. The wound closes up and heals. "You will have to wash the blood off, but it'll be as good as new by tomorrow."

Healing energy. This is the first time she's seen it. Honestly, she didn't know it existed until now.

With everyone distracted by Saira's dramatics, Ava turns to the dark chamber. The dragon's mind is present in the Sonder now. It wasn't before. Now she can feel it. Tendrils of power reach from the creature. Ava walks toward the beast and calls out to the dragon, *Aathmika.*

Miss Wyntryn, she replies. A deep, guttural voice.

She jumps backward. The dragon spoke to her. *Do you understand me because my ancestors share the blood of drag-*

ons?

Rather, you understand me because of our ancestral tie.

Ava gulps and walks toward Aathmika. The creature now lays on the stone, pushed against the back wall. Ava asks, *Are you trapped here?*

No.

The ground shudders beneath her. She reaches her hand out to the dragon's face. Her fingers grace the rough scales.

Miss Wyntryn, you are in danger. Your heart will soon be pierced by your own hand.

She sends back, *What does that mean?*

Aathmika retracts her head, lifting it toward the ceiling and revealing the pale scales on her neck

"What does that mean?" she asks. The dragon lets out a loud breath and tucks its wings against her sides. "Aathmika, why would I pierce my own heart?"

Four pairs of eyes watch her from behind. She glances back at them. Rais' narrow for a second. Saira is skirting the edges of the dragon's den, searching for the talisman she assumes. He won't find anything here. Ava backs away from Aathmika and goes to Rais. She can see the question burning in his eyes, but she doesn't want to tell him. He will only take it as a sign to hide her away. He's protective enough as is. It will only get worse if he hears the dragon's warning.

"She spoke to you," Rais finally says.

Ava shrugs. "Must be a family thing. She just introduced herself." His brows lower. She makes a show of looking in the cave for Saira. "Should we tell him he'll find nothing?"

"Nah. Let him get clawed again," Nina says.

Bryn's presence is quiet, but Ava can tell Bryn has

something to say about Nina's comment. The forest nymph seems protective of life and energy, whether it's tarnished or not.

They wait for Saira to finish his search. He eventually convinces himself there's nothing there and leaves the darkness, head hanging. The doors shut on their own and the five of them retreat down the tunnels. They don't stop until they reach the city of night. The bioluminescent home of the night nymphs.

Even under the spell of the city, her mind can't shake Aathmika's words. *Your heart will soon be pierced by your own hand.*

Chapter Thirty-Six

Willow

"If she wants a war, then she will get a—" Stygian stops midsentence. She turns to Willow with a smile. A soldier just ran in and whispered something into Stygian's ear. The resulting scowl could cause a bird to simply fall from the sky.

The temperature rises in the room and sweat grows on Willow's brow. She wipes it away. "Willow, darling, you had a vision on the bridge, when you fell to your knees, didn't you?"

"Yes." Stygian always wants to know about her visions. Whether they have anything to do with Goldryn or not. Some may never come true. She has no way of knowing. They may all be a trick of her mind, nothing rooted in reality. Willow believes they're real, but she's used to people doubting her. Stygian often doubts her.

The Queen waves the Goldryn soldier aside. "Throw the bodies in the ravine past Cataclyse Point." The ravine along the border of Iyer City. Stygian sits back on her throne and grips the arms. Willow raises her chin. "Tell me what the vision was of."

Stygian has never been able to see into Willow's mind. If she were to lie, Stygian would never know. It's the perfect opportunity to manipulate Stygian. Plant a seed that would never get there on its own.

Her fingers fiddle with the fabric of her dress. She forces herself to stop fidgeting and pushes her shoulders back. "I saw Ava, lying on the battlefield. Then I saw the people in this city running through the gates."

"Running from what?" Stygian asks.

Willow gulps. "You."

Stygian's laugh is breathy. The Queen brushes her hair from her face. "Why would they run from me?"

"I cannot say." Willow looks at the windows that crown the room. Outside the sky is blue. Stygian has locked her up inside and claims she isn't trustworthy. Willow may be here forever. Maybe her blatant lie has some truth to it. There very well could be a future where the people of Goldryn run from Stygian's rule. Willow could have run and she didn't. *I could be with Nina right now. Instead, I'm here, stalling an inevitable war.*

Clouds cover the sky. Willow blinks idly. "They are afraid of you."

"I have done nothing to them," Stygian says. The lie is meant to give Stygian confidence. So that she doesn't worry about attacking anytime soon. Further the arrogance that will lead to possible demise.

"Not yet." Willow turns from the dais. The concrete between the tiles is stained with Anya's blood. She can't be here. What was she thinking? She can't stop Stygian. Her gaze stays on the tiles as she walks through the room.

"Willow," Stygian says. She keeps walking. "Willow, come back here."

Flames rise in the doorway, blocking Willow's exit.

She stills, staring at the flickering purple. Tears well up in the corners of her eyes. What has she done?

"Tell me, why do they run from me?"

Willow faces the flames. "I would not know. You are a great Queen."

"Do not patronize me." Stygian's hand brushes Willow's hair to the side. When did she get so close? "If you are lying to me about this vision, I will find out soon enough. When the flowers bloom in the north, right?"

"Right." When the flowers bloom in the north.

If only that was a lie.

Chapter Thirty-Seven

Raiden

A blue haze spreads over the city. He stands at the edge of the path leading back into the tunnels. Ava is by his side. She stares down at the night nymphs roaming the sacred streets. "Do you have some time?" Rais asks.

She glances at him. "What?"

He clears his throat. "If you have some time, we can explore the city."

"Oh, I forgot about that. You wanted to take me to the creative district?"

"Are you okay?" he asks. His voice is quieter than before to keep the others from hearing. Ava nods, but her face is drawn.

He turns to Nina and asks her to take Bryn and Saira back to Metarock. If Ava's going to attack Goldryn, then they won't have much time together. War is chaos and there's no telling what the future will bring. Nina shrugs and tugs Saira along with her. Bryn watches him curiously but follows Nina along the outskirts of the cavern.

"Why did you ask them to go?" Ava asks.

"What? Do you not want to be alone with me?" He

wishes his tone wasn't darkened by his worry. He meant to say it with a smile, but he can't force emotion.

Ava bites her lip and air blows through her nostrils. "You are ridiculous, Rais."

"When did you decide to call me Rais again?" he asks.

She rolls her eyes, but he can feel her real emotions through the Sonder. Is she nervous? Ava sighs and says, "I think when I forgave you. I just started thinking of you as…" She rubs her neck. "As my—I don't know. I just started thinking of you as Rais."

His chest tightens, and he turns his face away from her. A quiet laugh escapes him. She was going to say, my Rais, wasn't she? He watches her closely. Muscles in her jaw flinch with her nerves. "You gave me that nickname you know."

"I did?" she asks, with a smile.

He steps past her and leads her down into the city. "When we were kids. You claimed that because you had to say my name so often you wanted something simpler."

She watches the nymphs pass around them. He leads her through the streets to the creative district. "Can I ask you something?" she asks.

"Anything," he says.

"Why didn't you keep your promise?"

He stops in his tracks. She keeps walking and has to turn back for him. "Did I not keep a promise?" He rakes his brain, trying to find what it is she's referring to.

"You promised to never leave me."

He takes a breath. "I never left. You left me."

"I know. I guess, even when I was angry at you, I hoped you'd come to find me. I don't know why. I just wanted you there." Her eyes glisten. "I hated you and wanted you… I understand how I've been selfish. Blaming you for things that are out of your control."

He folds his arms across his chest. "You have every right to hate me. I am not a good person. I try to be, but I have my faults. But I promise you, Ava, I will always be here for you. I will always protect you, even if you do not need my protection. I think of you every second of every day. You can tell me to leave, and I will, but I will never stop caring. You have my heart. That has always been true."

"I don't want you to leave. And I should hate you, shouldn't I? For some reason, I don't. I can't. No matter how hard I try. So, I suppose you're lucky. Because you're stuck with me. I never want you to leave me." A smile is painted on her lips.

"Good."

Music drifts through the streets. Ava turns to it and reaches for his hand. "Dance with me?"

"I thought you hated dancing," he says.

"I never hated it. Disliked is a better word," she says, pulling him toward the sounds.

"Then what changed?"

"In Goldryn I went into the city with Willow and Aliras. It was … unforgettable to say the least." She practically glows when thinking back to it. *Does she know what Aliras did to me?* If she did know, he imagines she wouldn't mention him so casually. She seems to care for the Goldryn soldier, so he won't bring it up.

He runs to keep up with her. The music comes from the waterfall at the back of the city. A gathering of irregulars stands on a bridge that stretches over the water. They play various instruments with delicacy.

Ava pulls him into the throng of people. Crowds

are a nightmare for him, but he'd gladly run into one with her. She lets go of his hand and spins. When was the last time she smiled like that? He genuinely can't remember. Her arms float around her as she moves with the sounds. She's beyond gorgeous. A radiant smile that could melt ice. He crosses his arms, watching her from a distance. Content with seeing her enjoyment.

"Come on, Rais." She grabs his forearm and tugs him to her. His hands slip down to her waist. She rests her hands on his shoulders and forces him to move with her. There's no point in arguing with her. He supposes he needs to loosen up a bit.

From a building near them, a nymph releases neon powder. The bright yellow dust falls onto them. It covers the street, and everyone gathered near the waterfall.

Her happiness breaks through his anxiety, and he joins her in the movements. They turn and dance together underneath the neon lights of the cavern. Her smile is enough to brighten his mood. "You're smiling," she says.

"I am."

She stops moving and her hands slide around his neck. She looks up at him and grins. "I like it here."

"I couldn't tell," he says. Her eyelashes are bright yellow now. He imagines his are too.

"If we survive this war, then I want to turn the manor into a school again. I think it would make my mother happy."

He runs his fingers through her hair. "You know you can do things that will make you happy too."

"I know. That's why I won't run the school as my mother did. I'll find someone else to run it. I want to move to Metarock. I like it here."

"I do too."

"Then you'd stay here with me?" she asks.

He closes his eyes and leans his forehead against hers. "Mhm." She doesn't remember their plan to move to Aysand. But she's queen now, so she couldn't go with him even if she wanted to. He can stay here though, with her. As long as she'll have him.

The talisman burns against his skin. It whispers into his mind. Tendrils of darkness wrap around his waist and pull him into the Sonder. He fights against it in his mind. All while his forehead is barely pressed against Ava's. He wonders if she can hear the whispering too. It doesn't ring anymore. Doesn't deafen his ears with the sound of silence, but it still calls to him. Asks him to release the dangerous energy. The soul within the talisman left him alone for a few days. Now that it's back, he doubts it'll leave anytime soon.

"Is this what it was like before I died in that accident?" Ava asks. The tendrils slip from him and return to the amulet. Those wretched whispers disperse like rats at the sound of her voice.

Rais lifts his head to meet her eyes. "Not always."

She kisses his jaw, and her fingers trail from his throat to his sternum. Tingles spread across his chest. Her smile fades and she steps away from him. "That's because reality always breaks through. Then we remember we're not the only people in the world. I am queen now and there's a war coming. A war I might start. And you are a mage, who lost his title because of my recklessness."

"Ava—" Can she sense it? The soul within the talisman seeping into his own?

"We should get back," she says.

Bryn waves to him in the foyer of the inn.

"Hey," he says. Their rooms have already been paid for, so there's nothing else here for him.

"I can go get the horses ready, if you want to say bye to Ava," Bryn offers.

He holds back a smile. "Thank you, but I already said goodbye." Bryn blinks at him as if he's said something foolish. "What?"

"I'm wondering why she likes you is all."

He rolls his eyes. "Go get the horses ready. I'll meet you there." No one has to convince him to go see her again. It just seems odd to say goodbye again when he'll see her at the manor later this week.

Nina left for the manor this morning. She alated there. Since Rais has the talisman, he must travel by horse. Bryn offered to stay with him.

Rais would have dragged Saira along with him, but Ava decided to send him back to Grymyr. Evidently, he's pledged his loyalty to her because Levites trusted her. She trusts Saira's word enough to have him return to the belly of the beast. Rais doesn't know all the details, but Saira is letting himself be captured by the Society to spy on behalf of Wyntryn.

Rais leaves the inn and jogs to the stairs. He leaps up them as quickly as he can. He doesn't have much time before he has to leave. It's a long journey home.

Ava didn't repromote him, which he doesn't quite understand, though she did give him some responsibility. Nothing more than a commander's role, but it's something. He's supposed to go back to the manor and gather the mages there. They're going to attack Iyer City, one of the smaller cities near the Wyntryn border. Ava wants the battle to be on her terms and in a landscape, Wyntryn mages are used to.

Ava told him of the plans last night after she met with the protectors.

Rais knocks on the fortress' main door. The guards open it and let him through. He assumes she'll be in the war room, so he jogs through the halls until he finds the right room.

The door is closed when he gets there. He presses his fist against the door. He should knock. Rais chews on his lip. Hopefully, it's only Ava in there. He moves his hand to the doorknob and goes inside. Ava stands alone in front of a map. She looks back at him with a smile. "Oh, hey. I thought you would have left by now."

"I wanted to see you, in case something happened before you got to the manor."

Ava comes over to him, and he drops his bag to the floor. "You are not allowed to say goodbye to me, Raiden Hynrule." She must have forgotten their goodbye last night.

"Why is that?" he asks.

She looks up at him with wide eyes. She's mere inches from him. The distance slowly receding. "Because nothing is going to happen to you. I wasted enough time away from you. I can't lose another moment."

He hums his disapproval. "Then you shouldn't have sent me off on my own."

"Are you scared?"

He brushes his fingers across her upper arm. "You are a menace."

She rests her forearms on his shoulders and holds his neck. When they were younger, she was not this forward. He leans down and kisses her. Her fingers hook into his short hair. Her lips aren't chapped anymore. Metarock must be treating her well. He pulls from her. Only inches separate them. "Unfortunately, I do have to go."

"I'll see you soon," she says.

"I'll see you soon," he confirms. Though he isn't convinced by the affirmation. The darkness has been growing in his chest. It's threaded itself through him and has a good hold of him. Ava may not admit to sensing it, but he can see the worry on the edges of her mind. Rais doesn't trust anyone with the talisman, so he has to keep it on. He only hopes that it won't destroy him before he can use it to save Wyntryn.

Rais leaves the fortress and goes down to the stables to meet Bryn. If they move quickly, they can be at the manor in three days.

He rides Oberyn out through the tunnels and down the mountainside, Bryn close behind on the thoroughbred, Robin.

His eyes catch on a small bloodroot plant. Five stems stick up from a crack in the rocks. Small white flowers with a yellow core. The first flowers of spring.

Chapter Thirty-Eight

Ava

The Plane of Verity blankets her in comfort as she steps through into the snow. It's near dusk now. Every window on the manor glows yellow. Few people roam the grounds. It's been five days since she last saw Rais. She meant to leave Metarock yesterday but moving the weapons from the underground armory took longer than expected.

Tomorrow they send their first squadron of mages into battle. Stygian has yet to attack, which leaves Wyntryn with the upper hand.

In the manor, the protectors who have arrived wait for her in the ballroom. They have gathered the mages there to go over the plan with everyone. Ava would go there, but she must talk to Rais first. She listens for his mind in the Sonder. It's often difficult to find him because he has a knack for putting up walls. She figures he's either in his room or the study on the second floor.

She checks the study first. When he isn't there, Ava walks back down the hall and climbs the stairs to the third floor.

No sound comes from the other side of Rais' door. She knocks anyway. Last time she stood here she cowered away. This time she didn't think twice about knocking. The door swings open and Rais keeps his gaze from reaching her. What's wrong with him? Ava pushes the door. It hits his chest, and he backs away without a flinch. The energy around him isn't warm or electric, it's cold.

He runs his hand along his neck and paces. Ava waits for him to speak. He stops pacing and stares at her. His mouth opens, then closes. She wants to yell at him to spit it out, but she holds her tongue.

"I know energy can take the guise of many forms, but I—I'm scared, Ava. It used to go away. I could snap out of it or fight back, but it's… not leaving."

"What are you talking about?" She can't put his phrases together. They don't make any sense. She pulls herself into the Sonder and reaches out to his mind. The energy around him pulsates and withers. It's not normal. She's never seen an aura like it. Certainly not around him.

"It's the talisman."

The dragon's scale, of course. She felt a difference in his mind when he possessed the arrow. The souls of these talismans don't agree with him. Even so, that doesn't explain what he said. What's not leaving? No matter how hard she tries to understand, the Sonder always surprises her. There are many things she didn't forget, but even more that she did.

"Ava?" he asks.

She blinks. Right, she never said anything. "It's attacking you?"

"I don't know how to describe it. It's as if the talisman reaches its claws out and grasps onto me. Tendrils of energy wrap around my mind and body and constrict.

I want it to stop, but there are only a few things that can make it go away." His eyes are full of desperation. She reaches her hand out to him. It only took five days for him to fall into this state. How could it take over his mind so quickly?

"What are those things?" she asks tentatively.

"Well… you—" He studies her face as if he may forget it. "In Metarock the same tendrils wrapped around me. Your voice snapped me out of it. And it was you who stopped the ringing."

Some part of his subconscious must listen to her. Enough to break through the spell cast by this tormented soul. "Rais, you need to take it off."

"I can't," he whispers.

"Why not?"

"We need the alliance with Eventyr, and I have to return it." His fingers grace her jawline.

Her brows push together. "We can put it somewhere safe until we visit Kalenti Alberona."

"What if we go into this battle, and we are vastly outnumbered? We gathered the talismans for a reason. If the dragon scale is this dangerous, no one else should possess it. I need to keep it on because it could be the difference between us living or dying."

"It's already killing you," she says. His hand stills beneath her jaw. She grabs his hand, then tightens her fingers around his. "Take it off."

"No."

She purses her lips. "Then don't ask for my help. Don't risk your life over this. We are powerful with or without them. If anything, we are better off without the talismans. If they can destroy your mind or anyone who possesses them, then I want them far away from here. You aren't thinking clearly right now. You need to take it off."

He pulls his hand from hers and steps back. "We should go down to the meeting. I'm sure they're waiting for us."

"It isn't safe," she says. Her voice barely audible. His white hair falls in front of his eyes. She pushes the locks away and meets his eyes. "Please."

"I'm okay now that you're here." Rais cups her jaw again.

"Don't you dare think touching me will distract me from that talisman around your neck."

"I would rather you be distracted by me," he says. She tries to fight it, but a fire blazes through her. It warms every inch of her body at his touch. His words. Gods, she hates him. He has her so worried she could rip that amulet from his neck, but he would never let her do that. And now his eyes look over every inch of her, teasing her.

"I don't believe you're a good enough distraction," she muses.

He frowns. "You must not be looking close enough."

"I've looked pretty close." She lifts her chin. The tips of their noses brush.

His breath is hot against her upper lip. "Not everywhere."

She presses her lips to his and his arm slides across her lower back. He pulls her to him, and she runs her hand up his chest. This time she touches the amulet. The power vibrates through her skin. It is engulfing Rais. His mind envelops hers, and she's washed with the feeling of darkness. It's lush and cold, but with her body against Rais, the darkness isn't threatening.

Being this close, there is no denying it's consuming

him.

His lips break from hers. "I think I can find a way to control it."

"Were you listening to my mind?" she asks, their bodies still pressed together.

Rais runs his thumb along her collarbone. "No. I felt you touching the amulet."

"How will you control it?"

"I think the talisman is scared of your touch. I stopped hearing it when you touched the amulet. Maybe if I think of you, it will have no power over me."

"I thought you said you thought of me every second of every day," she points out.

He chuckles. "I do."

"Then your plan won't work."

"I'll have to think of something else then." He stares at her lips.

"Let's get downstairs," she says.

Chapter Thirty-Nine

Ava

The next morning, Ava sits in the study. Rais leans against the fireplace. There's nothing but ash within it. The air outside is getting warm enough to keep the manor at a reasonable temperature without fires burning.

"Stay here, please Ava. We already lost Anya and Aran. We can't lose you too," Rais begs. Sweat drips from his brow. Rais told her he doesn't believe they will win this battle, or possibly any other without the talismans. She disagrees.

"No," she reiterates.

"Please, Ava." His eyes bore into hers.

She shakes her head. "No. This is my fight too. You are all more vulnerable without me. If I die on that battle-field, then I will die protecting my region — protecting you. What you've been going through these past few days with that talisman scares me. I will not leave you alone. Not if I can break whatever control it has over you."

He looks up at the ceiling; a tear falls down his cheek. "I can't lose you. Not again."

"You won't." She pushes off the couch.

"If this war never ends, one day I will." He sucks in a breath. "It's selfish, but I need you safe."

She presses her hand to the center of his chest, pushing him against the wall. "You hear me when I tell you if it comes down to me or my sister, I will be the one to live. I will fight with every breath I have. I will use every ounce of energy flowing through my veins. I will drag the entire city down before I let her take my life. I can't lose you either, Rais. I swear to you, that you will see me at dawn—standing over a battlefield where Wyntryn prevails. You need me, and I need you. Wyntryn is greater than us and I will not abandon this battle because you are worried about me."

His throat tightens as he looks down at her. "Can you at least stay here for now? I can send Bryn to get you if we can't win without you."

Ava doesn't want to fight him. She will give him comfort by agreeing to his request. But those are not at all her intentions. She won't leave her people alone out there. Not when she started this war. "Okay."

"Thank you." He reaches up and rests his hands on her cheeks. He leans down and presses his lips to her forehead. The talisman is a beating heart over his own. It pulsates with energy. Ready to blow. She can see it in the Sonder spindling within him, wrapping its tendrils around him. Hugging him as if he is the only one who can rescue the energy from its prison.

Ava leans into the wall where his back was pressed only moments before. She watches him leave the room and listens to the sound of his armor as he moves down the stairs. She hears the faint conversation between him and Bryn. It disappears as they leave the manor.

She breaks her mind from the Sonder to see Nina

enter the study. "You aren't waiting for that last group, are you?" Nina asks.

"Not a chance." She smiles, pushing off the wall. "There's something I need to retrieve before we go."

"What?"

There's no way she's avoiding that battlefield. No good queen would sit around while her people risk their lives. "A talisman," Ava says with a smile.

"Rais going to kill you," Nina says.

Ava leaves the study and moves down the stairs on steady feet. "He wouldn't dare."

She pulls her cloak from the rack in the foyer and slips it around her shoulders. Opening the door, she walks out into the snow. Nina follows behind her. To protect her or simply out of curiosity, she doesn't know, but she doesn't mind either. It's likely Rais told Nina to follow her.

"We do need you alive, you know," Nina says from behind.

"That's why I'm getting the talisman." Ava looks over her shoulder. "You're not going to stop me?"

"Absolutely not. Just ... you know, be careful or whatever."

Ava chuckles. "Yeah, thanks."

When she enters the pathway into the woods, her mind begs her to turn around, but she can't. She has to get the arrow. She barely stood a chance against her sister last time. If she went onto that battlefield without the talisman, she might get herself killed. Ava can't risk that outcome. Even if talismans don't always accept their possessor, even if it might destroy her mind, she has to wield it. To save the region she forced her mother to leave behind. That's why Rais refused to take off the amulet. If he can trust it, so can she. It still terrifies her.

Ava wonders where she would be now if her mother didn't die. If she never worked with the Society, if Levi never confirmed their identities in that car, or if Saira never fired that bullet. Would Levi be alive too? Would she be nothing but a girl, living in a stone manor in the middle of Wyntryn, in love with a boy with golden eyes? Would her father have stayed? Would she even be friends with Levi?

Ava glances at Nina who walks by her side. Nina scowls ahead. When she notices Ava looking at her, she shoots Ava a warning glare. Ava chuckles to herself. She doesn't need to worry about her past, nothing can be changed. She must keep going, keep fighting until she makes it out on the other side. If there is another side.

The snowy path begins to narrow. It's only been a few months since Stygian burned this forest to ash. Yet the trees are fully grown all around. Huge oaks tightly packed together. The small forest is thriving, wrapping around the clearing with vibrance. A life intent on protecting an ancient fountain tucked away at its center.

She stops at the very edge of the energy field encircling the clearing. It's too windy and loud to hear, so she sends a thought to Nina. Stay here or go to the edge of the trees and wait for me.

Nina gives her a look, but she can't go into the clearing with Ava. Nina seems to understand and backs down the pathway.

Ava turns back to the clearing. A solid sheet of white blocks her way. Held up by what, she doesn't know. This whole world is run by magical energy. It runs through the living and the dead. This place is held up by the spirits of irregulars. She forces her foot through, and then the rest of her. Until she stands in the empty clearing, before the large stone fountain. Voices and visions don't attack her right away. She slides into the Sonder, watching as blue orbs appear in the air around the fountain. They bob along invisible currents in the air. The wind thrashes the trees beyond her, but the air is frozen here.

She moves to the edge of the fountain and drops to her knees on the soft grass. As she goes to reach her hand into the water, a raspy voice coats her mind. *Child, you do not belong here. Leave before you are unable.*

Pressure builds around her skull. She fights against it and presses her fingers through the surface of the water. It burns her skin. The very particles attack her. Ava fights the tears and grazes the bottom with her fingertips. She feels for the arrow across the smooth bottom.

We have warned you, it rasps into her mind.

Sharp pains shoot through her skull, and she cries out against it. She thrashes her hand around, searching for the arrow, but she can't find it. Ava falls back into the grass, bringing her shaking hands to her temples. She tries to build the walls in her mind as Rais taught her. Desperate to block the invaders.

"Please," she begs them. "I need it to fight against Goldryn. I am not strong enough on my own." She gasps out as the pain begins to reverberate through her body.

The daughter who tried to kill her mother. A child of deceit. A friend of lies. We would rather see you fail. Its voice ricochets through her.

"You helped me in Rebynrock," she shouts into the clearing. "Ancestors, you worked through me. Work through me now as you did then. I have sinned and I have lied, and I have hurt those I loved. I've lost my memories for it. I've lost my best friend for it. Let me avenge my cousin and uncle, our bloodline. Let me redeem myself in the eyes of my ancestors."

The pressure in her mind retreats, and the source of the raspy voice in her head leaves. The orbs in the clearing move away from her. Ava forces herself to her elbows, and then onto her knees. Sitting at the edge of the fountain is a smooth obsidian arrow. Carved from the very mountains in that land.

She reaches for it, then wraps her fingers around the arrow. The thrum of the metal moves through her bones. It soothes the pain her ancestors inflicted on her. Ava stands. "Thank you."

Ava steps out into the blizzard that awaits her. She holds the arrow close to her chest and fights through the angry storm. As she approaches the edge of the wood, Nina waits for her just beyond the tree line. As soon as she exits the small forest, the storm breaks. The skies are clear.

Nina sits on the stairs at the front of the manor. There's something wrapped in brown paper beside her.

"Good. You're still intact." Nina's eyes are brighter in the early spring sun, causing them to become drops of honey.

"I am," Ava says. Her head still spins.

Nina tosses a package into the snow before her. "That was on the doorstep when I came back. Has your name on it."

Ava murmurs thanks to Nina, then goes inside with the package.

Ava opens the package to find a bow and a quiver filled with arrows. A note is tied to the bow with a blue string. *Found this in Eventyr. You should keep practicing, my lady.*

A gift from Aliras. He told her once if she could master a bow and arrow, then she could shoot fire arrows. She assumed he was joking. A way to make fun of her. This must mean he was serious. She never got good at using a bow, but she could.

She sets it aside on her bed and holds the talisman out before her. She brushes her fingertips across the thin metal. She had warned Rais of this very talisman in Rebyn-rock. It had changed the very aura of his mind. Now in her hands, she can't imagine what it will do to her.

There are stories that the original Wyntryn, Kaatar, had become a mad king. After fusing his blood with that of a dragon, he died. When he came back to life as an irregular, the fusion of blood caused his mind to slowly dissipate. He was driven into madness.

Those five souls who fused themselves into the talismans had a similar fate. The minds within each object became twisted and damaged.

It is no secret that the mad king of the Dragon Isles was afflicted by the talisman he got his hands on. That's why his daughter, Natalia, took it from him and hid it in the Wyntryn mountains. After ridding of the talisman, she sent a letter to Rais telling him of its location. Even the Queen of Eventyr, Kalenti, had suffered a maddened state. Although she eventually found a way to control the talisman's temptations.

These stories don't give her much hope. To survive the powers of the talisman, she will have to be careful with it. It might destroy her before she gets a chance to save her people.

Rais insinuated once that she could be a talisman herself. She's never hit a bottom to her power, but she isn't sure how the talismans work. If they are simply vessels of summoning energy or if they're something other. Like a filter for energy to flow through — an amplifier.

She sets the arrow aside, then pulls the wrappings

off the bow and quiver. The bow has a dragon carved into the wood. The quiver has a dragon image as well. Except the quivers embroidered with gold and dark blue thread. It matches her mage's coat perfectly. Aliras must have had these customized for her a while ago. There's no way he found such specific pieces in an Eventyr market.

Ava goes to her armoire and pulls out the blue metallic armor that Eieran brought to her. He said it was custom-made for her before her mother's death.

She told Rais she would stay at the manor, but her people are out there fighting. She needs to be there with them. What kind of Queen abandons her people?

She pulls off her tunic and leggings. She puts on a tight-fitted black shirt and pants before overlaying them with the armor. It's a feat to get it on. Though her weapon skills are nonexistent Armor is more than necessary.

There's a holster on the armor that fits her dagger perfectly. She goes to her bed and grabs hers. It slides into the opening perfectly. Ava straps the arrow talisman to her belt. It will be there if she needs it. She puts the quiver on and then secures the bow on her back.

Her crown sits on her bedside table. A ruby in her life of ash.

There's no one here to tell her what to do. Anya and Aran were her family. She could have confided in them, but she left them behind for her sister. Traded their presence for their killer's. Ava can't do the same to her people. Her power could be the difference between losing this battle or winning it.

Ava grabs the crown and looks in the mirror. She puts it on, then adjusts it so that it sits comfortably on her head. She looks herself up and down, then takes a deep breath. There's no avoiding the past now. She is her mother's daughter. This war is starting because she decided to attack Goldryn. If they don't succeed, then the blood is on her hands.

She alates into the forest beyond the fountain. Snow litters the shaded ground. Brown speckles the snow around two mounds of dirt. Gravestones litter this area of the forest, but there aren't gravestones for her cousin and uncle. Instead, pebbles are neatly piled atop their graves.

Ava presses her fingers into the dirt where her family lies. "Ayatha Itzal malla reyani Anya Petrichor ta Aran Petrichor fin." She asks the goddess of death to carry her family safely to the end.

Wyntryn is not religious. Gods and goddesses are an eastern continent belief. Willow was the one who taught Ava about them, and she shares a blessing as a safety net, in case they are real. The ancient language was spread across all civilizations in Kanaleigh, but the beliefs are separated by cultural divides.

Her people believe that when someone dies, their body and energy return to Kanaleigh, and their soul rises to join the night sky. That's why she asked for Anya and Aran to be buried without her. She wanted them to join their ancestors. Before the burial, the bodies are burned to ash before because fire helps the souls reach the stars. Then they place the remains in the ground so that their body and energy can rejoin Kanaleigh.

Ava stands from her family's graves and listens to the forest. The quiet whispering has returned, but this time it's not coming from nowhere or the back of her mind. It's coming from Rais.

He told her there's been darkness lurking in the distance, following him. This ringing is not the voice of silence, but the voice of the talisman speaking to his unconscious mind, controlling him without his knowledge. What she doesn't understand, is why she's hearing it.

Ava closes her eyes and pictures the Goldryn border. She tugs on the energy around her and enters the Plane of Verity. If what she believes is true, she needs to get to him. She and Rais have always been connected, but this is more than him reaching out when he's drowning. The talisman is slowly destroying his mind. He needs to take it off.

Chapter Forty

Raiden

Mages gather outside the manor. The sun is past its peak, an hour or two from dusk. Everyone will know soon enough that he has the talisman.

"Rais!" Eieran calls from across the clearing. His cousin walks to him. "You know, I wish I could still call you Golden Sparrow. It was cute."

Rais lifts his brows. Sure, that's exactly how he wishes people to see him. "Where do you need me?" Rais asks.

Eieran pats his shoulder. "I got Hyacin and Osidias on the second line of defense. I was thinking you and I should get there first with the mages that specialize in stealth. They're gathered over by the trees." Eieran points to the far side of the clearing. "With that talisman you can manifest some nasty storms, right?" Rais told the protectors in their meeting yesterday about the dragon scale.

"I suppose. Do you want me to alter the weather as a distraction?" Rais asks. It's a smart move. If they infiltrate the city without Goldryn knowing they're under attack, they can keep Stygian's main army away longer.

"When we get there, we're entering from the north-western gate. We have to get their archers down first. Be careful about how you attack, cousin, we don't want to kill these people."

"I will be careful." Rais looks out to the horizon. He can only be careful if he can control the talisman. Hopefully, their ancestors are on his side. "If Stygian orders her people to start killing us, then we have to protect ourselves."

Eieran narrows his eyes. "I know."

Rais joins the group of mages at the edge of the clearing. Erka is one of them. Nadia is there too—the owner of the inn near Rebynrock. He's glad she decided to join them.

Bryn runs up to his side, a bundle of herbs in their hand. "Are you fearful?" Bryn asks.

"Yes, as any sane person would be," he says. Though Rais has not felt sane since he put the talisman around his neck.

A young mage with blond locks stares up at him. "What should we expect? Most of us have only fought against Atane. Not people."

He glances over the faces that now stare at him. He coughs nervously. "We do not know what we are alating into. But we do know that we are Wyntryns. We also know that our enemy, Queen Stygian, has killed two of our protectors. Anya and Aran spent their lives loving and protecting us. If you are nervous or afraid, remember they are with us. Our ancestors fight at our side. Think of the family you have lost in the wars Goldryn has waged against our region. Fight for your friends, your family. Fight for your home. Wyntryn survives because Wyntryn is one."

"Wyntryn survives, because Wyntryn is one," they

repeat back to him.

Blue filters into his vision as the Sonder surrounds him. Tendrils of darkness tug him away from the manor. They beckon him to unleash his power here. The young mage asks another question, but Rais looks to the trees. The darkness rises in the distance. He fights against the urges forced upon him and grapples onto a line of energy leading into Goldryn. He alates to the edge of a ravine outside the northern Goldryn city. The stench of death is in the air. Rais looks down into the ravine to see dozens of rotting Atane.

The Wyntryn mages appear around him. He hadn't meant to lead them here yet. Eieran hadn't given him the order. He only knew the darkness was digging into him and that he doesn't have control over it. He figured here, where the battle will take place, he can safely release the bottled-up energy.

Bryn steps through the Plane of Verity to his side. Eieran arrives last and steps in front of the crowd of mages. He pulls out his sword and holds it at his side. His cousin gives him the side eye. "I'll lead us to the gate. Nadia, stay behind with Rais and Bryn. Their roles are vital to this mission, so protect them." Eieran raises his sword, and he stalks off toward Iyer city.

The mages follow Eieran across the hill.

Rais didn't know Eieran gave Bryn a task of their own. He's curious what it'll be. Bryn sits down on the ground and pushes their fingertips into the dirt.

It doesn't take long for Eieran and the mages get to the city gates. Instead of breaking through Eieran waves his hand at them. Bryn closes their eyes, and the ground visibly shakes beneath them. Vines grow from the ground by the city gate. They wrap through the stone and break the bricks apart. The gate falls inward, and the wall begins to crumble around it. Bryn continues to pull the city walls down. Brick by brick. Shouts echo from the city and Rais stares at Bryn. Their abilities are magnificent.

Eieran's voice enters his mind. *Now.*

Rais pulls on the energy from the talisman and taps into the air's electricity. He spreads the energy he harnesses across the open sky and electrifies the air. He pushes clouds over the city and yanks on bolts of lightning. The lightning falls around the edge of the city. He uses the talisman to hold onto the storm. Meanwhile, he uses the Sonder to search for Goldryn guards along the city wall.

Each time he locates an enemy's mind, he focuses on them and strikes lightning close by. Bolts this size are deadly. He must be careful where his lightning strikes or he could cause unnecessary fatalities.

He keeps this up for more than thirty minutes. In that time two more squadrons of Wyntryns arrive. No one notices them near the ravine, but Rais knows Stygian is on her way. It won't be long before she arrives with her army. He must hold on until then. He can't lose control. Not yet. Tendrils of darkness wrap around him in the Sonder. They tighten around his chest and stomach. Rais coughs on his own breath. The talisman is trying to overtake him, but this time it isn't only in his mind. It's attacking him through the Sonder. He already knew the soul inside didn't align with his, but he didn't expect it to physically hurt him.

Rais loses control over the storm, and he falls to his knees. Lightning begins striking the Goldryn soldiers. Rais tries to retract the energy back into himself, but nothing happens. Energy rattles through him into the atmosphere. His mind grows fuzzy. *Stay in control.*

Saira told him to bow to the talisman's power. He

shouldn't take the energy—he should let the talisman give it to him. Rais gives up the fight and lets the tendrils sink into his skin. The darkness wraps around his mind and tightens like a snake. He screams, but he can't hear himself. Was it out loud or only in his head? Someone grabs his shoulder, but Rais can't see who. His vision is gone.

The tarnished soul consumes him.

He grasps for the amulet at his neck, but his fingers can't find it. Is he even moving? He can't feel his fingertips. Rais tries to take control of the storm again, but it doesn't work. It's not the same as at the manor. He thinks he stands back up, but he can't tell. People shift around him. Screams sound from the valley below. Heat like fire burns against his skin. The darkness twists through him like a blade.

His mother's voice whispers into his mind. *Silent bird, fly through the night. Open your mind to mine. Hear the call and follow the stars comforting our cries. The ones on our path light the way. Sweet, sweet ringing. Silent bird, fly through the night. On the wind, we rise and rise. Hear our singing. Tame your heart and open your mind. Sweet, sweet ringing.*

Chapter Forty-One

Ava

Ava alates into the center of the storm. She spins on her heel watching the thrumming of battle. Sword's clash. A stark stench of death hangs heavy in the air. Lightning strikes fall all around her. They must be coming from Rais because they don't have the same green hue as Eieran's. Ava searches for him in the crowds of pulsating bodies. Blue and purple uniforms practically fuse together in the dusty air. If she can't see him, then he can't find her.

"The Queen is here!" someone yells.

Ava doesn't know if they're talking about her or Stygian. An arrow flies by her head. Ava's heart lurches. Her hand brushes the arrow at her hip. She can't use the talisman here. There are too many of her people. What if she loses control and can't focus the fire? She leaves the arrow where it is and draws on the energy around her, lighting fire in her hands.

A Goldryn soldier runs at her with a sword. She flicks her hand, and he goes up in flames.

"Ava!" She turns to Genevia. "It's Rais, something is happening to him. Bryn can't stop it. He needs your help." Genevia gasps for breath. Her face stricken with panic.

"Where is he?" she asks. This uncontrolled lightning has to be coming from him. The bolts strike randomly, sending rocks and people flying. More dirt flies into the air with each strike, adding to the already hazy atmosphere.

Genevia points away from the city to the edge of the battlefield. A cry escapes her lips at the sight. She runs toward him, but there are hundreds of people between them. It's not safe to alate here. She could end up pierced by a sword. She has to go through.

Goldryn soldiers try to block her path. She sets more aflame with barely a thought.

He's not far from her now. A Goldryn soldier crosses her path. She tries to set him aflame, but he wears armor that won't catch fire. The soldier raises rocks from the ground and sends them flying at her. She ducks and one crashes behind her. Another scathes her elbow, one of the few places not covered by metal armor. Blood spews from the wound. Chunks of stone rise from the ground again. Too close for her to avoid. She gathers energy and blasts it in front of her. The rocks hit the barrier and slow down. They crash into the dirt barely three feet in front of her.

Something hits her back. She turns and sets the other soldier on fire. A rock hits her head, and she falls into the dirt. Her mind begins to shut down, and her senses collide into one. Genevia lets out a battle cry and slices the rock thrower's throat. The world goes dark.

Chapter Forty-Two

Willow

Stygian is down in the throne room yelling at her mindless soldiers. That gives Willow at least a few minutes. Willow scales the stairs to Stygian's chambers. The talisman wasn't with Stygian this morning. If Willow can get it, then she can leave the city and bring the talisman to Nina.

Willow twists the doorknob and throws the door open. Stygian's chambers are ransacked. The glass door is shattered, a broken chair on the deck. Chunks of glass and clothes are thrown around the room. Stygian has utterly lost her mind.

Willow goes to the bathroom. She steps to the window and presses her back against the glass. She takes five steps forward and bends down to her knees. What Stygian doesn't know about Willow's abilities, is that she can see everything in someone's mind. Not only memories or thoughts, but Willow can search someone for specific things. All she needs is to be touching them for long enough. She drags her fingers along the edges of the tile and lifts the square stone up. Underneath is a small box.

She pulls it out and lets the tile drop back down. Willow opens the box and grabs the talisman. It's a small pink gem wrapped in gold wire.

She holds it in her fist and leaves Stygian's chambers. That was much easier than she thought. Luckily today Stygian had something to distract her. Willow carefully descends the steps. At the bottom of the steps, she presses herself into the shadows.

"You will gather the army and send them to Iyer city now! That witch is trying to steal my crown!" Stygian lets out a guttural scream and sends a sphere of purple fire into the wall. Then Stygian fades into the Sonder.

Willow shuts her eyes. Did Ava attack Iyer city?

There's no time to question it. She must get there now. If Wyntryn is attacking Goldryn, then Nina's in danger. There's no time to stall. If Willow can get the talisman to Nina, she can use it to protect her people.

Willow pulls herself into the Plane of Verity. She searches for a breach in Stygian's charms. There's a flow of energy that will take her directly into Iyer city. She grasps it and alates.

The streets are empty. All the soldiers fight on the hills outside. The walls around the city have been reduced to crumbled rock.

She tightens her fingers around the pink crystal and runs to the broken wall. Nina must be out here somewhere. Willow only has to find her.

At the edge of the battlefield, near the ravine, is a sphere of pulsating lightning and darkness. Clouds whirl around it. Is that Rais' energy?

The battle has mostly subsided now. Some soldiers still spar and energy is thrown around the hillside, but nearly everyone stares at the darkness. Willow pulls herself into the Sonder in search of Nina. She finds her mind near the cloud of darkness.

Willow pushes past the soldiers. They don't even notice—or care—that she's there. Willow runs across the torn-up ground and jumps over fallen soldiers. Once she's closer to the gathering darkness, she catches sight of her. "Nina!" she shouts over the thunder. Nina looks around until she spots Willow. She seems okay. There are no visible injuries.

Nina runs to her and sweeps her off her feet, pulling her into a hug. "Thank goodness you're okay. I was worried you'd be here," Nina says.

Willow pushes away from Nina and grasps her hand. Willow places the taaffeite talisman onto her palm. Though some still fight in the field, Iyer City's defenses have been destroyed. It would be smart for Stygian to retreat. And whatever is happening with that darkness can't be stopped by the talisman. "You need to run. Take this and go," Willow says.

Nina looks down at the talisman. "Is this—"

"Yes. Stygian left it in Goldryn to protect the city in her absence. She doesn't know I took it or that I even know where she hides it. This will not be the only battle in this war. Take it far away from here."

Nina kisses Willow's cheek. "Only if you come with me."

"I—"

"You can't," Nina guesses. "Then come find me when you're ready."

"I will," Willow promises.

Nina hardens her expression, then glances at the gathering darkness. "Save him."

Willow looks to the darkness—to the lightning. It is

Rais.

Chapter Forty-Three

A sound resonates around Ava. It's the cry of the child within her. Swaddled in hope and disparity. Those growing pains never subsided. Not even now, as she lays upon the battlefield. A girl who was forced to become a queen. Forced to face terrors that life should have protected her from. But here she is, her hair knotted, her skin slick with sweat, and blood clotted on her elbow. Her face worn, covered in dirt and grime. She lays in the dirt, shivering. The sun is hot on her skin, but she is cold.

Terribly cold. She stares into the brown land, and not a foot away is a single strand of lavender. A small vibrance in a sea of bland. Like her blue dress on the night of the rising moon ball. Bright in that dull apartment in Grymyr. A tear slides across her cheek as she closes her eyes. She sees his whitish hair in her mind. A memory of his soft smile and the lines on his face that reflect those of someone much older than him. They have both suffered more than anyone should ever have to suffer. Seventeen and eighteen, barely even old enough to live on their own. Leaders in a war they didn't start. Tying up the loose ends of centuries of conflict between their ancestors.

With the Sonder, Ava searches through the nearby minds. She can't give up now. She must fight. For her people, for her mother, for herself. She pushes her mind through the battlefield. Then she finds him, a familiar mind. Shrouded in darkness. Something eating away at him, drowning him in the unfamiliar.

She gets to her knees, then to her feet. "Rais!" Ava's voice crackles from her throat. A wildfire grows in her soul with the rise of her panic. She cannot let that darkness take him. If she loses Rais again—no. She will never lose Rais. Not ever.

Ava stumbles across the torn-up ground. Rais. Soldiers try to block her path, but she won't let them knock her down again.

Her lungs fight against her. She might throw up, but she has to get to him.

Ahead a man is crouched over Rais. She fumbles for the bow and pulls it before her. She notches the arrow into place and pulls back. The man is covered in the deep purple of the Goldryn uniforms. "Get away from him!" she shouts.

Lightning slides around the two of them. It slips into the air, sparking and bending. Darkness flies in arcs around Rais and the Goldryn soldier. Ava watches in horror as Rais' lightning is consumed by the talisman's dark energy. She runs toward them, but she's thrown back by the energy. It billows in huge waves.

The dark lightning spreads wider and wider consuming the ground. Dirt flies into the air and whips across her face. This energy is wild and untamed—tainted by the talisman. Willow's voice cuts through the air, shouting something Ava can't make out.

Ava falters and resets the bow. She can't miss this time. Her gaze goes to the Goldryn soldier, and she pulls her arm back but lets it drop. What if she hits Rais instead of the soldier?

"It's Rais!" Willow shouts. She screams it over and over, but Ava can't tear her gaze from the Goldryn soldier standing over him.

A hand grasps her shoulder and shoves her to the ground.

"What's wrong with you?" Stygian shouts at her. Ava flinches at her voice. Is she causing this? Did Stygian push Rais to this point of breaking? Stygian stands over her. "He is going to destroy the whole city if we don't stop him!"

"It's not Rais doing that," Ava insists. She knew that talisman was going to break him. She should've taken it when she had the chance.

Stygian rips the bow from her hands. "There is no soldier, sister. It's a vision I gave you, but if you won't stop this madness, then I will."

Stygian lifts the bow and pulls back. Ava jumps to her feet, but the arrow is already flying.

Lightning falls to the ground and disappears into the Sonder. Rais turns to her and the Goldryn guard fades away.

His eyes go wide, and his fingers stretch around the wound. She shot him. Stygian drops the bow to the ground and Ava flings fire into Stygian, sending her flying into the mud. No. Not again. She can't lose him too.

The world blurs and Ava screams, but the arrow has already hit its mark. Ava watches as he falls to the grass. His electricity dissipates from the air. He grasps at the arrow and begins to pull. "Stop Rais, wait!" Ava calls to him, running in his direction.

His eyes are black. His mind is almost unrecognizable. He is fading away.

She sprints to his side.

His body convulses, blood flowing from the wound in his chest. His breathing is ragged. Darkness consumes his mind, blanketing the space around them with endless pressure. She drops to her knees beside him, searching his mind with her own, fighting the consuming darkness for him. His hands are pressed against the wound, but it's too severe for his efforts to do anything.

"No." She moves his hands and presses around the wound. Why won't the blood stop? "No, no, no."

Oh gods, please let this be a dream.

She begins to shake, pain ricocheting through her head. "No. No." Ava wraps her fingers around the amulet and yanks it from his neck. She flings it onto the torn-up ground. Not even caring if someone takes it. Rais is bleeding out.

His eyes look through her, the gold rings are nothing but a pale whisper in the dark. What can she do? She's not a healer. Bryn is nowhere in sight and the bleeding won't stop. It won't stop. Why won't it stop? Ava presses around the wound with panic. "Rais?" she asks. He stares past her. Bryn can heal. If Bryn can get here, then Rais will be fine. Ava just has to bring him back to reality. Remind him of who he is. "Do you like me?" her words wobble out. His muscles flinch against the pain.

"You need to kill me," he gasps.

She cries out at his words, her hands shaking. She brushes his hair back, but her hand is covered in blood. It stains his white hair red. "No, you say everyone likes you, Ava. You're the best." Her gut falls, and her chest heaves.

"And I say, no. Do you like me?"

"Please—" His voice is distant, his mouth open. Blood dribbles down his chin.

"Say it please, please Rais." *No. No. No.* "Please." She can't lose him. Not yet. Not ever.

Part of her knows what's coming, but she doesn't want to believe it. She wants to live in the memory of his blissful heart and caring soul. She wants to go back in time to when they shared a conversation in the light of the city— in her father's old apartment. Right before Rais kissed her in the hallway. She wants to dance with him in the library and sink into his warm presence. She wants to go back to the manor, to when they were nothing but kids. When they breathed in aromas and fell over in endless laughter. She wants Rais to have a life of adventure, of the blissful happiness he's dreamt of. She wants to hand the crown to someone else and travel the world at his side.

His hand reaches up to her face. "Please end the darkness. It won't go away."

She shakes her head. "You're supposed to say that no matter what you will always be my person," she whispers to him. Tears stream down her face. She brushes his cheek as his eyes beg her to do the unthinkable. Her body fights her, as she reaches for her dagger. The dagger he gave her. Her hand shakes as she brings it to his chest, centering it over his heart.

She wants to live a lifetime with him. To make up for the time they spent away, to make up for the memories she lost. She wants to love him and hold him. To jump from cliffs together and bathe in the salty ocean. She loves him and he loves her. But he lost himself to the talisman and he's bleeding out on the grass. Underneath their ancestors, who are doing nothing to save him.

"I—I can bring you back. You will be free from the darkness."

He closes his eyes, fighting to breathe. "No. This is my end. You do not need me anymore."

"I can't. I won't." The tears stream faster as her body shakes with the words, at the mere thought of losing him. "I need you. You are my everything. I can't live in this world without you." She sees the lights of the city, his face bending down to hers. She feels his lips against hers, and the way the world bent with them as they fell in love.

His hand falls slack beside him, and his coughing grows worse. Blood soaks him. "It hurts, Ava." His voice falters. "I can't take it anymore. There's no stopping the darkness." The tears on his face are red against his skin.

Willow is close by. Ava turns to the people gathered nearby. "Willow!" she screams. Her hand holds onto Rais' shoulder. He mumbles nonsense into the air. Willow breaks from the crowd and stumbles toward her. Tears stain her skin. "Is there any way we can save him?" she asks.

Willow shakes her head. "It pierced his heart," she chokes out.

Ava nods hurriedly. "But I—I can bring him back to life."

"No. Alys already did. He died in the fire that killed his parents." Willow kneels close enough to lay a hand on Ava's shoulder, but Ava shakes her off.

She chokes on the air. Ava turns back to him and twists the dagger in her hand. He coughs up blood. His eyes find hers. "It's… okay," he forces out. She shakes her head.

"I can't."

He reaches for her hand and forces the dagger above

his own heart. It doesn't have to be this way. It shouldn't have to be, but his eyes are filled with pain. Blood pools around them and soaks into the grass. In the Sonder, his mind is steeped in darkness. "You will always be my person, Ava."

She closes her eyes and prays for forgiveness. "And you will always be mine." The words fall out, piercing her mouth like shattered glass as she slides the dagger into his heart.

His breathing stops, and his shaking subsides. She opens her eyes to see him staring back at her. No, he's not looking at all. His eyes are open, but it's as if they are empty. Panic rises in her at the sight of him. Her heart breaks apart, and she screams into the night.

Ava holds tight to his body, pulling it against her and rocking him in her arms. Her face is wet with tears. Her lungs jump with her sobs. An echoing, earth-shattering cry for her love. For her Golden Sparrow. Ava slings her head back and lets out another scream. The world goes distant and all she can see is a deep blue burning fire.

Every Goldryn left on the battlefield who can burn does. Faded in her peripheral are the blue blazes of the enemy soldiers.

The only person she has in this world is Rais, her loyal, protective, kind Rais. Her person. The only person in her life who will ever really know who she is. And he is gone. Left to join their ancestors, walking through the stars. Taken away by the malicious darkness that seeps through this world.

Ava clings to his body desperately, holding her face against his. With every second it grows colder, and she loses more control of herself. Falling further and faster into nothingness. She lays him back on the grass and presses her fingers to his temples. She knows what Aathmika meant now. She would slide a dagger into her own heart. Rais was her heart.

All she wants is to live a lifetime with him. All she wants is to love and hold him.

Lavender hair swings near her face. Willow grasps her shoulders and pulls her away. "No!" Ava yells. "Please don't take me away, he needs me!"

"He's not here anymore. You can't help him." Willow hushes her.

"No!" she cries out, fighting Willow. Her hands search for Rais, grasping at the air and the ground to get to him.

Willow struggles to her feet and pulls Ava to her. "It's okay, Ava. He's safe now. It's going to be okay."

Ava crumples into her. Her fire dissipates with her. "I just want to hear his voice." She says barely loud enough to hear. "I just want to hold him."

Stygian stands behind them. A sweltering rage replaces the deep sadness within her. Ava pushes off Willow and turns to her sister, blocking Rais' body with her own. "You did this," she grits out.

Stygian flashes a smile. "Darling, you almost shot him yourself. Aimed and all."

"How dare you."

"How dare I?" Stygian gestures to herself. "I am only trying to help you."

"Do you think you're innocent?" Ava asks. Stygian doesn't respond. "Do you think people look to you as a savior?"

"What are you trying to say?"

"You are so blind to your own evils. You claim you do this for my benefit. Kill the one person I can trust. How is that innocent? How does that help me?" Ava yells.

"I am not your enemy, sister. You started this war," she says.

"Of course, you are my enemy! You imprisoned me in Goldryn for disagreeing with you. You killed my cousin, my uncle, and now Rais. You claim it's because of my crimes against your region, what of your crimes against Wyntryn? You ransacked Rebynrock, then blamed me when I protected my people in their own home."

"I was helping Rebynrock. I did not hurt a single person there."

"You filled the streets with your soldiers. Enemy soldiers, with weapons. If you meant no harm, why were they threatening innocent lives?" Ava shouts back.

"It wasn't Goldryn. It was the Society who attacked you. And it was you who killed my people. I will do anything to protect my reign," Stygian says.

"To protect your reign. Do you even hear yourself when you speak?" Ava asks.

"Remember you started this war, sister."

"What?" Ava gapes in disbelief.

"It was you who sent letters to your cousin behind my back. Letters with information about my kingdom. You who altered my memories. It was you who started this battle and—"

"Because you threatened me and my people. You treated me like I was the enemy when I am your sister! I went to you for refuge."

"And you took advantage of me. You became a spy. You act like you did not start this war. You've been building an army in Wyntryn. Recruiting mages and training them. Calling back your people from the refugee camps in Goldryn. How is that not an act of war?" Stygian asks.

"You say that like you didn't threaten me in Rebyn-rock."

"I offered you an alliance."

"How can I trust that? You killed our cousin and uncle in front of me. You just made me kill Rais…" Ava gasps. Her voice breaks at the thought that Rais is really gone. At the thought that she pushed that dagger into him. "You made me kill him…"

"You disgust me." Stygian steps closer, eyes narrowing.

"I disgust you? You are a horrible, evil woman. I am not your sister. I am nothing but an ant for you to crush."

"Stop it," Stygian warns.

"You murdered our own family! And you blame this war, on me?"

"Stop it!" she screeches.

Ava juts her finger at her. "You act like you aren't as broken as the rest of us. You try to act like you are perfectly stable. Not damaged in any way. But I can see through those walls. What mother did to you, to us, is horrible. Why fight against me when we have both suffered the same horrors?"

She slams purple flames into Ava, throwing her back into the grass. "You know nothing of what I have suffered! You killed our mother!"

"Kill me. Do it," Ava dares. Stygian's eyes burn with an unrelenting fury, but she doesn't move. "Do it, sister. See if I care." There are no more tears. Nothing left for her to give. "Do it!" Stygian doesn't move. "Kill me, please! Do you think I want to spend another day of this life alone? I have no one left. So, kill me." Ava rips her fingers through the grass. "Kill me!"

Stygian stumbles backward. She looks down at Rais. Her chest heaves at the sight. Then Stygian turns to Willow, standing not ten feet away from them. Stygian walks to Rais' body and twists her fingers around the amulet nestled in the dirt.

"No!" Ava screams. But it's too late. Stygian yanks the necklace from the ground and twists it in her hand.

"Sister, you deserve a fate worse than death," Stygian says. Then she alates away, disappearing in a blue mist.

Vines reach up from the dirt and wrap around Rais' body. Ava runs to him. She falls to her knees and grasps at the vines. They wiggle and thrash across him. She breaks one and grabs another. But the broken one grows back. The vines begin to sink into the ground, pulling Rais with them. Ava screams, grasping at the vines. Her soul is collapsing in on her.

Then, he's gone. Nothing but dirt beneath her torn hands and bloody fingernails. Ava leans against her hands. She curls her fingers into the dirt and hyperventilates. Air rips through her lungs. She can't bare another second.

Willow stands behind her. As if she's a ghost. Her pale dress flitters in the wind. There's no ringing in Ava's ears now. No sound in the silence. It is only her and the wind. Until Willow's voice joins the mix.

Ava doesn't look at her as she speaks. She doesn't even bother to listen. Willow reaches out to her, and Ava stumbles away from her hand. "Do not touch me," Ava says. Willow stills and takes a step back. The past is haunting her. She is reliving her nightmares.

Chapter Forty-Four

Ava

Ava stares at the dirt where Rais disappeared. Broken vines litter the ground. She picks them up and chucks them into the ravine. Bryn did this. Bryn took him. It had to be. No one else has a power like that. Not anyone Ava knows of. Her breathing is ragged, and tears soak her skin. An ache ravages her head. She picks up her dagger from the ground. The one with his blood on it. Why did she listen? She could have waited for someone to help. He was begging her, and she couldn't deny him. There was so much blood. So much pain. She pulls her arm back and throws the dagger as hard as she can. It clatters against the rock on the opposite side of the ravine.

When she finally turns around, hundreds of soldiers watch her. Eieran walks past her and presses his hand against the ground where Rais disappeared. The Goldryn soldiers have either alated away or burned with her fire. Her people stayed.

Rais isn't the only one they lost, but he's the one every single mage here knows.

Ava's mind swelters with anger. Stygian did this.

Her own sister did this. A hand grasps her wrist. She faces Eieran.

"Be rational," he says.

How can he say that? How can he be so calm after Stygian has ripped so many people from this world? First, she took Aran, then Anya, and now… She can't breathe. Ava rips her arm away from Eieran. "I—I killed him." She sucks in a breath and looks down at the blood on her hands. The blood that pooled from the arrow's wound. From the dagger.

Eieran's voice is deathly quiet. "No. It is not your fault."

Ava's eyes widen, and the tears stutter to a halt. "If she wants me to be the villain, then I will become her worst nightmare," Ava whispers.

Eieran narrows his eyes. She can see the pain in his expression. He's trying to stay composed for her and for the mages who've survived. Ava cannot even fathom composure at this point. Every nerve in her body is on fire, and the world is crashing down around her.

Ava pulls herself into the Sonder and alates before Eieran can stop her.

She steps out into the frozen landscape. The mountain rises above her. Ava scales the side of the mountain as quickly as she can. She drops down into the small ravine and runs through the winding tunnels. Metarock opens before her, and she runs past the guards. One of them shouts something, but she keeps running. Past the stables and manmade fields.

She stops in front of the carved doors. The mages there recognize her and let her through. Her legs move before she can think to run. She goes as fast as she can through the tunnels, past the city of night nymphs, and down into the armory.

The intricately carved doors rise above her. She presses her palms against them and recites the phrase Rais had used. The cavern shakes and the doors move inward. There's a groan as the dragon twists itself to face her.

Aathmika seems to sense the pain and anger rushing through her because the dragon presses its nose to her. Ava holds her hand against the face of the creature. "Aathmika, I need a favor," she says.

The dragon shifts as if reading her mind. It tilts its body to the cavern floor, then stretches its wing out. Ava grazes her fingers along the white scales until she reaches the wing. She places her foot on the wing and boosts herself onto Aathmika's back. She shifts forward until she's at the base of Aathmika's neck and holds on. The dragon shivers beneath her and lets out a low hiss.

Where are we going, Miss Wyntryn?

"The City on the Sea."

Aathmika chirps and moves through the dark cavern. Ava can't see a thing, but she knows this is away from the tunnels. Aathmika lifts her wings and stretches them wide. They swing down and the dragon lifts into the air. Ava's muscles tense.

The dragon continues to flap its wings, and they move up through the air. Ava can't see, but she assumes what's above them is Metarock. The dragon is flying up into nothing.

Ava looks up and there's a reflection of light casting a low glow. It looks like water. It can't be. "Stop! We're going to hit the ceiling!"

Aathmika continues to rise through the air, and when Ava thinks they're going to hit rock, the dragon's head breaches the top of the cavern. Water sprinkles down on her. She tightens her grip on the dragon's back as the surface of the water hits her. She's pulled through. Ava looks below them in shock. Water droplets spiral down. Aathmika flew through a lake. Somehow, it's not a lake at all. It is water suspended in place. An entrance to the dragon's lair that's been disguised as a lake.

The dragon lets out a bird-like call and they rise into the skies. Ava reaches her hand out and touches the clouds. They are nothing but air.

Rais is nothing, but air. She chokes on a cry and holds back the tears begging to fall. Ava doesn't have any mercy left in her. If Stygian wants to take her head, then Ava's not going down without a fight.

Aathmika tilts in the sky and turns toward the Goldryn coast. Then they dive. Air rushes through her hair throwing it back behind her. Her stomach tightens as they go down. Then the dragon shifts its wings, catching the air. They float back up into the sky and move steadily over a mountain peak.

From this high up, Ava can see the ocean in the distance. Soon, the palace on the sea will crumble into it and all she will hear is a sweet, sweet, ringing.

Acknowledgments

This book has been a challenge for me. It was more difficult than the first because it came with pressure. This time I wasn't going in blind, with no clue how people may react to it. I've seen reviews for *These Shattered Truths*. There's been the pressure of outdoing myself and proving that I am capable of being an author.

There was a point where I lost the sense of wonder and the excitement of writing because I let someone's words get to me. Those words made editing a nightmare. With every sentence I read, I doubted myself a little more. I felt like I would never be enough for this person. That I could never write something they would be proud of. It wasn't until I finished formatting this book that I realized … it doesn't matter what others think. I wrote this. I love these characters, this world, and especially this book.

If you have ever felt like you couldn't live up to someone's expectations of you, trust me, you are and always will be enough. The only opinion that matters, is your own.

Before you close this book and move on to your next read, I would like to acknowledge some people who helped me create this book.

Thank you to my siblings, Parker, Micah, and Drew, for reminding me that I am capable of doing anything I set my mind to.

Thank you to my wonderful developmental editor, Natalie Camarratta, author of *Falling & Upris-*

ing.

Lastly, thank you to my beta readers, ARC readers, and everyone who has bought, read, or supported my books in any way.

I hope everyone can look around them and see the Sonder. See the differences in all individuals and appreciate everyone's unique diffrences.

Pronunciation Station

Unfortunately, telepathy is impossible in our world. So you can not see into my mind and know exactly what I'm thinking. This page is for those who read the weird words and names in this book and think, *my brain is simply refusing to comprehend this.*

Aathmika (Ah-th-me-kuh)

Alate (Uh-late)

Aliras (Uh-lie-russ)

Alys Wyntryn (Al-iss Win-ter-in)

Atane (Uh-t-on-a)

Ava Beckett (Ava Beh-ket)

Aysand (Eye-sand)

Bryn (Burr-in)

Eieran Hynrule (Ee-err-on Hh-eye-nn-rule)

Erka (Err-kuh)

Exceail (Ex-cee-ill)

Eventyr (Eh-ven-teer)

Genevia Cross (Gg-en-eev-ee-uh Cross)

Goldryn (Gold-rin)

Grymyr (Grim-er)

Hyacin Moore (Hi-uh-sin More)

Kalenti Alberona (Cal-en-tee Al-ber-o-na)

Kanaleigh (Con-ah-lay)

Levites Grenier (Lee-vv-eye-tiss Greh-nn-eer)

Metarock (Met-uh-rock)

Oberyn (Oh-burr-in)

Osidias Donsen (Oh-sih-dee-us Don-ss-en)

Petrichor (Peh-treh-core)

Rebynrock (Reh-bin-rock)

Raiden Hynrule (Rr-eye-den Hh-eye-en-rule)

Rais (Rr-eye-ss)

Saira Grenier (Ss-eye-rah Greh-nn-eer)

Sonder (Ss-ah-nn-der)

Stygian Liones (Stig-ee-en Lee-oh-ness)

Wyntryn (Win-treh-in)

Ygrette (Ee-gret)

Ancient Language

The ancient language is the original tongue used by civilizations of irregulars in Kanaleigh. It is a universal language used
to harness energy and elements through the sonder. The language remained prevalent in the lands until the Great War. but
was mostly eradicated after the most recent resurgence of the
war (approx. 20 years prior to These Shattered Truths).

Alate — to travel through the Plane of Verity

Atane — wild beast or untamable animal

Ayatha — goddess

Chessya — to bless, to feel blessed, to be faithful

Drogon — dragon

Feya — fire

Fin — destination, end, final

Itzal — goddess of death, darkness, destinations

Gana — realm, region, plane of existence

Malla — to be possible, to express possibility, to have permission, to give permission

Mata — beings beyond their world, ancestors, gods, and goddesses

Mey — relating to or belonging to oneself; relating to or belonging to many

Pheyani — to fly, to be one with the air

Ra — the origin of something, where something begins or starts, family name.

Reyani — to rise, to lift through the air

Rynal — the goddess of life, light, and beginnings

Sonder — the plane of existence (Plane of Verity) that irregulars can access with their minds

Ta — a way to connect words or meanings, used in the place of words (the, in, is, it, to, etc.)

Tyral — the goddess of relationships, land, and war

Vaye — to possess, to own, to hold

Verity — walking amongst the many, collection of souls in one place

** not all words appear in book **

Words ending in YR or YN – in relation to location, territory, or region. Also commonly included in the names of ancestral lines. For example, Wyntryn. Both a location and family name.

For more information on the ancient language of Kanaleigh, go to **www.sirisandford.com**

Explore the Sonderverse

You can go to Siri Sandford's website to learn more about the sonderverse. You can view special information and details about chararcters, regions, and upcoming books!

www.sirisandford.com

Items available on the website's shop:
Signed copies
Sonderverse bookmarks & stickers
Art prints
Keychains
Talisman jewelry
Book boxes

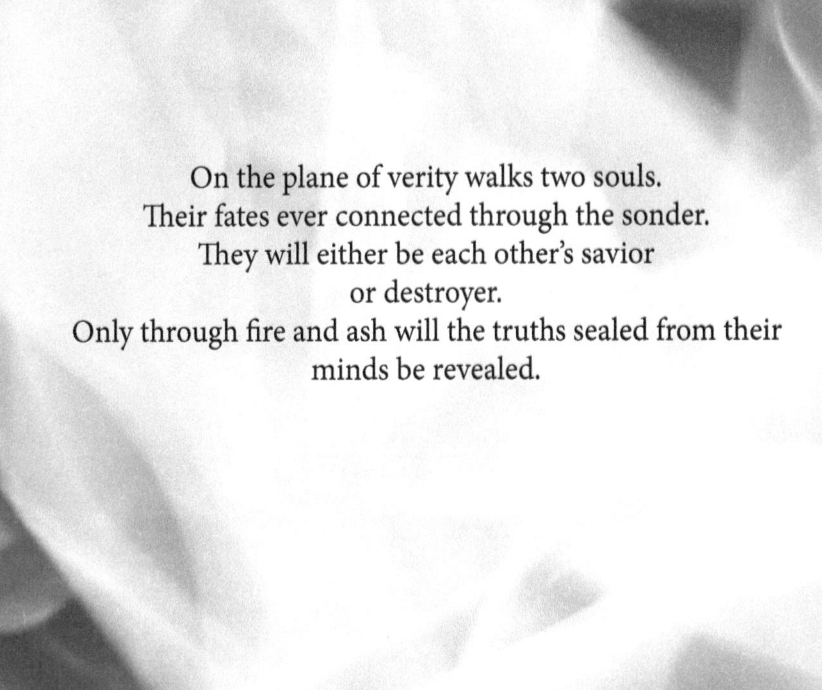
On the plane of verity walks two souls.
Their fates ever connected through the sonder.
They will either be each other's savior
or destroyer.
Only through fire and ash will the truths sealed from their
minds be revealed.